THE CLIMATE
OF THE COUNTRY

a novel by

Marnie Mueller

CURBSTONE PRESS

Printed in the United States on acid-free paper by BookCrafters
Cover design: Les Kanturek

This book was published with the support of the Connecticut
Commission on the Arts, the National Endowment for the Arts,
and donations from many individuals. We are very grateful for this
support.

Library of Congress Cataloging-in-Publication Data

Mueller, Marnie.
    The climate of the country : a novel / by Marnie Mueller. — 1st ed.
        p.   cm.
    ISBN 1-880684-58-6 (acid-free paper)
    1. Japanese Americans—Evacuation and relocation, 1942-1945—Fiction.
2. World War, 1939-1945—Conscientious objectors—United States—
Fiction. 3. Tule Lake Relocation Center (Calif.)—History—Fiction.
4. Japanese Americans—California—Tule Lake—Fiction. I. Title.
PS3563.U354C58   1998
813'.54—dc21   98-24112

published by
CURBSTONE PRESS   321 Jackson Street   Willimantic, CT 06226
            phone: (860) 423-5110   e-mail: books@curbstone.org
                    http://www.curbstone.org

To the memory of my parents

Donald Elberson 1912-1981

and

Ruth Siegel Elberson 1916-1993

who taught me that commitment and candor
are not mutually exclusive values.

Question #27: Are you willing to serve in the armed forces of the United States, in combat duty, wherever ordered?

Question #28: Will you swear unqualified allegiance to the United States and faithfully defend the United States from any and all attack by foreign or domestic forces, and forswear any form of allegiance or obedience to the Japanese emperor, or any foreign government, power or organization?

AUTHOR'S NOTE

By January 1943, 120,000 people of Japanese ancestry, American citizens and alien residents alike, had been forcibly living for almost a year, under Executive Order 9066, in what were called relocation camps. During the first month of 1943 the United States government developed a plan to recruit Nisei—American citizens who were second-generation Japanese Americans—directly out of the camps to fight for the Allies in Europe and to do intelligence work in Asia. In their effort to make the strategy acceptable to the general American population, Washington required that all Japanese American adults, both citizens and noncitizens, male and female, sign oaths proving their loyalty to the United States and forswearing any allegiance to the Emperor of Japan or to the people of Japan. Refusal to sign carried a penalty of up to twenty years' imprisonment and possible expatriation and/or repatriation.

This attempt to distinguish between loyal and disloyal evacuees set up wrenching conflicts for families living together in the camps. Issei, or first-generation residents, who were not allowed to become citizens of the United States by law (Japanese Exclusion Act of 1924), understood they would be people without a country if they forswore allegiance to Japan. Their children, the Nisei, who were citizens by birth, feared being separated from their parents and sent to other camps if they answered differently from their parents. And many people, young and old, were so outraged by this latest affront that they answered in a "disloyal" manner simply to make a stand. The people who answered "no" on two specific questions regarding absolute allegianc were dubbed "No-No's" within the camp population. They were subsequently transferred out of their camps and relocated to the newly designated Tule Lake Segregation Center in northern California where many "loyal" residents remained from the original Tule Lake Relocation Camp days.

THE CLIMATE OF THE COUNTRY

Chapter One

Denton and Esther Jordan were stopped at the gate by a young man in army uniform, his cheeks red and raw under the harsh searchlights. He held a machine gun across his waist.

"What's going on?" Denton asked as he rolled down the window, letting a gust of frigid air into the car.

"I'll have to see your identification first, sir. I'm not authorized to talk, sir, till you've identified yourself."

The soldier dropped his r's, so 'first' came out as fust, and 'sir' as suh. He was one of the boys they'd brought up recently from an Arkansas boot camp to guard Tule Lake when it became a segregation center. As far as Denton was concerned they were all racist rednecks, and rumor had it that they were trying to force themselves on some of the Nisei girls. But Denton wasn't about to argue with a boy who carried a machine gun.

He got out of the car, and hunching against the cold wind, unbuttoned his coat and dug into the back pocket of his trousers for his wallet. Stinging particles of sand blew up off the surface of the packed-down dirt. His hands smarted as he riffled through myriad scraps of paper looking for the identification card he wasn't even certain he had. They'd never asked for it before.

Even stooped forward, Denton was taller than the soldier, and just as slender. The soldier wore a wool cap, but Denton was bareheaded, the wind flattening his dark hair back from his high forehead.

Watching from the car, Esther was annoyed that, as usual, her husband wore no hat, no gloves, no muffler. Why couldn't he remember to take care of himself? Because he was so preoccupied with everyone else's needs that he neglected his own and his family's, was why.

She slid over to the driver's side and called out to him, "Ask about the children. Ask what's going on."

"The children are fine, ma'am," the soldier answered her directly.

Denton continued going through his wallet, the papers now dropping out.

"Damn it," he hollered, squatting down. He grabbed as the wind sent the scraps skittering across the road and the same gusts pitched dust into his eyes. Denton looked up. "Can't you tell us what's happening in there, soldier? For my wife's sake."

"I've got to see your I.D., sir."

"Sure, sure, soldier. I'm sorry. We're just worried about our daughter." Finally he found the year-old, dog-eared yellow card identifying him as Denton I. Jordan, Director of Business Enterprises. "Here you are." He stood and handed it to the soldier. "So how about it? Can you tell me what's going on?"

"In a minute, sir." The soldier turned and walked toward the guard tower. Denton started after him.

"Denton, no," Esther called. "Don't make him mad. I have to get to Parin as quickly as possible."

Denton spun around, sending more sand into the air. He stood for a moment, his face washed out in the light that was as intense and shadowless as the midday sun.

"What the hell were we thinking of? We shouldn't have left her alone tonight of all times."

"We didn't leave her alone. Nancy can hear everything through the wall. Don't accuse me." How dare he fault her? She and Nancy McIntyre always traded babysitting duties by listening through the thin walls of their barracks for any sounds of trouble. When he began to take responsibility for his daughter, then he could make accusations.

"Esther." Denton came toward the car. He leaned his head against the window frame, reaching in to touch her, to twist a curl of her thick black hair. "I wasn't accusing you. I was questioning my own judgment." She shifted away from him, moving over against the passenger door. Her strong profile, which hours earlier he'd admired in the movie's silvery light, had become haughty and stern. "Esther, please," he pleaded, but he saw she was gone from him. He knew she was frightened, but why couldn't she contain her anger and suspicions just this once?

2

"Sir." The soldier had come out of the guard tower and was walking toward the car.

"Esther, please don't act like this. I can't..."

"I'm all right." She smiled so falsely that he felt more forlorn than if she hadn't bothered.

"Thank you," he said, in his softest voice, wanting desperately to appease her. "Very much."

"Sir."

Denton turned to the boy. "Did I pass inspection?"

"Yes, sir, and there's a message that Director Andross wants you at Administration Headquarters as soon as you come in." He handed the I. D. card back to Denton.

"Now, how about it, soldier? Can you tell me quickly what happened?" Denton said, getting into the car, conscious of Esther's continuing hostile silence.

Esther stared straight ahead, wishing she hadn't become so angry. Even so, her rage threatened to erupt again. He had no right to blame her. All she'd asked for were a few private hours together after months of seeing him only when he arrived home after ten or eleven at night, exhausted, complaining, and worried.

"There was a pretty big altercation, sir, between the no-no's and the administration. What they say, sir, is that over a hundred of the Japs come into the administration area armed with four-foot pieces of lumber and baseball bats. They come on foot and in pickup trucks they got from the motor pool. One of the guys, a big Jap, I heard, run down a staff member with the pickup truck. 'Most killed him. They say the Japs was everyplace, at the hospital, in the bushes outside the project director's house. Scared the director's wife near to death. They was drifting around all over the place. Then a whole bunch, around fifty Japs or so, got into the gate around Andross's house and started yelling in English, 'Get Andross! Get the *keto*!' or whatever it is they call white people. They say they attacked 'cause they're still riled up about that farmworker fellow who died, and they was yelling about the strikers and 'scabs' out at the farm. But I wasn't there. I was in my bunk, but I could hear the Japanese music coming out over some kind of transmitter. By the time I got called to the gate, it was pretty much calmed down. Didn't take nothing to get them in line, I hear, once we moved in with the tanks and equipment. Not so brave as they like to think, them Japs ain't."

Jesus Christ, Denton thought. He looked over and saw that the six tanks and the dozen jeeps that had been lined up outside the gate for the last couple of weeks were gone. Ted Andross had been threatening for a month to retaliate against the militants, "to mow them down and bend them into submission, if we have to." The opportunity had finally arrived. If he hadn't let Esther talk him into the movie, he'd have been here tonight. He could have interceded and it wouldn't have had to come to this. Denton started the car, and rolled up the window with a terse 'thanks.'

"Bastards," he whispered.

The kid knocked on the window. "For Christ's sake, what the hell does he want now?" Denton muttered, and lowered it again.

"I forgot to tell you, sir, the Mrs. should go to the Community Room straight away. That's where the kids are. They took them there for protection, in case it got rough." He dipped down and peeked in at Esther. "She want to go?"

"Esther?" Denton asked. She remained in profile to him, staring out the windshield.

"Yes, I would like to go, soldier," she said, looking at the boy, avoiding Denton's gaze. "Can someone drive me there so my husband can go to his emergency meeting?"

Denton found her hand. "Give us a minute, soldier." He closed the window. "Esther, tell me what I should do, should I take you to the Community Room?"

"No, it'll be more efficient if one of the soldiers drives me," she said in a cold voice. She held herself stiffly, but he saw her face giving way to the strain.

"Come here," he said, moving over to put his arm around her.

"I think I should go to the Community Room, Denton. I'm too upset," she said, beginning to cry. "I simply wanted an evening out of here."

*   *   *

Esther waited on a wooden bench in the sentry house. The sooner Denton went to the meeting, the sooner he'd be back home, or so she hoped. One never knew with Denton these days. There were evenings when he'd return to the barracks to have dinner with her and Parin, and Esther would leave them to go into the kitchen for a minute, only to return to find their three-year-old daughter, her thumb shoved deep into her mouth, alone at the table. He'd wandered out again and sometimes he wouldn't show up for hours. When she asked him where he'd been, he would say he'd remembered something at the Co-op office, or a resident's birthday party, or a piece of business with the block manager. But she didn't want to focus on her anger at him any more. She felt ashamed of her own behavior in the car. She knew he was as worried about Parin as she was. She shuddered in the wind-chilled room, and pulled up her coat collar to cover her ears.

"Do you know where that driver is?" she asked another young soldier.

"There he is, ma'am," the private said.

But Esther had heard the motor, too, and was already up and striding across the rough wooden floor. She climbed quickly into the jeep and gripped the metal frame as they took off along the cinder road leading into the camp, the army vehicle rattling and shaking as it bounded and rocked over the ruts in the dirt road. They passed the military police barracks, turned right, and there she saw it—an army tank looming in the entry to the motor pool garage, a tank almost as tall as the one-story building. Tears blurred her vision.

Parin, please don't be too frightened, she cried inside. I'm coming. They turned right again, and drove along the west side of the hospital. There was light in every window.

"Busy here tonight," the soldier shouted over the noise of the jeep. "They stormed the hospital. People got pretty banged up. Tried to take the head doctor, Stanforth, and the head Jap doctor hostage, I heard."

"Were they successful?" she shouted back. She knew there had been complaints about both Dr. Stanforth and Dr. Oshimoto.

"Don't think so. Don't think it amounted to much, once we came in."

The trip from the front gate to the Community Room had never seemed so long. Beyond the hospital, except for the searchlight beams, the whole area was eerily dark. Even the stars were obscured by thick cloud cover. There was a dull sheen overhead from the reflected glare of the searchlights. Was Parin warm? Had Nancy remembered Parin's knitted afghan? Parin would be terrified without it. Please let Parin be all right.

She jumped down from the jeep as soon as it came to a complete stop in front of the Community Room. Later she couldn't remember if she'd thanked the driver. Grabbing the splintery banister, she bounded up the sagging stairs. Two soldiers were stationed on the porch, to the right and left of the double door.

"My daughter's inside," she called breathlessly.

Opening the door she was overwhelmed by blazing light, humid heat, the smell of food and wet wool. She moved swiftly down the hall. Black and orange construction paper chains crisscrossed overhead, and the corridor walls were decorated with cutout witches and goblins from last week's Halloween party.

The main room was jammed with close to fifty people, mostly women, a few children and one or two men, their belongings piled on the ten-foot-long activity tables. Children were asleep on the tabletops in a jumble of pillows and blankets and on pushed-together chairs, while adults sat in clusters, talking quietly among themselves, or dozed with their heads down on a table, or lay curled on the floor. For a moment Esther recognized no one in the mass of Caucasian faces. She scanned the room but couldn't see her daughter, her daughter's lopsided glasses, her wispy, blond hair. Damn it, where was she?

"Esther, over here," Sarah Topol waved and called from the far corner where she sat holding her own newborn, Annie.

Esther saw Parin bunched forward on a dilapidated davenport, her blue afghan clutched to her chest, staring straight ahead. Her wire-rim glasses reflected the light, so her dark eyes were hidden as Esther rushed to her. Parin's round face was expressionless, her little lips tightly closed. Nancy McIntyre was dozing beside her, Nancy's youngest boy asleep with his head on her lap.

"Parin, dearest," She knelt before her small daughter, tentatively holding her hands out to her.

"She wouldn't move," Sarah whispered. "She's been like that since we arrived."

Esther could smell Sarah's breast milk as she leaned down to Parin.

"Thank you, Sarah, she'll be all right. Parin sweetness, it's Mommy. I'm here. Daddy and I are back." Parin looked at her, but still didn't register Esther's presence. Through the child's smudged glasses, Esther saw that Parin's lazy eye had slipped inward toward her nose. It happened when she was exhausted or frightened.

6

"The poor little dear must be terrified."

"Yes, I know, Sarah."

"We tried everything to get her to relax."

Esther sat on the floor beside the davenport. "Please, dearest, it's Mommy." She pulled Parin down to her, but the child was dead weight, her body stiff. She cradled Parin in her lap, wrapping her arms around her daughter, hoping this was the right thing to do, breathed into her hair, inhaled the metallic scent that children's perspiration always seemed to have, and the distinctive odor that was Parin's own. She rubbed her hands along the flannel pajamas that were rough and stiff from being washed in the cloudy mineral-filled water of the camp, felt the sturdy three-year-old body beneath the cloth. Rocking her daughter, oblivious of the room and the movement of people around them, she was flooded with desire for Parin. She slipped her hand up under the pajama top, caressing the smooth, warm skin. She swayed rhythmically from side to side, until finally she felt Parin's body sag and dissolve into her own.

"That's right, dearest. Let Mommy comfort you."

After a time Parin shuddered and whimpered. Only then was Esther assured they were both safe again.

Chapter Two

When he entered Project Director Ted Andross's smoky office, Denton sensed the meeting had been going on for some time.

"Where the hell have you been?" Herm Katz demanded, lumbering to his feet. The bandage across his forehead didn't quite cover the edge of a raw wound. His complexion was paler than usual beneath the large freckles on his face.

"Went to the movies," Denton said, surveying the room, doing inventory of who Andross had invited in. A lot of power in one room. Andross was lucky as hell to have them all here tonight. Herm Katz, civilian Director of Internal Security. Sy Topol, Community Analyst. Bill Nakamura, Nisei and president of the Co-op Board of Directors. Toki Honda, Issei, and general manager of the seven Co-op stores. Nebo Mota, Kibei, a member of the residents' Negotiating Committee—the *Daihyo Sha Kai*—and spokesman for the militant *Hoshidan*. And once active participant in the Co-op, Denton thought sadly.

"Sorry about it, but Esther really wanted to get out."

"Too bad she picked tonight. Could've used your help," Herm said grimly, dragging a chair over for Denton. He settled it between himself and Bill Nakamura before collapsing back into his own chair, pressing his hand to his forehead. Herm loved personal drama.

Bill Nakamura acknowledged Denton with a nod, but he didn't give way with his customary eager smile. Bill looked like the Ph.D. candidate he had been before Pearl Harbor in his brown wool sweater and wire frame glasses, notebook open on his lap and pencil poised.

"What happened to you?" Denton asked Herm, wondering if he was the staffer who had been run down.

"Ask him," Herm pointed to Nebo Mota.

Nebo Mota sat to the right of Herm in the semicircle in front of Andross's massive mahogany desk. He wore a white shirt and trousers, uniform of the *Hoshidan*, but he had removed the white head band. Denton guessed Nebo must have thought better of wearing it in Andross's presence. Wise move. Mota was handsome, especially with his hair newly shaved off in the cause of militancy. His head was narrow and oval, his cheekbones broad and high, and his mouth was sensually full-lipped. He sat erect, with his feet hooked around outside of the chair legs, his thighs bulging under the thin, tightly stretched fabric of his pants. His brown leather bomber jacket hung over the back of his chair. Tough customer, Denton thought. How much Nebo had changed since they'd worked together in the Co-op; the enforced answering of the loyalty questionnaire had altered everything. Now Nebo was like a column of steel, a fortress of anger and resistance.

No one spoke. Bill Nakamura took off his glasses, pulled a perfectly pressed and folded handkerchief from his pants pocket and polished the lenses. At the far edge of the semicircle, closest to the door, Toki Honda, in starched white shirt and dark suit, sat rigidly in the straight chair, with his arms folded across his barrel chest. His thick black hair was combed back with pomade. He stared at the floor, lips pressed tightly together. Sy Topol sat between Bill and Toki with his elbows on his knees and his head in his hands. The tail of his wrinkled green shirt had come loose and straggled over the seat of his pants. Denton wondered what Sy's interpretation of this gathering would be.

The tension was palpable in the office as Ted Andross rustled through papers on his desk. Even after the altercation outside his house, the director had taken the time to dress in an impeccable black three-piece suit. His thinning chestnut hair was wetted down and parted low on his left temple, cutting a severe white line of flesh through the slick strands. A confrontation was either about to happen or had just taken place, Denton couldn't be certain which.

"Good you could find your way to my office, Jordan," Andross said, finally acknowledging Denton's presence. "I already told the others, but I'll repeat for your benefit, that I asked the Co-op fellows in here, along with our famous liberal contingent of staffers, because you have your fingers on the pulse of what's going on in camp. This is the last meeting we're having tonight. You missed the one with Colonel Benedict and the members of the maintenance and service staffs where we went over the new rules of this camp. We're under martial law. Until further notice the army is in charge. Mr. Katz

9

answers to them for internal security matters. The army will immediately start building a fence between the administrative area and the evacuee section. No internee can pass through without showing a work or school pass. No assemblies of more than twenty people will be allowed. No motorized vehicles can be used by internees. Starting tonight, there's a curfew from seven p.m. to seven a.m., enforced by the army and possibly by Mr. Katz's Japanese American internal security staff, if he can get them off their backsides to do it. They didn't do very well tonight. No Japanese may be spoken publicly. The *Tulean Dispatch* will be published only in English and all minutes from meetings must also be in English. That goes for your Co-op minutes, too, Jordan."

Denton went cold with rage. Every single thing he had worked for over the past year and a half had gone down the drain tonight in a few stinking hours. He could see satisfaction on Andross's face, in Andross's pale blue eyes, as his gaze darted from man to man, not settling on anyone.

"What about the fish delivery for the Co-op?" Denton said, seething inside. He was surprised at how calm his voice sounded.

"What about it, Jordan?" Andross picked up a pencil and tapped it impatiently on the desk top.

"We have five hundred pounds of fish freight coming in tomorrow morning by train. We have to unload it on the platform outside the gate and put it into trucks to carry to the store. Our Co-op drivers are all Japanese American. You said they're not allowed to drive motor vehicles."

"I'll talk to Colonel Benedict tomorrow. He has the final word."

"The train gets here at six in the morning. The fish'll spoil if it sits around for more than a few hours."

"Maybe you'll just have to send it back."

"I can't send back five hundred pounds of fish, sir, and expect the wholesaler to supply us again, especially not these days. There's a war going on, after all." He knew this dig about the war would irritate the hell out of Ted Andross.

Out of the corner of his eye, Denton saw Bill Nakamura support him with a tiny nod. Denton glanced over at Toki Honda, but the older man revealed nothing.

"I know there's a war going on, Jordan. I'm usually the one to remind *you*. But right now we've got one going on here in camp,"

Andross said as he scribbled on a piece of paper. "I'll have somebody out at the train with a truck, if I have to go myself. Will that satisfy you?" He forced a smile, but it wasn't friendly.

"I appreciate it," Denton answered.

"Now, it's getting late," Andross said, "so I'll tell you what happened here tonight. Two hundred hotheads decided to take the law into their own hands. They came into the administration area armed with weapons and terrorized our civilian population. They even went after the hospital staff. They had the audacity to attack my residence, but that's another matter." He stopped, shook his head as though to clear it. "I decided not to allow chaos and anarchy to reign, so I called in the army."

Denton knew Bill Nakamura and Toki Honda weren't going to challenge Andross's description of events, but he suspected they might have a somewhat different version, at least more nuanced. And Sy Topol wasn't going to give his hand away in a mixed group like this. His job was to observe and document life in camp through an anthropologist's eyes, which suited Sy's personality perfectly, Denton thought. He was a little too soft, too pliant. You never quite knew where he stood. But Herm—why the hell wasn't Herm speaking? Herm always had an opinion. Just then Nebo Mota began to talk.

"It is well known that the *Daihyo Sha Kai* came repeatedly to Director Andross over the past two weeks with a number of requests."

"Demands," Andross asserted.

"Demands, yes, sir." Nebo Mota acknowledged what he could have let slide by. "First, we came with the demand that Seiko Kitamara, the farmworker, be buried in a traditional manner."

"This is old business. You know that, Mota. I said no at the time and it is still no." Andross shot up, sending his springback-chair thudding against the wall, and he came around to the front of his desk. Crossing his arms over his narrow sunken chest, he stared at Nebo. Nebo didn't flinch.

This is going to get nowhere, Denton thought. The bastard is doing it again. No compromises, just jumping on people the minute they try to talk, making things worse. Anger welled up in Denton. There was complete silence in the room. Denton saw he would have to intervene.

Denton shifted in his seat. Everyone turned and looked at him, including Andross.

"Sir," Denton said, leaning forward, his elbows on his knees, mimicking Sy's relaxed position. He clasped his hands. "Maybe we could hear Nebo's version of the event this evening."

"If you insist, Mr. Jordan." Andross propped himself against the edge of the desk, looking down at them coldly.

Denton turned to Nebo Mota. "So, Nebo, what do you say?" Denton didn't smile. He had to be careful not to appear either fawning or patronizing; Nebo Mota could see through an organizing technique in a second.

Nebo ignored Denton's question and went right on with his own agenda. His face was hard. His eyes stayed on Denton's.

"Second, we demanded the right to *nihongakko* schools to teach classes in Japanese culture."

"I told you I couldn't permit it." Andross straightened to his full six feet, pointing his finger at Nebo. "The newspapers would have a field day and Washington would be down on my back in a second. Anyway, it's a moot point, what with the new restriction on speaking Japanese."

"We need the classes to repair the damage done to our people during this incarceration."

"Relocation," Andross snapped.

"The forced jailing of our people based on the race of our ancestors," Nebo persisted.

Denton glanced over at Bill and Toki. They showed no reaction, but he knew they both recoiled from Nebo's militancy and direct style.

"We demanded the release from the stockade of the men detained when they refused to answer the loyalty questionnaires." Nebo looked pointedly at Herm Katz. "And the release of the members of the *Daihyo Sha Kai* leadership who were thrown in the stockade after our demonstration supporting the farmworkers. And we demand the release of the men you jailed tonight."

"It was necessary to haul in certain people and you know it. And about tonight, don't play innocent with me on that. Not after the way your hotheads scared my wife," Andross said, his voice rising, his forefinger jabbing at Nebo. "We've been over and over this. I don't owe you a goddamned thing."

Denton felt like taking that finger and crushing it. He looked to Herm for help, but Herm studiously ignored him as he massaged his temple beneath the wound. Sy listened with a neutral expression on his sallow face.

"Our people are in the stockade for the crime of speaking out," Nebo said. He stood up. His muscular body was taut, his fists clenched at his side. "They were jailed for refusing to sign a false and unnecessary loyalty oath. I believe to refuse is their American right. They were imprisoned for demonstrating for higher wages and for supporting the farmworkers' strike. Also an American right."

"You are being unreasonable," Andross said, his voice low and full of warning.

"We also insist that you honor the demands of the workers who remain at the farm in defiance of the scab workers who were brought in."

"Your damn striking farmworkers can go to hell. They were committing treason by not harvesting that crop, and they're doing the same by refusing to return to camp. The replacement workers we brought in from other camps are loyal to this country."

Andross pushed off the desk with his hands, and strode through their semicircle, heading for the door.

"We demand that you reinstate the farmworkers and pay them what privates in the army make or at least what you are paying the scabs. We demand that you send the 'loyal' scabs back to where they came from," Nebo continued, his voice rising.

Andross went out the door, slamming it behind him. They could hear him walk to the outside door and into the night.

The room was silent. Nebo remained standing. Denton noticed that dried blood was streaked across the sides of his pants, as if he'd wiped his hands there.

"Herm, for God's sake, can't you say anything?" Denton said to his friend.

"Look, Dent," Herm raised his head. "I don't have a damn thing to say to Mota after what happened tonight."

"What happened?"

"His rebels turned my jeep over with me in it, that's what happened. I went to try to talk to them and they flipped my damn jeep."

Toki Honda cleared his throat and began to speak in Japanese to Nebo Mota. He seemed to be accusing Nebo. As he spoke he unbuttoned his jacket and crossed his arms over his chest, tucking his hands into his armpits. He didn't move a facial feature, but the ruddy color that rushed up his flat cheeks gave away his feelings. Denton thought he recognized the word *sendosha*, meaning agitator, and *kyokoha*, meaning obstinate faction.

Nebo answered in heated, staccato sentences. He walked over and positioned himself in front of Toki with his legs apart, his hands dug into the pockets of his white pants. Toki cocked his head back to appraise the younger man; even sitting in the simple wooden chair, he exuded authority and confidence. Before Pearl Harbor he'd been a successful wholesale produce marketer in Tacoma. The respect he had built in his home community had carried over to his work in camp as general manager of the entire Co-op operation. Toki oversaw all the outlets: the general store, shoe factory, appliance center, fish store, barbershop, beauty salon and tofu factory.

Toki continued addressing Nebo Mota in Japanese. Though Toki maintained a calm exterior, his mouth barely opened as he shot the words out. Denton could see he was furious.

Nebo's voice lifted in a whine, as a sneer twisted his lips. Denton recognized the name of Bill Nakamura and Toki's full name, Tokuro Honda.

"Just a minute," Bill said, standing. He was trembling. "You cut it out, Nebo. That's enough of your insults."

"I said nothing I've not said before," Nebo said in English, whirling around to address Bill.

"Let's try to stay calm," Denton said, also getting up. "Let's not let the director turn us against each other."

"No, let's not let that happen," Sy Topol said.

He actually opened his mouth, Denton thought in amazement.

"Can't we just sit down, talk this out like old friends?" Sy continued.

Jesus, Denton thought, he's an idiot after all.

Herm Katz had his arms folded on his knees and his head on his arms. He was not going to be any help.

And then Toki Honda, in one smooth motion, rose and slapped Nebo Mota across the face. Denton later wondered why he'd not seen it coming. Herm looked up, confused. Sy Topol stood. Roosevelt stared down from behind Ted Andross's empty chair. Bill Nakamura leaped over just as Nebo lunged for Toki, grabbed Nebo's arms from behind and held them.

"*Inu*," Nebo spat out. "Traitor to our people, informer."

"I am no informer," Toki said in English in his most sonorous voice. Toki prided himself on his English. At five years old he had come to this country with his father, and two years later started to work after school and on weekends as a runner for a Caucasian company in Pike Place Market. Toki had told Denton that by the time he entered high school, he had reached his goal of mastering the language. He'd said he taught himself "the King's English" because he didn't want to walk around like an ignorant Issei, confusing l's and r's and trying to communicate without helping verbs.

"You are the one who does us disservice with your radical, strong-arm tactics," Toki Honda continued. "I listened to you. I supported the actions of the *Daihyo Sha Kai*. I thought perhaps there was value in what you had to say. Maybe I have been passive and subservient for too long under these difficult circumstances, but you go too far. You frighten our people, causing them to turn against each other."

Denton knew Toki said this in English so that all those present would understand, the *hakujin* included.

Nebo struggled against Bill, but Bill was taller than Nebo and kept hold of him. Bill's eyes were fierce behind his glasses; his smooth pale brown complexion had a grayish cast. "Don't talk to your elders that way, Nebo. Is this what you learned in Japan? To disrespect your elders? Honda, Tokuro-san is a man to be respected."

"He does nothing at all for our people," Nebo said. Abruptly Nebo stopped resisting Bill, and stood calm and stony in his grip.

How could it have come to this, Denton wondered in disbelief. To have fought like this in front of Caucasians was unthinkable. He'd known Toki for a year and a half and had never seen him lose control in even the smallest way. But Toki looked as if he could hit the young man again at any moment. His square face was set rigidly, his jaw jutting forward. He behaved like a father whose son had turned against him. Denton recognized the primitive rage that only a family member can engender.

The door banged open in the exterior office, followed by loud voices and footsteps.

"Let him go, Bill," Denton urged.

Bill Nakamura dropped Nebo's arms. Nebo whipped around in fury as if to attack Bill, and then, thinking better of it, he swaggered to the chair he'd vacated and sat down, his legs stretched and spread provocatively before him.

Only Bill and Denton hadn't made it back to their places when the door opened and Andross came in with three Military Police.

Denton thought, They're going to throw them in the stockade. He began forming his arguments against it.

"This meeting is adjourned," Andross said. "These officers will escort Misters Nakamura, Honda and Mota back to their barracks."

Denton was afraid the three men would resume their fight on the way home. He knew they would be shamed by being escorted to their residences by soldiers. What if the anger broke through Toki's immense self-control again? Denton was shaken by what he'd witnessed here, but he should have expected it. Things were getting progressively worse in the camp. It wasn't yet as bad as it had been during the loyalty questionnaire episode, when the masked strong-arm boys were beating people to coerce them into signing "no" on the questionnaires. And it wasn't as bad as when those residents who prided themselves on being loyal Americans had informed to the administration against "disloyal" neighbors. During that time Bill Nakamura had asked Denton to hide his daily journals in Denton's barracks. Bill had feared that if the young thugs came looking for him, and found his writings, they would say he was *inu* and beat him up or harm his wife Mitsue and his little girl Dori. It wasn't that bad yet, but it was getting close.

The soldiers filed out of the room again, to wait for the men in the outer office.

"The *Daihyo Sha Kai* will be here tomorrow to finish this meeting," Nebo Mota said to Andross as the others made ready to leave. Mota hadn't budged from where he sat, legs stretched out, hands clasped behind the back of the chair.

"No more threats, Mota, if you know what's good for you," Ted Andross said. His fingers fidgeted down the buttons of his vest. "As far as I'm concerned we've finished every damn bit of business."

"I think, sir," Denton said, "we're going to have to find a way to talk this out."

"Goddamn it, Jordan." Ted Andross suddenly slammed the flat of his hand against the wooden wall beside the door. The wall trembled.

16

"I'm sick and tired of your interfering with my authority," he shouted. "You weren't here tonight. You don't know how god-awful it was. I'm about to, I'm..." Andross stopped. He took a deep breath, and massaged his hand. "You'll have to excuse me, gentlemen. I don't usually let myself go this way. I apologize, Jordan. But we're going to have to call it a night, so—if you please." He extended his injured hand toward the door.

Without a word they filed out. Denton nodded to Andross as he passed, thinking, People's anger had to go somewhere, for Christ's sake. Didn't Andross know that yet?

"Have a good long sleep, gentlemen. Maybe tomorrow you'll see things more clearly," Andross said, as his parting shot.

"You bet," Denton answered, mostly to himself.

*   *   *

Denton stepped outside into the cold and scanned the dark empty parade ground. All was silent except the lonely thud and clunk of metal clamps against the wooden flag pole. One of the soldiers came out behind him and Denton, thinking of Esther and Parin for the first time since he'd gone into the meeting, asked where the children and women were. "Far as I know, they've all been sent back to their barracks, now that everything's under control, sir." I'll be home in a few minutes, Denton thought. But before he left he wanted to say goodbye to Toki, Bill and Nebo in front of their escorts, so the soldiers would understand that these men had good friends on the Caucasian staff; what he didn't want them to get wind of was his rift with Nebo Mota.

Chapter Three

The upheavals in camp and Nebo Mota's defection from Denton and the Co-op had begun with the forced signing of the loyalty questionnaires.

Nebo's mother went mad the night the order was announced in public meetings around camp. When she returned to their barracks, she ran against the wall of their room with all her strength, and sliding to the floor she began screaming that she had lost her husband and she would not also lose her god, the Emperor Hirohito. At midnight she still hadn't stopped shouting. Yoshi Kitari, the block manager, came to Denton's apartment and begged him to come back with him. "You know Mota. He respects you. He needs your help." When Denton arrived he found tiny Mrs. Mota crouching on the linoleum by the coal stove, disheveled and disoriented, rocking and wailing hoarsely in Japanese. Her hair had been hacked off unevenly at chin length. At her feet a scissors lay among the long strands of chopped-off hair. The blue flannel shirt Nebo wore was torn and soiled, and his own wavy black hair was disordered. Catching sight of Denton in her room, Yuri Mota fled to her army cot in the corner, where she curled up like a baby and continued muttering in Japanese.

"What can I do to help?" Denton asked quietly, being careful not to touch Nebo.

"She won't sign," Nebo said, his eyes to the floor. "She says she'd rather go back to Japan."

"Is there anyone she'll listen to?"

"I'm the one who has responsibility for her."

Denton knew the story. In the fall, Nebo's sister and brother had obtained permission from Washington to leave camp to attend the University of Chicago. Yuri Mota had been too frightened of living near the "white people outside" to accompany her children. Nebo said he didn't mind being his mother's caretaker because he had spent so many years away from her while studying in Japan. He said it was his turn to fulfill his *oya on*. Denton understood, too well, the necessity of caring for one's mother.

"I plan to sign 'no,'" Nebo said, lifting his head to stare belligerently at Denton. "I can't leave her alone here. I can't ask her to renounce her God. I'll expatriate if necessary."

"You don't have to be that honorable," Denton said softly. "We'll find some way to convince her."

"No," Nebo said, glaring at Denton. "We don't need your help. This is family business."

"Nebo, we've been friends for close to a year. You've come to my apartment, eaten with my family, played with my child. Let me help you."

"I can...not...leave...her...in...here...alone." Each emphatic word came out almost as a threat. "If I don't sign no, they will separate us. They'll send me to another camp."

"Nebo, I'll make arrangements. I'll talk to the project director. He'll let you stay here with her." Denton wondered if what he said was true. Could he really talk this new guy Andross into helping out with this? "I'll tell Director Andross I can't do without the best organizer in the whole damn camp except for yours truly," he said, trying to ease the tension with a little joke.

Nebo's mouth trembled as he shook his head no.

Yuri Mota had pulled a khaki regulation army blanket over her hunched body and head. The woolen fabric muffled her ongoing monologue. At least she's calming down, Denton thought. She'd soon be asleep. Denton wanted to tell Nebo that he knew what it was like to be all alone with such a burden. But he couldn't be that personal with Nebo. In the time they'd worked together, Denton had learned how proud Nebo was.

"Damn it, Nebo, what will you really do if she decides to repatriate?"

"I'll go with her. I enjoyed my years studying in Japan. At least *they* never incarcerated me."

Stabbing pains suddenly shot up the back of Denton's head. Oh, no, he thought, not this, too. A white zigzag of light vibrated in both eyes. He'd have to get out of here and find some aspirin. His only hope was to catch the migraine at this stage. Otherwise he could lose days of work.

"I've got to go, Nebo. But we'll talk about this tomorrow. I'm sorry, but I'm feeling a migraine coming on. I've got to get some medicine."

Although nearly blinded by the auras, Denton saw Nebo's surprise at this abrupt change. "Honestly, Nebo, I can barely see. I'll come back tomorrow, or I'll meet you at the Co-op in the morning at seven."

"No need," Nebo said coolly, his black eyes growing opaque. He shoved his hands into his blue jeans pockets and looked at Denton as if to say, You can go to hell as far as I'm concerned.

Denton knew the hurt that lay behind the arrogant posture, but he couldn't respond sensibly or compassionately because he was losing control of the migraine. Waves of nausea were making him dizzy. He would begin to vomit at any moment. He had to get outside.

"I'm sorry, Nebo, I'm so sorry, but I have to get out into the air," he said, as burning liquid rose up his throat and into his mouth. "Forgive me."

Denton reached his car, which he'd parked in the firebreak, and there he heaved his dinner onto the icy crust of snow. His nausea passed long enough for him to get to the hospital for pills and back to his barracks and into bed.

He lost three days of work with that migraine. Esther left each morning to teach at the Junior High and Parin went off with her babysitters. As he lay alone in the darkened bedroom in their apartment, his ears rang and he couldn't move his head from side to side without bringing on an episode of vomiting. He couldn't even keep plain water down. Every time he thought of Nebo, he grew desperate. He remembered how he'd recruited Nebo. It had been early on when they were organizing the Co-op and Denton was just coming up against the divisions between the American-born Nisei, the Japanese-born Issei and the American-born, Japanese-educated Kibei. Denton needed to bring the Kibei into the Co-op to make it an organization for everyone in camp, and Nebo showed leadership potential. He was smart, didn't toady, and had his feet firmly in both cultures. When Denton approached him, laying out the concepts of the Co-op, one man one vote, participatory democracy, Nebo looked straight at him and said, "To what end? To subdue us further?" Denton didn't give up; he worked on Nebo over many weeks, describing how the five dollar membership fee would go toward buying power in the outside marketplace, and at the same time would purchase a piece of the store for each member. He explained how the membership could end up with a chain of stores where they could get items not available through the camp administration or the Sears Roebuck catalogue, items ordered by other Japanese-Americans who knew their needs and tastes, products that would be suited to their way of life inside this place. And to top it off, there would be a patronage refund to all members at the end of the year. In the end, Denton finally convinced Nebo that he was being honest in his desire to help people through the Co-op.

But Denton was terrified he was losing Nebo Mota. Whenever he emerged from sleep to a twilight state, he thought—through a miasma of pain—of how he had taken Nebo under his wing and taught him about organizing techniques. He remembered feeling he was passing knowledge on like a father to a son, though that was screwy, he thought in his foggy state. Nebo was only seven years younger than he. More like an older brother to a kid brother. Yes, more along those lines.

"You've always got to go into the meeting knowing what each party wants and what cards they're holding," Denton saw himself tell Nebo over coffee after dinner while Esther did the dishes in the next room. "You don't want to be surprised needlessly. There are enough ambushes even after you've done meticulous legwork. And always keep your primary goal in mind. You want people to join the Co-op and stay there, because it's the one place in this prison where they can still participate in democracy. It's the one place they can regain a semblance of control over their lives." Nebo eventually became the manager of the general store, and he was superb at the job.

Denton lay in the darkness, undone by sadness and loss, with his heart pounding at the base of his throat.

When Denton could finally keep a cup of consommé in his stomach, could face the daylight glaring on snow and could get himself into the Co-op, the Nebo Mota who greeted him in the store aisles was already a changed man. Nebo continued to work as the manager, and he came to all the meetings. He showed up every day at eight o'clock in the morning and he stocked the shelves. But he was no longer innovative in developing selling strategies, he took no pride in the product displays, and he alternated between subdued hostility and nitpicking during Co-op board meetings. And in March, Nebo signed "no" to numbers 27 and 28 of the loyalty questionnaire; "No" he would not serve in the armed forces, and "no" he would not renounce his allegiance to Japan and the emperor.

An eight-foot man-proof fence was constructed around the already-existing outer fence of the camp, "disloyals" from the other nine camps were transferred in, and a majority of the Tule Lake "loyals" were moved out. Throughout the transition Denton and Nebo had maintained a formal but cordial working relationship, giving Denton hope that he could reach Nebo again.

Denton was in the main Co-op store when a phone call summoned him to Andross's office. A farmworker's truck had crashed and Seiko Kitamara, an Issei truck farmer from the Sacramento area, was dead, and Ray Sato, the driver, was in the hospital with a broken leg. In the early days Denton had conducted labor arbitration sessions for the men who worked out on the camp farm, and he knew Kitamara and Sato well.

Denton drove immediately to the administration building. Taking the stairs to the porch two at a time, he arrived just in time to file in with the other men summoned. Denton was shocked to see Nebo Mota dressed in the white uniform of the militant pro-Japanese *Hoshidan*. Once inside Andross' office, Denton was further surprised to find that Nebo had also become a member of the eight-man Negotiating Committee, the *Daihyo Sha Kai*, whose job it had been to speak on behalf of the residents to the administration ever since the loyalty questionnaire troubles. They were a group of elected representatives who had become increasingly hard-line, and, judging by Andross's expression, the director was not happy to have them in his office.

The eight men settled into the usual semicircle in front of Andross's desk. Everyone but Nebo was dressed in rolled blue jeans, work shirts and thick sweaters, indicating they'd come directly from work. Even with their growing animosity toward the director, if they'd been given enough notice, the older men would have worn suits to the meeting.

"Gentlemen, the funeral will take place on Saturday—God willing that the ashes arrive—in the Buddhist church near the widow Kitamara's block, and only close friends and family will be permitted to attend," Andross said, beginning abruptly with no welcome, no courtesies to these guests in his office.

Denton was struck anew by how little this man understood of Japanese culture.

Nebo stood.

"There's no need to stand, Mr. Mota," Andross said.

"We feel that the widow was coerced into having a private funeral," Nebo said, remaining on his feet. "Her original wish was to have a camp-wide funeral to properly honor her husband."

"The rules and regulations don't allow it," Andross said.

"There are rules and regulations for the funeral of a prisoner?" Nebo asked, his voice feigning innocence.

Andross began to tap a rhythm on his desk with his thumb.

"Are these rules written?" Nebo asked.

"And if they are, Mr. Mota?"

"Then we would like to see them."

"Operational rules and regulations are not for public consumption, Mr. Mota." Ted Andross flushed, betraying his lie.

"We could write to the Spanish Consulate and ask them about that, Director Andross."

Denton waited for the challenge to sink in. The Consulate had been named by the Japanese Government to intercede when Japanese interests within the United States were threatened.

Andross's thumb fell silent. "The Spanish government's role is to protect Japanese citizens in this country, nothing more, Mr. Mota."

"Mr. Seiko Kitamara was a citizen of Japan. He didn't renounce his allegiance to his country of birth."

The seven other representatives hummed agreement, nodding.

"We're not asking any more than you would for your own people under similar conditions," Nebo continued. "We request a funeral where all neighbors may embrace the grieving."

Andross stood. "That's quite enough for today, Mr. Mota. I have already denied the request. Thank you, gentlemen. I think our meeting is adjourned."

Nebo didn't move. "We will have a public, traditional funeral even if the project director doesn't give permission. It is what the widow Kitamara wishes."

"Mota," Andross seethed, leaning forward, his weight on his knuckles on the top of his desk. "You and your committee are putting pressure on the widow to get her consent. Leave the poor woman alone to grieve. I've heard from reliable sources that it's the fault of the drivers in the motor pool that Kitamara is dead. They were racing down a rutted road, trying to beat each other to the turnoff and the truck Kitamara was in skidded into the ditch. It is their irresponsibility that caused his death. It is on their souls. I am not going to reward such wanton disregard for life and furthermore, I am not going to be browbeaten into doing your bidding."

When the door closed behind the committee members, Andross was slumped in his desk chair, a hand shielding his eyes.

"We're going to have a riot on our hands if we don't accede to some of their demands, mark my words, sir," Denton said.

Andross answered without looking up, his voice flat. "I don't want to hear any of your sob-sister cant, Jordan. I'm in charge here. They cannot have their Jap funeral. If I don't draw the line somewhere, we'll have anarchy."

The next day the farmworkers refused to return to work harvesting the fall crop, going on strike to demand compensation for the widow and her family, a mass funeral, higher wages and safeguards against accidents in the future.

As threatened, the mass funeral took place on Saturday afternoon. Nebo, his *Hoshidan* militants, and the *Daihyo Sha Kai* stood guard at the perimeter while five thousand residents gathered for the public ceremony. They congregated in the administration's parade grounds, in open defiance of the project director. Denton tried to attend, out of respect for the family, but for the first time in his tenure in camp he was turned away. Nebo himself stood before Denton, imposing in his white uniform in the bright sunlight, his face browner than his newly shaved head. He bowed to Denton. "I'm sorry, Mr. Jordan-san, but it is not necessary that you attend today. We can take care of this matter ourselves." Denton wanted to yell, "I fought for you. I stood up for you," but he saw that Nebo would not hear him. He bowed to Nebo, and without saying another word, turned to leave.

"Did you know that your project director broke the strike?" Nebo called after him.

Denton wheeled around. "What the hell are you saying?"

"He brought in farmworker 'volunteers' from the other camps to work."

"You mean scabs?"

"If you don't know about it, maybe that's where you should be spending your time, meeting with your great director. They say two truckloads of 'loyals' arrived last night from the train station at Klamath Falls. They were driven directly to the farm. They say more are on the way. It's rumored that he's promised to pay them a dollar an hour, what our men were earning in a day."

"Where did you get this information, Nebo?"

"Not from the project director. And not from you," he answered, his voice cruel with reproach. Nebo bowed deeply before walking away.

Denton felt as though he'd been bludgeoned as he watched Nebo's progress across the parade ground, through the throngs of people, until he reached the stage the leaders had erected, and marched up the stairs. Another headache threatened, but Denton could tell it wouldn't amount to much. Above them the American flag whipped in the wind, and beyond, in the distance, Denton saw the double line of chain-link fence topped by barbed wire. His eyes smarted. If he hadn't gotten that headache back in February, if he'd been able to stay with Nebo in his barracks through that night while Nebo was still raw and vulnerable, Denton could have kept him in the fold, could have convinced him that they would find a way around the loyalty questionnaire quagmire. But he hadn't, and look where all his cultivation of Nebo's leadership qualities had brought them.

The loudspeaker system squawked, and Nebo, at the microphone, began to address the crowd in a passionate voice.

Back in Andross's office, Denton confronted the director with the information.

"I had to save the crops. We're dependent on them," Andross said, admitting that he'd developed the plan secretly, consulting no one on the staff. "I had no recourse, gentlemen, but to bring in 'loyals' to do the work."

"An old American custom, strikebreaking," Herm muttered.

"What was that, Katz?" Andross was tight-lipped.

"I don't think bringing in scabs has helped matters, judging by the mess we have out there on the parade grounds," Herm said.

The blare of the loudspeaker entered the office. "Now I've got to clean it up. I'm in charge of security in here."

"So you are, Katz. So you are," Andross snapped.

"It would help if you could resume negotiations with the workers," Denton said.

"Oh, it would? I hear you did labor arbitration at camp early on. Do you think you could handle it, Jordan? Do you think you could defuse the situation in time to get those crops in before they're all ruined?"

If you'd be willing to give a little, Denton thought. "I'd be willing to try for the sake of all of us," he said.

"Well, for the sake of all of us, *I* wouldn't," Andross answered.

Chapter Four

After the three Military Police departed to escort Bill, Toki, and Nebo back to their barracks, Denton walked through the night with Herm and Sy. Off in the distance an occasional light shone from the staff barracks.

"Hey, Denton, wait up," Herm called out.

Denton had marched ahead of the other two men. He stopped. They joined him and the three walked in silence, Herm's six-foot-four presence on Denton's right, Sy's small, skinny frame on his left. After a few minutes, Denton realized he was ahead of them again.

"Why didn't you say a goddamn thing? What the hell was going on in there? What does that man think he's doing, humiliating people over and over?"

"Hey, Denton, hold on. You don't know what happened out there tonight. That Nebo's no angel," Herm said.

"I know he's not an angel. But at least he's speaking up. At least he's articulating people's concerns. What do you say, Sy? You're supposed to know what people are feeling."

"Well," Sy said, and then lapsed into one of his impregnable silences.

"Well what?" Denton shouted at him.

"I really don't want to go into it tonight, not at this hour."

"Why don't you? Why didn't you say anything in there?"

"Stop it!" Herm yelled back at Denton. "You're acting like a lunatic. Can't you hear what Toki Honda, your own Co-op manager, says? Can't you see that Bill Nakamura is being hurt by this? Nebo and his henchmen are trying to intimidate everyone. They would have killed me tonight, Dent. These radical heroes of yours would have killed a guy who's always been fundamentally on their side."

They'd been over this very same argument many times in the past few weeks. Denton had disagreed with Herm, with Esther and with

27

Sy, when Sy was willing to take a side. And he disagreed with Bill Nakamura, too; Bill thought that the militants were ultimately making life worse for people. On the other hand, Bill supported many of their positions, particularly the farmers' work stoppage and their demand for a decent wage. After all, Bill said, the Issei farmers had come here and cultivated three thousand acres of land that had never produced anything more than potatoes and horseradish. Now the land grew every vegetable imaginable, and the local farmers were hanging around watching what the Issei did. "The next thing you know Washington will be kicking us out of here," Bill had said sarcastically. "They'll say we're posing a security threat, eighteen thousand Japs in one place, plotting how we can take over their farmland."

"It isn't as simple as you'd like to make it," Denton said to Herm.

"Simple?" A strong gust of wind practically blew away Herm's last word. "Who's making things simple? C'mon, Dent, let's go to my place and have this out. We've got to talk this through and I can't stand out here in the freezing cold much longer. I'm gonna drop."

"I'm for it," Denton said. "Sy, how about you?"

"No, no, I can't. I've got to get home and check on Sarah and Annie." He'd already backed away from them, pulling his hat down and his coat collar up, all but disappearing into the darkness.

Denton felt a momentary pang, knowing that he, too, should return to the barracks and see how Parin and Esther were doing. But he'd be out of Herm's in no time. Better to go over this with Herm instead of driving Esther "to distraction" with it, as she would say.

"You're sure about that, Sy? It might do us good to talk this out." Denton said. It would be best if Sy were with them; if they both got home at about the same time.

"Naw," said Sy. "Sarah's a little postpartum as it is, if you know what I mean. See you fellows tomorrow." He walked toward the family apartments. He hesitated when he'd gone a few steps as though, on second thought, he wanted to join them. But then he waved without looking around, and continued on to his apartment.

Denton and Herm didn't try to talk as they made their way to Herm's room. The powerful wind came from the north. Though it was barely November it felt like January. Esther had said the other day that she didn't know if she could stand another winter in this place. Even when they'd stopped up every crack and hole in their walls last winter, the wind had still drafted through.

Herm Katz lived alone, half a mile away from the family section, in barracks more rudimentary than the Jordans'. Denton followed Herm up the three steps to the walkway that ran the length of the hundred-foot, tarpapered one-story building. Each strip of barracks contained four apartments; Herm's was at the eastern end of the row. Denton stopped to look out across the firebreak that separated the administration from the evacuees. From here he could see that the searchlights had been turned on around the entire perimeter of the camp. For a mile to the east their beams lit the roofs of row upon row of the evacuees' barracks, latrines, mess halls, community rooms and laundry rooms; each block seemed exactly like every other when you couldn't see the personal touches of gardens, fences, false facades and statues. Each was as desolate as the next in the night—black buildings, black shadows, on black sand. The same view stretched for a mile to the west, and to the north, too.

"Make yourself at home, buddy," Herm said, stamping in and going straight over to the potbellied iron coal stove. He clanged open its door and threw in two shovels of coal from a pail standing to the left. "I'm so cold I could cry. This sure isn't the life, I can tell you." Kneeling down to poke the embers, he looked over his shoulder at Denton. "I don't think I'm gonna last, Dent. I think I'll be following Sylvie out of here. She was right to leave when she did."

Denton sat in the standard cushioned, blond-wood Sears Roebuck chair found in every staff apartment. He kept his coat on. The room was so cold he could see his breath. He didn't want to hear this from Herm. When Herm's wife Sylvia had left in September with their six-month-old boy, Davy, Herm had been devastated, but he'd said to Sylvia and to Denton that he had to see this thing through into the spring. He felt a commitment. He was afraid of who might come in after him, especially with Andross's repeated threat of calling in the army. "A bunch of racist bastards," Herm had said. "We might as well be in Germany with those guys. With one little shift of policy, they could do the same to our friends here as the Nazis are doing to my people."

Herm came over and sat on the edge of the matching Sears and Roebuck sofa. "I've come to the end of my rope. I was hanging by my teeth before, Dent. Really." He grimaced, almost closing his puffy eyes. Herm's whole face looked swollen with fatigue. His skin was pasty-white beneath the large freckles. There was dried blood on his chin,

29

which must have dribbled from the gash on his forehead and been missed when the rest of the blood had been wiped away. "I'm ashamed—you know that, don't you? Ashamed to be a quitter in this way."

Denton got up and walked around the small room. Herm had a kitchenette with a hot plate, a sink and an icebox along the inside wall that backed his bathroom. A narrow cot was pushed against the wall under the only window. Denton stopped at the coal-burning stove and stood with his hands over it, his back to Herm. Some heat was coming up. He didn't know what to say. He felt as if Herm were leaving *him*; as though he, Denton, had failed Herm in some way, had failed to notice his distress, had failed to protect his friend. He cleared his throat. "Is there any way I can convince you to stay?"

"Look at these, will you," Herm said, holding his hands up. The backs were scratched and dirt was deeply embedded in his knuckles and caked under his fingernails. There was a raw abrasion on his left wrist, blood-red and streaked with the black lava sand.

"They got like this from crawling my way out from under the jeep. You know what it felt like to see those angry faces at my window and windshield? All of them hating me because I was white. Hating me because I'm goddamned in charge of security at this camp. At least until tonight I was; after this they'll have the army to contend with. They'll get no sympathy out of those army men from what I can figure. A real bunch of rednecks." He let his hands drop to his knees. "How could they be so stupid? They've got a sympathetic guy in me. I've proven myself over and over, so what do they do? They attack me, turning my damn jeep over, trying to kill me. They had me pitching and rolling like a boat on Puget Sound before the whole damn thing went over on me. No, siree, I was betrayed tonight, and I'm only human. It's one thing to be monkeyed with by Andross, but to be attacked by the very people I thought I was doing good by? Sorry, Dent, it hurt too much."

Denton kicked lightly at the base of the stove. "I wish I'd been here. I'm sure I could have made it work out differently."

"You think you're god almighty, don't you? Yahweh himself. I love you, buster, but you've got an inflated view of your own power. And you're not addressing what I brought up. Stay with the topic on the floor. What about it? What about these hotheads turning on me, Herm

30

Katz, who's been on their side through this whole ordeal? What about that, Dent?"

"But that's part and parcel of our commitment to working here. If you choose to do for people, you've got to take the consequences. It's not all glory in this business."

"I hoped you wouldn't say that, Dent, but I would have staked my money on just that holier-than-thou answer."

"That's the way you answer a serious statement? What the hell is the matter with you?" Denton kicked hard at the stove.

"Don't go high and mighty on me, Dent. You're turning your back on all you believe in when you take their position. It conflicts with your pacifism. And with working your butt off to get those men to work together."

"I warned Ted Andross," Denton sat back down on the chair opposite Herm. He shook his fist at Herm. "I said if he didn't give in to some of their demands there would be a riot. You can't take everything away from people and expect them not to react."

"You're not answering me. I call the question. Stay on the topic. What about your pacifism? These fellows are militarists. And tonight they used violence against me."

Denton spoke under his breath. "That wasn't violence, that was reactive behavior."

"What?" Herm shouted.

Startled, Denton looked up to see his friend's hazel eyes glaring at him from under his bandage. The bruise was darkening under his eye and over his cheekbone.

"Sorry," Denton said. "I'm sorry."

"Don't give me your goddamn liberal sorry. That was violence out there, pure and simple. Who knows where it would have led if the army hadn't stepped in. I'm grateful they did." Herm stopped and pinched the bridge of his nose. "I'm still upset," he said quietly. "But you're going to have to come to terms with this. You cannot be a pacifist and still go along with them." He covered his face with his big hands.

Denton laughed nervously. "How about we put this talk off for another day? Let's have a drink, what do you say?"

But Herm kept his face covered. Denton wondered if Herm might be crying. The only man Denton had ever seen cry was his older

31

brother Huey when Huey had come back from the war in Europe with shell-shock, and all he did was weep. The doctor said Huey would stop crying eventually, which he did, but then Huey disappeared into catatonic muteness, relieved only by shrieking escapes to the dark, spidery place under their back porch where he would remain until the ambulance came to take him away. That happened more times than Denton wished to count.

"So when is it you're thinking of taking off?" Denton spoke to the top of Herm's bowed head, to the disorder of his auburn curls.

Herm didn't answer. The room was warming up. Sand spit lightly against the windows. The wind seemed to have let up some. There were times when it hurtled for days across the flats of the dried lake bed, bashed against the buildings, whipped up the firebreaks as if it had a life of its own. Not tonight. But it was still coming from the north. That meant it would be cold tomorrow. The sound of the wind and sputtering sand made him sad, and the memory of Huey gave him a hollow feeling inside.

Denton shifted in his chair, leaned back, and waited. It scared him to think of Herm not being here. They were a team, Denton the more politically radical, Herm driven by his complete decency, his compassion, his clear sense of right and wrong. They'd been friends since May 27, 1942, a year and a half earlier, when he and Herm had been assigned to meet the first trains of evacuees. He remembered how the train moved slowly down the line, on the far side of State Highway 139, which ran between the hastily erected camp and the high, craggy outcrop of Castle Rock. He and Herm were late and they came racing across the highway but they were caught on the camp side as the train rolled to a stop. Window shades, shut for the duration of the nighttime trip from the coast, snapped up one by one. Framed in the mud-spattered, soot-smeared windows were two young women holding infants, a man about Denton's age, a small girl in pigtails. A teenager reached over and opened one of the windows, then moved back to give an elderly couple an unobstructed view of their destination. The old man wore a brimmed hat, the woman a straw bonnet with a sprig of silk flowers attached to the crown. They blinked their eyes in the bright morning sun, their faces expressionless until the moment when they saw the high chain-link fence with three bands of barbed wire stretched along the top and the watch towers with armed soldiers standing guard. The old woman shrank against her husband's body as she stared up at the tower. The man spoke to her, but his murmurings didn't seem to bring her comfort.

Young mothers who struggled down the train's stairs with their new babies and small children, and young men who in a sane world would be getting off at a college campus were hard enough to bear, but the frail old men who trembled as they leaned against his arm were the ones who hurt Denton the most. He'd said so to Herm during that grueling day as they processed close to four hundred arrivals. "Yep," Herm had answered, "I agree." Herm told Denton that every time he helped one of those guys down he thought of his Great-Uncle Osaf in Poland, and hoped there was some sympathetic soul giving his uncle an arm to lean on. "That's how I can tolerate participating in this degradation," he said. "I'm doing it for my Uncle Osaf."

The evacuees were fingerprinted and had their mug shots taken, and then it was Denton's job to accompany family groups to their new homes. He walked with them across the endless dusty parade grounds and firebreak toward the blocks of new barracks. Each barracks was constructed of quarter-inch-thick boards over wooden frames, and covered with tarpaper that was nailed to the walls and the peaked roof with batten strips. Line upon line of these long, black buildings stretched north for a mile, each topped with four cylindrical tin chimneys, held in place by guy wires. Each block consisted of fourteen barracks bordering two sides of a large open rectangle. The hundred-foot-long by twenty-foot-wide barracks buildings had been partitioned inside to make four apartments; each apartment was a single room, twenty by twenty-five feet. Roughly fitted windows were positioned up under the eaves, and the door to each room opened out from the side of the barracks. Up to six people were to live in a room. At the north side of each block, a building the size of two barracks was designated as the mess hall and another barracks served as a recreation hall. Down the center of the block were separate tarpapered, cement-floored structures for the women's latrine and shower room, the men's latrine and shower room, one laundry room, and an ironing room. A coal bin stood outside at the head of the laundry room. Nine of these identical blocks made up a ward. The wards were separated by vast firebreaks, which were seventy-foot-wide open lanes of black sand. By the time the evacuees started arriving, four wards had been completed and additional wards were being constructed at the north and south ends of camp.

Denton was so busy helping people lug their huge suitcases and awkward cloth bundles that he barely noticed their reactions. It was only when a family arrived at its assigned building and Denton opened the door of their stark twenty-by-twenty-five-foot room that the reality struck. Suddenly he saw through their eyes: the splintery floor; the sheet-rock dividing walls between family groups, that didn't reach the ceiling; the steel cots with empty, unstuffed mattress covers on top; and the potbellied coal stove in the center of the room. Nothing more. He caught the shock on the Issei women's faces that first day, just before they hid all emotion. After that he learned not to enter the room with the family. Instead he remained outside when they went in; their pain was too excruciating to witness.

Each night after meeting the trains, Denton would fall exhausted onto his cot in the staff dormitory, with Esther and Parin in another dormitory, and sleep deeply and without dreaming, only to awaken before dawn to a high, piercing keening. They're crying, he thought, they want to go home. By the time color streaked the gray sky, the wailing would have died down. After a couple of mornings he asked Herm if he had heard the crying. They sat across from each other in a makeshift mess hall filled with people who had arrived the night before. There were squalling babies, children who sat in stunned, sleepy silence, and mothers who cajoled their children and sullen husbands into eating the unappetizing food. He saw one man spit into his plate. When Denton asked his new friend the question, Herm leaned closer and said, "It's the wind. I heard the same thing. It's not crying. There's not enough privacy in this damn place for them to grieve." Herm shook his head and continued eating, scowling as he spooned up the bland oatmeal.

"You think you'll take off right away?" Denton asked, trying again. He wished he could say something profound, insightful, to change Herm's mind. But nothing came to him.

"I don't know yet." Herm's voice was muffled by his hands.

"Maybe you could take a visit home. See Sylvie and Davy. That would help."

"I miss them. You're right." Herm sighed. "But that's not it. I've been sucked dry. I'm useless here except maybe to keep the peace, but I can't even do that anymore. It's gotten out of hand. Tonight they broke the camel's back." Gingerly he touched the bandage over his wound where blood was beginning to seep through. He opened his eyes. "You should get out of here, too. Your wires are frayed. We're neither of us much good for anybody."

Denton stood up abruptly. "It's late. I should have gone straight back home."

"The biggest favor you could do for Esther is to get the hell out of here."

"And the evacuees? Who's going to defend them if we both leave?"

"They can damn well take care of themselves."

"That's not what you used to say."

"I used to be a different person. I used to believe I could make a difference. Not any more."

"I'll miss you."

Herm stood up painfully. "Thanks for saying that. I'm not taking off tomorrow, you realize. Sylvie always complained that I couldn't ever get out of the house when we were going anywhere. It drove her crazy. How could I expect to accomplish anything if I couldn't even get out the door?"

Denton nodded as he buttoned his coat. "See you tomorrow, then."

"Hey, I've got an idea before you go," Herm said, hobbling over to the icebox. "How about that drink you mentioned? So we end the evening on a better note."

Chapter Five

Denton stood at the bottom of the barracks stairs gulping in the cold air before starting home. He was tipsy, reeling from the scotch. The wind had picked up, but the sky was clear, with no clouds, just moon and stars and black oblivion. Pulling his watch from his pants pocket, he got a jolt. It was almost three o'clock. How the hell had the time gone by so quickly?

He set off, bent into the wind. He could hear Herm, "The biggest favor you could do for Esther is to get out of here."

There had been a time when Esther wasn't always after him for this or that failing or slip-up. They had once thought their love was a romance linked to the political and social changes in the country, a love between intellectual equals, a mixed-religion love that broke down barriers of prejudice and defied the odds.

He remembered their first date on Christmas Day and how he showed up at her Grandmother Leah's house in Oakland to find Esther sitting outside on the stucco stairwall waiting for him. She wore a navy blue dress with a white dickey, looking beautiful in the late afternoon light; her olive skin was dark against the white collar, her black curly hair cut fashionably short. The low slanting sun was warm and he was so filled with stage fright that he was sweating up his wool suit jacket. He'd felt like a nothing sort of fellow coming to meet this illustrious family of Jewish intellectuals; Esther's father, Dr. Harry Kahn was an immigrant who had worked his way into the position of State Chemist and her mother, Dr. Judith Kahn, was a respected and feared biology professor at Berkeley. It was said that she was brilliant and demanding, and could make a fraternity man grovel and weep. Even though he almost had his own doctorate in economics and had met Esther while proctoring her labor economics final, which gave him a little leverage, all Denton could think about was that he was a mere Gentile from the Ballard section of Seattle, the second son and middle child of a failed Colorado rancher turned accountant, son of an adulterer and his bitter wife, and the younger brother of a shell-shocked soldier.

Esther came to meet him on the walkway, smiling broadly, causing the dimple in her left cheek to dig deeply in.

"Hi," she said breathlessly, linking her arm in his. He noticed that she was almost as tall as he was. He liked the feeling of physical equality.

"You ready?" she asked. "We only have to say hello and then we can go to the movies. I hope you don't hate them."

"Why should I hate them?"

"They're quite overwhelming." She glanced nervously over at him. "And very Jewish."

"I know that, Esther Kahn," he said, pressing her arm into his body, relaxing in the realization that she was jittery as well. "What I don't understand is why they gather together on Christmas?"

"They all get the day off. Mother says Christmas is a state-provided opportunity for busy Jewish professionals."

Savory, dense aromas enveloped him when they entered the house. Different sized tables had been pushed together to make one that snaked through the small living room and into the dining alcove. Layers of white linen and lace covered the uneven surface and the place settings were a hodgepodge of linen napkins, old china, silver, and crystal glasses. To Denton it all spoke of a European refinement even though nothing seemed to match, including the thirty or so assorted kitchen and dining room chairs that were crowded cheek-by-jowl around the table. The parlor's overstuffed red velvet easy chairs and sofa were shoved against walls and windows. Every bit of leftover space was bursting with aunts and uncles, cousins and grandparents talking at full volume. He didn't think he'd ever seen a house so packed with people and all of them related. He shunted aside an image of his own dark, silent and austere home; he was a new person walking in here.

Leah Siegal, the diminutive grandmother, came through the swinging mahogany kitchen door, limping on a raised oxford shoe. She was in her eighties and well under five feet tall. Full-bosomed with squared-off shoulders, she had a face like Edward G. Robinson's sitting atop a thick, short neck. She held Denton's hand between rough, warm leathery palms, while she looked up to examine him carefully. Esther had told him Grandma Leah persisted in running a secondhand clothing store, even after sending all five children through the university on its earnings, so that her husband could continue with his private scholarship. "An old Jewish tradition," Esther had said. "The women make the money so the men can study forever."

"So this is the professor who gave our Esther a B on her exam," Leah Siegal chided, an ironic smile twisting her full wide mouth.

"Grandma," Esther pleaded, leaning down to hug her.

"What? He gave our Esther a B?" A man in his fifties, a cup of punch in hand, called from where he stood in the archway to the living room. "I am paying half of that girl's tuition. I don't expect to see any B's. There never have been any before in the history of this entire family."

Esther was laughing. "That's what I told him, Uncle Hyman. Mr. Jordan said the writing was fine but the thoughts were flawed." She looked over at Denton with a mock accusatory look. "Why don't you explain to my uncle, Dr. Hyman Siegal the oral surgeon, why my ideas on Thorstein Veblen's theory of conspicuous consumption, particularly the analysis of Darwinian postulates as applied to society were not worth an A?"

"Ridiculous," a woman said as she came down the wood-paneled staircase into the hallway. Her gray-streaked black hair was pulled back into a bun. She bore a resemblance to Leah Siegel in that she was stocky and anchored in her carriage, but where the old matriarch was welcoming, this woman's demeanor was severe.

Esther sobered. "Mother, this is Denton Jordan. Denton, my mother, Dr. Kahn."

She's everything she's rumored to be, he thought, as he shook her hand, looking into cold gray eyes behind steel-rimmed glasses.

Grandma Leah insisted that they stay to eat. "So you shouldn't run out to the movies on an empty stomach."

By the end of the meal there was nothing but praise for Denton's eating ability. He had stuffed himself with brisket and boiled potatoes, cabbage and three helpings of kugel.

"So you're not Jewish, young man," another uncle said, a lung doctor whose face was shining and flushed from the sweet purple wine.

"He seems Jewish," Aunt Ruth the librarian said.

"He eats like he's Jewish," Grandma Leah said.

"He argues like he's Jewish," Uncle Hyman yelled.

By now Denton, feeling both pleased and discomfited at being the center of attention, was laughing helplessly. Esther had her napkin over her mouth and was laughing so hard tears were coming down her cheeks.

"But he listens like a Gentile-man," Esther's idiosyncratic father quipped quietly at Denton's left. Throughout the dinner the dark haired, slender man had been regaling Denton with his intense theories about evolution. "When have any of you ever stopped talking so as to listen through to the end of my ideas?"

"He wants to court your daughter, is why," a fat aunt called from the dining alcove.

"So he gives a B, if he wants her so much?" Uncle Hyman said.

"You're sure this boy isn't Jewish, Esther, and trying to pass?" the librarian said, her pale blue eyes glinting with humor.

Denton tramped across the barren camp in the freezing darkness remembering how their teasing had made him feel like a small boy being tumbled in the grass yelling, "Don't tickle me!" and all the time hoping they would never, ever stop. Even Judith Kahn's judging look from down the table hadn't dampened his pleasure.

Esther had been kind to him, as though she sensed his insecurities and didn't hold them against him, as though she wanted to make life easier for him. No one had ever done that for him before. One night at a tea dance, he led her in a foxtrot, feeling masterful, with Esther, slender and graceful in his arms. As they dipped and glided across the ballroom, and she nestled closer to him, pelvis to pelvis, she said, "I can feel your hip bones." She squeezed his middle. "Your ribs are sticking out. Don't you eat?" His skin prickled with the heat of shame. "What is it?" she asked, stopping in the middle of the floor. Patterns of light and dark off the ceiling's rotating mirrored globe swirled around them. "You're not eating, are you? Your cheeks are hollow," she said, touching his face.

On the balcony of the hotel, looking out to the bay, he confessed to her that he was skipping meals to pay for their dates. Tonight he remembered how awful it had been to have to admit to her that there wasn't enough money in his family to pay for school. "We'll just have to economize," she said, matter-of-factly. "It's more in keeping with our beliefs, anyway, don't you think?" He'd embraced her and to the strains of the band reaching them from inside the hall, they'd twirled and side-stepped elegantly at their own private dance. He'd whispered, "But I'll never stop dancing with you. We won't join the revolution unless we can dance." What he couldn't tell her was that even if there had been money, no one in his family cared enough to help him pay his way.

And she'd been such a good sport. When Denton got a job in the Farm Security Administration, Esther agreed to spend their honeymoon in the Farm Security Camp in Arvin, California, in the San Joaquin Valley, the same camp that was memorialized in Steinbeck's *The Grapes of Wrath*. Esther wrote thank-you notes for gifts of Franciscan-ware, silver, and crystal seated on a shabby canvas chair set on the dirt floor of their tent. They stayed up late those nights, talking over their work: Denton's attempts to convince corporate farmers to hire the displaced Okies, Esther's plans for getting nutritious meals into the scrawny children and their emaciated parents, Denton's struggle to figure out how to apply the principles of the co-operative movement to landless dust bowl farmers, and his pleas to the camp administration to set up a soup kitchen for the bindlestiffs who tramped the countryside and came up to the gate for handouts.

They were proud of the life they had chosen, proud of being involved in the remaking of the country, and when Parin was conceived and born, they were thrilled that their daughter was started in Arvin camp. "She can point to the *Grapes of Wrath* whenever they ask her at school where she was born," Denton bragged when they brought Parin back to the tent, and their colleagues and the Oklahoma farmers crowded in.

It was during the first week of December 1941 that things began to unravel in the world, and—he saw it with stark clarity tonight— how in an uncanny way the world crisis paralleled the subsequent difficulties in their private life. He and Esther had taken Parin up to Grandma Leah's so they could be by themselves for a few days' break in Monterey. Denton would always remember sitting in the car overlooking the ocean when Roosevelt spoke the fatal words over the radio; "This date will live in infamy..." There was a stunted, twisted cypress tree framing their view of the Pacific through the windshield; he could smell salt and the resinous odor of pine. Esther felt soft and vulnerable in his arms, and he didn't tell her then that he knew he wouldn't be fighting, that he'd already had discussions with pacifists in Berkeley. Judith Kahn was an ardent Zionist. Harry Kahn sent money back to Vilna to save Jews; and Denton was certain they would see his pacifism as a betrayal. He was afraid to find out if Esther would feel it was a betrayal, too.

That's exactly when their problems had begun, Denton thought, as he arrived at their darkened barracks. Even though they had been enthusiastic when they'd come up here to Tule Lake, the issue of his draft status hung over them. Esther was thrilled to be teaching again, and he was involved in building the consumer co-op system throughout the camp; they told everyone they felt they were making a contribution, but privately Esther was subdued with him, and it had been that way since he'd gone to San Francisco to file as a conscientious objector. Oh, sure, Esther insisted she believed in what he was doing and had respect for his taking a profoundly difficult stand; she said, if she were a man she might make a similar choice. But there was a moment of telling silence when direct discussion of the war came up, whenever acquaintances talked about what was happening to Jews in Europe. Esther would retreat from the discussion, growing conspicuously quiet, even getting up and leaving the room.

Long before America entered the war, Esther's mother, who was active in Jewish rescue programs, had related shocking tales about concentration camps and massacres of Jews, stories that were not verified by Washington and never appeared in the newspapers or the Movietone News. "Our great Roosevelt is turning a deaf ear to this, conveniently for him and his career," Judith had said. After Denton declared to his draft board, after they had lied to Harry and Judith at Esther's request, saying Denton was 4-F because of his migraines, Esther didn't want him to go to the apartment with her. When Esther returned from her own visits, she no longer told him about Judith's reports from Europe. "How is Judith's work progressing? What has she heard?" he would press. "Honestly, Denton, it was hard enough to hear it from her. I don't feel like repeating it. Maybe later." But later never arrived.

Even enjoying her work in the Junior High, Esther had grown increasingly angry with him and melancholy, and it was only when Herm was around and cracked jokes about her being "Esther, Queen of our People, protector of the Jews" that she reminded Denton of her younger self.

And now Herm was leaving. How was Denton going to continue without Herm, his one Caucasian friend in the camp? He and Herm had kept each other's spirits up. When one would falter, discouraged by the cultural divide between them and the internees, tired of Japanese politeness, frustrated by the Japanese refusal to say what they meant, the other would be there with dark humor or a cogent reminder of the reasons they had committed themselves to working at Tule Lake.

This time he had no decent argument left. He couldn't convince Herm that staying made sense. All he could say to Herm was that he had a duty to sacrifice himself, as a radical, as a person who believed in the internees' right to self-government and self-determination. But he'd argued that for hours tonight over drinks and Herm wouldn't buy it. And Herm was correct; Denton couldn't defend the violence used against Herm and still call himself a pacifist and a conscientious objector.

The door creaked from the cold when he opened it and went inside.

The light was on over the sink. There was a note from Esther on the counter. "Denton, dearest, wake me when you get in. Love you, Esther."

Sobered, he felt worse about not coming directly home. He started to undress in the kitchen. Maybe he could slip into bed without waking her and in the morning he could fudge the time.

"Denton, is that you?" Esther's whispered call came from the bedroom.

"Yep." He picked up his shirt and pants and went to the door.

Esther turned on the lamp by the bed. Her long black hair, a lustrous mass of combed-out curls, fell on her shoulders. She wore a pair of his old gray-blue pajamas she'd made over by cutting off the collar and turning the material to create a scooped neck. "You're home at last," she said, squinting from the light.

"Yep, finally."

"Was it awful? What time is it?" she asked, reaching for the clock.

"It's late," he said, wishing he could grab it from her hands.

"My lord, it's after three. You poor thing." She put the clock back. "I didn't get to bed until one myself. Parin had an awful time. She wouldn't cry and wouldn't cry in the Community Room, but when we got here and I put her down and left the room, she began shrieking."

Denton dropped his clothes on the straight-backed chair, and too tired to bother with pajamas, he tucked in under the covers. The sheets were cold on his side of the bed, but he could feel heat coming from Esther.

"I wonder why she waited until she got home to start crying." He reached over and found her hand. It was warm.

"I don't know why." She pulled her hand away. His was freezing and she wasn't in the mood for handholding. She could smell liquor on him. When had he had time for a drink? She was the one who'd had to comfort Parin, to make some sense of her daughter's fears. Parin hadn't been able to say what she was afraid of. She kept calling for her babysitters, Mr. and Mrs. Takaetsue. "Mrs. Take, Mr. Take," she repeated over and over, which made Esther feel worse. Mr. and Mrs. Takaetsue were her true loves because the Issei couple spoiled her as they spoiled Japanese American children. Esther had to be the one to discipline her daughter. She resented it, though she could never say as much to Denton. He wouldn't approve.

"How did it go tonight? You still haven't told me." She reached over to stroke his body, running her hand down his chest. She shouldn't have rejected his hand. She loved the feel of his chest—smooth with very little hair. She remembered the first time they'd made love in his boardinghouse room, and how she'd lost herself in the astonishing satiny quality of his naked skin on her naked skin. But they barely touched in a sexual way anymore; it seemed too dangerous, fraught with possible conflict, and Denton was always fatigued these days and too preoccupied with the troubles in camp. The rare times they would get as far as trying, Denton would lose his erection before or shortly after he'd entered her. He would begin a litany of apology, saying he was sorry for always disappointing her, and she would assure him that he didn't always disappoint her, and that it was her fault too. "Maybe we love each other too much," he would say, nuzzling into the place where her neck met her shoulder. "Maybe so," she would answer, thinking he was becoming amorous, kissing him, digging her face in under his arm to smell his acrid odor, and she would imagine the other strong odors of sex, of the hair around his penis, of his semen, and the way his saliva tasted different after orgasm, but she soon found that this secondary flirtation was not a prelude to loving, and she learned to stem her own erotic longings. She had lashed out at him a few times for his "deception," and it was awful, leaving her hating herself and him.

"It was pretty rough, I guess." He felt better when she caressed him. He wished he dared to hold her. He would love to feel her body against his tonight. He wished they could just cuddle together without all the other complications.

"What do you mean, 'rough, you guess.' How was the meeting? Who was there?" Esther said impatiently.

She found a pack of Chesterfields in the night table drawer. She lit one, inhaling deeply, blowing the smoke in a straight column toward the ceiling. Denton felt wordless with fatigue. When she offered it to him, he took the cigarette without touching her skin. He dragged on it and handed it back. He turned on his side to face Esther as he exhaled, propping his head on his hand.

"Herm's leaving." It hurt to say the words.

"Oh, no," Esther exclaimed. But maybe we can leave, too, she thought; without Herm, maybe Denton cannot keep on. Esther looked at her husband, considering him carefully. Some people said he was like a dark-haired Scott Fitzgerald, with his long nose, high intelligent forehead and wide-spaced eyes. But his eyes were too dark and penetrating, too sorrowful and kind to belong to a self-indulgent boy, and his mouth was too sensitive. When he laughed, which he used to do often and with real abandon, he was a person unlike anyone she had ever met. His laughter could fill a room and every heart. But these days he rarely allowed himself to laugh.

"He said he didn't believe in what he was doing anymore."

"I'm not surprised," she said.

"What do you mean?"

"He's been discouraged for a while. Last week when he came to dinner, before you got here, he was so excited, saying Sylvia had written that Davy had spoken his first word and it was 'Da-da.' He asked me if that was just a reflex or could Davy remember him. I said, How could Davy forget such a nice father? He looked relieved but then he got this tragic expression on his face. He said he thought he should get out of here, that he wasn't doing any good for his family or the people here."

"I never noticed," Denton said. "As far as I could see he's been going on as usual. We're all a little tired from this turmoil." He waited for her to agree with him.

"You're supposed to be the great organizer, Denton. You're supposed to understand human dynamics. Why didn't you know what was happening to your best friend?" She stubbed out the half-smoked cigarette without offering him another draw.

"Esther."

"What is it?"

"I feel awful about this."

"I know you feel awful. But what I don't know is, why do you feel awful? Because you're losing a friend? Or losing a worker bee? Or losing another true believer?" An entire part of her was threatening to crack open; a place where she forgot she had ever loved him.

"I'm struggling to do my job here under horrible circumstances, but I can't do it all alone."

"Oh, but you think you can. That's just it."

"What do you mean by that?"

"Nothing." Esther got up. She felt around for her slippers under the bed, found them and put them on. She reached to the foot of the bed for her pink chenille robe.

"What's going on?" he asked.

"I want to sleep," she said, walking to the door. "I need my sleep for tomorrow. I have to wake up at dawn to take care of our unhappy daughter. I have to be cheerful and charming to the Takaetsues so they won't think I'm a shrewish mother, which they already think, but I don't want it to get worse. Then I have to walk out of here into that relentless wind to see if school will be open or not and whether or not I have a job anymore. If you know anything about the status of the schools, I'd appreciate your telling me."

"As far as I know they're open," he said sadly.

"Thank you for that piece of information. Then I certainly can't stay awake all night. You'll have to comfort yourself."

"Esther, come back to bed, please."

"No."

She went out to the couch. She hoped the woolen afghan and her robe would provide enough warmth. Without turning on the light she lay down and arranged the afghan over herself; her body heat would build in a moment. Already she was happier out here, away from Denton. She knew where the conversation would have led if she'd stayed there beside him. He would have lambasted Andross, as if Andross were the crux of the problem and had single-handedly ruined the good work Denton had single-handedly done. Not that Denton would ever say he'd done it all himself. No, he would talk about how Bill Nakamura, the Co-op president, had brought in the membership, and how Toki Honda, the general manager, had the respect of the Issei and Nisei communities because of his standing in the world prior to camp. Denton would say modestly that they had done the work, and that he, Denton, had only made it possible for them. He had been available, had the time, the knowledge of co-op principles, and was the one paid by the administration to see that the pieces went together properly. Damn his modesty. Damn his organizing skills. She knew that the underside of his humility was terror: if he wasn't vigilant every moment the entire Co-op operation would fall apart. It *was* crumbling, and he blamed himself; proof of his egotism. She began to cry. What was she turning into? What kind of bitter wife? She'd fallen in love with him for his organizing skills, for his original ideas, for the complexity of his mind. He understood what motivated people and what actions would follow from their needs and desires; like a chess master he could plot long sequences of moves. She had loved his ability to control, yet not seem to be controlling. What had gone so terribly wrong between them?

Denton came out of the bedroom and sat down on the edge of the couch, but she shifted away from him. She knew without opening her eyes that he wore his robe. She could smell it, the wool that had absorbed his odor over the years. That maroon robe had been her first anniversary gift to him when they were living down in Arvin migrant camp. Their salaries were minimal, and the bathrobe was a luxury item. It was too hot to wear in the San Joaquin Valley, but she'd said, "Someday we'll be moving north again." They did eventually move north to San Francisco, where he began to wear it, and when she tried to take the robe from him to wash it, he refused.

"I like it wrinkled and soiled. I'm a simple man."

"Simple and smelly," she'd said.

"The best kind," he'd countered, smiling seductively.

"You're right, that's the way I like my men." She'd laughed and pulled him down onto the bed that night and they'd made love.

"Nice and dirty," she'd whispered later. "The dirtier the better."

That's the way it had been, she thought, overwhelmingly erotic.

There had been a time when they could barely get their clothes off fast enough, when the passion was that insistent.

"Hi," Denton said, putting his arms around her and nuzzling in under her chin.

He hadn't bathed today. He gave off the warm muskiness that she loved. Leaning away she looked at him again. In the wedge of light from the bedroom, she saw that his face was drawn, blanched to a flat beige. A deep crevice had formed between his brows, and his jaw line sagged. She felt pity for him, her anger evaporating into empathy.

As he held her, he felt her resistance give way and, grateful, he kissed her. She had the softest lips of anyone in the world. He took her hand in his, lifting it into the light to examine her fingers. She snipped her nails to the quick, and used no polish, just as she wore no makeup but lipstick. Her lower knuckles were red and shiny. She often complained, as everyone did, of how hard the mineral-filled water was. He kissed the curl of her fingers.

Esther thought, How strange marriage is. How was it that after five years of being together, she could one minute feel she hated him and had made a horrible mistake by marrying him, and the next she could be consumed by love for his lips, the curve of his cheek, his tiredness, the seriousness of his vocation. No one ever told you about this part of living with a husband, this violent seesawing within the span of a day, or even within an hour.

He held her close for a while, not saying anything. He didn't want to talk. He had her back, that was all he cared about. He got so damned frightened when she turned mean and angry, so terrified when she retreated from him into herself.

Esther returned to bed with Denton, and they lay together, he wrapped around her. She remembered the days when they could sleep like that for an entire night, or when she or he might wake in the middle of the night from a nightmare with heart pounding and one of them would wrap tenderly around the other, soothing the heart to a normal beat and softly talking the terrors away. Tonight he slept soundly while she lay awake staring at the searchlights that swept intermittently past their window.

Chapter Six

In the end, when she decided to lie to her parents, saying that Denton had been classified 4-F, she convinced herself and Denton that it was easier for her to go to Berkeley without him, so on that January day she stood alone before her mother and father in the apartment where she had grown up.

"They won't take him because of his migraines," Esther explained.

"Never heard of such a thing," Judith answered dismissively.

Harry sat at the table in the dining area sliding his dark-green fountain pen back and forth across the pink damask cloth. He wouldn't look up at Esther, and she was left to stare into his black hair that glistened under the table lamp, that hair she loved the texture and smell of; she remembered grabbing it as a small child and not wanting to let go and burying her nose in its gleaming thickness. He was either too grieved by the news or too cowed by Judith to help her. Esther wanted to scream at him to put the pen away, to stand up for her and Denton.

"Well, it's true, Mother, and Denton is very upset."

"Did *he* bring it up?" Her mother turned away and walked to the window, parted the blackout drape and the lace curtain and looked down to the dark street.

"What do you mean, 'bring it up?' Of course he told me."

"You know that's not what I meant, Esther."

"What *do* you mean, Mother?"

"I mean, did he volunteer the information about his headaches to the draft board?"

"You don't lie to the draft board."

"People have been known to."

"Denton doesn't lie."

"I'm deeply disappointed." Judith turned to glare at Esther, her heavily lidded eyes huge behind the lenses of her glasses.

"I know you are, Mother."

"You cannot conceivably know what I am feeling in this regard. No one can." With that she went to the table, picked up the book she had been reading, slipped the leather marker between the pages and closed it. "I think I'll read for a while. Please don't disturb me, Harry." She smiled coolly at her husband before going through the French door to their bedroom.

Esther watched her mother's shadow on the curtain behind the glass panes, thinking, you are only disappointed that you cannot report to the women at Hadassah that your son-in-law has gone to liberate your people. That is all you care about. Your "people." Your daughter, your granddaughter, your husband, none of us matter in comparison to the Jews of Europe.

She thought of what Denton had said when she'd been packing his suitcase for the trip from the Valley to the San Francisco draft board.

"I know that to your parents what I'm doing is immoral, but I don't believe in killing. And it is legalized killing."

"Is this because of what happened to Huey?" she had asked, placing clean underwear neatly on top of an extra shirt.

He was silent for a moment and she almost regretted bringing it up, knowing how pained he was about his brother, but she had to know once and for all.

"No, it's not about Huey. If anything, Huey's failure makes me want to go to prove myself, to show myself I'm not as crazy or weak or vulnerable as he was. It's nothing that easy, honey. I don't even understand it fully myself, but no matter how many times I go over it, I come up with the same thing. I have no right to take another life."

When she didn't say anything, Denton said, "I think it's better that we face the music and tell Judith and Harry, no matter how hard it is. I'll do it myself."

"No!" She said, shoving a pair of rolled socks into the valise and slamming it shut. He didn't understand how furious her mother would be, and how to Daddy it would be a deep, unhealable wound that his Gentile son-in-law refused to fight to save their people. He didn't understand that her decision to lie was predicated on saving her father that pain and saving herself and Denton from her mother's wrath.

"What happens if I end up in prison? What will we tell Harry and Judith then? It's a real possibility."

She nodded, but still couldn't meet his eye. "I know," she said, though she was sure it would never come to that. She'd asked questions of a Quaker woman at Berkeley who told her that because they had had a child before Pearl Harbor, and because Denton was thirty, he probably wouldn't be called up, and if he didn't get called up, they wouldn't punish him for being a conscientious objector. "I'll deal with that eventuality when the time comes. Until then I'm going to lie to them." She lifted the valise from the bed and held it out to him.

"I wish we could be truthful, but I won't interfere," he said, as he took the suitcase from her. "It's your choice what to tell them."

"It isn't a choice," she said curtly.

Daddy's pen continued to slide back and forth in the deathly quiet of the apartment. She ached to sit down beside him and place her hand over his big-knuckled, brown hand and halt the obsessive movement that kept his pain and anger contained and didn't allow him to speak to his beloved daughter. She wanted to lean close and whisper in his ear that Denton was a good man with the highest of principles and that she, deep within herself someplace, admired the difficult stand her husband was taking. She wanted to tell Daddy that it was because Denton was so much like himself, gentle, pacific, loving, not wanting to fight in any man's war, that he had declared himself to be a conscientious objector; she wanted to confess that though Denton *did* have violent headaches, the army didn't even know about them. But Harry wouldn't look up and she couldn't sit down and tell him the truth. It wasn't that kind of a world anymore and her loyalties must now be to another man.

Chapter Seven

When Esther woke to Parin's cries Denton had already left, even though it was only six-thirty. She called out to him, but he didn't answer. "How the hell did he get out of here without my hearing?" she wondered aloud as she grabbed for and lit a Chesterfield before sitting up groggily. The dawn was gray in the window. The sun hadn't even risen over the eastern hills.

"I'm coming, dearest," she called, as she stepped onto the icy linoleum. Her voice was hoarse, and she was exhausted. Her body felt like overcooked meat, thick and tough. She found her slippers. When she stood to put her robe on, she ached all over. Why was she so tired? "I'm coming, dear one." Parin was shrieking as loudly as she had the night before. Esther took two more deep draws on her cigarette and carefully put it out, saving it for later.

She found Parin on her stomach on the floor in the middle of the living room with her torso under the blond wood coffee table and her head under the blond wood-framed couch. Only the bottoms of Parin's pajama feet stuck out, black and grainy with dust, kicking up and down to the beat of cries that had fallen into an incessant, repetitive pattern.

"Parin, come out." Esther tugged on her daughter's warm ankles. "Will you please?"

"No, no, no." She kicked at Esther, catching her on the forearm.

"You stop that, young lady, this very minute." She grabbed the flailing calf with one hand and squeezed—too hard, she knew, but she squeezed harder, her fingers pressing in relentlessly.

"Ow, you hurt, you hurt me." Parin tried to kick with the foot Esther held, and when that failed she struck with her free one.

Esther caught and gripped the free leg, digging her fingers into the fabric, into the pliant flesh beneath. She wanted to hurt this child, hurt her until she stopped crying, hurt her until she said she was sorry, until she told Esther she loved her.

"Mommy, Mommy, Mommy."

The voice penetrated, the defenseless voice. She heard her daughter's cries.

"I've stopped. Parin, I'm sorry. Come, dear one. Come, please." She released her grip and began to caress the leg gently over the flannel, moving from the injured calf up to her knee. What had she done?

Parin lay still and silent before slowly crawling out from under the table. Her glasses were crooked. Her face and pajamas were filthy with the black dust from the floor.

"I'm sorry, Mommy." She looked pleadingly at Esther. Tear rivulets marked paths through her black-streaked face.

"Come here, sweetheart. Mommy's sorry, too." Esther held out her arms and took her daughter into them. The child's body was at first unresponsive and then gradually, as Esther petted her, she relented and sank against Esther's breast and shoulder.

"I'm sorry, Mommy, I didn't mean to."

"It's fine, Parin. Fine. Just let's have a little quiet period. Let's be quiet now, please, my dearest."

Esther could feel Parin's heart beating too fast. Her own was racing as well.

*   *   *

As usual there was no hot water available from the tap. Esther heated some on the stove. As she poured it into the wash basin for Parin's sponge bath, she thought of the wicked stepmothers in fairy stories, who threatened to scald their children. Those tales had fed her own childhood fears. When she was six or seven years old, she'd passed through a phase when she'd been terrified that her mother was going to burn her with a poker or scald her with hot oil. Whenever she was alone with her mother in the kitchen, which wasn't too often because Judith spent as little time as possible in the kitchen, Esther would repeat to herself a litany of made-up prayers to ward off these evil acts. The prayers developed into silent chants and magical counting. If she could reach the number ten before her mother carried the pan of boiling water from the stove to the sink, she was safe. If she could drink her milk in seven gulps, she was protected for the day from the poison her mother had put there. If she could hold her breath and count to thirty, she bought herself two days, or whatever time elapsed until a new fear overcame her.

As Esther emptied the last pot of water, she turned and saw Parin eating her oatmeal at the table. Parin was shut into her own thoughts, not watching Esther at the sink. Or had she averted her eyes? Was her daughter saying comparable chants, creating similar magical spells to ward off her own mother's cruelty?

"Parin?"

The child looked up and immediately smiled.

"Come, let's get you washed," Esther said, running cold water from the faucet into the steaming basin. She dipped in the most tender part of her wrist. It was fine, no danger to her child. She lifted the heavy basin from the sink, and carried it into the bathroom with her daughter following behind.

Esther sat on the closed toilet seat with Parin in front of her, the washbowl at her feet. Esther reached down and lathered the wash-cloth. The bathroom was back to back with the McIntyres' since they shared the primitive plumbing for both the kitchen and bath. As she wiped the soapy cloth through the accumulated film of grit on Parin's face, she could hear steady bickering going on next door. Paul hadn't left yet. Did that mean there was no school? A minute later she heard him yell, "I have no time. I'm up to here with all of this. I'll try to get back for lunch." A door banged. School must be on, Esther thought. If the Takaetsues didn't arrive in half an hour, she would take Parin to the Topols' apartment and ask Sarah to watch her.

"Mommy?"

"Yes, dearest."

"Nothing," Parin said as she nudged herself deeper between Esther's legs, her head arched back on Esther's shoulder.

Esther laughed. "Nothing? I can't believe my chatterbox has nothing to say." She lifted Parin's bare arm and washed underneath, lightly running the cloth into her shallow armpit.

"That tickles, Mommy," Parin murmured but didn't drop her arm and didn't shrink away.

"Let's see if the other side tickles, too." Esther shifted carefully, not to jar the heavier weight of her daughter's body as it relaxed in pleasure.

"Okay." Parin let her other arm be lifted.

Esther wiped down her side and across her narrow chest, over her stomach, which still protruded slightly even though Parin had this last year grown out of her baby fat into the solid sleek body of a little girl. Parin let her face slip against Esther's and Esther reveled in the moist softness of her child's skin, the fresh scent of soap mixed with a trace of perspiration. A rapture akin to sexual desire came over her, a need, as compelling as pain, to hold the child so closely that she could again incorporate Parin into her own body and at the same time envelope Parin in her arms, crushing flesh against flesh. She could have sucked and bitten at the child's skin, consumed her with her mouth and arms and thighs. But before she could do harm, the impulse subsided and she found herself bending her child forward ever so slightly and grazing her back with the damp cloth.

"I guess that about does it, my clean lady," she said, brushing her daughter's bangs off her high forehead. Again she felt the welling of love; as strong as the anger that had overcome her in the living room. How she feared that anger, the way it could rise up unexpectedly and threaten to do injury. She feared it most when she was alone with Parin.

*   *   *

Esther made her way along the cinder street of barracks with Parin's hand in hers. The wind was tunneling fiercely from the west and she had to keep her head down. Parin was running to keep pace and kept tripping and twisting in Esther's grasp. She wore a bulky red coat and matching leggings, donations from Judith Kahn's Hadassah Refugee Fund; Judith had given them reluctantly the last time they'd been in Berkeley, fretting that it meant two fewer items for European Jewish children.

We should go again, Esther thought; she was due for a visit. Though she dreaded seeing her mother, it would be good to get out of here for a week.

Gray sky and muddy light made the camp seem drearier than usual. Much of the snow cover had blown off, exposing patches of black sand between the rows of barracks. All of Esther's dreams these days were filled with this monotone of flat black, gray and white earth. In the dreams she was a child of Parin's age crying in this desolate landscape. At first she'd thought it was Parin in the dreams, but eventually she realized this was a small version of herself, like the studio pictures taken of her when she was four—brown-skinned, round-cheeked, with dark hair and sorrowful eyes, nothing like Parin's cheerful and slightly comical demeanor, her flyaway blond hair, and light brown pupils that sparkled through her thick lenses. But even Parin's ebullience was being dampened by this place.

Bent forward, fighting the wind, Esther trudged on. She wanted to be fun-loving again, the way she'd been at the University of California after she and Denton met. The thought of Berkeley brought sunshine and the smell of eucalyptus to her, as she saw herself, head flung back, laughing. At what? At something Denton had said, seated beside her on the stone bench beneath the Campanile, looking out over the bay toward the new Golden Gate Bridge, scarlet in the sunlight.

"Mommy?"

Esther returned to Tule Lake.

"What is it?"

"Where're we going?"

"To the Topols', I told you."

"We went by." Parin's face was framed by a red cap that Esther had knitted to match the coat. Soft spikes of hair stuck out around the collar of her coat, and her glasses were covered with a film of dust.

Esther saw that they had indeed passed the Topols' barracks. These damn places all looked the same.

"Good girl for being so observant. Big people get lost sometimes. They need careful watchers like you."

Parin raised her shoulders. "Mommy?"

"Yes, my helper."

"I'm people now, aren't I?"

Esther laughed. "You surely are people now. Yes, you are."

Sy came to the door dressed for work in his three-piece suit, but still wearing his slippers. He looked haggard with fatigue, and Esther guessed he wasn't getting much sleep these days.

"Morning," they greeted each other as Esther pushed Parin ahead of her into the room, out of the cold.

The Topols' apartment was the coziest of the administration homes, Esther had to concede that, though she found it a trifle overdone for her taste, and fusty this morning from a melange of baby formula, ammonia from dirty diapers, and sweet talcum powder. Sarah had slipcovered the furniture in a bright chintz, hiding the ubiquitous cowboys and Indians tearing across the Sears and Roebuck upholstery. In the beginning they joked that the War Relocation Authority must have thought they were furnishing one hundred teenaged boys' rooms. Sarah had put down carpets, which meant she had to use a carpet sweeper three times a day to keep the black sand under control, and she'd made dainty white antimacassars for the two chairs and the davenport. Esther suspected that with the new baby to care for these niceties would soon be relegated to a trunk to wait for easier times.

"Esther. Parin." Sarah emerged from the bedroom with baby Annie in her arms, wrapped in a yellow satin quilted bunting.

Sarah bent to kiss Parin on her forehead. "How's my sweetest three-and-a-half-year-old today?"

"I'm fine," Parin beamed up at the round-faced smiling woman.

"And you, Esther, exhausted?"

"No, not at all." Sarah was always insisting that she looked exhausted, from working at school, from attending a meeting with Denton. She succeeded in making Esther feel she looked bedraggled and old. It seemed an insult somehow, even though today she really was tired.

"What time did Denton get home last night? Sy said he left him arguing with Herm at midnight."

"Maybe later, Sarah," Sy shuffled uncomfortably. "I didn't have my watch."

"He didn't come in much after that," Esther said, but thought, what the hell had Denton been doing for three goddamn hours? From midnight to three he'd probably been solving the problems of the world with Herm, without regard for his wife and daughter.

Esther smiled at Sarah and Sy. She would *not* satisfy Sarah's curiosity. "Do you think Parin could stay with you today until I find out about Mr. and Mrs. Takaetsue's status? Apparently they're not letting evacuees into the administration area without work passes. I don't know whether that includes the school children, but I must at least show up at school if they do. I'll go by the Takaetsues' afterward." Esther put her hand down on the top of Parin's head. She was leaning against Esther's leg; before leaving the apartment, she had become upset again when she'd learned that the Issei couple wouldn't be taking care of her today.

"Of course. I love having my Parin here keeping me and Annie company. Don't we, Annie fanny?" She spoke into the bundle of baby. Annie gurgled and began to coo. "You see, Parin, sweetheart, we both want you. It'll be a party."

It was all a little too cloying for Esther, but Parin seemed reassured. Esther knew she would never be as maternal and domestic as Sarah. She was like her mother in that way. She couldn't endure being at home alone with a child. Even down at the Farm Security Camp during Parin's infancy, with people continually coming in and out, available for conversation, she'd envied Denton and the others, women, too, who were working in the camp, in the recreation center, in the school. She'd been stuck feeding, diapering, and eternally scrubbing on the galvanized metal rubbing board. Motherhood was a boring, demeaning, twenty-four-hour job as far as she was concerned, but she certainly never told anyone else how she felt. She knew such opinions were so unacceptable as to be blasphemous. She had learned this when she cried to Denton that she was going crazy being with the baby all day while he was always out. He'd looked at her incredulously. "But you wanted to have a baby," he said. "Yes," she whispered angrily, hoping she wouldn't be heard in the next tent, "you wanted a baby, too, but you wouldn't be happy changing diapers every day of your life." He said he understood, which relieved her, but she also saw a flicker of distaste in his eyes. She was more careful after that. Some days she felt guilty about her deficiency. Today she only hoped the schools were open.

"I'll drive you over to the school, Esther." Sy offered, once Parin was settled with crayons and paper on the floor.

"That would be wonderful. It's bitter out there."

"About as dreadful as the collective psyche of this place."

"It's awful, isn't it?"

"The worst it's been," he said, putting on his overcoat.

Sarah kissed him goodbye. He spent a moment poking his finger into the baby's mouth, saying nonsense words.

Though Denton was suspicious of Sy and complained that he never took a stand on issues, Esther liked him. He had the same introspective Jewish look as her favorite cousin Herzl. Esther allowed herself the thought that perhaps Denton didn't like how obviously Jewish-looking Sy was. If she'd said as much to Denton, he would adamantly deny any such prejudice. He was married to a Jew, after all, and his best friend, Herm, was a Jew. Still, she wondered. She didn't like herself when she harbored such distrust of him, but then, she often didn't like herself these days.

"Denton's having a hard time with all of this," Sy shouted as they walked toward his Plymouth.

"Aren't we all?"

Sy helped Esther in on her side. He remained beside her open door, his black hair blowing wildly in the wind.

"Circumstances are affecting all of us. But Denton has something else inside, maybe from his past, that's tangling things up a lot worse for him."

"You're talking like a psychoanalyst," Esther said.

"That's my fate, I guess. Always looking for the underlying motivation. Don't want to talk about it, do you?"

"No, Sy, I don't. And I'm freezing, if you don't mind."

Sy drove west toward Highway 139 and then turned south around the bottom of the administration barracks, before turning east again toward the evacuee area. The sun was a hazy platinum disk in the overcast sky. They drove in silence.

Sy stopped the car at the northern edge between the administration area and the evacuee section.

"Is it okay if I leave you here?"

"Of course, it's only a block more."

He put his hand on her arm. "Are you all right, Esther?"

She kept her head down as she gathered her purse and bag of books. She didn't want him to see her sudden tears.

"Don't be silly," she said. "I'm certainly doing better than ninety percent of the people over on the other side of the divide. Let's both get to work and stop dwelling on our own problems." Her tears had receded.

"You sound like Denton," Sy said, smiling kindly.

"Not the worst person to emulate, don't you think?" she said, opening the door to the cold air.

"Of course, Esther. I apologize. I shouldn't have pried."

Chapter Eight

Army vehicles, mostly jeeps and two tanks, were parked along the southern perimeter of the firebreak, and army personnel were questioning long lines of residents, children on their way to school, and adults coming over from the evacuee side for work. Esther scanned the nearest group for the diminutive Takaetsues but didn't see them.

She walked past the high school where groups of youngsters and a few Nisei teachers were waiting outside. A soldier with a gun stood at the door. If there were no classes today, it would be the first time that school had not convened. Even in the bewildering, bleak days in the beginning, when staff and residents alike had been ripped from the familiar and felt unsure of the future, the school had been open. Even when they'd had no supplies, the teachers had found ways to hold classes.

When they first arrived at camp there were no blackboards, no books and no paper or pencils. The only seats were splintery, wobbly benches. There were no tables. Esther couldn't cajole anyone into building her even a few simple desks for the students. She fought with Harry Morrisey, the man in charge of construction, until Denton asked her to stop. He said Harry couldn't do anything because he had to answer to the Army Corps of Engineers who were overseeing the entire camp, and Denton couldn't afford to alienate any of the conservative people on the maintenance staff. She backed off, but, determined to have control, she took her own kitchen table and placed it at the front of her classroom. But how to teach without books and blackboards? In the project director's office she happened upon a delivery of large sheets of newsprint destined for the camp newspaper. She didn't ask for permission. She waited until the office staff went to lunch and simply carried off a large stack. Back in her classroom she attacked it with an ice-pick, punching holes in the corners of the paper, through which she threaded string, and hung the stack like a calendar from nails she pounded into the front wall. When Hiroko Onji, a Nisei woman assigned to teach in the classroom next to Esther's, arrived for work on the last day of May, she stood at Esther's door with hardened face and suspicious eyes. Esther turned from where she was preparing sentence diagrams with crayons on the makeshift instruction sheets, smiled, and shrugged. "It's the best I could do," she said to the dour young woman. "Given that we haven't a darn thing to work with." With that Hiroko smiled ruefully and asked Esther if perhaps she could borrow Esther's idea and if Esther could tell her how she too could get some newsprint. Against all odds, they had found ways to teach the children.

Esther spotted Hiroko in a circle of junior high children at the school door. Beyond them, in the newly created no man's land between the school and the evacuee barracks, she saw a small formation of *Hoshidan* dressed in their white pajama-style slacks and shirts and head bands. It was long past the hour for their dawn calisthenics and their daily worship of the rising sun.

Esther suspected that they had come to intimidate the children and the Nisei teachers with their presence, trying to persuade them not to attend the *hakujin* school or to teach in it. They had been hounding Hiroko for the past month, badgering her with the fact that she made only $19 a month while the white teachers made $120. Their tactics only made Hiroko more angry and stubborn about remaining in the camp's school.

"They've closed the schools," Hiroko said when Esther joined her. Her broad face was set in its most determined expression. A dark green knit muffler covered her ears, crossed under her chin, and was tied in back. She wore a fitted grey wool coat that emphasized her waist and made her look even thicker than she was.

The students, who had parted when Esther walked up, pressed in on them. Tall, skinny Sally Hiro looped her arm through Esther's. Danny Honda hooked onto her other arm. His pudgy face was troubled as he watched her.

"Has Superintendent McIntyre been here yet?" Esther asked.

"Yes," was all that Hiroko said, her lips drawn back in frustration and anger.

"What did he say?" Esther looked around quickly. There were no other teachers and students. "Where is everyone? Inside?"

"They left," Sally Hiro whispered.

"That's right," Hiroko said. "Apparently the teachers from town were notified not to come in. The other Caucasian teachers, the single ladies, must have stayed in their dormitory. So their students went home. I worried that you had stayed home, too, but Mr. McIntyre said he hadn't seen you back at your barracks. I took the chance and waited for you. I told the children you would be coming." She smiled, her dark eyes warming for the moment. "I was correct."

"Of course I'm here."

"There are soldiers inside the building. With guns." Hiroko shook her head sharply. "They bring guns into the children's classroom."

The bastards, Esther thought. Aloud she said in her most cheerful voice, to avoid alarming the children more than they already were, "What do you suppose we should do? Shouldn't we have our class anyway?"

"Yes, yes, please," Sally Hiro squeezed her arm and Danny Honda moved in closer. Nancy Nakamata, a beautiful girl of thirteen, with clear smooth beige skin and black hair in thick braids that stuck out below her plaid kerchief, begged, "Please, Miss Onji, say yes, ple-e-e-ase."

"Do you think we should?" Hiroko said. "There's an army order that says no school."

"An order that says I can't visit with some friends?" Esther asked. Maybe they would get in terrible trouble, but when she saw Hiroko's expression of pleased defiance, she thought, what the hell do I care? She would tell anyone they met along the way that she was going to see about Parin's babysitters.

"But where? We can't go to the recreation room in our block, because the hotheads have taken that over for themselves, for their renegade *Nihongakko* schools. They'll probably try to use it all day. I bet they'll even kick the ladies' art group out." Hiroko rubbed her hands together and stamped her feet. "They already tried this morning to get the children to go to the Japanese school."

The children watched in silence. Young deer on the alert for danger, their eyes observing and darting. The hotheads had been intimidating and threatening them for some time, insisting that the children had to learn Japanese and Japanese customs if they were to consider themselves loyal to their families and culture. They claimed that everyone would be shipped off to Japan when the war ended, whether Japan won or not.

"I guess we can't go to the Recreation Room, then, if it's their territory. Why not someone's room? Is that a possibility?"

"Yes," said Hiroko, smiling. "We can go to my room. My mother is at work in the mess hall and Pop is no doubt playing goh in the bachelor quarters. If not, this horde will discourage him from staying," she laughed.

The children squealed. "Is this real, Mrs. Jordan?" Danny Honda asked, his perpetually worried brow furrowed more deeply.

"Yes, Danny, if Miss Onji-san invites us, it would be impolite to say no." She smiled to let him know this was a joke. But Danny didn't laugh, or even smile. His father, Toki Honda, was a serious man. Like father, like son, it seemed.

When they rounded the corner they found that the High School students and teachers she'd seen before had dispersed. Walking across the divide, they encountered no problems. The army didn't seem to care about anyone going into the evacuee area. But as they passed the *Hoshidan* phalanx, shouts of "*inu*" and loud barking were directed at Hiroko, and the young men shouted "*keto*" at Esther. She flushed with embarrassment at being called a "hairy one." She was ashamed to have the children hear it. When she was far enough away, Esther glanced back. The *Hoshidan* were walking slowly in their direction. She began to move faster, bustling the children along like a mother hen.

At the firebreak between Wards 1 and 6, the children walked ahead and Hiroko fell back to wait for Esther.

"I think they're following us," Esther said.

"They'll get a piece of my mind if they try to come to my room. They can taunt me, but I won't let them upset the children. It's enough that they bother the boys and girls in the mess halls and recreation rooms. They've started breaking up the teenagers' dances. Cowards. They think they are big men."

As they cut between Blocks 6 and 13 on their way to Hiroko's Block 14, Hiroko said, "What do we do with the children? We don't have any schoolbooks."

Hiroko was four inches shorter than Esther, but a fast walker, taking an extra step to Esther's every two.

"Did that ever stop us before?" Esther grinned down at her colleague, feeling her anxiety ease away.

Hiroko smiled and then frowned again. "But what can we do?"

"I thought ahead." Esther touched her bag of books. "I brought a copy of *The Yearling*. I've been meaning to read it to my class, half an hour each day. We can begin this morning by reading a very long segment. From there we'll play it by ear."

The center of Block 14, sheltered from the wind by barracks, was deserted. In the morning there were usually groups of women standing talking or carrying baskets of dirty clothes to the laundry room, and tiny children racing about. Today the curtains had been drawn on all the windows. Esther imagined eyes peeking out, watching their progress, wondering what she was doing here. In the past she had felt welcome; she was one of the favorite teachers, and people's trust in Denton and his work in the Co-op served her well. But since the loyalty questionnaires she had been reluctant to come into the evacuee area, even though it was known that she had refused to participate when the project director had called on teachers to administer the signing. This morning as never before she felt the chill of being an unwanted intruder. She no longer heard the taunts of the *Hoshidan* militants, but she sensed the climate of hostility in the emptiness of the block, in the faceless windows, in the silence. She was glad when they arrived at #5D and she could enter the safe privacy of the Onji room.

Chapter Nine

Esther had been in the Onji family room on a few occasions—twice after school for tea and to work on lesson plans, and another time when she and Hiroko were enlisted to chaperon a high school dance and Esther and Denton came by in the car to pick her up. That was early in the life of Tule Lake and Hiroko hadn't yet met Denton, though she'd heard of him. "All good reports," she'd smiled at Esther. "Even Papa has nothing bad to say." Denton had cemented the good impression by joining Tosuro Onji, Hiroko's father, in a cup of bootleg sake before they left for the dance.

At the dance, Hiroko declined when Denton invited her onto the floor, but—she later told Esther—after she watched Esther and Denton take a few flashy turns to the music of Woodie Ichihashi's swing band, she couldn't deny herself the pleasure. Hiroko confessed to Esther that she was often disappointed in the northwest Nisei boys she'd met at the University of Washington. "They were so stiff when they danced," Hiroko complained. "The Sacramento jitterbuggers that I've met in camp are different, but those Nisei boys in Seattle were afraid to be themselves in white company or even with their own people. They were always too careful, damn it." When Hiroko had divulged her unhappiness, Esther had admitted to feeling similarly about the few Jewish boys at Berkeley. She didn't mind that they were so studious, but they were afraid to let their fun-loving sides show around the Gentiles.

Esther and Hiroko took turns reading *The Yearling* to the children, who sat on the swirling floral pattern of the linoleum-covered floor with their ankles crossed and their backs as straight as fence posts.

The children were enthralled with the novel. Observing their rapt expressions, Esther realized how well she had chosen. Their eyes softened at the lush description of inland Florida, the marsh and hummock country. She saw their clear identification with the boy,

Jody. Many of them came from farms. They must miss the rural, crop-growing life as much as their parents did. If nothing else, she thought, they must yearn for the green. There was barely a touch of verdancy here, save in the small gardens some of the people planted in front of their barracks. They must miss the smell of turned earth, the fields, the rivers, the dirt roads. Over the camp the sky was still beautiful, with grebe, ducks and geese flying over, and because of the constant swirling dust, the sunsets were splendid. But where in this entire place could a child lie down to watch the cloud formations floating by? Where could they lose themselves for a day? They had spoken to her of their yearnings on a day of rare introspection when she had encouraged them to talk of their lives on the outside. At first she'd worried, when they hadn't been particularly forthcoming, whether she had opened a wound too carefully covered; wondered whether it wasn't better to allow them to keep the memories deep inside, safe and forgotten. But soon the discussion had become animated. They spoke of kittens and puppies, and swings in old trees, and walking to schools that had blackboards. They described warm kitchens where they ate with their entire families, so different from the mess halls in camp. Their faces quickened with delight and their eyes sharpened with memory. In the days and weeks that followed, she'd decided she had been right to broach this topic because the children lightened noticeably and were more eager to learn. Earlier, they'd obstinately complained that this was not a real school, because a real school had books, notebooks, desks, inkwells and blackboards with chalk and erasers. After the discussion they let go of their resentment, only wanting to learn more about grammar, fractions, geography, and the history of the Indians before the European colonists arrived.

Esther's thoughts were interrupted by the sound of the hotheads' *banzai* salutes coming closer. The children shifted position, became distracted. Helen Hituri, a chubby, anxious girl, looked toward the window, and then whispered to Sally Hiro who sat beside her. Hiroko continued reading but her worried eyes met Esther's, unable to hide her concern. They wouldn't dare, Esther thought. They had never entered a classroom. The *Hoshidan* would talk with the children as they left school in the afternoon, but the young men never entered what they perceived as government property.

A sudden sharp rapping on the door startled Esther and the children, too, who began to whisper among themselves.

A man's angry voice called out in Japanese. It was as though violence had entered the room. Esther thought of the armed soldiers they'd left behind in the school building.

Hiroko responded to the man in Japanese but remained seated.

The man outside the door replied more angrily yet.

"What is it, Miss Onji?" Esther asked. She felt she was the only person in the room who didn't understand, though she knew most of the children didn't speak Japanese.

Hiroko put the book down on her chair and walked to the door.

Sam Kiritari, a usually joking sort of boy, leaned toward Esther and said solemnly, "He wants to come in."

Esther rose and followed Hiroko to the door. She told the children to remain seated.

Esther immediately recognized Nebo Mota, dressed in militant whites, with a brown leather bomber jacket and a black knitted cap against the cold. He'd come to their apartment on many occasions: for dinner, for small parties, for informal meetings with Denton. He'd been aloof but polite, and sweet to Parin. Denton had told her that the young Kibei had admitted to being uncomfortable, that he didn't trust Caucasians and didn't think he'd like being in a white person's home. But he'd grown accustomed, had liked "little Parin-chan," and thought Esther was a "fine lady." This morning Nebo Mota stood a few feet away from the bottom of the Onji steps, his eyes filled with distaste for Esther's very presence. Twenty feet behind him stood a phalanx of fifteen young men in white.

"Ah, Mrs. Jordan-sama," he said. "I wondered if you might be here."

"I am, Mr. Mota-san," she said. Of course he knew she was here. He'd watched her walk from the school. "What may we do for you?"

"I'm here to say that if there is to be a dissident school, it should be ours."

"And who is ours?" Hiroko broke in before Esther could reply. Hiroko's arms were crossed belligerently over her yellow sweater.

The cold air was beginning to penetrate Esther's own sweater.

"Our people, Onji, Hiroko-san. People of Japanese blood."

"Don't impose yourself on these children, Mota-san. It's unfair to them."

He continued in Japanese, shaking his head vehemently. Even without understanding the words, the fierceness of his impassioned monologue reminded Esther of a younger Denton when, working in the San Joaquin Valley, he had stood up to the farm owners on behalf of the displaced Oklahoma farmers. She had thought Denton so brave and handsome in his rolled-up white shirtsleeves and his worn-to-shiny gabardine pants, and that determined look on his face—yes, so like Nebo Mota's expression. Maybe this was why Denton persisted in his stubborn support of these men; he identified with them, with Mota himself.

"We teach them what they would be learning on the outside, and you know it, Nebo Mota," Hiroko said. "You may disagree with *our* persisting under the current circumstances, but these children are innocent and need to be educated. They must keep pace with the children on the outside."

Esther began to shiver. She looked back into the room to find the children as riveted as they had been during the reading of the novel, though now their concentration was tinged with fear. Should she return to them and continue reading, keep them occupied, or did Hiroko need her here? Esther stepped out and pulled the door shut behind her so the children would not hear more.

"That's unfair, Nebo Mota," Hiroko answered another stream of his words. "And disrespectful. I must ask you to leave."

He continued without stop.

"It is filth you speak. Get out of here." Hiroko rushed down the steps and grabbed two fistfuls of dirt and snow and flung both at Mota. Specks of black dotted his face, and he broke off and wiped his hand across his eyes. "Get going, leave us alone," Hiroko shouted again before she made an about-face and marched up the stairs toward Esther.

Nebo Mota, his face impassive, bowed deeply before turning and striding across the square toward the young men who waited for him. They stood at attention, their white uniforms in stark contrast to the black buildings. When he reached them, he raised his arm and shouted "*Banzai!*" They raised their arms and returned the call.

Just like fascists, Esther thought. Why couldn't Denton see the parallel?

She and Hiroko remained outside, silent, until the young men had disappeared at a trot around the line of barracks.

Not another soul was out under the lowering gray sky. The square was ominously still. Word of Mota's visit to the Onji house had to have already passed through the entire block, if not the entire ward. Rumors were like mice in the camp these days, they could get in through the tiniest holes. Knowing that people were hiding behind the closed curtains, she was surprised that the children had been allowed out for school. Though on second thought, she shouldn't be surprised, because school took precedence over everything else in this community. Bombs could have dropped the night before and the children would still have been washed, dressed and sent out to learn, just as she would have been sent by her own mother. In her home, education was primary as well. She knew both the power and the burden of it.

"What was that all about?" Esther asked.

Hiroko shook her head and looked at Esther. There were tears in her eyes. She was trembling. "Can you take over the reading?"

Esther sat in front on the red-painted kitchen chair. She knew the children wouldn't ask for an explanation if it weren't offered. She found the place where Hiroko had left off and began to read. "The pines were becoming scattering. There was suddenly a strip of hammock land, and a place of live oaks and scrub palmettos." She glanced up to find the thirteen-year-old faces soft with relief and concentration, transported again to the flatland of Florida, walking toward the marsh with its sawgrass, with the old dog running ahead to splash knee-deep in the water.

In the rear of the room Hiroko had opened the top drawer of a dresser and with her back to Esther, she found the handkerchief she'd been rummaging for. Her shoulders shook as she dabbed at her eyes.

They dismissed the children at noon after trying, with great frustration, to give a lesson in algebra. They didn't even have sheets of newsprint on which to illustrate the formulas. When Esther told the students not to return after lunch, that she and Miss Onji would have to assess the situation and let their families know, Sally Hiro pleaded, "Please, Mrs. Jordan-san, can't we just come back and hear more of the book?" And Sam Kiritari, his eyes large behind smudged glasses, reasoned, "We can take turns reading aloud ourselves so you don't have to work so hard. Really."

Esther and Hiroko told the disappointed children that they would have to check with the administration, but Esther knew there would be no classes.

As the subdued boys and girls got their coats and hats from wall hooks by the door, tied scarves around their necks and slipped hands into mittens, Esther thought how beautiful they were. They seemed much younger than thirteen-year-olds. She touched each one on the shoulder, head or cheek as he or she went out the door.

Esther and Hiroko stood at the door watching them walk across the square, kicking up spirals of dust. In a sky the color of a battle ship, a line of geese flew, their wings flashing white against the dark grey. "See you tomorrow, Misses Teachers," the children called from the far side of the square before scattering to go to their respective blocks. As they separated, they began to run, and became like large pieces of colorful confetti, darting and dashing, yellow and green and bright red and blue, in the wind. For a moment, before they disappeared, there was joy in the ward.

When they re-entered the room, Esther sensed that Hiroko wanted her to leave, but she had to find out what had transpired between Hiroko and Nebo Mota.

She sat down on the ocher-and-green brocade-covered daven-port, and traced the pattern with her finger, remembering Hiroko telling her that this fabric had come from their house in Seattle.

Hiroko stood by the table pretending to read silently from *The Yearling* which lay open before her. This wasn't like Hiroko. She would consider such behavior insulting to a guest if anyone else had done it.

"May I make you some tea?" Hiroko finally offered, without looking up, when Esther didn't budge.

"No, thank you, Hiroko, I'll be leaving in a moment. But I must know what Nebo Mota said."

Hiroko shook her head.

"That's not the way we are, Hiroko. We're colleagues, friends."

"He was shameless in what he said about you."

Esther felt a flush rise up the back of her neck, up her cheeks. It hurt to think of herself as insulted, no matter what the circumstances.

"I guessed as much, but please, tell me. It's better to know than to imagine."

"I've always believed that the messenger intends the hostility if the news is bad."

"And who is the messenger in this instance, you or Nebo Mota?" She saw the twitch of a smile pass over her Hiroko's lips. That touch of sadistic pleasure in all of us, she thought. Even so, it hurt. "Please tell me. I'll imagine worse possibilities if you don't."

"He spoke terrible lies," Hiroko said softly.

"Go on." Esther's heart raced. This was like those awful times at the university, when she heard, second and third hand, the anti-Semitic insults the sorority girls spewed about her and her mother. "That haughty Jewess and her arrogant mother." In those days she hadn't understood that any so-called girlfriend who carried the message, who would come expressly to tell her, was also suspect. But this was not true of Hiroko, Esther assured herself. If Esther weren't insisting, Hiroko would never tell what Nebo said.

"He said you and Denton were not to be trusted."

"I've heard worse before. Go on."

"Oh, Esther, please, no."

"Please, yes, Hiroko. We're both strong ladies." But she lied. She felt like the fragile, embattled college girl, not the twenty-eight-year-old woman she was now. She reminded herself of the envy of the Gentile sorority girls when she appeared on Denton Jordan's arm at the tea dance in the Student Union. He was the catch they were all swooning over, and by finals she had gotten him. Or rather, he had chosen her, an Independent on campus, the brainy Jewish girl. They had hated her even more as a result. And how she'd gloated. How superior she had finally felt.

"He said..." She looked directly at Esther. "That you and Denton especially are here because you feel superior to us, that you think you are teaching us your superior ways. That you're worse than the others who let us know directly that they think we are beneath them."

The tenor and force of the accusation took Esther by surprise. She couldn't find a retort. There was no answer.

Hiroko went on. "That's when I told him he was being disrespectful, that he had to leave."

"What do you suppose the children thought?" Esther said, feeling again the rush of blood up the back of her neck. The children hadn't seemed to react, but one never knew.

"I don't think they understood. They aren't exactly proficient in Japanese, you know, and he speaks a rather modern version. Even I have trouble." Hiroko smiled. "Please, Esther, know and trust I have no such thoughts." She closed the book and came around the table to sit beside Esther. "I've admired you since that first day. I regard you and Denton highly for what you've done here, the help you've both given in the face of all this hardship."

Esther didn't answer. For the second time today she had to fight back tears. She abhorred crying in front of others. It was humiliating and undignified; tears were for the privacy of home. But she couldn't hold them back. She kept her head bowed.

Hiroko touched her arm. "Esther?"

Esther shook her head. How could she explain to this woman that she was so miserable that if she had her way she'd leave camp for good? How could she say this to her colleague while Hiroko had no choice but to continue living here? Hiroko's parents had refused to fill out the loyalty questionnaire and because they hadn't registered, they could even be deported. Hiroko had committed herself to staying with them. Hiroko was the prisoner, but at this moment Esther felt more like the captive. She had tried and failed, and she wanted to leave. She had tried to be supportive of Denton and he was acting like a mad person, unwilling to listen to reason from anyone. She was failing with her daughter in front of Sarah, the Takaetsues, and Denton. Each day it was worse with Parin. The child didn't love her, though a child was supposed to love her mother. Parin cared only for the Takaetsues and for Denton. She became a sunny child whenever Denton entered her life, though that was increasingly seldom. Perhaps that was why. Maybe if she made herself scarcer, Parin would love her. But how much less could she be with her daughter? Already she knew people looked askance at her. The Takaetsues certainly did. Oh, what did she care? They could all go to hell, including that rabble-rousing, do-no-good-for-anyone Nebo Mota. With that thought, Esther's tears stopped. In a few moments she could stand, put on her coat and galoshes, and be out of here.

"I know he would say I'm imposing my views," Esther said, "but I think Nebo Mota is doing everyone a terrible disservice with all his agitation. He's making it more difficult for everyone."

"Of course I agree with you, Esther. You saw how I reacted. Most of us feel the same way. But it's difficult for some, particularly older people like my parents, when they are caught in the middle of factions and loyalties and their own confusions about right and wrong. But you know all that very well. We've spoken of it many times."

Esther thought, Does Hiroko really speculate about these concepts? She liked Hiroko very much, but the woman wasn't a great intellectual; she had only taken education courses at the university. The cruel, arrogant thoughts went through Esther, fueled by her anger at Nebo and her shame at being caught crying. In some pocket of her mind and heart she knew she didn't really disrespect this woman, but another wave of vengeful thoughts overtook her. She had never really had an intellectual conversation with Hiroko, and if she were honest, she would admit she had not gotten any innovative ideas about teaching from her friend. Why was she bothering with Hiroko's opinion? Now Esther's tears dried completely and she was ready and able to leave the room.

She stood rather abruptly, judging from the look of surprise on Hiroko's face, and said she had to look in on Parin.

"Will you come back this afternoon, Esther, so we can talk more and plan what to do with the children?"

"I don't know if I'll be able to," Esther said, snapping her galoshes shut. She grabbed her coat, missing the sleeve a couple of times before getting her arm in. "I have to check on the Takaetsues and then I think I should spend the afternoon with my daughter. She was very upset last evening. We weren't home and she was moved out without knowing where we were." Tears threatened again. She had to leave.

"Goodbye, Hiroko." She turned away before Hiroko could touch her or try to make any soothing response.

*   *   *

Out in the wind and cold Esther could no longer control her tears. She looked around frantically, fearing that someone might see her. The worst case would be if she encountered Nebo Mota again, though she knew deep inside that if she met him her tears would disappear instantly, replaced by bitter indignation. She let them fall, down her cheeks, over her jawline, into the collar of her coat. She hadn't cried this hard since childhood, when she had sobbed herself to sleep, or when, to seek relief from her sadness, she'd go up to the eucalyptus groves above the university where her mother taught and would lie flat on the ground staring up at the sickle-shaped leaves against the blue sky or the rolling fog. She would cry until sated and then, exhausted, she would listen to the metallic rustling of the leaves and wish that she would die and rise up among them so that she could be soothed forever by their music.

Esther stopped walking and stood still in the center of the wasteland. In the distance, beyond the administration area and the chain-link fence with its barbed wire on top, rose the craggy profile of Castle Rock, a dramatic outcropping that changed color continually with the light. The early morning sun stained the sandstone a deep burnt sienna, and by evening, with the sun behind Castle Rock, it was a complex picture of black shadows with edges of red light. This noon, in the flat gray atmosphere, it seemed grayness itself, dull and unimposing. In the early days, the internees were allowed to go up there and climb to the wind-and-water-eroded ridges. In June of 1942 a cross had been placed on the summit by the camp's Young Men's Christian Association, and Esther had climbed Castle Rock with Hiroko. Looking west when they reached the top, they had seen the three-thousand-acre spread of the camp's farm with its rows of pale green new plantings alternating with stripes of black earth, and to the southwest, if it had been visible that day, they would have seen Mount Shasta. But what had discouraged Hiroko from ever taking the walk again was the view to the east, north, and south—Tule Lake Relocation Camp, stretching out two miles in each direction in all its bleak, black ugliness. "This is not an escape. I didn't climb up here to witness our sorrow," Hiroko had said before turning and abruptly beginning the descent.

Esther resumed walking across the firebreak. She had to get out of here, but the only place she could afford to go was down to Berkeley to stay with Mother and Daddy. Sometimes the visits were painless—there had been occasions when her mother even appeared happy to see her, to share some information or ideas with her. Perhaps this would be such a time.

Chapter Ten

"**P**arin, I said sit down. The food is hot. It's time to eat."
Esther took a mouthful of mashed potatoes, while Parin
continued to stand on her chair at the table. Esther swallowed slowly,
telling herself that she was not going to let her daughter goad her into
anger, but as she cut her tough steak she felt her resolve crumbling.
She was too tired to deal with this child's behavior. When Esther had
arrived to fetch her from the Topols', Parin had been on the floor
playing with Annie, talking baby babble with her. She hadn't looked
up when Esther called hello, but had continued her nonsense
conversation. It had been one insult too many in a day of hurts. "Parin
Jordan, I'm speaking to you. You answer when I do." Parin immediately came over to her, putting her arms around Esther's legs and
her face into Esther's coat. Esther had seen the disapproving look on
Sarah's face, but for once she hadn't cared. It was easy for Sarah, always
rewarded for being a good mother, a good housewife. But what
happened when a woman wanted something more than that, when—
as in her own family—the rewards were given for having a
distinguished career, academic credentials, and respect in a scholarly
community? Yes, what happened when the work of such a person
found no respect or was taken right out from under her as it had been
today? Sarah Topol, with her self-righteousness, could never
understand Esther's feelings about this.

"Parin, if you don't sit down and start eating, I don't know what
I'm going to do." Esther struck the end of her fork as hard as she could
on the tabletop.

Parin winced but didn't sit. Instead she turned her back on Esther.
"When's Daddy coming? Is Daddy coming tonight?"

"Parin, I detest your whining. Do you know how unattractive you
are when you whine and simper like an idiot child? Do you know how

ugly it makes you? Do you know how grotesque your face becomes?" She felt her fury pushing the words out. She knew they were too cruel, but somehow they satisfied and she didn't want to stop them. She would have to hurt her daughter with them if that's what it took to make her obey.

"Mommy, is Daddy coming home?" Parin repeated in the same singsong voice.

"You know Daddy is coming home. Daddy always comes home. He may be a little late because he has a meeting," Esther said, feeling the fury radiating from her own eyes, hoping that her daughter would turn and see how enraged her mother was. "Parin?"

But Parin didn't turn. Instead, as though knowing how close Esther was to losing control and wanting to push her over the edge, she began to climb down from the chair.

Esther rose abruptly, and grabbed Parin by the collar and slammed her into the chair. "Don't you dare try that, young lady," Esther spit out in a raspy whisper, conscious of the McIntyres on the other side of the thin wall. She brought her face down to Parin's. "You sit when I say to sit, do you hear me?"

Parin didn't cry out. She merely shrank back and put her fingers to the collar of her dress and tried to pull it away from her neck where it was digging in so tightly that her veins were distended and her face was red.

"Oh, God," Esther said, yanking her hand from Parin's neck, and backing away. Rage seized her, owned her; her arms, chest and jaw were pulsing and cramping with this madness. If there had been a carving knife in reach she felt she would have plunged it into her daughter. She had never descended so far into fury.

She didn't move for a moment, working to contain her violent impulses. She saw her daughter avert her eyes, but she knew that Parin was urgently aware of every sign. She remembered how as a child she had known the meaning of each breath her mother took, each movement, no matter how tiny. Esther knew that she shouldn't make a sudden gesture, that she should speak to Parin first and then kneel down and gently touch the child.

"Dear one, I am so sorry," she said. "Mommy is so sorry."

"It's okay," the little voice squeaked.

"No, truly, I didn't mean to hurt you. I love you more than anybody in the whole wide world." She knelt and put her hand to

Parin's cheek. Parin didn't move away, but she did stiffen; Esther felt it.

"It's okay, Mommy." Still she didn't look at Esther.

Just then the front door opened and Denton came in. Esther hadn't been expecting him. She felt as though she'd been caught in some unseemly act. Had he heard anything?

"Well, ladies," he hollered, laughing, his arms outstretched. He looked more vigorous than he had for some time, with his dark hair falling over his forehead and his cheeks flushed as though he'd been outside all day.

"Daddy!" Parin scrambled out of her chair and across the small room to be scooped up in her father's arms and hoisted to his shoulder. She grabbed him under the chin from behind. Hunching forward, she put her cheek to his, and pressed her face so tightly against his that her glasses fell off. Denton caught them just in time.

She never, ever greets me like that, Esther thought, as she watched her handsome, seductive, charming-to-everyone-else-in-the-world husband laughing and jiggling his squealing daughter. They galloped around the room, grazing the shade of the standing lamp, weaving through the narrow space between the davenport and the easy chair, sidestepping the scarred coffee table. Their faces beamed pleasure. Parin's high forehead matched his. His long straight nose would one day be hers, his mouth as well.

"Be careful, Denton, don't excite her too much. She'll never get to sleep."

"Oh, yes, she will. She'll go right to sleep tonight, won't you, button-nose?" He reached up and grabbed hold of her nose, catching it between his thumb and forefinger.

"Help!" Parin shrieked in pleasure, leaning closer.

"Denton, stop it," Esther stood up. "Just stop it right now."

The laughter immediately left both her husband and daughter. They stared at her, their faces flushed, their chests rising and falling from the exertion.

At least they stopped, Esther thought.

"Thank you," she said. "Really, Denton, it was too noisy for the McIntyres. You know how every sound goes through these walls."

"They don't care about a little horseplay once in a while, honey." Parin had started to tickle him under the chin and he was grinning. He walked toward Esther, his hand outstretched. "Come on, honey, join us." He slipped his arm around her waist, pulling her close. Parin's foot caught her collarbone.

"No, stop that." Esther yanked away. "Goddamn it, I don't want to play your games, Denton. Leave me alone."

Before she turned to walk to the bedroom she glimpsed the stricken look on her daughter's face. Silence had again replaced her laughter. Parin's face remained with Esther as she strode into the darkened bedroom and without turning on the bedside lamp, lay down.

Denton slowly and gently lifted his daughter from his shoulders. He held Parin close to his chest for a few moments until he felt her relax against him, and only then did he carry her to the table and place her on the chair in front of her dinner plate. She reached up for him, but when he said, "No, button-nose, I have to go see to Mommy," she immediately acquiesced. He watched her as she picked up her spoon and began eating the mashed potatoes and peas he was certain must be cold by now.

"I'll be back in a minute, chicken," he whispered to her. She nodded.

It was only then that he realized he was still wearing his overcoat, but he decided to leave it on. He didn't have much time.

He stood in the doorway of the bedroom. The wedge of light from the outer room fell across the bed and over Esther's lower body, so that her face, breasts and arms remained in shadow, though he could discern their outline, and he could see her dark hair on the white pillow. Her arm was thrown across her eyes. In this picture framed by light and shadow he was hauntingly reminded of his mother and how she spent most afternoons taking long naps in the bedroom with the curtains drawn. Sometimes the excuse was a headache. Other days a hazy look would cross her face, her eyes losing focus, and she would murmur in her faint voice, "I'm suddenly feeling so lazy. I think I'll just lie down for a few minutes."

Hours later, four or five, his father would come home from work and ask about her. "She's lying down," seven-year-old Denton would say, always the one to speak for the children. Bessie was too little and twenty-year-old Huey had returned from France too damaged to speak for himself, much less for the three of them. So it was always Denton to whom his father would repeat the dreaded words, "Maybe you should go up and see about your mother." Denton would think,

"Why don't you go up yourself?" But he knew that his father disliked entering that darkened, moist, breath-smelling room even more than Denton did. He knew his father abhorred walking over to his mother's deep-breathing body and touching her cool, damp arm. Usually it took numerous attempts to pull her out of her stuporous sleep. "Mama, are you awake?" "Mmm?" would come the dreamy, far-off voice from another world. When he was certain she was awake, he would escape the room. On the second-floor landing in the dim hall light he would be engulfed by revulsion and an ineffable sadness. He would hate himself for those feelings, and then relief would flow through him. He had done his duty. It was over. The evening could proceed.

"Esther, are you awake?"

"Of course I'm awake," she said in a harsh voice. "I'm not your mother."

He had once told Esther about his mother's naps. She, too, had witnessed them on one of their visits to his home. "It must have been awful," she'd said. "So frightening for a small child to have her disappear like that."

"It was," he'd said, tremendously grateful that he'd been able to tell her of his disgust and that she had not judged him to be a terrible person.

Denton went over and sat down on the edge of the bed beside Esther. She pulled a little away from him, but not too far, he noticed. There was hope.

"What is it?" he asked. "I thought we'd made up last night."

"Did we?"

He shrugged, not knowing what to answer now. Last night she had come back to bed. She had seemed affectionate; she'd even fallen asleep in his embrace.

"Please, honey, don't leave us out there all alone," he said.

"Why not? You always leave us alone," she said, dropping her arm back to reveal her eyes.

He could see them, dark and angry.

"That's different."

"What in hell do you mean different?"

He wished she'd keep her voice down. He didn't want Parin hearing this. Or the McIntyres. But he didn't dare tell Esther to speak more quietly.

"Please, Esther, we can't leave her out there." He tried to touch her again, but she shifted further away. He was dead with fear inside. This reminded him of something, not his mother's sleeping exactly, but something similar.

"Then you go out and sit with her."

"Esther."

"What is it?"

"You know I have to leave." He stopped. "I've got to go pick up Bill and get to the Co-op meeting. I've got to leave in a few minutes. I just came to get some papers."

"Of course. Then go," she said, turning on her side away from him. "I'll be out in a minute."

They remained in the near-silence. He could hear the radio playing next door.

"Esther, damn it, don't do this. We need each other, now more than ever."

"Listen to him," she said bitterly. "Listen to the man who didn't come home until three in the morning."

"Oh, lord, so that's it." He put his head in his hands. "Did Sy say what time I left him at the Administration Building?"

"He didn't have to. Sarah made certain I knew what time he got home." Her voice was flat, but at least she was talking to him.

"I don't know why I did it," he said. "Herm and I got talking. I needed someone to talk to. I thought Herm needed somebody to talk to. His head was banged up. He'd been through one hell of a time."

Esther turned over. She stared at him. She maneuvered herself up, sitting with her back against the wall, her trouser-clad legs tucked under her. She did this with a frightening dispassion, as though she wanted to get as far away from him as possible.

"What do you think I wanted and needed last night?" Esther asked.

"You mean that you also needed someone to talk with."

"Good for you, Mr. Organizer. Good for you. You discovered the underlying need of your most intimate community member."

"Don't be nasty to me," he said. "Don't put on that school marm voice."

"And don't you turn it against *me*," she said, her voice rising. "*I* am not to blame that you didn't see fit to be a husband last night or any other night for that matter."

"Esther, be quiet. Don't do this." He imagined Parin sitting at the table holding her hands over her ears, or blocking out this fight between her parents with loud humming.

"Why don't you just get out of here?" she whispered viciously. "I can't tolerate looking at or listening to you. Get out of my sight. Go out and take care of those people who need you and want you and adore you. Get out of our apartment. I don't want you anymore."

He grabbed her. She struggled in his arms, but he didn't release her. She wanted to be held tightly when she got this angry, with him, with herself. She'd once told him so, and he remembered now. She'd said, When I get that angry, I feel as though I'm breaking apart; just hold me.

Finally she stopped battling and fell heavily against his body. "What's happening?" she whispered. "I feel as though I'm going crazy."

"You're not going crazy," he said. But he thought, This is very bad.

"I think I'm going to go down to San Francisco with Parin," she said after a long silence, during which he had begun to worry that it was getting late. The meeting was to start at eight o'clock sharp. They'd been granted permission to break the new curfew, but they had to finish by ten. And they had a lot of business to take care of.

"You are?" he said. "When did you decide this?"

"Today. I need some time away. The school is closed. What am I going to do here if I'm not teaching?"

He knew that this conversation required his complete attention. Concerned as he was with what Esther was saying, he could not concentrate on it right now. He had to get to Bill Nakamura's house, and then on to the meeting.

"You're not listening, I can tell," she said.

"I'm listening, honey."

"No, I can tell, my time is up. Time for the meeting agenda." She slid down and slipped out of the circle of his arms. Her feet landed with a slap on the linoleum floor. She walked around him and over to the light in the doorway. Standing silhouetted, her face in shadow, she said, "I'm going to stay with Mother and Daddy. It'll be better. Anything has to be an improvement over this." She went into the living room.

Chapter Eleven

Denton left the car at the Administration Building and went on foot to pick up Bill. Because the residents weren't allowed vehicles under the new strictures, he didn't want to drive into the blocks unless it was absolutely necessary. It spoke too blatantly of his own freedom and mobility in comparison to the others.

The afternoon wind had settled down, but it was turning even colder, and the sky was overcast, with no hint of a moon. It felt like another early snow. He wondered how that would affect the crops out at the farm after the delay caused by the work stoppage. He'd heard that the potatoes were rotting and that the cabbage would go in a week's time. Inevitably the Tule Lake farmworkers would be punished if the crop was lost. Denton had also heard earlier today that a group of renegade striking workers had refused to leave the farm and had set up a lean-to of scrap lumber to sleep in, but if it turned much colder, if it snowed, they would freeze out there. But that was not his business anymore. He had enough to occupy him here.

He'd had to use all his powers of persuasion to get Andross and the army commander-in-charge, Colonel Benedict, to allow the shareholders' meeting tonight. The new rule against mass gatherings, as well as the seven o'clock curfew, had threatened its going forward. When the Colonel agreed to allow the curfew exception and permit the meeting as long as it was held indoors and was not a rally, Denton was careful to keep a smile off his face. He said thank you and goodbye and was on his way before Andross could advance any arguments.

All day the army had been constructing the chain link fence separating the administration area from the internees. So far it ran a few hundred yards from the western perimeter along the firebreak toward the center of camp. Temporary searchlights shone down on the gate, turning the immediate area into a circle of glaring white surrounded by black night. At the makeshift sentry box, a soldier with a bayoneted gun waved him through.

Denton cut across the new no-man's-land that divided Caucasian from Japanese American as never before. When he reached the barracks he turned right into the north-south firebreak between Ward 5 and Ward 1, walking along the line of tarpapered buildings that stretched out for a mile to the north and a half mile to each side of him. The smell of food from a mess hall mixed with the stench of a backed-up septic system. He'd heard that on top of everything else the latrines in Blocks 10, 12 and 40 were unusable. Director Andross was accusing people of sabotage.

Denton remembered how in the early weeks after the internees arrived, the hospital was receiving cases of serious constipation among the women residents. With delicate questioning the cause was discovered. The women's latrines had no dividing walls between the toilets. Everyone—other women, and their children, both boys and girls—was present as the women sat. Children stared, and even when they didn't, the lack of privacy was incapacitating. Many women waited until the middle of the night to go to the latrines, disrupting their normal bodily rhythms. Denton hated to think how insensitively Andross would have dealt with the problem if he'd been Project Director then. Fortunately, Al Bennett had been in charge. But Bennett was quickly ditched by Washington because he was deemed too egalitarian, too 'lenient' in his dealings with the evacuees. It was a sorry day when Al Bennett left.

Leaving the firebreak, Denton walked through the dark shadows between barracks and out into the cold light of Block 15. A few stragglers were leaving the mess hall at the far end of the block, where tonight's meeting was to be held. The mess staff had to clean up after dinner, so there was still some time to talk with Bill. He opened his coat and fished his watch from his pants pocket. It was only seventen. He needn't have rushed away from Esther. But that was a different matter. He must put it aside for the next few hours.

Denton walked between Buildings 15 and 16 to the Nakamuras' corner room and then a few steps past it onto the cinder road just as an army vehicle roared by. Across the firebreak was Ward 5 and beyond that the new Ward 6 that had been constructed for the overflow of disloyals from the other nine camps. Herm had told Denton that just before dawn the army ran raids with bayoneted guns in Ward 6, picking up suspected participants in the incident. Herm said they'd locked over a hundred more men and boys in the stockade. Word had it that they hadn't gotten Nebo because he'd been sleeping in a barracks other than his own, but Denton thought Andross had known it was better not to turn Nebo into a martyr.

Denton leaned against the outside wall of the Nakamuras' room. He could hear the steady, staccato tapping of Bill's typewriter, and over it the squeals of Bill and Mitsue's daughter Dori, high piercing laughter from the child. She was a year younger than Parin. He had made Parin laugh tonight. He hadn't heard her laugh, full out, in a good long time. He hadn't laughed in a long time, either. He used to be a real laugher. Esther loved to tell a story that in Berkeley, after they'd been to a movie, people would come up to her the next day and say, "We know you were at the movie last night. We heard Denton's laugh."

The sadness he'd been keeping at bay finally overtook him. He could see his daughter watching from the table as he left. She'd had a sagging, disheveled look as though the stuffing had been pulled from her. He would make her laugh in the morning. He wouldn't leave until after breakfast. If he got back early enough tonight, he and Esther would have a long talk. Maybe they would talk about work the way they used to do. He would ask about what had happened at school; it was always good when they could talk about work. He tilted his head, looking up into the cloud-filled sky. He stayed like that for a while.

Denton went through the gate Mitsue had constructed to protect her summer garden. He walked up the three wooden steps and knocked on the door.

"Coming," Mitsue's voice sang out. Bill's typing didn't miss a beat.

The door opened and Denton was enveloped in a rush of warm air heavy with the sweet, fresh scent of pine soap.

"Welcome, Denton," Mitsue bowed slightly in greeting. She was American-born and university-trained, a consummately modern woman, but as she had laughingly explained to Denton, having been among the more traditional Issei for a year and a half, she had picked up certain rituals. "All those years of rejecting Mama's Japanese ways and here I am. Though I think the transformation is completely lost on Mama."

Denton slipped out of his shoes at the door.

"Excuse me for not shaking hands," Mitsue said. "I'm bathing

Dori and my hands are wet. Come in, don't let more cold air in." She waved him past her.

Her flat cheeks were flushed pink, and strands of hair had come loose from the sleek roll she wore off her forehead. There were beads of perspiration around her hairline, Denton noted. He always noticed every detail about Mitsue, because he thought she was beautiful. Not that he'd ever lusted for her. She was Bill's wife, and he honored that. He had never committed adultery—unlike his father, he thought bitterly—but he did admire great beauty when he saw it. It was what had attracted him to Esther, after all.

Dori sat in a metal washtub in the very center of the room, to the right of the standing coal stove.

"I can't take her to the latrines or the laundry room for her bath," Mitsue said, re-tying a red-patterned bib-apron over her pink sweater and dark green trousers. "Everyone is crowding into our section because they can't use their own facilities. Did you smell those foul latrines in the next block?"

"I sure did. It's criminal and sickening." He sat down at the table. "Don't let me bother you, princess," he said to Dori.

Dori stared, her black eyes riveted to his.

Denton laughed. "She's as single-minded as her father," he said. The sound of typing continued without hesitation from behind the floor-to-ceiling bookshelves that partitioned off their tiny sleeping area.

"I heard that," Bill called, from the other side.

Denton wished he would hurry. They had a meeting agenda to go over.

"Would you like some tea, Denton?" Mitsue asked.

"Not now, thanks," he said. "Finish up with her majesty before the water gets cold."

Mitsue pulled her daughter's round, gleaming body to her own and kissed her loudly on the cheek. "Good girl. Isn't she good, Denton?" Mitsue looked over her shoulder at him. Dori peered around her mother's head.

"The very best, besides my own girl, of course," he said.

He checked his watch. They still had forty minutes, and he and Bill could go over the essential points in fifteen. Maybe tonight he could even slip in a resolution about the latrines.

Mitsue lifted Dori out of the water, and wrapped her in a large yellow towel. Only Dori's black hair showed at the top. Holding Dori in her lap, Mitsue dried her daughter's feet and then helped the child step into her pajama suit, fitting her feet into the slippers.

Denton remembered when he'd met Mitsue. Though it was a day of flat white, high-desert sunshine, a strong cold wind blew down off the Cascades, filling the air with choking clouds of black lava dust. Meeting the trains, Denton was on the lookout for leadership, spotting people who seemed to be spontaneously taking charge and those to whom others gravitated for help. He needed men or women who spoke both Japanese and English, through whom he could communicate. Denton immediately singled out Bill in the milling crowds, and recruited him to assist with the five hundred other people entering camp that day. Mitsue was left guarding their bags and holding her one-year-old daughter while Bill went to comfort frightened elderly Issei arrivals who understood no English. But Dori was squirming and shrieking, and Mitsue was having a hard time on her own.

Denton felt guilty for having deprived her of her husband, so when it came time for Mitsue to be fingerprinted and photographed, Denton offered to hold the child. Without a word, and barely a look, Mitsue put Dori in his arms. The baby pushed at him with angry strength, arching her back, squalling in a penetrating scream, red and wailing like a fire engine. Denton held tight, afraid she might fling herself out of his hold and tumble onto the sandy ground, while Mitsue knelt to open her huge suitcase. She riffled through, pulling out diapers, sweaters, baby dresses, a rag doll, and finally a bottle. Slowly she repacked everything but the bottle. He became impatient with her deliberate slowness, while all around them there were people with more pressing demands. He was starting to become very angry at the baby in his arms, at himself for getting caught up in this, and mostly at the beautiful young woman bent over the suitcase, when she stood and turned to him. She had been crying. She had used the time to gain control, to compose herself. Her face was streaked where the tears had run through the train soot and lava dust, and her eyes were bloodshot.

"Why don't we find a seat for you inside? We can get you processed later," he said.

"There's no room anywhere," the young woman said, as though defeated.

"Come on. Follow me. Your husband is helping out. The least I can do is offer you some peace and quiet in my office until he's finished," he said, and picking up her suitcases, he directed her toward the administration building.

"Kiss, kiss, kiss," Mitsue's voice broke into his thoughts as she came toward Denton holding Dori horizontally at her side.

Dori scowled as she was edged closer, but when she was within kissing distance her little lips puckered and she touched them to Denton's in a soapy smelling, satin caress. A raw place opened in his chest as he watched Mitsue carry Dori on her hip like a fat loaf of bread, across the room and around the bookshelves into the bedroom where Bill was now scrolling the paper from his typewriter.

Lulled by the hum of bedtime conversation between mother, father and child, Denton's thoughts drifted to the issues at hand and the imminent Co-op meeting and what he wanted to discuss with Bill before they went out. He'd had a talk with Toki Honda in Toki's office at the Co-op. Toki had been closemouthed when Denton had tried to engage him in a discussion of how he intended to handle the shareholder's meeting.

"I plan to carry on as usual," Toki said. He sat rigidly in his chair with his hands resting lightly, palms down, on the desk top.

"No discussion of what went on last night?" Denton asked. Denton didn't think it could be ignored.

"Whatever you like," Toki said, his face stiffening.

"I think we should discuss the disturbance. It's there anyway. It's going to drive the meeting. Better to put it on the table."

Over the year and a half of working together he and Toki had learned to be open and direct with each other, but now, he saw, they were back where they had started.

"The membership is coming to hear about their dividends and to elect new officers," Toki said in his most formal voice.

Denton usually sprawled comfortably with one leg over the arm of the wooden office chair, but today he kept both feet on the floor and his shoulders hunched forward, trying to appear deferential. His elbows were on the arms of the chair, his hands clasped.

"Is it possible that they see this meeting as a forum for their opinions and thoughts about what went on last night?"

Toki remained silent. He wouldn't look at Denton.

"Toki," Denton said. "The Co-op meeting is the one place people feel free to speak."

"Do they?" Toki's eyebrows rose, as his voice dropped to a deeper tone.

"What do you mean by that?" Denton realized that he might have missed Toki's point.

"There are rumors."

"There are always rumors. What's this one?"

"That there is an *inu* among us."

"Meaning me, I presume." Denton wasn't surprised. He was an easy target. It had happened before. A year ago the accusations had bothered him, but after a while he'd grown to take a certain comfort in them. At least they meant that people weren't accusing each other, turning against their own as had occurred in Andross's office last night. To Denton's way of seeing, hostility directed outward at the Caucasian organizer was a healthier state. "Well, it's not true."

Toki nodded.

"You know what this means, that they're accusing me?"

"I believe in this instance it's more serious."

They had been interrupted by Mary Makado, the young woman who worked the counter. She needed help in the store. No other staff had shown up and she had a line of customers. Denton left after half an hour, seeing that Toki would be busy for a good time more.

"A penny for your thoughts," Bill stood in the bedroom doorway. He wore his best gray suit, white shirt, tie, and slippers. His affable round face looked tired. He'd pushed his wire-rim glasses up to the top of his head, revealing puffy, strained eyes.

Denton took his watch from his pants pocket. "Put your shoes on and let's get out of here. What were you working on anyway, the great American novel?"

Bill yawned, dropping his glasses down onto his nose. "Nothing so enduring. My contribution will be a stunning analysis of the impact of rationing on current Co-op sales."

Denton laughed. "Well, someone has to do the real work."

"While others entertain."

Denton knew that what Bill typed in the next room had nothing to do with Co-op sales, but were his daily diaries about life in the camp. Bill had been working on his Ph.D. in American Literature at the University of Washington when the Executive Order had been issued. In the early days of evacuation, when he'd been in Pullyap Assembly Camp, a sociologist from Berkeley had approached him about keeping these journals. Since then, Bill took an hour or two every day to record his random thoughts, political observations and personal feelings about being in camp.

Bill had remained in Tule Lake after the loyalty questionnaires, even though he, Mitsue and Mrs. Ikura, his mother-in-law, had signed "yes" to both crucial questions and even though his mother, father and four brothers had left camp. "I can't run away and let our people turn against each other," Bill had said. "The tactics of the strong-arm boys, the beatings they carried out on their own people, well, I can't let that happen again, here, or anywhere." Denton had argued with him, insisting that he had to take advantage of the opportunity to get out, that it would be much more difficult later, and that if Bill would apply for leave clearance Denton could see about getting him a job with the Co-op's wholesale operation in New Jersey. But Bill had been obstinate about his decision to remain, and Mitsue, though she had some reservations because of Dori, supported him in his choice.

Bill went to the door where a line of shoes stood—his, Mitsue's, and Dori's galoshes. He picked up a pair of highly polished brown wingtips and brought them over to the table, sitting down across from Denton. Denton began to tap his foot nervously. He wished he knew what Toki had been alluding to. He repeated his cardinal rule to himself: Never go into a meeting without knowing what each party is thinking.

"Toki doesn't want to get into any of the underlying issues tonight," Denton said.

"No?" Bill began tying his second shoe.

"What do you think?"

Bill shrugged.

"I think it's a perfect forum," Denton said. "I told him as much."

"To what end, Dent?" Bill straightened up.

"To air the stuff. To let people have their say."

Bill shook his head. "They're not going to talk."

"They always have before in the Co-op. It's the one place they feel comfortable."

"Not anymore."

"What do you mean?" Was this what Toki had been going around the mountain about?

"They've lost their trust in it."

"In me, you mean?"

"Sort of," Bill sighed. He glanced over his shoulder toward the curtained-off room where Mitsue and the child were humming a tune together. "There's talk," he said quietly.

"What kind of talk? Be straightforward with me."

Bill nodded, gesturing that Denton should keep his voice down as well. Denton knew how to read faces. He could see Bill holding back, not wanting to hurt, not wanting to say.

"Nebo and his fellows have got a new tack. They're trying to cast doubt on you by saying..." Bill stopped.

"Go on."

"Saying you've been stealing money from the Co-op all along. That the only reason you seem to be on our side is to make a profit off of us."

"But there are always rumors going around about everyone. They peter out eventually."

"Sure, but..." Bill looked around the room.

"But what? Spit it out." Denton began to feel as guilty as if he had actually stolen money. Esther would get a good laugh out of this. She had several times accused him, in the heat of arguments, of not caring enough about money. She'd said money told you what you thought about yourself, that it was a clear indication that you didn't think you were good enough, if you didn't fight to earn at least a living wage.

"Nebo is smart. I tell you, Denton, you taught him his organizing lessons too well. He's saying that where there is suspicion, there has to be some truth to the accusation. His campaign is working, I'm afraid. In a mere twenty-four hours, it's begun to work."

"But what's so clever about that?"

"Let me finish. When people say, But Jordan-san is honest, he's always been straightforward with us, Nebo counters by saying that you're so honest as to be *too* honest, and thus suspect." Bill shoved his hands into his pants pockets, rocking his chair onto the back legs, his eyes to the floor.

"I didn't think there was such a thing as too honest."

"In my candid opinion? In your case? You're too honest to see base motives in the people you've dedicated yourself to helping."

"Every single one of you is lecturing me and I'm tired of it," Denton said, staring down at his own clasped hands. "I have my way of seeing things and doing them. Are you telling me I'm not doing a good job? That I'm messing up?"

"Of course I'm not saying that. I'm saying Nebo is going too far and you're not helping us when you don't face that."

"I know Nebo is no innocent," Denton said. "He'd try most any trick to get his way. I just think Andross should give in to some of his, the *Hoshidan* and the *Daihyo Sha Kai*'s demands. They—you—have constitutional rights, to a burial of your religious choice, to fair wages, to labor arbitration..."

"Japanese culture classes?" Bill's eyebrows rose.

Denton thought that he wasn't so sure he liked his friend as much as he had. He could see him as a conservative old man toeing the line in some university bureaucracy. Where had his liberal pal gone?

Denton looked down at the tablecloth. It was a cheerful design of watering pots and flowers, blue, yellow and red, behind a green trellis. Another example of people putting color into this dreary place. Flowers, ribbons, sculptures made of the shells found in the sand of the old lake bed. Always making the best of things. He supposed that was what Bill was doing, explaining to him how they all had to make the best of a very bad situation.

At that moment Mitsue lifted the green curtain covering the door and stood framed by the darkness behind her. She blinked in the brightness.

"Are you two through with it?"

"We'd better be. We've got a meeting to go to and we're late." Denton slapped the tabletop. "Your husband and I just disagree on some major points. Nothing new in that."

"All I'm trying to say is that Nebo Mota is a troublemaker. He's making life miserable for all of us."

"Or you could say he's articulating problems that should be addressed."

"Strong-arming Mrs. Kitamara into a mass funeral she didn't want? Rioting like an adolescent the other night? Landing hundreds in the stockade? Bringing on martial law? Breaking down the talks between the farmworkers and Andross?"

"Andross would never talk with them and you know it."

Ignoring Denton, Bill continued. "And this 'status quo' tactic. This total slowdown being set in motion by what's left of the Negotiating Committee, all three of them. It's going to kill us."

"You mean leaving the stinking latrines as they are?"

"That, yes. They're telling people not to co-operate with the administration, not to do any of the work that keeps the camp running smoothly. To force the administration's hand, so Andross supposedly has to give in to the demands if he doesn't want the whole place to collapse, or people to come down with diphtheria or worse." Bill shook his head in disgust.

"We can't live like this," Bill continued. "What happens when all the latrines go out? Or when the mess crew slacks off more and some child gets sick? Andross is not going to give. There is no indication that he will."

"That's what I've been saying. He's the problem in all of this."

"I beg to differ with you. Nebo Mota, that arrogant Kibei, is the problem. It was the tactics of Nebo's precursors, those militant strong-arm boys, during the loyalty questionnaires, that got us to this place. I only wanted to point out that it's a narrow line we walk," Bill said, looking at his wife and back at Denton. "Contrary to what you say about constitutional rights, we don't live in a free country in Tule Lake Camp. Certainly not these days."

"I'm not being helpful—that's what you mean," Denton said. He saw Mitsue nod ever so slightly.

"Moderation is what we need. Otherwise this place will blow sky high. We've all been through too much. May I be candid with you, Denton?" His smooth brow furled with concern.

"Shoot."

"I don't think you can take much more strain either."

"You think I should hightail it out of here?"

Bill smiled as he took his overcoat off the hook by the door and slipped his arms into the sleeves. "That's a whole other discussion, no? I for one don't particularly look forward to life around here without your ugly face."

Chapter Twelve

The meeting had already begun when they arrived. They'd been stopped at the front door by a private with a machine gun slung over his shoulder. He hitched it higher when he asked for their identification. Denton dug out the ragged piece of paper that identified him as Director of Business Enterprises. Bill pulled out his own I. D. that said he was an evacuee, which was obvious, and a block manager, which was less apparent. The boy let them pass.

The mess hall was filled to capacity. The tables had been moved and stacked along the side walls. Extra folding chairs had been set up in rows. With more than three hundred people in attendance many men and women stood against the back wall beneath a double line of men's hats hanging from pegs. Overcoats were draped over the backs of chairs and hooked over the low two-by-four crossbeams that ran the length of the room. The smallest children lay across laps, wrapped in blankets, while other children quietly played with toys in the main aisle. The seven-member Board of Directors for Ward 5 sat behind a long table at the front of the room. Toki stood at a podium to their right, addressing the assembly through a microphone. A murmur went through the body when people noticed Denton and Bill's arrival. Toki beckoned them to the front. Denton was about to demur, since he didn't usually sit with the Board, preferring to sit in the audience as an observer. Bill pressed his arm. "Come. There aren't any empty seats in front. Join us at the table this time."

Seated between Bill and Arthur Nagasaki, the Co-op treasurer, Denton looked out over the room. Sumiko Honda, Toki's wife, caught his eye. He waved to her, their daughter Sally Murayama and her artist husband, Frank. Toki's son Danny leaned against Sumiko's shoulder, his eyes already closed in sleep. The talk subsided when Arthur Nagasaki stood to give the treasurer's report. The news was good. There would be a substantial patronage refund for the past quarter. Applause followed his report. He returned to his seat beside Denton, all smiles. As he sat down he tugged his brown suit jacket over his large belly.

Toki rose again. "I'm afraid I have some unfortunate news," his authoritative voice boomed through the squawk of the microphone. "The shoe rations may be held up as much as a month. And the Office of Price Administration has said they will only allot us three-quarters of our request for sugar."

Loud, angry mutterings arose in response. Bill banged the table with his mallet. "Please maintain order and respect our hard-working general manager." A smattering of applause for Toki followed, but Denton sensed Toki's discomfort with the uproar, especially before his family.

When Toki was finished Bill introduced Ate Kashimoto, the manager of the tofu factory. The old man remained seated. "No report tonight," was all he said. Denton knew him as a difficult person, a taciturn, traditional sixty-year-old Issei who often insisted on speaking Japanese to Denton, even though he knew Denton barely understood a word.

Then it was time to begin the nominations, and Toki, as rules chairman of Ward 5's membership group, was recalled to lay out the election procedures. As he described the nominating rules, Robert's Rules of Order, and the general nominating process, Denton allowed his thoughts to drift from these well-traveled roads, so familiar that he could recite word for word what Toki was explaining. He gave himself the luxury of remembering the better early days of building the Co-op enterprise, when he, Bill, Freddy Huzaka and Teru Kanasawa had sat together and plotted their strategy. Freddy Huzaka, an Issei businessman, had known merchandise, had pointed out that the best products to concentrate on in the early months were dry goods—fabric, thread, pots and pans, things people had had to leave behind. Bed spreads. Linoleum. All the items that the women hungered for to make their barrack homes livable. Teru Kanasawa, a Nisei Bill's age, who had been recently transferred to Minidoka Camp when he'd signed "yes" on the loyalty questionnaire, had been one of the great organizational minds. His leaving was a big loss. Teru had known how to go after the Issei without alienating the Nisei and how to go after the Nisei without alienating the Issei and Kibei. With input from Denton, Bill, and Freddy, Teru handpicked the Co-op leadership.

It was Teru who knew that they had to have Toki Honda as the spokesman for the Issei. Toki had leadership abilities and a thorough knowledge of the wholesale business. The only problem was that there was lingering suspicion of Toki in Tule Lake. Because of his respected position as a Japanese American leader in his community back in Tacoma, Washington, Toki had been rounded up by the FBI in the first days after Pearl Harbor and accused by them of treasonous acts. He'd been incarcerated in the Missoula Internment Camp where he'd survived relentless interrogation by the federal investigators. But when Toki arrived at Tule Lake in July of 1942, a group of Issei women gossiped about him mercilessly, accusing him of having ratted on their husbands to the FBI. When other men, interned at the Missoula camp, were finally released and reached Tule Lake, they vouched that Toki had never given in to government pressure, that he'd been one of the more honorable men there. The rumors died down, but Denton knew that Toki still nursed the pain of humiliation from the whispering campaign, and Toki still worried that people harbored doubts about his reliability. It didn't help if Toki was being linked with Denton in Nebo's rhetoric, and if word about the slapping incident in Andross's office had gotten around camp. Denton recalled how Nebo had dared to call the older man a traitor to his face. Linkage of past and present rumors might explain tonight's jeering response to Toki's report.

Denton's ruminations were interrupted when the rear door opened and a group of five youths, Nebo Mota among them, pushed through the standing crowd in back. Toki continued to talk even though the audience had turned to see who had entered. The young men strode across and positioned themselves behind the last row of chairs on the right side. They didn't wear their militant whites; instead they had on brown leather jackets which they kept zipped, blue jeans with wide rolled up cuffs and dark knitted caps. Denton recognized Tony Kato, another Kibei, who was nicknamed "hard soul," and Mike Kitamano, a Nisei teenager who had recently attached himself to Nebo and followed him everywhere. The other two he didn't know, but they looked young enough to be members of the bugle corps for the *Hoshidan*. None of the members of the negotiating committee accompanied this group. Was Nebo becoming too militant, too wayward for them? Denton wondered. Nebo stepped into the aisle and without asking permission shouted loudly in Japanese.

Toki, who had been assiduously ignoring the new entrants, even as Nebo interrupted, stopped speaking and turned a frozen glare on Nebo Mota. The room fell silent, expectant.

"*Watakushi wa, kare ni tsuite, konban hanasana kereba,*" Nebo said.

"You are out of order, Mr. Mota-san," Bill rose from the table. "You must wait your turn as everyone else does. And you know the new rules. Japanese is not to be spoken for the duration of the period the camp is under martial law." He sat down again.

Nebo responded in Japanese.

Eyes turned fleetingly to Denton.

"Speak English so the accused man can hear, Mr. Mota-san," Toki Honda demanded.

Nebo answered in Japanese.

"You know better than anyone, Mr. Mota-san, that without Mr. Jordan's good services, we would not have the Co-op. Now, please sit down and wait your turn. We are under a time limit because of the curfew. Please, for everyone's sake," Toki was growing calmer as he spoke, which told Denton that he was getting increasingly angry.

Nebo walked down the center aisle, stopping halfway. He delivered what seemed to be a political tirade in Japanese.

Toki spoke next through clenched teeth. "Just wait a minute, young man. You respect your elders. If you had complaints about this meeting beforehand, you knew very well how to handle them procedurally, instead of coming in here and trying to steamroll over everyone. And I say it again, without Denton Jordan's intervention with the director, we would not be having this meeting tonight."

Denton thought, Uh-uh, Toki, don't take my side too much. Not these days. Don't let yourself be seen as a lackey.

A young woman stood up in the middle of the room. She was dressed neatly in a gray suit and prim white blouse. Denton recognized her as Esther's colleague, Hiroko Onji. "Mr. Honda is correct. This interruption is out of place. We have to do the business of the Co-op. This is just another strong-arm disruption."

Nebo looked over and glared at her.

"Tell me what the hell is going on," Denton whispered to Bill.

"What I told you," Bill hissed. "He's been saying you're a cheat, a robber, a spy, and you should be expelled from this meeting of Japanese people."

"Let No-No-boy speak." An elderly Issei man stood up in the far back left corner of the room and Denton recognized Gozo Horokawa. Horokawa began to talk switching to Japanese in mid-sentence. The entire room turned to listen. His voice rose in anger and anguish. He was small and wizened but he had an aura of dignity and gravity. Denton leaned toward Bill for a translation, but none was forthcoming. Satisfaction settled on Nebo Mota's face, and Denton suspected that the old man was speaking against him. Denton glanced at Toki and saw that the general manager was moved by what this man had to say.

Horokawa had been a farmer from outside of Tacoma. Toki had known Gozo Horokawa before they came to Tule Lake. Denton knew why an awed silence had settled over the room. Gozo Horokawa's was the worst near-tragedy to come out of the loyalty questionnaire debacle and the army recruitment. The old man had tried to kill himself when his only son had decided to enlist in the army's language school to train for intelligence work against Japan, to fight against his father's homeland—Gozo Horokawa's only homeland since he wasn't allowed to be a citizen of the United States. That night Horokawa beat his son and his wife and tore their room apart. Shortly before dawn Sy had called Denton to help him, but Horokawa hadn't let them in. They'd had to get Herm's security force to break the door down. What they found was wreckage. The linoleum had been ripped up, the bedspreads and curtains lay torn, dirtied and crumpled, and Mrs. Horokawa's painstakingly constructed sculptures, made from the tiny caracole shells she collected around camp, were smashed and thrown from one end of the room to the other. No one was there but Horokawa himself. Mrs. Horokawa and the boy had escaped during the night. The man's head was a bloody mass from being battered repeatedly against the wall. The white sheetrock was streaked with red. Horokawa's clothes were in tatters, there were long bloody knife wounds down his arms, on his thighs and calves, across his torso. He had maimed himself, slit his own skin, attempting to destroy himself. It was a sight Denton would never forget. Weeks later, after hospitalization and when he'd been transferred to the stockade, Horokawa had tried to hang himself. Sy had wondered aloud why he hadn't taken a kitchen knife to his jugular right away, but Denton had thought that Gozo's first fury was a circular rage of helplessness, a way of punishing the authorities through the self. The rage only congealed into a solid hopelessness in the stockade. In that prison within the prison, Gozo Horokawa had tried to find release. But he was discovered before he could succeed.

Denton watched transfixed as Gozo Horokawa talked and gestured with sharp movements and harsh, guttural sounds. The scars on his face had healed into bumpy lines.

"Is he talking about me?" Denton whispered to Bill.

"Obliquely," Bill murmured. "About all of you who've seemingly come to help."

"Sy Topol?"

"He's not mentioning names."

"Sy and I found him that morning."

"I know." Bill looked at him gravely. "I'm afraid this isn't good, Denton. You wanted people to lay it on the line. That's what Horokawa is doing and I don't think you'd like it."

Abruptly, the Issei stopped talking. He waited for a moment in the ensuing silence, then he bowed and sat. The room was still, but before long a murmur began and gradually got louder. People began arguing with each other, shouting. Bill banged the gavel to no avail. Nebo remained in the aisle. He looked completely pleased with himself. People rose from their seats shouting at Toki, telling him that the old man was right and that Nebo was right, which Denton took to mean that Nebo was right about Denton, that he, Denton, was here to make trouble, or to steal from them, or to spy. It was probably a little bit of everything. But his name was no longer used, eyes didn't focus on him. The men who spoke in English mentioned only "members of the administration," and that they shouldn't be invited to attend public meetings of the evacuees. They said this was a meeting of the co-operative membership and if any person wasn't a member of the Co-op, then he shouldn't be here. Denton was a member, but he didn't think it would help to state that fact.

"Order, order." Bill picked up his heavy coffee cup and pounded it rhythmically on the tabletop. The dregs of brown liquid leapt over the edge. But the noise continued unabated.

Toki's family sat stunned and frightened, staring straight ahead, the one spot of silence in the erupting room. Danny sat up and looked around groggily until Sumiko put her arm around him and cradled his face into her shoulder.

"What good does it do to have the administration representative among us?" a young man in the center of the meeting hall yelled above the noise. It was Bob Okura. Denton knew him well, had considered him an ally.

"It only takes up our time in arguing among ourselves," Okura was saying over the commotion in the room. "It only makes people like Mr. Horokawa-san more disturbed than he already is. I can't speak to the role of the member of the administration. I've trusted him in the past. I don't know if what Nebo Mota says is true, but I think we must be able to talk this over among ourselves without feeling that it will get back to the higher-ups. Though who can tell who is the real stool pigeon among us?"

Denton realized that this had gone too far and he had no alternative but to get out. Toki would never ask him to leave; not even Nebo, or anyone else in the meeting hall, would directly demand it, but if this meeting were to be saved—that was his priority—he would have to leave.

"I'm going," he said to Bill.

He didn't wait for his friend to say, "Stay," in politeness, in camaraderie, out of loyalty. He didn't remain to hear Bill agree that it was time for him to leave.

Though no heads turned, he could feel eyes upon him, sidelong looks, while people continued to speak, though the noise level had lowered significantly by the time he reached the back of the room. As he walked past Nebo, Denton made himself glance over. Nebo stared right through him. Nebo's cold opaque look fell like a physical blow on Denton. It hurt worse than Nebo's excoriation of him in front of all these people.

Outside the double door, pulling on his coat, he was slapped in the face by the cold night.

"What's going on in there, sir? Trouble?" the soldier asked.

"No trouble, son," Denton said. "Just some good all-American debate. Old tradition in this county."

"Yes, sir," the boy answered, looking frightened. Denton noticed the soldier was out here alone.

"Where's your partner?"

"It was our time to change guard, sir, and ain't nobody come to relieve us, so he went back to the sentry house to check on it."

Denton buttoned his coat and turned up the collar.

"Hope your relief comes soon," Denton said, starting down the stairs. "Be seeing you around."

Chapter Thirteen

Denton decided he'd pick up the car at the Administration Building and drive back home instead of walking the entire way. He was suddenly feeling exhausted. His legs were leaden, so heavy that he wished he didn't have to make it all the way to the car on his own, wished somebody would miraculously drive by and pick him up. But there wasn't a soul out here, save the boy on the porch, since nonessential vehicles were forbidden and the curfew was in force. Maybe if the other soldier came along in his jeep, he could hitch a ride.

In truth he was glad to be out of the meeting. They would be there at least another hour. He didn't feel up to the arguing. Didn't feel up to the concentration it would take to listen to all sides, to what was going on beneath the spoken words, trying to interpret and store all the information so he could talk it over with Herm in the morning and get his take on it before going over the whole mess again with Bill and Toki. Maybe he was like Herm after all, just fed up. Maybe he should get out of here as everyone was telling him.

He clenched and unclenched his fists as he moved along. Goddamn it, he couldn't give up. There had to be a way to deal with this. He'd go and talk to Nebo. Ask him what he really wanted, what he thought he was gaining from starting rumors against Denton. What could he be up to? What good could it do Nebo's cause to alienate the one Caucasian on his side? But Nebo had never been a very trusting soul. Denton remembered when he'd been recruiting Nebo to join them in building the Co-op, and Nebo responded, "To what end? To subdue us?"

Denton dug his hands into the pockets of his coat and hiked his shoulders to bring his collar higher. He and Nebo were clearly in the same boat. No humor left. Holier than thou. He had to admit it, both he and Nebo were on some kind of path where they didn't want to listen to anybody else; they were like twins—fraternal, not identical, but the same. Hope surged in Denton. If they were so alike, he should be able to find a solution and remedy this fiasco, bring it back to where they'd been before the loyalty oath questionnaires, when Tule Lake had been a place where imprisoned people made decent lives and a semblance of community for themselves. But he knew better.

The dignity the internees had gained from making the Co-op work, from showing their ability as entrepreneurs even under the harshest, most humiliating conditions, from demonstrating that even incarceration couldn't keep Japanese Americans down—all this had been vilified, wrecked, demeaned by the government's insistence that they sign those idiotic loyalty oaths. That was the rotten reality. Anger came over him again, wiping out the surge of hope he'd felt moments before, and as it did he thought he glimpsed figures running out of the shadows of Block 14. They were dressed in white pants and they were coming toward him. For a split second he believed that they were racing to embrace him, to say they wanted him back in the meeting, that they'd voted and decided he was the best Caucasian in the whole place and they needed him.

Then they were circling him, silently, menacingly, moving in closer and closer, four or five of them. Too many of them. He couldn't see their faces in the dark. Fear buzzed in his jaw. "Hey, fellows, wait a minute," he called. Nobody answered. He started to run, to dart between them, to get the hell out of there when a powerful blow landed in the middle of his back. He staggered, his knees buckling. Catching himself, he whipped around to see who had hit him when someone grabbed his arms and wrenched them back and up, throwing him forward. A thudding punch to his stomach knocked out his breath. He couldn't call out or breathe in. He tried to kick, but he met air. The person constraining him tightened his hold suddenly, yanking Denton's arms in their sockets. His legs doubled under him from the pain, but the man jerked Denton's arms yet higher, keeping him from falling. More punches, sharp vicious jabs, to the stomach, to the chest, to the ribs, to the lower back, to the...he couldn't tell anymore where they landed. Total silence descended on their tiny world, only his own grunts and the grunts of his attackers disturbing the eerie quiet.

All he saw was white and shadow, white and shadow, no features. Punishment, punishment, dirty punishm... and he was on the ground. Alone. Trying to breathe and not to faint. Trying to believe he would come out alive. Trying not to vomit because it hurt too much, but he did vomit and a wrenching, burning pain went up through his belly into his chest and out his mouth—'where laughter should have been,' he thought before blacking out.

He dreamed he was a child, his hand in his mother's, his foot rising to take the high step onto the trolley car. Too high. Why was the step in this new city so high? He wished his father was with them. His father could lift him up and the trolley man wouldn't be angry at him, the ticket-taker wouldn't scowl, his mother wouldn't tell him later that he had humiliated her. But he couldn't lift his leg up, couldn't...it was too heavy and too light at the same time, and his arms were being torn right out of their sockets by his mother. The trolley took off without them while he vomited on the pavement. Vomited on his shoes, on his knickers, on his mother's long black wool skirt. Wet, vomit-soaked wool, yellow slime against the black. Cold. The smell of vomit. Hard pavement. Denton tried to open his eyes. The dream stayed with him as he looked into the darkness. He'd been afraid of the dark as a kid. He groaned as he tried to move his body, an adult man's arms and legs and torso and back. The vomit smeared slickly against his cheek, and underneath it the ground was hard, cold. He remembered what had happened and began to cry. He wept as the small boy in the dream did when he'd humiliated himself, throwing up in the city street, in the new city. After his father had to sell off the farm and move them there in defeat. His mother would ask him then, when he threw up in the street, "What are you trying to do, shame me like your father did?"

Denton struggled to sit up. The tears kept flowing down his face, burning along the path they traveled. He smelled so bad. Where could he go to get cleaned up? As soon as he had that thought it became his sole motivation; find someplace to clean this slime off his face. He turned over on his knees and with tremendous effort he stood up, being careful to keep his movements minimal, his breathing shallow. Every inhalation brought an agony of sensations, through his chest, into his abdomen. He would go to Herm's. That's what he would do, even if it meant that Herm would say, "I told you so." But what if Herm insisted that Denton go to the military police? Herm would have to do that; he was in charge of security for the administration. He'd get in trouble if he didn't make Denton talk to them.

Like an old man, Denton stood there huddled against the cold, against his own pain, against his loneliness. What the hell am I going to do, he cried silently, looking up at the stars that appeared and disappeared behind swiftly scudding clouds. He felt like the wounded coyote he'd once come upon on a night hike in the Sierras. Denton had been by himself on a high plateau, euphoric in the full-moon night when the coyote's whimpering had come to him on the wind. Looking down over a meadow, he'd seen the animal, golden in the brilliant light, a blackness flowing from his underbelly onto the low-growing, gray-green grass. Denton had sat transfixed under the bleached night sky, as the animal stood, and turned and turned in place, his head down, yelping and biting and snapping at his wound, until he fell to the ground and the life went out of him.

Denton began limping back across the rutted expanse of firebreak. He moved between Blocks 15 and 16, out into the square, across and down the line of barracks, returning to the Nakamuras' room. That was it. He must have known all along. He'd go and ask Mitsue for help. There would be no recriminations from Mitsue, no "I-told-you-so's."

Mitsue opened the door immediately. He knew when he saw her expression just how bad he looked.

"Denton, what happened? Where is Bill?"

"He's fine, Mitsue. He's still at the meeting. I left early."

She came to his side and put her arm in his. "Please, let me help you."

"I stink," he said, about to start crying again. He held back his emotion, not allowing himself to melt into her kindness, into the warmth of her body, and the sweet soapy smell emanating from her. "I'm sorry, I threw up."

"Come, sit down. Let me try to clean you up." She led him over to the table where he'd been sitting earlier watching Dori having her bath.

"I can do it," he said feebly. "I just need a basin and a cloth." His voice trailed off, like the whimpering of the coyote on the plain. He wished he could go to sleep. But he wanted to say something else. He had to tell Mitsue...but what the hell was it? He couldn't remember. He couldn't remember anything.

"I insist that you sit here and let me take care of you. You look terrible!"

"Am I that bad?" he whispered.

"I'm worried about you." Her voice softened. "I'm going to wipe off some of the vomit and a little of the dirt, but I think I shouldn't touch too much. No, no, don't you touch." She grabbed his hand as he was about to rub his cheek. "It looks like sand or gravel in the abrasions. Someone must clean it professionally and paint it with mercurochrome, I believe. Oh, my."

Denton insisted on seeing himself. Looking into her hand mirror, he couldn't believe he was this man with the swollen, cut lip and bloodied, blackened cheek. A solid glob of blood was coming out of his nose, lapping over his upper lip. His hair was matted with blood, slime and bits of undigested food.

"What did they want to do, kill me?" He was seething now as he sat waiting while Mitsue heated water on the hotplate and murmured words of comfort to him.

"You'll be fine, Denton. It doesn't look as though any bones are broken. We must just get you washed up a bit."

A rage rose in him, burning away her gentle words. He had visions of stabbing one of the men or boys who had attacked him, and of bashing two of their heads together and hearing their skulls crack, watching their brains flow out and rejoicing. Were there five of them or more? He thought he remembered five figures though there could have been more. One person held him. At least four people took turns punching him. The man who held him he would grab around the throat and strangle, then smash his head against a cement block to finish him off. These were things he'd sometimes thought of doing to Bobby Paterson, a schoolyard bully who'd tyrannized him, and for a single shattering moment he remembered having had these same thoughts long, long ago about his mother.

Mitsue came to the table with a yellow washcloth and a red bowl filled with warm water. In her presence, the madness fell away, leaving only shame and guilt for such thoughts, and that too was soon wiped away by each searing brush of the cloth on his face. Even administered by Mitsue's delicate hand, each touch was almost unbearable, but he accepted it as his punishment. A pacifist could not have such savage fantasies.

After she had washed his face and his hands, Mitsue left Denton for a few minutes to find a neighbor who could stay with Dori so that she could accompany him to the hospital. He told her she didn't need to and that perhaps she would have trouble getting past the military police, but she insisted that he must not go alone. She would tell the army men that she was the one with the emergency. Seeing how determined she was, he stopped protesting. And he knew the thugs would never beat up a Nisei woman. While he waited for her to return he sat looking at his injured hands like a chastened school boy, and realized that he did need her help to the hospital, because he was afraid that out there alone in the wasteland of camp he would split into pieces and fly apart. Sometimes overwhelming sadness would wash over him, then the rage would return, then he'd feel as small as a seven-year-old boy with the hollow, fragile bones of a bird. That was the most frightening sensation, as though his body had shrunk, had abandoned his adult self, was as light as a feather, and that he could be blown off his feet with a gust of wind.

Now, for the first time, he thought of Esther. What would she be thinking? Would she decide he was sitting around talking and drinking with Herm? It gave him a certain grim satisfaction to know he would have his wounds to show as evidence against her accusation. But she would be all the more justified in wanting to get out of here. Well, who knew. Who the hell knew what was going to happen after this?

Chapter Fourteen

Alice Hamilton, the new Caucasian nurse, had just gone off duty when they met her outside the main door of the hospital.

"What the heck happened to you, Mr. Jordan? Hello, Mrs. Nakamura." She was as tall as Denton. She moved him around into the light by the door to get a better look. Though she was carrying her uniform over one arm, she still wore her crisp, winged nurse's cap. She shifted her uniform to the other arm. "Oh, lord. This needs some attention. What happened?" She looked from Denton to Mitsue and back, her gray-blue eyes wary when they met Denton's.

"We came by for tea." Denton laughed and then grimaced from the pain. "Damn."

"Denton was beaten up by a group of hotheads," Mitsue said in an outraged voice.

"Mitsue, please, I don't know that." He didn't want it down in the records.

"I don't care. That's who it was. Miss Hamilton can decide how to report it, but I want her to know what I think. I'm fed up. Just fed up." She reached for the door to go inside.

Denton started to tell her she didn't have to wait, but when he saw the stubborn set of her mouth he realized it would take too much of his energy to get her to go back. He recalled the proud girl he'd met at the trains, the young mother thinking he didn't know she had cried. Tonight she was his strength.

Alice led them through the wide, brightly lit halls of the rambling wooden barracks towards the back. They passed the maternity ward, then the children's ward, both dark. Denton had not been in the hospital since he'd come to visit Raymond Sato after the farm truck accident. It was the precipitating moment in this whole mess, Denton thought, as he followed Alice and Mitsue around a corner.

The hospital was hot, the one building in camp that was warm enough. He unbuttoned his coat. He thought of the loyalty oath debacle, the frustrations that had built and converged like rain-swollen tributaries of a river causing it to flow over and ravage the surrounding land. Kitamara's mass funeral and the so-called riot were the direct result of the administration's mismanagement. But tonight Denton found himself resenting the demands of the Negotiating Committee, their capitulation to the more militant *Hoshidan*. A suspicion crept into Denton's exhausted mind and body. What if their goal really was simply to stir up trouble, as some people were saying? What if their goal was complete anarchy? What if they had no positive agenda other than creating chaos and disruption, what then? Then that would mean he was a damn fool.

Denton sat on a cot against the wall of a narrow examining room, while Alice Hamilton stood in the far corner with her back to him, placing items on a cloth-covered tray. She had brought Denton and Mitsue to Joe Miller's office in the far reaches of the hospital. Mitsue stayed out in his waiting room.

"Dr. Miller and Maggie went into Klamath Falls for a few days. Did you know that?" Alice kept working as she spoke.

"Nope."

"May I call you Denton?" She looked over her shoulder and smiled.

"Of course, if I can call you Alice."

"Sure thing."

He smelled the alcohol of the sterilizer and another strong medicinal odor escaping from her work area. He watched as she moved, stooping to get cotton batting from a low shelf, standing again to tinker with something metal that he could hear but not see.

"He got roughed up in the disturbance when they took over the hospital last night. Maggie insisted on getting out of here for a while. I think Dr. Miller didn't want to, but he went along with her. He's a nice guy, Dr. Miller is, don't you think?"

"I like Joe a lot. He's one of the more committed." He wished she'd stop talking. She probably thought she had to keep him entertained to get his mind off what had happened.

"That's the way I see it, too." She said, tucking a long strand of reddish-blonde hair under her nurse's cap. She quit talking and went about her preparations. The room was silent except for the soothing clatter her movements made.

He'd never taken much notice of Alice Hamilton even though the men—Herm, Sy, and even Joe Miller—had commented on what a looker she was. She wasn't flashy, they agreed, but if you observed her closely you could appreciate her attributes. Shiny blond hair, smooth pale skin, and a body that could be described either as solid or voluptuous. "That gal could compete with Ava Gardner," Herm had said. Tonight she wore a gray flannel straight skirt that hugged her behind and a sky-blue pullover sweater. It looked good with her hair, Denton thought. She turned just as he was imagining the texture of her hair and he noticed her breasts, revealed by the soft cling of her sweater.

"Okay, Denton, this is going to be painful. I could give you something, but then you'd be out for a while and groggy when you came to. What do you say?" She placed a tray of metal utensils, gauze and cotton on the cot beside him, pulled a small table over and set the tray on top.

"I don't want anything. I hate pain, but I'll bite the bullet."

"It's your choice." She stood directly in front of him, her breasts at his eye level, and drew her hand across his brow, combing his hair back off his forehead.

He could tell from the way her hand moved through his hair that it was still sticky with vomit.

"I threw up."

"You don't have to tell me, I can smell it."

"Jesus," he said, ashamed.

"It's okay, I've smelled worse." She grinned.

She had a slight overbite. He'd always thought an overbite was sexy. She smelled like warm milk, almost like a baby.

She began to work on his face, to clean it with the medicinal-smelling solution that obscured her own personal odors.

"Are you okay?" she asked, her face close to his.

"Not as bad as I expected. Burns a little is all." It was as though his skin had gone numb. Her touch was so light and her face so close to his, and he felt the pressure of her leg against his thigh; all of it was more overwhelming to him than any pain she could inflict on his poor cheek. A part of him had been broken tonight, and instead of feeling guilty about the sensations moving through his body, up his thighs, into his groin, aroused by a woman other than his wife, he simply gave himself to the pleasure of it. He let his body relax. He hoped her breast might graze him accidentally, or that he could once again smell the milky freshness of her body, or that she would brush his hair back off his forehead another time.

He longed to touch her round, full breast, or lay his face upon the sweater's knitted texture and breathe her in, and then take her sweater off, pulling it over her head, loosening her straight silky hair so it would fall over her shoulders, over the straps of her white satin slip and brassiere. He would reach his hand inside and cup her warm flesh.

"Okay, Denton, I think I've done about all I can for now." She straightened and stood back a step, inspecting her handiwork. He was glad he'd folded his jacket over his lap. He hoped he wouldn't have to stand for a minute or two.

"You've got some sand stuck in there, but it looks more like beard stubble than dirt. I hope it's going to just grow its way out in a couple of days to a week. I'll give you some of this stuff to keep it disinfected." She held a bottle of amber liquid. "I want you back tomorrow or the next day at the latest. I need a look at it. Come in the afternoon when I'm back on duty. Two p.m. until ten, got that?"

He nodded, not yet trusting his voice.

"What I want to know," she said, sitting down close beside him on the cot, but not touching him, "is how am I supposed to file the report? What do you want Andross to know about this?"

He looked over at her. She grinned, exposing the tips of her front teeth. He noticed the slight indentation on her lower lip where her teeth must rest when she slept.

"What would you say?" he asked.

"If it were me?"

"Yep."

"You're smart, Denton. Okay, I wouldn't say it was *Hoshidan* or No-no boys or anything like that. I wouldn't know after all, now would I? I'd probably say I tripped and fell, skidding my face across the sand. The abrasions could pass for that."

"And why wouldn't you state your suspicions?"

She smiled widely. Shrugging, she said, "I don't know. I'm funny that way, don't want any more trouble for these people than they've already got."

"Could it be that your sympathies are with the No-no boys?"

"Could be," she said, and stood up, leaving him alone on the cot. "Maybe I spent too much time down in Manzanar before getting here.

So what'll it be?" She carried the metal tray over to the high worktable and stood with her back to him.

"I guess I tripped over those damn ruts out there, left by the tanks the other night," he said, intrigued and curious about what she'd done in Manzanar Camp.

She nodded. "Now that we know each other, take off your shirt. I'd better check for any broken ribs."

Her hands were cool, her touch firm but delicate. He wished he weren't quite so thin. He was sure she liked her men with more meat on them than he had.

"Well," she said, stepping back. "Don't think they're broken, but I'd like to tape them as a precautionary measure."

He thought he detected a roughness in her voice. Was she feeling what he was? Was she as reluctant to stop touching him as he was to have her hands stop moving up and down his chest?

"It's going to hurt like hell when we take this off," she said as she wrapped him in white adhesive tape. "But you have mercifully little hair on your back and chest."

Did she like that or not? he wondered as he felt her breath on his shoulder. Did she prefer hirsute men?

"I'm a brave guy."

"I bet you are."

When she was done, she carried the roll of tape to the standing metal and glass cabinet. "You can put your shirt on," she said, without turning. "No lying around in the bath. You can sit with the water below your waist and sponge-bathe your uppers. But try to keep the tape dry."

"Kind of like my powder," he joked feebly.

"Yep, soldier. Kind of like keeping your powder dry," she said as she went about her business.

*   *   *

Denton was surprised to find Mitsue, not in the doctor's office, but sitting with Bill on a wooden bench out in the main reception area. The night nurse had left her post and no one else was in the room. Bill's head rested against the wall. He had removed his glasses and closed his eyes, his round, eager face gone slack in sleep. Denton had never seen his friend so unguarded. He was used to seeing Bill's face

109

alert and eager for the next encounter or argument, and registering impatience when the speaker didn't get to it quickly enough. Mitsue, who had removed her coat in the warm room, dozed with her head slipping off Bill's shoulder down to his chest.

As soon as Denton began to walk toward them, Bill's eyes blinked open. He rose, carefully shifting Mitsue off his body. She remained sitting, rubbing her hand over her sleepy face.

"Denton, what the heck did they do to you?" Bill scowled as he came close to examine Denton's face.

"Just got myself a little roughed up." Denton tried to laugh, but his skin had tightened from the treatment and it felt as though his face would crack.

"I'll say. Mitsue said it was Nebo's fellows." He shook his head in disgust.

Alice came out into the waiting room just then. "Hello, Mr. Nakamura. Would you and Mrs. Nakamura like some tea or what passes for coffee here?"

"No, thank you," Mitsue said, getting up from the bench. She looked exhausted, her complexion pale in the harsh light. Her lips and eyelids were puffy. "I must be getting to bed now that Denton is safely taken care of. You two can talk tomorrow, can't you?"

"Sure thing," Denton said, though he wanted to know more about the meeting. Maybe he could ask a few questions in the car. "Let's get going. I'll pick up my car and drive you back."

"There's no need, Denton," Mitsue said.

"It's the least I can do, Mitsue, for all your help. I don't know what I would have done without you."

She put her arm through his. "You would have done just fine, Denton."

He felt his ribs as she leaned into him. Alice had told him tomorrow would be sheer hell. Already the ribs hurt more than when she'd poked around.

"Miss Hamilton says I need my beauty sleep, but it can wait half an hour. Isn't that right, Miss Hamilton?"

She was seated at the front desk, writing, her head bowed over the page, and she didn't seem to have heard him. The ubiquitous Roosevelt looked down on her from the wall behind the desk. Lucky fellow, Denton thought, he can watch the nape of her neck night after night. But, unlike in the privacy of the interior room, he felt ashamed of his desires in the presence of his friends. He couldn't believe it had been him in that room responding to her hands, to the smell of her.

She looked up as though she'd sensed his thoughts, and he felt himself redden deeply.

"Miss Hamilton, thank you," he said as coolly as possible. "See you tomorrow."

"Until tomorrow," she said, giving him her toothy grin. "Sleep well, all of you." She went back to her writing.

It was silly, but he felt rejected by her. She obviously hadn't been as excited as he had in that small room. He felt foolish as well as feeling like a man who had strayed. He had a sharp, horrifying memory of being in his mother's bedroom, clasped too close to her on the bed, while his mother said in her slurred voice, "Your father likes his women, any kind of woman, colored or white, slant-eyed or straight, as long as she spreads her legs for him." She put her mouth against his ear. "Your father used to want to do it twice a day until I put a stop to that. So now he goes wherever he can find it."

*　　*　　*

Bill and Mitsue walked with Denton to the Administration Building to pick up his car. They continued to protest his driving them home, but he insisted, saying it would be nearly impossible for them to get past the sentries at this hour. As it was he had to explain to the soldier on duty at Administration that they had been visiting his apartment, and he had to do the same as they crossed back over into the no man's land of the firebreak. But he barely noticed the inconvenience since it took his entire concentration to drive the car. Every bump of the road, every effort to turn the steering wheel was agony. His ribs screamed with each jolt. His shoulders were both painful and weak and his arms felt dangerously loose in their sockets. Denton counted off the blocks as he drove along the firebreak across the darkened camp. It hurt too much to talk. He feared that Bill would hear the suffering in his voice. But he did ask him about the meeting and Bill filled him in as they bumped and jostled along.

"We didn't even get to the slate. Nebo disrupted the meeting so much that people got fed up and began to leave in disgust about fifteen minutes after you did. I'll tell you, Denton, he's trouble. He doesn't care what people want. He wants what he wants. And that is to disrupt. I know what he would say if I got to talk to him face to face, if he's capable anymore of a private conversation, instead of lecturing and finger-pointing. He would say what you said, 'The people need to express what they're feeling about the disturbance. The people must say how angry they are at the administration. Only that way will we be proud of who we are, proud to be Japanese. *Banzai!*' Sorry, Denton, I don't mean to equate the two of you. You mean well; he only wishes to rabble-rouse. He is so full of hatred, I hardly believe he's the same fellow I've worked with this whole year."

Denton kept driving and kept quiet. He glanced over at Mitsue who dozed between the two of them, her chin lolling on her chest. Looking forward, he glimpsed a rabbit just as it ran through his headlights.

"You see that?" he said with effort.

"Sure I did." Bill's voice was flat.

"Just think, if it got in, it can get out again."

"I know Mitsue and I can get out, Denton. I know that very well. I could be out of here right now. I could have taken the offer from the University of Chicago to finish my doctorate. I could have enlisted. I chose to stay here and help folks."

Denton wished he hadn't tried to make the joke. He should be talking seriously with Bill, but in his present state he could barely absorb his words, much less challenge them coherently.

"The question is, what kind of shape will we all be in when we finally leave," Bill said. "As far as I'm concerned, what Nebo is doing is more demoralizing than anything Director Andross can order. Nebo is wearing me down. You and I have had our philosophical arguments about this. But I don't want to have these discussions anymore. I want Nebo to stop. How about you? Are you shifting your position after tonight? Are you changing your mind about Nebo Mota?"

Denton didn't answer. What could he say? That he'd agreed with Alice not to turn Nebo in? The decision sounded stupid in the face of Bill's vehemence.

They drove in silence, with only the sound of the car engine and Mitsue's deep breathing for accompaniment. Bill didn't repeat his question.

He stopped the car beside Bill's barracks. The moon was shining through the windshield, illuminating Mitsue's face.

"Mitsue," Bill whispered. She didn't stir.

"Wait just a minute, would you?" Denton asked. "I have something to tell you."

Bill sat back, his face in shadow. The sedan was cold. Every part of Denton's body hurt. But he had to do this.

"Alice Hamilton isn't going to report that I was beaten up."

"What!?"

Mitsue shifted, but didn't wake.

"Shh, let me explain."

"You'd better." Denton heard Bill's barely contained anger.

"She doesn't want to make more trouble than there already is. I agree with her."

"I cannot believe you. I'm furious. Those guys should be in the stockade. Nebo most of all. They are making our lives miserable. My life, Denton. My wife's life. My neighbors' lives." His voice had risen to a high pitch. This went beyond their usual disagreements. Mitsue began to wake up.

"I'm not sure I agree with you on that. I need time to think about this," Denton said. He kept his voice calm, so as not to show his grief at this fight. He didn't want acrimony with every friend he had here. Why couldn't they understand what he felt?

"I know we don't agree, Dent. But I'm afraid you won't see reason until somebody gets killed. Or at the least until we're all so intimidated that none of us will leave our rooms. That's what is going to happen, sure as the nose on my face. This is insane. I'm tempted to turn Nebo in myself."

"You wouldn't do that. Not to yourself, to Mitsue, to me or to Alice." Denton knew he wouldn't. Bill would never turn *inu*, no matter what he believed was right.

Bill looked away from him and stared out the windshield. Denton thought of Esther the other night, in the same car seat, just as angry at him.

"Where are we?" Mitsue's sleepy voice came between them.

"You're home," Denton said, when Bill didn't answer her.

"Home?" Her voice rose in a mix of hope and sadness.

"Yes, dear Mitsue," Bill said. "Denton drove us *home*."

The last word hit him with the intended rancor, as if it were altogether Denton's doing that they were here.

Bill got out of the car and Mitsue slid over, following him. Bill muttered thanks for the lift before slamming the car door shut.

*   *   *

Esther was awake and sitting at the table playing solitaire when Denton came into their apartment. She looked up as he entered, her eyes acknowledging only fleetingly the terrible condition of his face. She went back to her cards, turning them over three at a time, taking one out and placing it suit up on a line. He walked into the kitchen to get a glass of water. As he stood drinking, the only sound in the other room was the slap of the cards being put down. He went over to the opening between the kitchen and the living room and watched her. She still wore her daytime clothes. Her hair was coming loose from the roll around her head. Black curls had sprung from the pins that held them. He knew the pins, he'd pulled them out enough times in the early days, when they'd made love regularly. He'd liked plucking them out one by one, slowly, tantalizingly, or so Esther had said she'd found it. At least he'd done that much right, for a time anyway.

"Aren't you going to ask me what happened?"

"What happened?" she said without looking up.

"I slipped and fell."

"Hah." She continued to place the cards down, though with a sharper slap.

He wondered if it was possible to hate the woman you'd thought you loved, had married in passionate love, had been terrified at all times would find you deficient and decide to leave you. She pursed her lips as she placed the cards one on top of the other. As he had imagined Bill earlier, he could see how she would look as an old woman, her face permanently assuming tonight's stern contours. Fussy. She'd be a fussy, hard, maybe bitter old woman. She'd be scornful. Biting. He didn't think he wanted to know her then. Though he'd promised himself on his way back from Bill's and Mitsue's that he wouldn't think of Alice Hamilton once he got home, that he wouldn't spend time fantasizing about her, he couldn't stop himself from imagining her in her old age, blond hair silvered with gray, her face slightly filled out, her skin still smooth, and her expression welcoming. She'd have a bosom even then and he, an old man himself, could press his face into it for warmth and sensual pleasure.

Denton shook these thoughts away, ashamed, shocked that he could be thinking so intimately about another woman.

"Esther, please," he said.

She didn't look up from her solitaire.

"I didn't fall, I got beat up."

Her hand stopped and lay there, covering the red pattern of the cards. Her chest rose and fell with each breath. Denton couldn't help thinking how small her breasts were. But then he began to worry about her response. There was no telling what it would be, but one thing was certain—she would be appalled that he wasn't going to report the beating.

"I can guess who did it," she said, keeping her eyes on the cards.

"I don't know who it was. It was dark and I couldn't see them."

"But they wore white, or at least white bands on their heads, I'd bet on that."

"I guess you could say that."

"I didn't tell you, but this afternoon Nebo Mota came to our makeshift school. We held it in the Onjis' room when we couldn't get into the classroom. He came and threatened Hiroko, mostly speaking against you and me." Her mouth trembled as she spoke.

"I feel like a heel."

"Why?" She looked at him. Her eyes were filled with tears. "Why do you feel like a heel? Why don't you feel angry?"

Esther saw something in her husband's face she'd never noticed before. She saw him struggling to find the correct response. He shuttled from fear to worry to anger to sadness. He didn't know his own mind, or was he hiding even grimmer facts from her and trying to find the right emotion to cover the truth? His face is weak, she thought. She'd never felt that before. Even in its battered state she detected a flaccidness along the jaw bone, and there were his eyes; the pupils rode high, with the whites showing beneath them. She'd once heard a Chinese man in San Francisco say, "You can't trust a man when the dark of his eyes don't meet the bottom rims. That man is not honest." She'd always loved Denton's eyes before. They matched his dark hair and looked so striking against his light skin and ruddy cheeks. But tonight they skittered. She wondered if it was more noticeable when dark eyes shifted than when pale ones did.

Denton wanted to say, Can't you take me for who I am? Can't you just accept that I'm confused and afraid and don't know what I think anymore?

Instead he said, "I am angry. I'm angry at what's happening to this place. Angry that it's all falling apart."

115

"Well, that's something," she said, standing. She shuffled the cards together, breaking up the game she'd played for hours, to stay awake waiting for him. "But has Andross been informed?"

"Not yet," he said. His body was trembling. He hoped she couldn't tell.

"I see," she said.

"What do you see? What do you see, Esther?"

"You're not going to tell, are you? You're going to give the answer you did when you came in. 'I fell down.'" She mimicked him, using baby talk.

He hated her for doing that.

As for Esther, she became her husband as she imitated him. She felt his fear of petitioning the project director on his own behalf. Denton would never say, The bastards beat me up, I need your help. He was too weak to stand up for himself. Only when someone was weaker than he could he play the radical hero, posturing on their behalf.

"You don't know what I'll do," he whispered.

"Oh, yes, I do. I know only too well. And I can't stand it, Denton. I'm getting out of here. You're going to dig yourself in deeper. You don't ever want to leave here. You want to stay here and be more and more miserable and then you'll be as happy as a pig in mud."

"That's not fair, Esther." He heard his voice as a growl, like a wild animal, like the coyote on the plain. "I'm not evil." He hardly knew where he was as he spoke. The room had disappeared and he was out where the wind blew and the sky was frighteningly high up, far away, and there was nothing around him to enclose him, protect him. "You cannot speak to me that way. I do my best. It may not be good enough for you, but I try." Terror beat in his chest as though it had been trapped there and was frantically trying to get out. I want to be away from her, out of this apartment, he thought. It's dangerous here. He thought of his car. He could go out and sleep in it or drive away and find a person who would take him in.

Esther watched as he disintegrated emotionally before her. Part of her reached out to him, the part of her that still loved him, felt tenderness, perhaps even sexual passion. But there was another part of her self that watched, gloating as he withered and became a defenseless little boy. She found pleasure in his fall from grace, in his bruised face, his bloodied nose, his blood-matted hair. Then these two parts of herself merged again, and she was whole and she cared about him as she would for any suffering soul. It hurt her that he must ache in every bone and muscle of his body; she cared for the raw redness of his cheek, for the panic and aloneness in his dark eyes.

"I'm sorry, so sorry." She went to him and gently put her head on his chest, all the while feeling distanced from him, as if she were merely acting this role of concerned wife, playing at doing the proper thing. But before she knew it, the warmth of him came through his shirt and with it his smell, mixed with medicinal odors and dried vomit. The rough fiber of his coat brushed against her cheek when she shifted her face; all this made the world real again and the room almost benign.

"We'll find our way through this," she said, urging him toward the davenport. They sat. She began to unbutton his coat. "Here, let me help you."

Denton allowed her to assist him in getting his arms from his sleeves. It was excruciating. When she put her arms around him and held him lightly, he let her do that as well, even though the slightest pressure against his body gave him pain. But as she held him and said the right words, he found no comfort. Was it his inability to receive consolation? Or didn't she mean what she said? An immense exhaustion settled on him, weighting his body to the couch. All he wanted was sleep, though even the effort of lying down and closing his eyes seemed too great. He wished he could float like a mote of dust, suspended, not touching any surface that could hurt him.

Chapter Fifteen

When Mr. and Mrs. Takaetsue arrived in the morning, Esther greeted them with as much enthusiasm as Parin. For once she wasn't envious of Parin's unabashed joy at seeing the Issei couple, nor of the protective way they cared for her.

"Mrs. Takaetsue-san, Mr. Takaetsue-san." Esther made a slight bow to each.

The elderly couple bowed back, Mrs. Takaetsue standing a foot or two ahead of her husband. She wore a bulky, dark green wool jacket over full trousers, and a yellow knitted scarf wrapped around her pudgy face and neck. Mr. Takaetsue, shorter than she and skinny where she was plump, held his brimmed serge hat in front of him, at his waist.

"Good morning, Mrs. Jordan-san," Mrs. Takaetsue said, without smiling.

Her husband smiled, but didn't say a word to Esther, as usual. He spoke hardly any English and communicated to Parin either through his wife or in the private language he and Parin had concocted or in a simple Japanese.

Parin was beside herself with excitement, rising and falling from her heels to her toes, beaming up into the couples' faces.

"*O hai yo, Parin-chan,*" the old man leaned forward, and putting his hat on the chair, he reached out to Parin.

"*O hai yo, oji-san,*" she answered solemnly, taking hold of his proffered hands.

"*I kaga desuka?*"

"*Kekko, oji-san!*" Parin shrieked with pleasure.

"Parin, calm down," Esther said, placing her hand on Parin's head. "You'll be with them all day."

Parin turned, craning her face up to Esther, the left pupil of her lazy eye sliding toward her nose. Her glasses had slipped down. "Mr. and Mrs. Take stay here all day?"

"Well, let's see what we can arrange, dearest."

Esther wanted the couple to take Parin out of the house to the Community Room or even to their barracks. She couldn't have all of them in the apartment. Denton was still in the other room. He had tried to get out of bed this morning at his usual hour of six a.m., but had fallen back, groaning. He'd whispered that the pain was too great in his stomach and chest walls, that his face felt as though it had been scraped completely raw, with only bloody tissue exposed to the world. She'd turned on the bedside lamp to see how bad the damage was, and reported to him that he was lucky, that though the skin looked abraded, it was dry. No pus seemed to be forming and only his left eye was slightly darkened. His nose looked normal, if a bit puffy. "They did a good job at the hospital," she'd said. But he couldn't rise; he'd tried again, and given up. She knew if Denton remained in bed, he must be in unbearable misery. She gave him three aspirins and stayed with him until he was breathing heavily in sleep. When Parin had come to their door, Esther told her that Daddy had to sleep, that he'd been up all night at a meeting. She had turned the light off and pulled the shade on their window, so Parin couldn't see his injuries.

"I wonder if Parin could go out with you today, Mrs. Takaetsue?" Esther asked.

Mrs. Takaetsue had already unwrapped her scarf and was unbuttoning her heavy jacket.

"Out? It cold out, Mrs. Jordan-san. Too cold for little child, out all day."

Parin looked from one to the other of them, hope and worry on her face.

"I didn't mean outside, exactly. What I'd hoped for was a stay in the Community Room, perhaps?"

Mrs. Takaetsue nodded, though she looked skeptical. "What about lunchi?"

Esther hadn't thought of that. She didn't want them back here for lunch. She needed time to talk with Denton about her plans for leaving. She'd decided in the middle of the night that she would indeed go down to Berkeley. She would leave in the next few days if Denton was feeling better. If he agreed, she wanted time alone to take care of details and wash clothes for the trip.

"Let me explain. The school is closed. I won't be going to work. Mr. Jordan isn't feeling well."

"Daddy's sick?" Parin face was stricken. "What's the matter with Daddy, Mommy?"

"Sweetheart, it's nothing, just a little cold. You get little colds. He's sleeping in bed. He needs quiet."

"I'm quiet, Mommy. I'm quiet. Does Daddy have a fever?"

"Only a tiny one." Esther knelt down and ran her hand over Parin's cheek. She straightened her glasses and smoothed the knots in her brow. "You're such a little worrywart. That's what Daddy says, doesn't he, my little worrywart. Don't you worry. By tonight he'll be like you, bright and healthy and happy."

Esther got a faint smile from her daughter.

"But we've got to let him rest." Esther said, glancing up at Mrs. Takaetsue who was staring down at her, with an expression as worried as Parin's.

"I hear there big trouble last night, Mrs. Jordan-san." She plucked at strands of black hair that had pulled out of her bun when she'd removed her scarf. "Bad trouble. Bad men. No-no boys, they call selfs."

"He's fine, Mrs. Takaetsue, please." Esther looked at the woman meaningfully. She hoped Mrs. Takaetsue would get the hint and be quiet. Esther rose from kneeling.

"All right, I know." Mrs. Takaetsue nodded and scowled. "I understand. All the same..." She stood with her chin high, waiting.

Mr. Takaetsue made a funny face at Parin, and Parin took his hand. Esther felt the old envy steal in, at their understanding that didn't need words. But she mustn't dwell on this.

"If I write a note for the sentry, would you mind taking Parin to the mess hall in your block?" Parin loved eating in the mess mall. Esther didn't think there would be hostility directed at a child, especially if she was with the Takaetsues.

While Mrs. Takaetsue gathered Parin's coloring book, crayons and blue afghan, and stuffed Parin's rag doll into her knitting bag, Mr. Takaetsue, dressed in the coat and scarf he'd never removed, began to sweep the floor, loudly banging the chairs as he shoved them aside.

"I'm going to Mr. and Mrs. Take's house, Mommy?" Parin asked over and over in a high, squeaky voice as Esther dressed her in overcoat and leggings and tied the strings of her red knit hat.

"Parin, please. I've told you twenty times. Yes!" Esther cried, losing her patience. The old man was getting on her nerves, too; he would wake Denton with his noisy cleaning, and bring Denton to the bedroom door. She had to get them out of here.

Esther kissed Parin on both cheeks. "There now, skedaddle, and I'll see you at dinnertime. All ready, Mrs. Takaetsue-san?"

"Yes, Mrs. Jordan-san. We come back dinnertime." She didn't smile. Her face was stony as she bowed. Only her husband gave his usual broad grin.

At least while they were in Berkeley she'd get respite from this part of her life, Esther thought, watching from the front window as the three of them, the two elders on either side, and her daughter in the middle with her arms stretched up to hold their hands, walked bent into the wind toward the evacuee side.

But no sooner had she dropped the curtain and turned back into the living room than she felt a sense of loss, a longing for Parin, and she wanted to call the three of them home and have them settle around the table for tea and coloring. Maybe Mrs. Takaetsue would take out her knitting. She'd begun to knit in the camp. "Now I have time for this," she'd said. "Now I no have to cook. No much to wash and clean. Only Parin, and he help me with Parin," she said pointing with her chin to her husband. This was how they'd spoken together in the beginning. But over the year and a half, they'd grown more distant, Esther from them and they from her.

From the bedroom Denton had been half-aware of Esther's conversation with the Takaetsues, but now he listened attentively to the silence. Had Esther left with them? He almost hoped so. He was too exhausted and in too much pain to have a talk with her. He knew they had matters to discuss. Last night, right before he'd fallen into a dead sleep, she'd said that she was going down with Parin to see her mother and father. He'd been surprised to find he didn't want her to leave, after all the times in the past weeks he'd wished she wouldn't badger him about what he was planning to do and what he wasn't intending to do, and what his positions were on each issue. But lying here, unable to go to work, helpless in the darkened room, all he wanted was comfort from her. He imagined her hands fluttering softly over his face and shoulders; was he confusing her hands with Mitsue's or even Alice Hamilton's? He could still feel both their hands on his brow, and hear their soothing voices.

For most of his life, before meeting Esther, he'd been suspicious of a woman's caress. He'd shrunk from his own mother's touch. Even thinking of his mother's cool hand on his forehead could still make him shudder. As far back as he could recall, he would lie unmoving if his mother happened to place her hand on him, collapsing his chest to make himself smaller, or shifting to make her hand drop away. If they met neighbors or unfamiliar people on the street, his mother would say, "Let me introduce my son," and she would touch his arm, or his shoulder, or the top of his head, and he would be overcome with disgust. His aversion to the weight of her hand would grow until it threatened to take over his entire being, to turn him into a creature seething inside, while on the outside he remained calm and courteous. He would say, "Hello, pleased to meet you," in a normal voice, and smile charmingly, before abruptly kneeling to the ground saying, "My shoe is untied." Or he would pull away and say, "Oh, Mama, I've forgotten my books," and have an excuse to run back to the house if they were near. He never consciously thought it was her touch that repelled him. He ascribed it to his distaste for being presented so grandly as her son, or to her persistent exhortations that he act this way or that in public so as not to embarrass her the way—she insisted—her husband did. It was only years later that he had understood, after he'd married Esther and they were visiting his mother's home in Seattle. He'd been in the garden reading the newspaper, with Esther in the lawn chair a few yards away, when his mother came up from behind and put her hand on his shoulder to get his attention. An electric current of revulsion, of horror surged through him, and he'd had to drop his paper and lean forward to retrieve it to detach himself from her touch. He didn't know or care if she'd noticed. He had to save his own life. He watched her walk over to the rosebushes separating her lawn from the one next door, and begin to fuss over the blooms with those lethal hands, all the while keeping up a languid monologue about her flowers. She looked so petite, defenseless, not at all threatening in her person, but he'd wanted to take that hand caressing the roses and break it in his own or smash it with a rock.

He was surprised and frightened by the violent thoughts. "Denton," Esther's voice had brought him back to the sun-filled garden. She sat on the chaise lounge in her navy-blue dotted swiss sundress, with a look of concern clouding her face. "Come here," Esther had beckoned. He went over to her, still preoccupied by his mother's touch, and reluctantly took Esther's hand. But when his hand met hers the tension broke and the disgust left him. He was consumed with love for her and indebtedness. Standing there, he suddenly understood that not all caresses were alike, not all were his mother's, that some could be trusted, and even longed for.

He heard Esther moving in the other room. In the warmth of his memory, he called out, "Esther."

"I'm coming." Her voice was welcoming and slightly wistful, he noted with relief.

She stood in the doorway to his darkened room, as he had stood the other evening. Her body, framed by the sunny room behind her, was slender, well proportioned. A little full in the hips, too narrow in the shoulders and breast, but rather nice, he thought. He'd always thought that, he reminded himself.

"Hi, there," he said to her, lifting his less sore arm and gesturing her to sit beside him on the bed.

"How're you doing, buster?" Esther asked as she sat down. She held his hand but didn't speak, enjoying their closeness.

Denton, too, was filled with the old overwhelming love for her, one he'd all but forgotten, one he wished he could reclaim.

"I feel pretty awful," he said.

"I bet you do. For Denton Jordan to be in bed instead of out there tending to everyone, he has to feel like he's been run over by a truck."

"Just about. I'd say, just about."

"Can I get you something?"

"No, thanks."

"You'll tell me?"

He nodded, careful not to jar his head, as a spasm of pain and nausea rocked him. "What are your plans?"

"I don't have to leave right away," she said, thinking, perhaps that was true, that she could stay here as long as he wanted, go back to teaching in a few days when the school re-opened, or if it didn't, teach temporary classes in the Onjis' room.

"I don't want to get in your way, Esther, if you think you should go," he said. "I'll be fine by this afternoon. After this rest, I'll be up and around. You need to get out of here. Parin does, too. She hasn't been so good. I didn't notice it before." Should he be saying this much? Would she take it badly? Would she think he was accusing her of being a bad mother?

But she seemed fine about it. She was agreeing with him.

"You're right," she said. "We're not doing well, any of us. I wish you would come, too."

"I can't," he said. "I have to find my way out of this. See what I can do to straighten things out."

Esther frowned.

"But let's not talk about it right now," he said quickly. He caressed her hand and brought it to his cheek. He kissed her open palm.

"I love you, Denton." She leaned toward him, being careful not to put her full weight on his sore body. "Please believe that I do." She bent forward until her lips touched his. At least this still feels wonderful and true, she thought.

But as he kissed her, Denton's pleasure was obscured by another bad memory. He kept getting these flashes of intense, haunting thoughts that came on like the jagged auras of a migraine. He wished they would stop. This time it was the night after his father died. "Please, my little Denny. Do this for your Mama," his mother cried, as she begged him to come into her bed, the bed his father had died in, to sleep with her so she wouldn't have to be alone. She clung to him. He was rigid with terror at the prospect, but he guided her upstairs, his hand touching the back of her sweaty nightclothes. Denton lay beside his mother, on top of the blankets in his pajamas and robe, gripping the side of the mattress to keep from rolling into the center of the sagging bed and falling against her. He was afraid she might fling her arm over him, thinking he was her husband. He could almost feel the indentation his father's body had made in the mattress. He stared up at the ceiling, his eyes wide, but the room was dark and he slipped off into sleep only to wake over and over and over throughout the endless night.

Chapter Sixteen

Two days later Denton drove diagonally across the firebreak between Blocks 15 and 16. He never liked to keep to the official cinder road. It was a minor act of rebellion. He was using the car because Esther had asked him to, "Not that I believe anyone will attack you again, but I don't want you walking alone out there, and I don't want you exerting yourself needlessly."

It was funny how a person could forget certain things, he mused as he drove. He had honestly believed that his interest in Alice Hamilton was the only time he'd betrayed Esther in thought, but lying in bed this morning he'd remembered the social worker down in the Arvin camp. It was when Esther had moved up to San Francisco in preparation for Parin's birth; Esther hadn't wanted to chance having her baby in the primitive local hospital.

The social worker, who had been at the camp for months before Esther's departure, was a woman he'd barely noticed in meetings and at various social events. She was Jewish, he remembered; her name was Rachel Cohen, yes, that was it. Dark hair, green eyes. Pretty. Shortly after Esther left, Rachel had been assigned to accompany him on his inspection trips into the corporate farms and their work camps. She'd been brave when they were threatened by goons at the entrance to the Gigante farm, holding her own when they'd called her filthy names. On the hot dusty road in the blasting sun he'd noticed for the first time her straight back and narrow waist, full round breasts, and long legs. When they climbed back into the sweltering cab of the pickup, he'd smelled fear in her sudden perspiration, and had seen how her face had gone white under her tan. "I guess we showed them bastards," she said, laughing nervously at her own distress. He'd been caught by her eyes, the mix of vulnerability and bravery in them. He imagined holding her in his arms, sucking on those full breasts, slipping his hand between her legs. As the days went by his fantasies grew wilder and, correspondingly, so did his guilt. Esther gave birth, and once he could tear himself away from work to go see his new baby, once he'd been reunited with a happy, absorbed Esther, and had held his tiny daughter in his arms, the connection to the other woman evaporated, leaving no trace of his blinding lust. When he returned to camp a few days later, it had been impossible to imagine that he had ever been attracted to Rachel Cohen.

Esther would be leaving tomorrow, and with the memory of Rachel Cohen as a warning, Denton decided not to visit the hospital again to see Alice Hamilton. After a day and a half in bed and an afternoon of carrying out a minor work load, he looked normal save discoloration on his jaw and minimal swelling over his right eye. Cosmetically he'd gotten off easy, but his shoulders, ribs and stomach hurt more than ever. Deep breathing was agony; bending down was worse. Stretching was out of the question, and dressing was, fortunately, an activity he only had to do twice in a day. When he'd wakened he'd wished he'd gone to bed fully dressed, merely shucking his shoes. But as the hours went by, he'd pretty much forgotten his pain and he saw no need to go by the hospital.

He was on his way to see Toki, whom he'd missed at the office yesterday afternoon. Andross had left a message at the main Co-op; he wanted to see Denton immediately, but Denton couldn't visit Andross without knowing more about what had happened at the meeting and exactly how much of it Toki had communicated to the administration. He didn't care to be caught with his pants down in Andross's office.

Denton pulled in front of the main Co-op. He remained in the car looking at the front door with the emblem of the twin pines hanging over it. When Parin was born, he and Esther had sent out an announcement that showed two large pine trees with a small pine tree between them. He remembered sitting in their tent stuffing the crisp green and white cards into envelopes and passing them across the folding table to Esther to be addressed. Esther had been tired but her post-delivery complexion was glowing and her black hair gleamed in the lantern light, and curled moistly against her forehead. Parin slept in a basket at their feet. Life had seemed perfect then.

Denton got out of the car and, slowly lifting one foot after another, climbed the steps to the porch. He paused and gazed out across the block. He watched a group of women walking along on *getas*, moving away from the laundry room with baskets of steaming clothes as they chatted quietly among themselves, their heads bent toward each other, their small children running and toddling behind them.

The gentle peace of the scene struck him. That was it, wasn't it? What pleased him most deeply was this peaceful, domestic tranquillity. He could hear Esther saying, "Ironically, it is what continually eludes you." Maybe she was right. What he desired for everyone, including himself, was this quiet human interchange he saw before him. He considered himself a radical; he had dedicated his life to changing the system from the roots up. But he was unwilling to participate in physical violence for the purpose of achieving what every person in the country had a right to—a simple, decent life. That much was still true. But the question that had nagged at Denton over the past two days was, Did he let Nebo do the dirty work of his soul? Nebo spoke out radically while Denton stayed in the background playing the arbitrator. Even though he knew that working in the background was what a political organizer did, the thoughts continued to trouble him.

Denton turned from the soothing sight of the women. He opened the door and stepped into the bright warmth of the store.

Though there were specialty-service operations throughout the camp, this location functioned as a variety store, with dry goods, notions, appliances, furniture, toys, clothing, and packaged food supplies.

An Issei man and woman were at the checkout counter. Denton recognized them but couldn't remember their names so he only nodded, bowing slightly. They bowed back.

"Hiya, Mary," he said to the pretty girl who regularly worked the counter. She was adding on the new Burroughs machine. "How are you?"

"Things could be better, Mr. Jordan," she said, not looking up from her work.

"That's for certain."

Yoshi Yakamata, the store manager, was at work rearranging shelves of thread, needles, thimbles and clothing patterns. "Good morning, Yoshi," Denton called as he passed him on his way to Toki's office in back.

"Good morning, Mr. Jordan-san."

He felt Yoshi examine his face, but the man was too polite to let his gaze linger. He assumed that Yoshi had heard about the beating.

Standing outside Toki Honda's office, Denton watched Toki through the glass of the door laboring over the Co-op's inventory books. Come hell or high water, Toki always did the inventory on Tuesday. He worked in his shirtsleeves, his eyebrows drawn together in deep concentration. His left palm rested on his low forehead, and the fingers of that hand thrust into his thick black hair. Denton wished he'd known Toki before internment, when Toki had built his wholesale produce business on a daring mixture of experience, trust, cleverness and very little money—with only his devilish humor and atrocious puns to smooth the way.

Toki and his wife, Sumiko, had wed in an arranged marriage, but Toki had once told Denton, with a sly grin, that it was a love match, after all. He'd also told Denton, "She's an artist, my wife, truly. None of those lady shell sculptures for my Sumiko. You must come and see them one day." Denton had heard that Toki's son-in-law to be, Frank Murayama was an up-and-coming modern painter, that he'd studied with the new abstract artists in San Francisco before internment, but he hadn't known that Sumiko Honda was also an artist. One evening, early on in their relationship, Denton had accompanied Toki to the recreation room in Block 12, which had been turned into an art school, and Toki had proudly shown off Sumiko's beautiful wood sculptures, as abstract as Frank Murayama's splashes of wild color, but more subtle because they used no color except the natural shades of wood. They were shaped into the simplest of forms.

"I'm in awe," Denton had said truthfully to Toki. "I agree with you," Toki said. "Forgive me my immodesty in regard to my wife." Toki was not as enthusiastic about Frank's work. He confided to Denton that he didn't understand his future son-in-law's paintings and was somewhat worried about Frank's ability to support himself and Sally. But on the day of Frank and Sally's wedding, at the reception in the mess hall of Block 14, none of these doubts had been apparent as he toasted Frank Murayama, saying, "We are now truly a family of artists." A week after the wedding, when Frank and Sally still hadn't been allocated a room of their own, Toki had come to Denton's apartment. Toki had asked if Denton could step outside to talk. Standing together on the cinder path, Toki had said, "I didn't want to speak of this in front of your wife. I've come to ask if you could do something to help my daughter and son-in-law begin their private life. I've always believed it's the privilege of young marrieds to fulfill their sexual needs whenever the impulse arises." Then he grinned. "So to speak." But his eyes remained filled with sadness.

Toki looked up when Denton knocked.

"Come in, come in, good morning, Denton," he said, standing. He removed his reading glasses, rubbing the bridge of his nose. "Please, find yourself a seat. We missed each other yesterday. Forgive me, but I was attempting to make up for the damage caused by Nebo."

"So I heard. How did you do?" Denton pushed the chair from beside the door over to the desk and sat, trying not to bend forward, but still feeling pain in his ribs. "Sit down, old man."

"How accurate you are. I become more decrepit every day. Do you know that I can barely rise up from a crouch some mornings, my knees are so stiff." Toki sighed as he lowered himself into his swivel chair. He settled back, resting his arms on the chair arms. As he spoke, he watched Denton closely. "I did as well as can be expected. It was necessary to soothe wounded egos, and convince board members that the entire Co-op was not falling apart. But I've heard you had some trouble after you left the meeting."

"You want the story, don't you? The whole damn thing, no fudging?"

Toki raised his eyebrows, but he said nothing. Denton knew Toki would think it impolite to ask direct, detailed questions.

"Well, even though you're not going to ask, I'm going to tell you." Denton tried to laugh but found he couldn't. The memory of the night crept in. He felt the blows, heard his own grunts, felt the world turn topsy-turvy again. "I'm okay, honestly, but I did get knocked around. The obvious culprits are Nebo's fellows. But I didn't see any faces. What did you hear?"

"Any number of opinions abound in the community, as you can imagine," Toki said in his low, deep-toned voice. "Some say Nebo. Some say his men, but not on his orders. Some say it was army provocateurs disguised as *Hoshidan* so as to stir up matters even more. And there are people who say that Andross ordered the attack because you have sympathy with us." Toki stopped speaking. He picked up his glasses, took his handkerchief from his pants pocket and began polishing them.

Denton knew not to jump in, that Toki was collecting his thoughts, choosing the proper words. It gave Denton time to let what Toki had said sink in. So people felt he was on their side. Did they think he supported Nebo and Nebo's followers? If so, they must think he was an idiot for defending a man who had only contempt for him. Or did they think he was on the side of those, like Bill and Toki, who opposed Nebo's tactics?

"Of course, there are the rumors I'm not hearing, since more and more people believe I'm *inu*," Toki said quietly. The corners of his mouth twitched downward, but he quickly controlled the spasm. "He's being rather recalcitrant, isn't he?"

"Nebo?"

"No," Toki smiled. "I mean your boss. Our esteemed Director Andross."

"So you noticed."

"I noticed," Toki said, nodding his head slowly. "We haven't spoken of any of this, but I wish to say that I'm sorry I didn't pick up on your suggestion to discuss the disturbance openly at the membership meeting. If I'd put it on the table, maybe this wouldn't have happened. I'm deeply sorry. I feel I must take responsibility for losing control of the meeting and for your beating." He stopped as though wanting a reaction from Denton.

Denton often felt as though he was talking to a father when he had these meetings with Toki, when the conversation would take an intimate turn, when Toki would let him in.

"That's crazy," Denton said, gently. "*I* was wrong. The deterioration of camp morale and the erosion of trust between you and Nebo had gone too far for a general airing. Especially after that humiliating business in Andross's office. If I may be candid?"

Toki kept his silence, but Denton saw that he remained receptive.

"Andross's belligerence, his show of disrespect for all of you that night, exacerbated whatever rift there was between you and Nebo. It was unconscionable of Andross. You said he was recalcitrant. That's far too generous a description, Toki. Ted Andross is a damned high-handed despot."

"We're a polite people," Toki said, stifling a mischievous grin. "We know how to speak about our superiors." Toki had never before referred to anyone in the administration with such ironic disdain, at least not in Denton's presence.

"Well, Andross is why I'm here. We'll have to talk more about this, but I'm already late for a meeting with our dear director, and I need your help in deciding what I should say to him. I know he's going to ask me about the membership meeting and I don't want to say anything that reflects badly on us. Do you have time to go over it with me?"

"Yes, for this I have all the time in the world." He closed the ledger book and sat with his hands folded on top. "The inventory can wait a few minutes. This is too important."

Toki tapped the large black book with his forefinger. "Bill and I met yesterday about those rationing shortages I presented at the meeting. But Bill was too agitated to think in his usual clear manner. You'll pardon me for mentioning it, but he thought you planned not to tell Andross who beat you up or even that you were accosted. I told him if that was your decision, then I would stand by you. We almost had an argument over at his place. We only stopped because we suspected the walls had ears."

Denton was confused. "You think I shouldn't tell Andross?"

"After all, you only have suspicions, isn't that right?"

"I didn't see anyone. I can't identify faces. But why this change, Toki? You deciding to secede from the union?"

Toki didn't laugh at his joke.

"No, to back up a bit, I've decided this Andross gentleman is not a man we can talk to. He is thick-headed. He thinks the worst of us. He sees us all as if we had one face, and nothing is about to change his opinion."

"He's a bigot, that's what you're saying."

Toki bit his lip against his own smile. "There it is in your own inimitable nutshell, my favorite *hakujin*."

Pride and pleasure coursed through Denton at the affection coming from the man.

"I said to Bill that it would serve no one to go to Andross with this information. Of course, the director could well have heard of it through his own sources by now."

"I realize that. I'd like to take my chances though."

"Who in the administration knows besides your beautiful wife?"

Denton felt himself blush again. He hoped Toki wouldn't notice.

"I believe that Bill told me the Caucasian nurse at the hospital tended to you," Toki said, when Denton didn't answer.

"She won't tell," Denton said. "Keep this to yourself?"

"Of course."

"She suggested to me that she not enter it into the record. She didn't want to bring any more trouble to the table than there already was."

"I agree with that."

"Toki, why don't you want to go after Nebo?"

Toki's eyes got the old, wicked glint that Denton hadn't seen in months.

"Because I believe we can outfox Nebo Mota and the rest of the *Hoshidan* and the *Daihyo Sha Kai*, and protect the Co-op in the process. We can handle this ourselves without further interference from Director Andross or the military. We can use our brains and our organizing skills rather than resorting to more fists, billy clubs, machine guns and tanks. Of course, I would like to punish Nebo for harming you, if indeed he was responsible, but like you, the Co-op is of utmost importance to me, as is my own belief in self-determination."

Denton had to smile at Toki's comments about the Co-op. "But, outfox them? How are you going to do that."

"We've been petitioned by the *Daihyo Sha Kai*. They've asked to attend the next Board of Directors meeting."

"What do they want?"

"I'm not certain, but Bill and I have our ears to the ground. We'll know more by tomorrow. We plan to be ready for them this time."

"I do want you to answer one more question," Denton said.

"Ask it."

"Do I look like hell, or am I going to pass inspection in the Director's office?"

"You look tired as a dog, and as though you did a butcher job on yourself when you shaved this morning. You'll do just fine."

Chapter Seventeen

Denton sat in Andross's empty office staring up at the photographic portrait of Roosevelt. Lately it had been hinted that the government was doctoring the photos of the President, that Roosevelt was not well, that his polio was acting up. But who knew these days what was truth and what was rumor? In this place the tiniest whisper, the slightest innuendo could be blown into an article of faith in a matter of hours.

He turned painfully to look at the door. Where was Andross anyway? He'd called him in and then had left, saying he had to see to a small matter. That was fifteen minutes ago. Denton stood and walked to the window, feeling every muscle in his body. Alice Hamilton had been correct in saying he'd feel like hell the next day. But she'd neglected to tell him that he would be worse off on the third and fourth days. Maybe he should go see her after all. The thought sent a jolt of excitement through him, which he could do nothing to dispel. All the time he'd been in bed resting, he'd had the most lustful thoughts of the woman. The second morning he'd wakened with a large erection which Esther, who'd brought him breakfast in bed, had seen and commented on, saying, "too bad you're so sick, we could have a fine time. Maybe all you needed was a good rest." She'd grinned and teased, "What kind of dreams did you have last night, buster? Was I in them?" He'd felt as though he'd been caught in the act, but then he'd imagined entering Esther, feeling her insides close around his penis, tight and moist and pulsing, having her body move against his. And since Parin had left the house, he'd slipped his hand up between her legs. She was immediately thickly wet and ready, and she'd sunk down onto the bed and he'd rubbed her until she'd moaned and cried out in pleasure. He hadn't felt such pressing desire for Esther in months, and was sure if he hadn't been in so much pain he would have been able to really perform. Still, he couldn't trust himself to go in to see Alice, and he couldn't bear to think what people could do with a rumor about him and Alice. Toki would condemn him. Toki would never find himself in this predicament, consumed with erotic longings for a woman other than his Sumiko.

Denton watched as Sarah Topol pushed her baby carriage across the parade grounds toward the canteen. He recognized her by the red plaid coat Sy had bought for her on a trip down to San Francisco in the fall. Sy would never be torn like this. Denton softly beat a rhythm with his fist on the window frame. He'd prided himself on being as self-controlled as Sy, if not quite as cagey. Only a few times had anything like this happened to him, like the episode down at the Farm Security Camp. How had he gotten that one under control? It had disappeared when he'd gone up to see Esther and the new baby. Also, it had been a case of out-of-sight, out-of-mind. That was what he must do. He must not see Alice Hamilton. But hell, how was he going to arrange that? At any minute she, too, could be making her way across the parade grounds. Or he could run into her in the canteen, or she might show up at the Co-op. He imagined standing in the store, someone coming up behind him and touching his arm, saying, "How are you? I was worried about you." He could have cried from how much he wanted that to happen. He wanted to know if she also had been thinking of him constantly. But why would she? Who was he? She could have any man she wanted. Though he had sensed her interest; he couldn't have read it that wrong. But could she possibly feel as consumed by sexual craving as he was?

Denton remembered a night he had come upon his father sitting alone on the porch swing. His mother and sister Bessie had long since gone up to bed. Huey was out wandering the streets. It was a warm night, probably June since there had been the seductive aroma of roses. He had been surprised to find his father sitting quietly, letting the swing creak slowly back and forth. Denton had been about to retreat into the house, hoping he'd gone unnoticed, because there was a quality to his father's presence, to the sweet gentle air, to the scent of freshly cut grass and dark evening beyond, that made him embarrassed to intrude. But his father had called out, "Denny?"

"Yes, sir," he'd answered.

"I thought that was you. Your mother tucked away?"

"Yes, sir. I guess so, sir."

"What's this 'sir' business, Denny? Makes me feel so old." He laughed, not his usual rolling chuckle, but in a way Denton with hindsight would call wistful.

"I don't know." He really didn't know why he'd used 'sir' with him. Maybe because it felt too intimate out there, as if he was getting inside his father, and he didn't want to. He wanted to keep his distance.

Stan Jordan got up, went over to the porch post, braced his arm against it, and stared out to the lawn. "I hate these nights without a woman."

Denton's breath left him. His eyes darted in the darkness, looking for escape. He wanted to run down the porch stairs, throw himself onto the lawn and roll and roll as if he were five years old again instead of almost thirteen. He didn't want to be growing into a man, if this was what it meant, if this was what it sounded like. His father's desire sickened him.

Denton stood in Andross's office with his arm on the window frame—aping his father's posture—filled with unrequited desires, feeling his whole body yearning toward what he wanted and didn't have. Was this what his father had felt? Was this what it meant to be a man?

"Oh, good, you're still here. I'm sorry, Jordan," Andross said, entering the room.

"I was about to give up on you." Denton moved from his position at the window, oddly reluctant to leave these thoughts. He didn't usually allow himself memories about his father.

Seated across from Andross, in their customary positions, he saw that Andross was scrutinizing his face. He squinted at Denton, leaning forward across his desk. "Is something the matter with your face?"

"Yep." Denton touched his cheek. "I mangled myself with a razor the day before yesterday and I think it got infected. They say at the hospital that it may be from the damn dust."

"You should get yourself a new razor. Try the army's canteen. I bet you could get a Gillette there. What's the matter with your Co-op supplies?" He laughed. "Only fooling. You'd better get a good one, though. You could make yourself really sick with something like that. Whew, you do look bad. Sort of swollen up." He wiped his hand along his own cheek.

"Honestly, it's okay. There's no danger of it becoming worse."

"Glad to hear that. Now, let's get down to business. I thought we should go over the Co-op meeting you had the other night. I hear it was one big mess. That the Kibei riled things up."

"What did you hear?" Denton asked. Was he right in sensing that Andross was friendlier than usual?

Andross sat back. He looked directly at Denton.

"I hear Nebo Mota came in with all his *Hoshidan* cronies and intimidated almost everyone in the hall, so much so that Toki Honda couldn't get nominations from the floor for your slate of officers and that our illustrious Director of Business Enterprises was forced to take his leave." He smiled knowingly at Denton.

"I thought it best to get out of there, if that's what you mean. Toki was having enough trouble keeping control of the meeting without any more attention being drawn away from his agenda."

Andross clasped his hands behind his head. He rocked back and forth without speaking.

Denton kept his mouth shut. He decided to let Andross take the lead.

"I hear that Mota raised havoc in the hall after you left." Andross continued rocking.

"Who'd you hear that from—Toki?" Give it a try, Denton thought.

"Jordan, don't try to fool me. You know damn well it wasn't your friend Toki Honda. Toki Honda wouldn't show up alone in this office if his life depended on it. He is not going to let it be thought that he's *inu*. And he's not. I'll say that for Honda, he's loyal to what he believes in. And I respect a man who holds to his beliefs." He looked meaningfully at Denton. "Including you, Jordan. Even you."

"Thank you, sir," Denton said. He thought, What are you after?

"You're welcome, Jordan. No, I like a man who has principles. Who states them as forthrightly as you always have. I know I can trust what you have to say."

In the outer office, Stella Andross, Ted's wife and secretary, was rattling at top speed on her typewriter. Denton's ribs hurt, like his head. He should have brought along some aspirin; he couldn't afford to get one of his headaches. He felt too exhausted to keep this repartee going much longer, but he was afraid Andross was going to get the better of him. He couldn't figure out what the devil the guy wanted.

"Who gave you the briefing on the meeting?" Denton asked directly.

"You know I don't talk about that sort of thing." Andross shook his head.

"Not even to staff? Not that it matters." Denton shifted direction. "But if I know who's giving you the report, it helps me to understand what slant you're getting on the meeting."

"That's a point." Andross dropped his hands and sat forward. "A very astute point. A man's religion or politics or whether he had a fight with his wife in the morning, any of that, can color what should be an objective view of the facts, isn't that right? Wouldn't you agree?"

"Yes, I agree with that. It's what we community organizers always take into consideration. It helps to put ourselves in the other guy's shoes for a while, helps us have more empathy for his opinions instead of rigidly opposing his ideas." Two can play at this game, Denton thought.

"Hmm," was all that Andross said in response. He examined his hands.

Denton shifted gingerly in his chair. Even so, sharp pains shot up his right side. He winced.

"My sources say you got a little roughed up three nights ago. You tell me you got messed up with a rusty razor. Who's telling me the truth?"

"I guess you'd have to say I didn't want to make more of it than there was," Denton answered, thinking, So he's known all along.

"To protect a militant Jap?" Andross kept his voice low.

"I don't know who did it to me. Nebo Mota was still in the meeting, by your own source's account. He was making trouble for Toki, not me." Denton warned himself to hold back and not let his animosity for Ted Andross take over.

"You didn't see anyone?" Andross's voice rose with incredulity.

"It was pitch black and then I passed out."

"But you have your suspicions."

Denton saw that Andross thought he'd gotten him. He felt as if he were fighting for his job. It was a serious matter, his not reporting the incident, as it was for Alice. He would cover for her. He would say he lied to her.

"No more suspicions than you have. The obvious culprit would be Nebo, but he was in the meeting."

Ted Andross stood and walked around the desk. He grabbed a chair and turning it back to front, he straddled it, sitting face to face with Denton. "I heard you were a philosophical draft shirker, not one who refused to fight because of his religion." Denton had no answer for this man. This was not what they were discussing, but it was clear that Andross's intense dislike of him was based from the start on Denton's refusal to bear arms. Denton felt himself going cold inside.

"But that wasn't what we were talking about was it, Jordan? We weren't talking about conscience, or were we? Doesn't conscience, like a man's politics or his religion, operate in matters of this sort, when there are questions of national security involved?" Andross leaned closer. "I can't have things getting out of hand in this place. Do you understand that?"

How was he going to get past his own anger in order to fashion some rational response to this man?

"I thought I could handle it alone," Denton said.

"Handle it alone," Andross repeated.

"I thought I could find out who did it and go have a talk. Try to calm things down a bit, rather than exacerbating tensions more than they already have been. It's pretty bad out there."

"I'm well aware, Jordan. It's my job to be aware."

Then why the hell don't you try to do something about it? Denton wanted to say.

"I'm sure you're aware, but there's been a lack of communication."

"Such as?"

"Not understanding that we can't keep putting these people under more and more pressure. They're being made to feel increasingly like second-class citizens. Like the administration is against them. I didn't report the beating because I didn't want to cause more military police sweeps of the camp. Didn't want to be the cause of anyone else landing in the stockade."

Andross seemed to be staring at a spot on the floor between his and Denton's chairs. In a flat voice he began. "You still think I should be more lenient with them, should give in to their demands. Should try to understand Japanese ways." He looked up.

Denton shrugged. "I know you wouldn't go as far as I would. But I do believe it's better to compromise in situations such as we have here. I don't see what can be gained by freezing the sides."

Andross got up. He shook his head. "I see it exactly the opposite of you. I believe I've been doing it exactly right. To give more freedom is to ask for trouble." He walked over to the window and looked out, his back to Denton.

Denton had to turn to watch him and in doing so was reminded that he had to get himself to the hospital.

"I inherited this situation," Andross said.

"I know that," Denton said, but thought, You inherited a tense situation and made it worse.

"I got the worst of the lot here," Andross said. "I know there are a few good people among them, but essentially I got the traitors. You don't like me to use that term, but it's the truth. These are rotten-to-the-core double-crossers, ones who don't give a damn for this country, who'd commit treason with a snap of the finger. You can be sure I won't give them any slack. Not you, nor any of your liberal pals are going to convince me to change. I believe in my country too much. I come from a military family, Jordan. You may not know that about me." He glanced back at Denton. Then he placed his hands high on the frame at either side of the window, and spoke gazing out. "I had an older brother who went stark crazy from World War I, fighting the Huns. He came back and he wasn't the same man, ever again. He's still around. Still hangs out around the last small town we lived in. Outside the army base where my dad was last stationed. But he ain't worth nothin' as they say about Scotty in that town. Ain't worth nothin' in his head." He turned. His face, washed of anger, was soft and hauntingly sad. "For myself, I can't go to war. I won't bother you with the ugly reasons, but even with their taking anyone with two legs, I can't go. This is the next best contribution I can make, to my mind, and you can be damned sure I'm going to do a good job."

Denton wished he weren't listening to this confession that brought him too close to Ted Andross. It was easier to see Andross as the archvillain, a man unsympathetic on every count. Denton would never tell Andross about Huey and Huey's tears and his stays in state mental hospitals and his inability to hold a decent job, but the knowledge made him feel a secret empathy. Fleetingly, he thought how intriguing it was to have this similarity in their backgrounds and to have reached such diametrically opposing positions.

"I'm sorry about your brother," Denton said. "It was terrible for those fellows. I know that."

"No need to say you're sorry. I just spoke of it to let you know where I stand." He looked smaller, sapped.

"With a background like yours, you probably resent me even more because of my position on this war," Denton said. Being so direct made Denton uncomfortable, but it was the least he could offer in return for Andross's openness.

"I do, in my way," Andross nodded. He leaned against the window ledge. "I don't get it, not one bit, why you don't want to beat the pants off the Krauts, no matter what you think about war in general, no matter what your religious beliefs are or aren't. I hear your wife's a Jewess. What's her feeling about your not fighting?"

Stella had stopped typing in the next room. Denton wondered if she were listening.

"We don't talk too much about it, but she supports me in this," Denton said quietly.

Andross shook his head in disbelief. "I hear for Jewish people it's hell to pay over there. You must have some marriage, Jordan, some marriage." Still shaking his head, he shifted forward off the windowsill and returned to his desk.

Denton could barely breathe. He felt as though the room had gotten very dark, but when he looked toward the window he was surprised to find an intensely red sunset.

The director thumped the end of his pencil on the desktop.

"I'm not going to report what happened to you. I'm not going to make you pack your bags. But you're going to help me, Jordan. So let's have a little talk about it."

As Andross mapped out what he wanted and what he was willing to give, the light from the window turned from deep magenta to a dusky pink to a purple twilight. Stella stuck her head into the office and said she had to get back to the barracks to see to the children. She needed to know what to do with the letters and memos she'd been typing. She gave a significant look in Denton's direction, which Denton caught. Andross told her to put them in the standing file. They could go over them in the morning. "I'll see you at home, Mrs. Andross," he said stiffly.

Andross wanted Denton to watch out for things, to "keep an eye out," was the way he put it. "I'm not asking you to be an *inu* or anything of the sort, but I need a sharp eye out there to make certain things don't get out of hand again. In return, I'll go easier. I'll make some concessions, hard as it is for me, much as it goes against my grain, against my better judgment." He went on to say he would allow the Japanese language schools that he'd been so adamantly against. "Sy Topol has already agreed to be more cooperative in exchange, to work with me, keep me informed. Sy saw nothing wrong in that. Said that's what you've all wanted, not to be working at cross-purposes." Rocking in his spring chair, he moved in and out of the light from the desk lamp. The rest of the room was dark.

"What is it you want from me, exactly?" Why hadn't Sy come to him about this? Leaning forward, Denton put his elbows on his knees to relieve the pain in his ribs.

"Just don't work against me, Denton. Let me know what happens when it happens. Report, like you're supposed to, and don't involve any more of the staff in your lies," he said. His chair sprang into upright position. His face was a mask of light and shadow as he looked meaningfully at Denton.

Alice, Denton thought. He had found out about Alice.

"Don't you worry, the woman didn't rat on you. I just checked the hospital reports after I got my information and they didn't jibe. And I know that woman Hamilton. I know she's a harder nut than you are." He laughed. "And a damned sight prettier." He leaned back out of the circle of light into the shadow. "Just watch out. Your position here is precarious. For some reason I like you—honestly I do. I don't agree with your politics, and I can't abide your stand on this war, but I know a smart man and I know a man who deep down wants to do the best by people, who wants to keep the peace. Am I right on that?"

Denton had a powerful inexplicable desire to prove himself to this man. He wanted to impress Andross on Andross's terms, even while he loathed him. "You're right, I only want what's best for everyone. I don't want things to blow up here. If things become violent, people can only get hurt. I hate that they have to be here in the first place. My mandate to myself has always been to make life tolerable for them while they're here. Whatever I can do toward that end, I'll do."

"Even if it means letting me know everything about the activities of your protégé, Nebo Mota?"

Denton didn't move. He willed his face to show no emotion.

"Sure," he said.

"Okay." Andross slapped his palms on the top of the desk. "I'm glad we've had this little talk." He took his watch from his vest pocket.

"Not so little. Nice long chat, in fact."

He accompanied Denton to the door and started to open it, but stopped and closed it again. "Keep what I said about my brother to yourself, will you? I think we can afford to have a few secrets between us, don't you?"

Denton mumbled an assent. He wanted to be out of there, breathing fresh air. He felt he had lost a part of himself in this room. He had to get away from Andross before he lost the rest.

The reception area was dimly lit by the lamp on Stella's desk. He grabbed his coat from the bench and without stopping to put it on, he opened the front door and escaped into the crystalline night.

The sky was navy blue and star-filled with a faint pink streak of light low on the western horizon. Such beauty seemed indecent in the face of what was happening down here on earth, Denton thought, as he walked across the parade ground toward the hospital.

To hell with it. He had to warn Alice about Ted Andross. He couldn't allow her to suffer for something he had started. It was just as well that Andross had gotten wind of their conspiracy and that he had admitted to it. Just hearing Andross speak her name in the office had dried up Denton's infatuation. No more temptation for him, no more daydreaming. He could carry on with his work, and he wouldn't jeopardize his marriage, or give Andross more blackmail ammunition. He ran up the stairs to the hospital, but was overcome by pain and had to pause on the narrow porch to wait for it to subside. He looked out over the rutted parade ground, with its iced-over black puddles. The metal clamps on the empty flagpole rope began to rap against the wood as the wind whipped up. Something was brewing.

The door opened and closed behind him. He turned to find Alice Hamilton with a russet-colored coat thrown around her shoulders, over her white uniform. Seeing her he was again overwhelmed by messy passions, with a desire for her as great as any he'd felt, furious at himself for his weakness. Her hair fell loosely on the high shoulders of her coat. A nurse's cap sat pertly on her head. Her eyes were gray in the porch light.

"Hi," she said, coming to stand beside him. "I looked out when I passed by the door a couple of minutes ago and I thought I saw you here. Are you coming in for your follow-up treatment?" She stood so close that one empty sleeve of her coat touched his arm.

He longed to feel the warmth of her body beneath the layers of clothing.

"No, not now. I'm feeling fine, a lot of the pain has subsided," he lied. "I'm actually coming from a little tete-a-tete with the director."

"Hmm. Andross," she said, drawing a line on the porch with the toe of her shoe.

"Yep."

"He's learned I taped you up the other night."

He looked down at the top of her bowed head. "How do you know that? Who told you?"

"I guessed. We were pretty stupid. For such smart people, we didn't act too brilliantly on this one." She smiled up at him and nudged against him. "You worried?"

He directed his gaze back out to the darkened grounds. He hoped no one was watching them standing in the light. He knew he should not stand so close to her, should move away, but he couldn't.

"No, not really. I fessed up."

"Took the blame?"

He felt ashamed. "I hedged a little."

She laughed. "Don't worry. He can't do anything worse than fire me and I don't think he's going to do that. I don't care anyway. Do you?"

"Do I what?" He cleared his throat.

"Care if I get kicked out of here? If I'm gone?"

She's a hard woman, Andross had said. "I don't want you to suffer on my account."

"That's not what I meant," she said.

A vibrating silence hung between them. She laughed again. "What do you say you make it up to me by coming by next Saturday for dinner. Seeing as how your wife is going away tomorrow and you won't have anyone to cook for you."

"How did you know she's leaving?" he half whispered.

"We live in a small town."

"I was planning to use the time she's gone to catch up on work," he said. It sounded like such a feeble, cowardly excuse. Just tell the woman no, damn it.

"I'm not the finest chef, but I can put a simple meal together. Honest." She waited. "Hey, brother, look at me."

He noted how wide-apart her eyes were and how high her forehead was.

"Nothing bad, just a meal. Some political talk. I'm interested in what you have to say."

"No, I don't think so." He smiled, relieved that he'd refused. It was easier than he'd thought.

"Okay. But I'm going to leave the invitation open. I live in Block 3, closest to the dividing gate, Room 5, on the very end. I'll cook enough for the two of us. If you don't show up, I'll stuff myself. If you do, you get to eat your portion." She frowned. "Don't worry, mister, it's not all that serious. My, you are an intense man, aren't you?"

After she went back into the building, he remained standing on the porch, getting colder, but unable to move. He had acted like a tongue-tied teenager. With Esther it had not been that way. He'd immediately been able to talk with her, to argue with her about the grade he'd given her on the exam, to engage in political and academic discussions as he'd walked with her along the paths toward her student government meeting. She had been beautiful, alive, intellectually his equal, even his superior, but he had maintained a sense of himself with her, a powerful notion of what he had to offer. This woman destroyed it all, left him speechless, gasping for air. What in hell was the difference, and how was he going to get control of himself and the situation between them? By not going near her again. By not even letting her minister to his aching body. A surge of longing went through him. No. He would not let her get anywhere near him.

Chapter Eighteen

Herm offered to drive Esther and Parin to the train station in Klamath Falls, saying he had time to kill since "the army has, for all intents and purposes, usurped my job." Denton said he felt guilty about not taking them himself. He was so obviously agitated about work that Esther told him she didn't want to put any more pressure on him, and she wished he'd take a little time off, even if it was just having a night out with Herm. She felt generous now that she was getting out of here.

He sat beside her as she still lay in bed. She ran her hand lightly over his bruised and scraped cheek. "But don't have too much fun while I'm gone," she joked.

"I have so damn much work, it'll honestly be easier if you're not here." His eyes skittered back and forth, avoiding hers.

"Hold still a minute, Denton. Give me a moment of your precious time."

He looked at her. She could see it took all his will power even to remain seated on the bed. She knew he wanted to be up and out the door, on his way, dealing with the business at hand, pulling the pieces back together again.

"Okay," she said gently. "I got my fill of your beautiful eyes. But think of us once a day."

When it was time for Denton to leave, Parin began to cry. She held onto his leg, refusing to let go even when he said, "Please, button-nose, Daddy has to go to work. You'll be back in two weeks. You're going with Mommy on the train to see Grandmother Judith and Grandpa Harry."

But to no avail. She wailed louder. Esther came from the bedroom to find her with her arms locked around Denton's neck. He'd stooped to pick her up and she'd grabbed hold. Her face was buried in his neck. Denton looked over her snarled hair at Esther in desperation as he gently jiggled his frightened daughter.

"Parin," he whispered. But she screamed over his pleas. "Parin, chicken, I must go. I love you."

He grabbed the green and orange afghan from the davenport, bundled it around the clinging child, and walked outside into the cold air. Esther stood alone in the suddenly quiet room listening to the muffled screams receding. She went into the kitchen and began washing the few dishes Denton had left. A coffee cup. He'd reheated the brew from the night before. A plate with bread crumbs scattered on it. The water remained cold. She turned the tap full blast. It began to run warm. She looked at the clock over the sink. Six-ten; he'd been out there for four minutes. She turned the water off. No cries.

Esther walked across the living room to the window and parting the yellow curtains, looked out. Twenty feet from the house, Denton stood beside the car with his and his daughter's heads under a tent of the afghan, the rest of the blanket wrapped around her body and tucked under her bottom. Esther watched, trying not to feel anything, because she knew the only emotions available to her were anger and deep hurt.

That was how her day began. Afterward things had gotten better. Once Denton left, Parin had calmed down and was cheerful as they finished packing their valise. She brought items from Esther's and her own drawers, saying, "I'm helping, Mommy, aren't I?" Her face was open and clear as though it had been washed by her bitter tears.

"Yes, dearest, you most certainly are helping." Esther bent to hug her, surprised at the tenderness of her daughter's touch and the pliability of her small body. Her back was a marvel, Esther thought, as she ran her hand down the straight strong spine, feeling the bones, flesh, and muscle under the light sweater. "You're quite a wonderful big girl," Esther said, and held Parin away to look at her and was filled with a consuming love and joy.

She scooped her daughter up into her lap and the child snuggled in. She does love me, Esther thought, as she pulled her close.

Holding her, she remembered coming out of the anesthesia after Parin's birth and frantically asking the doctor, "How are her ears?" Esther had faded before she'd heard his answer. What she had meant was, Did the baby's ears stick out? Were they Jewish ears? She had a fixed idea that ears like her own and her cousin Herzl's announced one's Jewishness to the world. When she woke and the infant was brought to her, Esther held her up and looked straight at the scrunched-closed eyes, the red screaming face and the ears. They were flat. "I won't love her right away," she silently promised herself. "Not until I'm certain she can live." She'd seen too many babies die in the Farm Security Camp. She'd witnessed the agony of the farm women. No, she promised herself, in the privacy of her hospital room with the little mound of body now outside her own body, I will not love this perfect girl until I can be certain she will survive.

*   *   *

The train station, a clapboard structure built on a base of boulders, was filling up. Almost all the seats were taken when they arrived. Rows of slatted wooden benches hugged the walls and radiated outward from a coal stove in the center of the room. The ceilings were vaulted and beamed, the floors the same polished pine as the benches.

The evacuee trains to Tule Lake had passed through this station. Hiroko had told Esther that when they'd pulled into Klamath Falls in the predawn, she'd thought they had arrived at camp. She had peeked out the drawn shades to see the grim landscape of freight trains and run-down storage buildings in the gray light. She'd been relieved when the whistle had blown and they'd moved out again.

"We're lucky to have seats," Esther said to Herm, who had insisted on waiting with them until the train arrived from Portland.

"Will you look at all these soldier-boys," he said.

Parin crawled over Esther to snuggle her way in between Esther and Herm, and opened her picture book, her ratty-looking rag doll clutched to her chest.

"And will you take a gander at who's here?" Herm laughed. He picked Parin up and placed her on his lap, wrapping his arms around her so only her head showed.

"Are you sure that's no bother?" Esther asked, ready to take Parin back.

"Are you kidding me? This is paradise, holding this pip-squeak of a half-breed on my knee." He sang the words as he rocked a contented Parin from side to side. Her eyes began to slide shut.

"Keep rocking," Esther whispered.

The room became overheated, as more soldiers arrived and a

Negro porter heaped coal into the stove. She hoped the stuffy warmth would put Parin soundly asleep. She wanted the opportunity to talk with Herm about Denton. Unlike Sy, Herm didn't push her to confide; Herm absorbed, was a sounding board, and was forthright in his opinions. She liked knowing what he thought without worrying that he was keeping some judgment to himself. In the car she had resisted the temptation for fear that Parin would understand her concerns or at the very least sense her distress about Denton. Parin had antennae for even the slightest uneasiness either of them was feeling.

The waiting room was becoming noisier with talk and movement. A train had pulled in from the East. She'd heard it announced, and those making connections to the north and south were jamming into the already crowded room. The majority were servicemen in uniform, army men, in khaki shirts and trousers with long, heavy wool overcoats. Rather dashing, she thought. She wondered how Denton would look in that outfit, deciding that he would easily outshine any of the men in the room, young or old. She longed for a cigarette as she saw one serviceman after another lighting up. She would have lit up herself, but she thought it might make Herm uncomfortable to be with a woman smoking in public. Denton would appreciate that show of independence, but Herm was narrower in his views of what a woman should do.

She thought how strange it was that she was so fond of Herm, even with this limitation. She liked that he was Jewish. Not as intellectual as Sy, but very Jewish in his humor and warmth. Herm's bulky body made her feel cozy and protected. She liked that he was concerned about her and Parin, concerned enough to sit with them for the next fifteen minutes until their train was due and probably help them through this crowd of men and assist them in finding seats. She hoped they could find seats, that the train wouldn't arrive full from Portland. They said that with the troop movements all the trains were overcrowded these days. She started to worry, to fret. Just like Mother, she thought. If her mother were sitting in this room, with a soldier pressed close like the one on Esther's left, her mother would begin to repeat over and over, "What if we can't get a seat? What will we do, ride standing for eight hours? I don't think I can tolerate standing for eight hours." Esther sighed. Mother. Two weeks with Mother and Daddy. At least Daddy was easier.

"Glad Denton decided not to bring you here and left it to me."

Herm finally spoke. Parin was sound asleep in his arms, her chin on her chest, the brim of her navy blue, wool bonnet shading her eyes from the overhead lights. Her legs in red leggings dangled over his thighs.

Esther unbuttoned the leggings at her daughter's ankles. Parin's upper lip was beaded with sweat. She decided to leave her glasses on, not to awaken her.

"Why's that?" she asked, knowing the answer.

"Because of this." He waved his hand from right to left twice, indicating the room. "These service boys. He'd hate it."

"I know," she answered. Maybe it was because of the warmth of the crowded room that she felt herself relaxing, or was it the anticipation of being away from Tule Lake for fourteen days that made her more willing than usual to share with Herm what she usually considered family business? She longed to confide in him. "I don't know why it bothers him so much. He's made his decision. It's based on a principle of the highest order."

"All the same," Herm shifted slowly, careful not to disturb Parin. "A civilian does stand out here, like a Jew at the dinner table making a point nobody wants to think about."

Esther laughed. "Is that how you feel, Herm, deep down?"

He shrugged. "Yep, I guess so. Yep, pretty damned uncomfortable being here today."

"Then why should you be glad Denton isn't here? Do you prefer to suffer alone publicly? Or do you think your position is unassailable compared to Denton's?"

"Hello, Miss Sharp Tongue." He nudged her with his shoulder. "No, I don't like to be singled out as a traitor or a coward, but I've been *told* I can't go. No back and forth for me, really. No ambivalence, as Sy would say. I feel damn bad I can't be over there doing my part to beat the Nazis. It tore me to bits at first, Sylvie can attest to that. I cried. Truly. But once you get used to it, you can live with it. I'm still a man. I'd fight if I could. I know I'm afraid, but I know I could do it. But I don't think Denton can ever be at peace about it. I think that's half his trouble these days, this conscientious objector issue."

Esther looked quickly around to see if anyone had heard. But everyone was engaged in his own conversation, even the soldier on her left who kept falling against her. He was bent forward grabbing onto the tail of another soldier's coat to get his attention as he yelled at him, "Hey, buddy." The noise level was already high and it was rising. Only she and Herm could possibly hear what they were saying.

"What do you mean, his trouble?"

"He feels bad about not fighting. He doubts his motives. He worries about his angry feelings. He worries about his wanting to kill somebody, anybody, preferably Andross because that would be politically acceptable to Denton. He's worried every single day about the fury inside him."

"You know this? He's talked to you?" So that's what they discussed for three hours.

"Esther, doll, you should know better." Herm looked down at her, his hazel eyes warm with affection. "Denton admit to anything like that, even to himself?"

"I'm relieved," she said.

"Relieved?"

"Yes, that he keeps himself as hidden from you as from me." She was shocked at herself for talking this candidly, even with Herm, but it felt terribly good.

"All you got to do is look, Esther, sweetheart. He's in agony, your hubby. He's one big knot of guilt about not fighting, and angry at Andross or whoever he can focus on for messing up his one chance at redemption."

Esther felt herself tighten. Herm was going too far. She didn't like hearing this much criticism of her husband.

"You don't like my saying this." Herm turned toward her.

She didn't answer.

"Hey, I love the guy. He's my best pal. I have all the respect in the world for him. I'd never be able to take such a brave stand right now. But he's having trouble, Esther. I'm not criticizing him, honest to god."

"Denton believes in what he's doing," Esther said stiffly. "It isn't an easy thing to do."

"My point exactly. Especially with a Jewish wife."

She could feel his gaze on her. He's as bad as Sy, she thought, getting in there, prying where he shouldn't.

"Being Jewish is not the issue," she said. "Neither of us believes in religion. Religion is not a concern with us."

"No, but it's an issue with the rest of the world right now. Esther, there's a world war being fought over the lives of Jews."

"That's not about religion. It's a war of aggression. Plenty of other innocent people are being killed."

"Who the heck cares what it is precisely? Jews are dying because they're Jews." His voice rose. "And I know it's no longer about religion. In the Nazis' eyes we're a race."

"Keep your voice down," she said, irritated and embarrassed. People were turning to look at the three of them. "You're calling attention. And anyway, you're not making sense. I'm losing the line of your argument."

Herm sighed and slumped. Parin shifted in his arms.

"My argument is that I think Denton's having a rough time with his conscience, rougher than the rest of us. When I lie awake at night pondering where I stand on the infighting in camp, I keep coming back to Denton. I don't understand why he's siding with the militants. I don't get why he's not protecting himself from Nebo Mota, and why he takes such a belligerent stand against Andross. He leaves himself open, front and back. And I don't understand why he's so god-awful angry at everybody, me included, and why he doesn't listen to people who talk sense like Bill Nakamura and Toki Honda."

"He's never seen things the way other people have, Herm, you know that."

"I know, doll, but he's way off the mark now."

The stationmaster came into the waiting room and called out the arriving train.

"Five minutes, train from Portland, proceeding to San Francisco," he called in a bass voice that almost silenced the packed room. Then an even louder din of shouts for duffel bags and shouts of "So long" and "Good luck to you."

Esther quickly picked up her suitcase. She didn't know whether she was relieved or sorry to end their conversation. Herm lifted the sleeping Parin into his arms and they pushed through the moving crowd, trying to get to the front and out the door to the platform.

"I'm going to get on board with you," Herm shouted above the noise. "I'm going to help you get a seat."

"Thanks," she mouthed at him. It took all her willpower to keep from leaning against his massive body, into his rough wool coat, into his burly chest. He could be such a comfort at times. Denton so seldom was, anymore.

The whistle shrieked as the train pulled around the curve of track and into the station. Exhilaration took hold of the mass of people. There were more shouts and jostling. Esther and Herm tried to gauge where the steps would be when the train stopped. Parin woke up and looked around sleepily, slightly bewildered and frightened, but Esther had no time to soothe her as the train braked and the stairs to one of the doors were directly before them. Herm grabbed the valise from Esther with his free hand, and shoved her bodily toward the stairway. She held the metal railing and pulled herself to the car platform, reaching back down to Herm for the suitcase. He swung himself up, shouting, "Get the heck in there, Esther, look for seats."

The Negro porter came through the car door. "There's a few seats in this car, ma'am. How many are you, three?"

"Two, thank you. Just my daughter and myself," she shouted over the other voices as soldiers shoved past them.

"And the gentleman?"

"He's only helping."

"Hey, Esther, get on in." Herm was at her side, yelling. "You'll never get a seat."

"Pardon me, sir." The porter moved aside. "Let me take that, sir." He took the suitcase from Herm.

They followed him into the jammed car. Soldiers were pouring in from both doors, filling the aisles. It looked as though the car had already been full when it entered the station, and no one was getting off.

"Right here, ma'am," the porter said, standing by two seats in the last row. He picked up a folded jacket and two small dark valises and snapped off a sign that said "Reserved". "You take these two seats, for you and the little girl."

"But these are yours," Esther protested.

"You're not about to stand with the child all the way down to San Francisco, now, are you? I'm right, that's where you're headed?" He smiled, his smooth dark skin folding into deep wrinkles around his eyes.

"Thank you so much. How can I thank you?"

"By sitting yourselves down and getting comfortable." He smiled again, reached up and straightened Parin's glasses.

Esther thanked him again as he turned and made his way along the aisle, slipping between the standing soldiers. Herm handed Parin down and Esther lifted her over to the window seat.

"Looks like you're going to ride in luxury," Herm said.

"I'll have to give up Parin's seat if someone asks," she said, still not believing her good fortune. "I can always hold her on my lap."

"Watch out, you sound like Denton."

The whistle blew three times. The conductor called out, "A-A-A-All aboard, last call for S-a-an Fra-a-a-ancisco." The car jerked forward, throwing everyone off balance, including Herm. Esther threw her arm across Parin's body as the child flopped forward and then back against the seat.

"I'm off, Esther, doll." His face was sad though he was trying to smile. "Hope I'll still be up there when you get back." She felt the warmth of his big hand on her shoulder.

"I'm only going for two weeks. I'm certain that's all I can tolerate of Mother."

"You never can tell. Maybe all that good home cooking will lure you in."

Esther laughed. How fine it felt to laugh. "You haven't met my mother, nor have you tasted what she calls food."

"It can't be that bad." The train began to move.

Esther laughed again. "Oh, yes, it can. Ask Denton about my mother's meatloaf."

"Last call, a-a-a-l-l-l aboard," the conductor's voice boomed from outside.

"Be seeing you, Esther."

"Yes, Herm, thank you. We appreciate all you've done."

"Esther, doll. What's this formality?" He bent and kissed her cheek.

She felt herself blush as he leaned across her to kiss Parin.

"Take care, Chicken Little." Then he was gone, shouting, "See you in fourteen days!" They saw him in the window for a split second, waving at them. The train lurched forward and left him behind.

"He's not coming, Mommy?" Parin said, looking up at Esther, her face crumpling with disappointment.

Esther felt the vacuum as well. How pleasant it would have been to travel down to San Francisco with Herm at her side.

"No, sweetest, Mr. Katz had to go back to camp. Back to see Daddy, to keep him company."

"He's not coming with us?" she asked again.

"No, Parin, I told you. He has to stay and work, like Daddy. But you and I will be together. You're going to be my little companion in this. Isn't that nice?"

Parin scrutinized her and then nodded, but her glumness didn't lift. It shaped her lips, her chin and cheeks.

Esther untied her daughter's bonnet. She smoothed Parin's hair.

"Do you want to keep your coat on? Is it still chilly in here?"

Parin nodded. "Yes, it's chilly in here, Mommy."

Esther saw that Parin was trying with all her might not to cry, but she couldn't manage whatever pain inhabited her small chest, because her eyes brimmed and swam behind the thick glasses and a tear welled out and slid down her cheek. Esther could have cried along with her. She, too, was overwhelmed with emptiness, with the sense of belonging nowhere, not in the camp, not on this train with the troops of soldiers on their way from here to there and back again, nor in her mother's home. There was no comfort there.

"My little puddingface." Esther lifted her daughter onto her lap. The child came willingly. As though she wants to be near me, Esther thought, as though I can provide her with warmth and love.

She knew she could lose the extra seat by holding Parin in her lap, but she didn't care. She felt as if she could hold her baby for the entire trip.

"Excuse me, miss, is this seat free?" It was a handsome older soldier she'd noticed in the station.

Esther nodded yes but didn't speak, and the man looked knowingly at the child. He flung his duffel into the rack above and, without removing his coat, sat down beside them.

Esther didn't concern herself with the soldier but instead held Parin tighter and let the motion of the train rock them both. Beyond the window, the outskirts of the town stretched out: rutted dirt roads with patches of sooty snow along the sides, piled-up stacks of Red Cross supplies, the tiny backyards of drab, run-down houses that looked as if they hadn't been painted for years. The view wasn't much of an improvement over camp.

"How are you doing?" Esther asked Parin.

"Okay," came a peep.

"We've got to stick together. You know that. You're my only best companion."

"Yes, Mommy."

They rode in silence after that, Parin drifting into sleep and Esther returning to a sort of reverie. The train turned and the sun flowed through their window, warming, caressing, soothing the tension from her body.

Chapter Nineteen

It wasn't until Esther heard the conductor's call for San Francisco and saw that they were about to pull into the station that the old fear arose at the thought of seeing her mother. Why hadn't she prepared herself better, hardened herself for Judith's barbs?

"Parin, sweetheart, we're here."

Parin had been well-behaved throughout the trip, sleeping, playing patty-cake with Esther, talking to her worn rag doll.

"Are we in Fran Sancisco?"

Esther laughed, "Yes, dearest. We'll see Grandmother and Grandpa in a few moments."

This was followed by silence. Parin turned to her. "Do we have to see Grandmother, Mommy?"

Oh, lord, Esther thought.

"Yes, of course we're going to see Grandmother. We came down here so they can see their wonderful little granddaughter."

"Oh." She continued to stare at Esther.

"What is it?"

"I don't want to see Grandmother."

Esther barely contained her amusement. How easy life must be when you know exactly what you feel.

"Why not?" Esther smoothed her cheek.

"'Cause I don't like her, Mommy. She's not nice."

"No, Parin, she is nice, she just has trouble showing it to you. She loves you very much."

"No." Parin shook her head vehemently.

How does she know this? Esther wondered. Had Parin sensed her own fears?

"Parin, I promise you Grandmother does love you. And Grandpa says you're a potato dumpling. Do you remember that?"

Parin's face was transformed from rigid consternation to delight when she heard the words "potato dumpling."

"Pa-pa-pa-pa-potato dumpling!" she squealed.

"You remember the game?"

"Pa-pa-pa-pa-potato dumpling." Laughter this time.

Relieved, Esther began collecting their belongings. She helped Parin put on her coat. She tied the blue wool bonnet under her chin. "You look beautiful, you know that?" Esther said.

As Esther reached up to adjust her own hat and slide the long pin through, she felt relaxed and almost happy. Even with the threat of Mother and a nagging concern about Denton, she was more contented than she could remember being in a good long time. A shiver of excitement reminded her that she was going to see Daddy. Maybe she had made the right decision, to come down here.

The train jerked to a stop and bedlam broke out. Uniformed men filed from their seats and grabbed duffel bags from the overhead racks, throwing on their caps and heavy overcoats, all the while yelling to each other.

"Have a fine stay, young ladies," their seatmate shouted as he tipped his cap and backed into the surging line of men.

Esther carried Parin on one arm and their valise in her other hand as she maneuvered through the crowds on the train platform. She craned, straining to spot her parents in the throng.

"Help me look, Parin. Tell me if you see Grandmother Judith or Grandpa Harry." Parin was becoming too heavy on her arm and hip. "Hold tightly around my neck, sweetness. Help Mommy. You're too heavy for her." Parin, grabbing tighter, shifted some of her weight off Esther's numb and aching arm.

Esther stopped to look around; she saw nothing but the backs of heads and, high on the station wall, an enormous poster of Uncle Sam, asking that she buy war bonds for Christmas. She was being shoved from all sides. She decided to try the exit gate. Maybe her parents would be waiting there. If not, at least she could rest for a moment in the waiting room before setting off for Berkeley on her own.

But there at the gate was her father, hat at his chest, on tiptoe, his thick black hair combed back off his low brow, twisting his small head from one side to the other.

"Daddy!"

"There's Grandpa. Mommy, I see him. Grandpa!"

"Daddy!"

He heard them. "Ach, my loves." He flung wide his arms, knocking a woman in the face with his hat. "Ah, hah," he laughed.

Then they were in his arms. Esther was pressing her bowed head against his diminutive but strong, sinewy body, breathing the odor of cigarette smoke and perspiration permanently woven into his wool coat and suit jacket.

"My darlinks, my darlinks," he murmured into Esther's hair.

Esther always forgot that he spoke English with the pronunciation and inflections of his native Lithuania. She only heard it when they were reunited after being apart for an extended period. If she were asked what it was that she loved most about her father, she might even answer, His accent. To her, his curious way of putting words together told the story of his courage. It was shorthand for the tale of how he had escaped from the army. "For Jewish boys, it was a dangerous place. Not a shit were we worth in the czar's army," Harry would laugh. He was born in Vilna. When he turned eighteen his father had arranged work for him in a lumber camp where, within a week, Harry had jumped on the logs that carried him out of the country illegally.

"Daddy, how are you?" she asked, patting his mussed hair back behind his ear.

"Fine, I'm fine by me. You're looking a little peaked, the two of you. Even my little pa-pa-pa-potato dumpling!" Laughing, he grabbed two fat chunks of Parin's cheeks between his thumbs and index fingers, and jiggled her face back and forth while his granddaughter became hysterical with laughter.

"Please, Daddy, she's going to get sick from excitement."

"Ach, not possible. Not if her Grandpapi holds her in his arms."

The relief was so great when he lifted Parin from her arms that for a moment she had a delicious sense of weightlessness.

"Thank you, Daddy, she's getting big." Esther glanced around. "Where's Mother?"

Harry Kahn shrugged. "At Hadassah. Your mother wouldn't miss her Hadassah meeting even for the Dean of Arts and Sciences."

It was true. And Judith Kahn would certainly not consider the arrival of her daughter and granddaughter even remotely equivalent.

"Not to blame, Esther, not to blame."

"I'm not..."

"Shh. I know my daughter's face. Nothink on it can be hidden from me. But by your mother's Hadassah meeting, they're learning very important pieces of information. She'll tell you about them, I'm certain," he said, his face solemn when usually such a statement would light it with interior merriment. Silent jokes about Judith's austere demeanor were part of their private communication.

As they talked they had pushed through the crowds in the station, and were about to exit through the main door. Servicemen swarmed around them, army and navy, privates and commissioned officers, but almost no civilians except themselves; no wives, girlfriends or children meeting the soldiers.

"What is all this?"

"Our influx of men?"

"Servicemen to be specific."

"This is nothing. Our town is full up through the gills with them. Not to speak of the gills." He chuckled at his own silly play on mispronounced words.

"Daddy, please. Are you telling me the whole of San Francisco is like this?

"Right. In the last week, we've had a flood of them, you've never seen such a thing. Big Pacific Theater activities, I hear. Not to make your mother so happy. She'd rather Europe."

"They've recruited up in camp," Esther said. "For infantry and also intelligence work."

"In Japan?" He looked at her.

She nodded.

"Hmmm," he said, shifting his granddaughter from one arm to another. "Some conflicts it must raise."

Esther sighed, remembering what she had left. "Yes, quite a few conflicts. Here, let me take her, she's too heavy for you."

"Ach, don't insult me." Parin had her arms around his neck and her cheek on his forehead. "Such sweet pleasure you're going to deny me? So, you ready for the outside?"

The night was thick with moisture. Esther breathed the smell of ocean carried in on the wind. Conversation was muted out here beyond the doors of the station. It was very dark on the street and it took a few minutes for her eyes to adjust. The city skyline had faded into the night with the windows of the buildings mostly blacked out. Only the sailors' white hats and their white pants below their pea coats lit the way along the sidewalk. The waning moon, dark orange, was behind the train station, just lifting above the roof.

"So how's my favorite son-in-law?" Harry asked as they headed toward the trolley stop, moving slowly to accommodate Parin who now walked between them.

"Just fine, Daddy," Esther said, careful to control her voice.

"Not so fine, I can hear. But later we'll talk about it. Is that right, my lovely?"

"Of course, Daddy, we'll do lots of talking." She knew they would and it worried her.

*   *   *

The ferry shuddered as it left the pier. Three deafening blasts sounded their departure. A few yards off the pier it became too cold on the deck and they had to descend to the enclosed waiting room. Even down there the brackish wet air penetrated, and in the peaceful hush that lay between her and her father, Esther listened to and felt the vibrations of the motors through her spine. There were very few passengers, and all were civilians, mostly women, riding home to Berkeley after work in town. As they cut through the water, pitching deeply, she watched the young woman at the front counter as she collected money for the USO. Esther felt she knew her from somewhere. She tried for the length of the trip to think who it could be. Perhaps a girl she'd gone to high school with or known at the university. But the girl didn't seem to recognize her. It only added to the strangeness of being here on this ferry, gliding over to the Oakland dock, surrounded by nicely dressed Caucasians who dozed or murmured in the near-darkness. She thought back to the desert camp she had left only twelve hours before. She saw their cinder street, their wooden barracks. She thought of Denton driving off with the black dust kicking up behind the car. She saw the faces of her students, the inside of Hiroko's room. She felt as though she'd entered an alien country down here, one she had never before set foot in. But this had been home. Even six months ago, when she'd visited with Parin for a few days, she hadn't felt so strange. Tonight Denton, Hiroko, Herm, Nebo Mota, Toki Honda, and her students seemed to inhabit Esther's real country, one that was dark, sad, and tormented, but familiar. She was afraid she wouldn't know how to talk about her life in camp, because it had become...what? So alien to the people riding the ferry. Yes, she thought. That's what we are. A new country of aliens fenced off from our old land. Separated from the rest of America. Up in Tule Lake none of the rules from down here seemed to apply.

*   *   *

At the apartment, they ate a simple supper of scrambled eggs and fried potatoes and onions that Harry prepared. The kitchen was warm and Parin grew so drowsy her head dropped to the table.

"I want to go to bed, Mommy," she whispered with her cheek flat against the table top.

"Of course, but don't you want fruit?"

"No, Mommy, I'm too sleepy."

"I set up for the two of you in the alcove, *bubele*," Harry said as he carefully placed a shallow bowl of peaches on the table in front of his granddaughter. "You're sure no peaches for you, baby doll?"

Parin lifted her head and shook it.

"No, thank you, is what you say, Parin," Esther said.

"No, thank you," Parin said, her face sagging with fatigue.

Esther pushed aside the heavy brocade curtain that concealed the bed, releasing a hint of camphor; she felt the familiar thick fabric between her fingers and recognized the old sound of the brass rings slipping along the wooden rod. This was where she lay as a child silently begging her mother to stop belittling Daddy, to stop the nightly list of his failings. But Judith would go on and on ridiculing his research and admonishing him for the money he spent on books, for wasting her professor's salary on his "little, quixotic project."

Esther sat on the edge of the bed with Parin drooping between her legs. She slipped Parin's red sweater off, lifting her daughter's arms high, letting them flop down onto her own thighs. Parin's head fell forward as Esther unbuttoned her blue corduroy jumper. She had made the jumper as she had made all of Parin's clothing. Maybe I'm not such a terrible mother, she thought, if I can make her clothes. Judith couldn't sew a stitch. She slipped the jumper over Parin's head.

"Are you too tired to get into your pajamas?" Esther asked.

"Yes," came the tiny voice.

"Let's put you to sleep in your jersey and panties then. It can't

161

hurt for one night." Parin's head fell back onto Esther's shoulder, her soft cheek sliding against Esther's.

Esther wrapped her daughter tightly against her own body. You're mine, she said silently. You are all mine.

Esther tucked Parin in, pulling the white sheet and green blanket up to her chin. She slipped off her glasses and brushed strands of hair from her forehead. The strain of the trip showed on Parin's face. She was pale and pasty. Even dinner hadn't brought her color back.

"Sweetheart? This is where Mommy slept when she was a girl."

"I know." Parin tried to open her eyes, but they closed anyway.

"Of course, I've told you that before," Esther whispered to the already-sleeping child.

*　　*　　*

"Tell me, Daddy, how is your work?" Esther asked as she spooned sun-yellow peaches, preserved by Grandma Leah, from a dusky pink glass bowl to her mouth. They were delicious, not like the syrupy canned fruit they received in camp.

"The paying or the real?" He brushed his fingers through his thick black hair. For a man of sixty-three, he was astonishingly free of the signs of age. No gray hair, and almost no wrinkles on his deep-olive-toned skin, only faint etchings around his eyes, even though he smiled a lot.

"First the paying, to get it over with." She grinned at him.

"Barely tolerable. It's important for the war effort, but it doesn't stimulate." He tapped his head and then his heart. "It's for coming up with cheap forms of gasoline and crude oil." He poured dark amber, steeped tea into narrow glasses and, holding the rim, placed one before Esther.

"You do crucial work, Daddy. And they respect you," she said, trying to fend off the predictable litany.

"Esther, you're still a little girl. You think State Chemist of the great state of California is an honor. By them this is a job nobody wants, so they gave it to some stinking little immigrant."

"Stop that. It's an awful thing to say." She rose and took her bowl to the sink. She saw her reflection in the window and was surprised to find a grown woman. He was right. Sitting in this kitchen she did feel like a child. She turned. Her father had his head down.

"Daddy, please."

"I have other loves is all, my sweetheart," he said, looking up at her like a contrite child. For years her father had spent evenings and weekends behind the apartment building, in the garage he'd made over into an office, working on his intellectual life's passion, his theories of evolution.

She sat again and put her hand in his, feeling how smooth his palm was. His hands were oversized for his small body, as if his body had stopped growing prematurely but his hands kept on, as though the hands signified the man he was meant to be.

"That husband of yours will be pleased to know how from my reading of original sources, I've discovered, by my Russian source material, the co-operative theory of evolution."

"I know that, Daddy," she said, growing irritated. As always, he was going to start from the beginning of his tale of woe, as though she were a stranger who had to be initiated into his world of ideas. Then her father would begin his lament on how he should have become a biologist, should have begun his study of evolutionary theory at an earlier date. Maybe Mother was right to be furious with him about this.

"No, madam, it's finally my theory I've substantiated, that evolution, the survival of the fittest, is not a competitive venture, that the species do not battle between each other for their spot on earth, but rather they go together, give assistance to one another so that they can survive." His voice grew louder, rising and falling in pontificating waves. "But these Americans, these people who themselves they call scientists, have nothing of scientific curiosity. They don't want to know from a Russian theory, or an immigrant's ideas. No, they choose the side of xenophobia. Such a way, I can't believe." He tapped his forehead. "Such looniness."

"Daddy, it's because you're a chemist and not a biologist," she said, thinking how sadly ironic it was that he was married to a highly regarded biologist who taught at a prestigious University.

"No. They want nothink with a little Jewish man and his accent from Lithuania."

"That's not so. There are many Jewish scientists, Mother included. And foreign scientists. You know that. It's your credentials they care about."

"Exceptions they've been known to make. No, it's the visage that counts. The straight nose. The gentile hair. It's the same here like in Lithuania and with the Nazis. The same, Esther. Maybe if I introduce my son-in-law to these men they will accept my papers."

"Daddy! Why are you talking this way?"

He stopped, and sat staring at her with a forlorn face. "Oh, my darlink. Yes, make me shut my mouth." He slapped his own cheek sharply. "I miss my darlink. I speak from anger at losing you." He continued to stare at her as though consuming her, intruding on her most private self.

She was familiar with this staring, knew it as his way of saying, "You are a beauty, my daughter. How ever did I, a little Jewish immigrant, runt of a man, create such a beauty of a woman?" She often asked herself the same question when she wondered at Parin's blonde hair, at her smooth pale skin, and the sturdiness of her body. Because she's Denton's, she answered herself, it's all his doing, his blood.

The door on the lower landing opened and banged closed.

"It's your mother," Harry said, in his softest voice. He stood and began to clear the remaining dishes. He grew smaller and older before Esther's eyes. "I'd better find her some supper. She's going to be hungry."

"Daddy."

"I know, Esther. I know."

Chapter Twenty

J udith Kahn sighed as she reached the landing.

"Mother?"

"Esther dear, is that you?"

Judith appeared in the doorway. She was no taller than Harry, though in Esther's mind she always towered over him. She was squarish and densely packed, solid like a heavy crockery cream pitcher. Her gray hair, in her unchanging style, was combed back and knotted in a bun. Perched on her head was a brimless blue felt hat with the veil drawn up so it didn't interfere with the view through her steel-rimmed glasses; she could not abide having her vision impaired for vanity's sake. She wore a severe gray-blue coat with utilitarian steel buttons, which she began to undo.

"I am so exhausted," she said, walking over to Esther. "I thought the meeting would never end, though it was most informative." She offered her cheek to Esther. "Hello, Esther. I'm sorry I couldn't go with Harry to the train. Did he explain?" Their faces touched.

"Yes," Esther said. "He explained about Hadassah."

Judith turned and walked to the front closet. She sighed again. "There was no possibility I could change it. Even with more notice. They are cast in concrete, I'm afraid. Especially these days." Extracting the long pin, she lifted the hat from her head. A few strands of hair pulled free.

Esther thought, in a normal home I might have hugged her. Sadness permeated her. Had she already succumbed to hope in the few moments since Judith had arrived? Did she harbor an expectation that her mother would take her hand, touch her, if she went over and smoothed her mother's hair back into her bun? Therein lies the danger in this house, Esther warned herself. Therein awaits the hurt and humiliation. Don't hope for a thing.

"Is Harry here?" Judith asked as she unbuttoned the bodice of her dress. "Harry?" she called.

"He's here, Mother. He's cleaning up the dishes."

"Harry!"

When he still didn't answer, Judith went to the curtained glass door leading into the kitchen. "There you are. Why didn't you answer me?"

"Because I didn't hear you," Harry's voice emerged. "A little hungry, is it, after the meeting?"

"I am. Sara Finkel served us tea. That was the entirety of what she had to offer. At least the tea was better than Alma Klein's dry cookies."

Esther was always dumbfounded by her mother's complaints about other women's hospitality when Judith herself was a dreadful cook and had no conception of entertaining. The few times they'd had guests in the house, Esther had watched in abject mortification as people struggled through a meal of tough overcooked meat, tasteless vegetables, lumpy mashed potatoes and salad with too much vinegar. And the coffee! She and Denton had sat in the park one night, helpless with laughter, after such a dinner, when they'd gone for a walk to digest it. He said his mother had been an atrocious cook, but, as in everything else, Judith had surpassed her.

"Come, Esther," Judith said. "Come while I get changed. Harry, you'll take care of things in here?"

"Certainly. I'll have her majesty's dinner in a moment."

Esther turned to catch her father's wink. She smiled back. Their old conspiracy was intact.

"Don't mock me, Harry. I won't be mocked."

"Ah, *bube*." He shook his head as he went over to the icebox.

"Harry, I don't like '*bube*'. You know I abhor those little terms of endearment." Judith held the top of her dress closed with one hand. She scowled, the two lines between her eyes deepening. "I have had a terrible, terrible evening. I don't need to be humored in my own home after listening to how our people are being eradicated from this earth. Harry, do you hear me?"

Harry had remained partially hidden behind the icebox door, only his backside, legs, and hand showed. He stood, closed the door. He held two eggs in his right hand. His face was flushed a dark copper-brown from bending over and from the anger playing across it.

"My darlink, my hearing is excellent." he said. "And I know what is happening to my, excuse me, our people. I don't need from you or from your Hadassah ladies this information." He turned, walked to the stove, and with his back to them, took down the matches from the shelf, plucked one from the box and scratched it across the sandpaper until it flared.

Judith stared in disbelief at her husband, her grasp tightening at the neck of her dress. Esther stifled a grin of pleasure at hearing her father, for once, stand up to Judith.

"Why does he speak to me this way?" Judith said in a low voice, her lips trembling.

Harry didn't answer, but simply got out the skillet and placed it on the fire.

Judith turned. "Are you coming with me, Esther?"

"Yes, Mother."

As Esther followed her out through the dining room and across the darkened parlor, she heard her father say, "Dinner will be served in ten minutes." The oleo was already sizzling in the pan and the aroma of browning onions wafted out.

*   *   *

Their bedroom had a window facing the street. During the afternoons the leaves of an oak tree dappled the sunlight on the rose-patterned rug. Esther loved those trees and often when her parents were out of the house, which was every weekday afternoon when she was growing up, she would sit on the window seat with a book. Usually she would end up staring out, watching mockingbirds scramble and squawk, and woodpeckers work their way up the trunk and along the branches. With no one present in the house this room was a comfort to her. She would pretend it was her own, that she alone occupied the apartment. In those solitary hours, the rug, the maroon quilt, the heavy maroon and cream drapes patterned with dark green ivy, the tall bureau with its disarray of bottles, papers, combs and brushes all seemed to embrace her. The sound in the room was muted by the thick fabric, the windows kept out any exterior noise, and the angry, hectoring voice that emanated from this place at night seemed never to have existed.

Judith stood at the bureau with her back to Esther. She hadn't yet made any inquiry about Parin. Where does she think Parin is? Esther wondered. Does it even penetrate her thoughts that she might have a grandchild under her roof?

Judith asked Esther to help her off with her dress. "I'm getting to be an old lady. I find myself too stiff at times to lift the dress over my head. It's humiliating. Harry has to help me." She waited with her arms raised, her image reflected in the bureau's high tilted mirror.

As Esther struggled to lift her mother's dress over her shoulders, she caught her mother's familiar odor of bruised, overripe fruit. Intermingled with it was old perspiration embedded in the rayon fabric of the dress, the talc she patted and pressed over her body each day before dressing and the unclean odors from her slip. These smells were the very essence of Judith for Esther. She would know her blindfolded. Other mothers were perfumed, and, just as their houses always seemed to smell deliciously of bread baking or roasts in the oven, they themselves smelled of roses, lilies of the valley, or intoxicating, more sophisticated odors, like smoky rooms, whisky, or deep musk. Esther envied other girls their mothers for many reasons, but for this she envied them most. Any of their scents were far better than the smells her mother gave off, with their implications of uncleanliness, of being too busy to care about such plebeian matters, of not caring for the womanly luxuries of life. Esther often feared she would smell like her mother, that anyone—a stranger, Denton or Parin—would find her, as she did her mother, faintly repulsive.

Esther sat on the bed while Judith went into her walk-in closet to finish undressing.

"Where is Parin?" her mother called out.

Finally she asks, Esther thought.

"She's sleeping in the alcove." Esther fingered the beginning of a tear in the peach satin comforter that lay at the foot of her parents' bed. This had been Grandma Leah's dowry, brought from Russia when she emigrated. She smiled to think of Grandma. She wondered why the old woman had already given up her quilt. It was her most prized possession, even after seventy years in the new land.

"How is Grandma?"

"Not so well, Esther. Not so well."

"What is it? Mother, why didn't you write if something was wrong?" Her body tensed with panic. Grandma was her favorite, her sole protector besides Daddy.

"No, no, she isn't ill. As strong as ever at ninety. We'll all die before

Mother. No, it's the emotional pain that we're going through, with what we're discovering about the situation in Europe."

Here goes, Esther thought. She had hoped for a reprieve for at least this first night, but she should have known better, particularly after that brief encounter in the kitchen. Her mother would begin her guilt-provoking tirade on the destruction of the Jews. How did her mother happen to be the only one privy to this information? Ordinary newspapers never printed the horrifying reports of mass deaths that her mother regaled her with. Of course Esther was gravely concerned, but once Judith began her relentless, dogmatic recitation, Esther reflexively recoiled from her.

Judith emerged from the closet wearing a flowered housedress and bedroom slippers. She had removed her brassiere and girdle, to avoid wearing them out. Again Esther felt disgust for her mother. Judith's thick legs were bare of stockings, her leg hair dark against the pale skin, her varicose veins bulging after a day of carrying her weight. Esther was disgusted with the entire room. Tonight she felt oppressed by the heavy draperies, the patterned rug, and the dense bedding piled on the double bed. The whole apartment seemed shabby. Why couldn't her mother show some concern for her surroundings?

Judith stood before the mirror and perfunctorily whisked the hairbrush over her bun, catching up the strands of hair that had escaped when she removed her hat.

"I look hopelessly awful. I can't abide looking at myself these days."

"No, Mother, you look wonderful. A little tired, but really very good," Esther said. Maybe flattery would steer her mother away from the subject of the war.

Judith put the brush down on the dresser top with another long sigh. "I'm fully aware, Esther, of how I look to the world. But what do I care for that?"

Judith turned and stared hard at Esther. She smiled. "I'm glad you're home, my dear."

"Well, I am, too, Mother. Thank you." All resistance melted. A memory took shape. Her mother was braiding her hair and chuckling because the disorderly curls would spring out of the braids a moment after she'd entrapped them. Her mother's hand had been as gentle as her good-natured complaints about Esther's obstreperous hair. It was almost as though her mother had been proud of the curls' conduct.

She must have been six. That's when she wore pigtails. Just before the demands started, demands for her to be independent, to study, to be better than her cousins and the other children in the neighborhood, to excel in biology so that the science teachers couldn't gloat that Dr. Judith Kahn had a child who fell short in the natural sciences. But standing here before Esther was a mother who said she was glad her daughter was home, who needed her daughter, who was perhaps even fond of her. Esther almost rose and put her arms around her mother's shoulders for comfort. She stopped herself. Be careful. She can turn on you without notice. But no, Esther thought, this time is different.

"This European business is becoming overwhelming," Judith said, the obsessive intensity re-entering her voice.

Esther scrambled to retrieve her old defenses, thankful she'd not risen, relieved she still sat on the edge of the bed fingering Grandma's soft satin quilt.

"I can imagine," she said.

"I'm glad you understand. Your father doesn't. He refuses to hear, no matter what he contends."

"Maybe it hurts him too much to listen," Esther suggested.

"He can't hurt more than our people who are dying," her mother retorted sharply. "He is like our government. They refuse to acknowledge what we have proof of."

"Mother, I don't think Daddy is not acknowledging the problem."

Judith stared. "Are you taking your father's side in this?"

"It's not a question of sides. I think Daddy cares deeply, that's all."

"Harry won't sit for ten minutes and listen to me. You heard him out there. I need someone to talk with about this."

"What about the other women in the Hadassah group?"

"Honestly, Esther, they are not professional women. They are as incapable of writing a straightforward note to Rabbi Stephen Wise in support of his refugee work as they are of formulating a lucid letter to pressure the State Department. In the end, I must generate all our exchanges with this fundamentally anti-Semitic government, of whom only Mrs. Roosevelt cares. I had the honor of meeting with Eleanor, but the rest of the administration, including her husband, think we're bothersome. It is not an easy job."

"What did you meet with Mrs. Roosevelt about?"

Judith looked surprised. "To push the President on a refugee matter, of course. There is a possibility of getting Rumanian Jews out, but an offer of sanctuary is necessary. We've met resistance in the State Department in the person of Secretary Hull, who they report is married to a Jewish woman, but who I believe is virulently anti-Semitic. As you may know, being married to a Jew does not preclude anti-Semitism in the goyim." Her eyes darted to Esther's and away.

Esther didn't flinch. She refused to respond, to give legitimacy to the attack, but she thought, Oh, Mother, you gave yourself away that time.

"Not our Denton, of course. He's quite different. How is he? You haven't said a word about him since I've gotten here." Judith's face took on a concerned motherly expression.

"He's fine, Mother," she said, thinking, You nasty person. Butter wouldn't melt in your mouth, would it?

"You know I didn't mean that as a reference to Denton. We know that Denton isn't anti-Semitic."

"I didn't suspect it for a minute," Esther said, smoothing and resmoothing the satin quilt. The light in the room made it more rose-colored than peach, she decided. But in the sunlight it was definitely peach-colored. In Grandma's bedroom it had been peach. Definitely.

"And how are poor Denton's headaches?" her mother asked. She hadn't budged from where she'd taken up her position, just to the right of the bureau. The way the mirror was tilted, Esther could see the entire line of her mother's stocky, stubborn body, from the back of her head to her slippers. Esther watched the mirror instead of meeting her mother's eyes. To look at her mother would be to risk being seen into, inside, where the rage of years had festered.

"He's had some trouble with them in the last year, but nothing dire."

"Oh, no?"

"No. But one never knows when he'll be overcome by them."

"Yes, I do understand about headaches. Is he totally incapacitated by them when they overtake him?" Her mother's voice rose in calculated innocence.

"At times he's had to go bed for several days."

"Pills don't help? I have an acquaintance, Sophie Schwartz, who has migraines. She swears by certain little pills. I believe they have some narcotic in them, but she says one night in bed with them and she's cured. I told her about Denton's problem. She said perhaps he could try her tablets. Do you have a doctor up there, Esther? If not, I could get some from Sophie. Perhaps he'd like to try them?"

Esther clutched one hand in the other in her lap, clenching the hidden fist with all her might. If she didn't, she feared she would scream at her mother, or rise and strike her.

"He's tried a number of remedies, to no avail. Denton never knows when the migraines are going to attack, and even if he takes care of the pain, the nausea can incapacitate him, and his eyesight is often affected. A soldier cannot fight with affected eyesight. And a soldier can't be in action under a narcotic. It isn't allowed."

"Sophie didn't indicate that her headaches were so incapacitating."

"Maybe Sophie doesn't have real migraines." Esther concentrated on keeping her voice under control. Maybe Sophie doesn't know what the hell she's talking about, she thought. How was she going to get her mother to stop?

"Oh, yes, absolutely, there's no question about Sophie's having migraines."

"I don't know about Sophie, but I do know that Denton's headaches are violent at times. They can even impair his hearing. I wouldn't want to think of him under enemy fire unable to see or hear."

"Nor would I, dear. I hope I haven't upset you with this, because it certainly was not my intention."

"No, I'm not upset at all." Esther stretched her lips in a false smile.

"Good." She breathed deeply. "I think I smell food. Let's go out and see what your father has prepared. I'm quite hungry. Did I say that all Sarah Finkel served was tea?"

"Yes, you did." Esther stood and straightened her skirt.

"I don't think I could have eaten anything even if it was provided. It was a terribly difficult meeting. These are monstrous times we're living in." She went out the door.

*   *   *

Esther lay in bed, listening. Parin breathed softly beside her. She could hear her parents moving around their room. She heard Daddy come out and walk across to the bathroom. His slippers scuffed along the wood floor. Just as she knew her mother's smell, she knew his sliding step. It made her sad to hear it. His age told in the slowness of the slide. It used to be a slide and a tap, one following rapidly on the next, but tonight she heard no tap, only a shush, shush. He was becoming a defeated man. She thought of how tonight he'd looked into her face with love and longing. He missed her. She knew that from the day she left the house to marry Denton, he'd felt a great loss. He never said it, but she knew.

One night, a week before her wedding, she had heard him begin his walk across the living room linoleum. He stopped halfway. She waited, breathing shallowly. Why had he stopped in the middle of the darkened room? Lying there, her heart had opened and filled up with her father's sadness at this loss. She tried to imagine the house without her. He would have no one to greet joyfully in the evening. No one to joke with at the dinner table or in the morning as they all scrambled for coffee. Daddy would only have Mother.

She was brought back from her memories by the sound of the toilet flushing. Water ran in the sink. Her father was a meticulously clean man. She smiled to herself, thinking that he was probably the only state chemist in the history of California who had his fingernails manicured. Another way he and Mother had reversed roles. He shuffled back toward the bedroom. This time he didn't stop in the middle of the room as he had that night five years before. During that night she'd thought, What does it feel like to know you'll never marry the woman of your dreams, or, if her mother had once been his great love, how did it feel to have that passion dashed and know it could never be restored?

Esther reached over and felt her daughter's back rising and falling under her hand. Parin's body was warm and her back so very small. What was she dreaming about? The Takaetsues, or Denton, or herself? She wondered where Denton was, and how his wounds were healing. Had he eaten dinner? Was he sitting up with Herm going over every detail of the day? He used to do that with me, she thought. It was their favorite occupation, his and hers, turning over each action taken by this or that group, analyzing the actions from a psychological point of view. What were the individual motivations? What were the cultural implications? What political strategy should Denton follow? They had marvelous arguments that kept their lights on late into the night, until he or she would collapse, exhausted from the sustained exhilaration, or one of them would hold up two hands, palms forward in surrender, to say, I give up, I need to sleep. And usually they laughed. Yes, in the end, their warm feelings and their humor would rise to the surface. It was their genuine liking for each other, their rapport, their respect, their interest in each other that was the foundation that allowed them to argue. But where had all this feeling gone in such a short time? Esther turned on her side and moved closer to Parin. She stroked Parin's chubby little fingers. They were as soft as Grandma's satin quilt. Where had she and Denton begun to fail each other? She felt the tears slip from her eyes, just before she realized she was crying. They slid silently down over the bridge of her nose and onto the cotton pillowcase. They soaked the fabric until all Esther felt was sodden cloth against her face.

Chapter Twenty-One

Wives and sons and daughters of prisoners were complaining of inhuman conditions in the stockade, and judging from rumblings around camp, the population was growing angry enough to cause serious problems. With eighteen thousand people housed here even the army in full force would be overpowered if the majority rose up. Concerned about the situation, Herm petitioned Andross to get permission from Colonel Benedict for Denton, Herm and two residents to go into the army's stockade for an inspection.

Herm told Denton, "I said to Andross, Let a couple of us liberals and some residents visit the stockade and bring word out that it isn't as bad as people are saying. I overrode his objections by saying I had to see it in my official capacity as civilian head of internal security."

"And?" Denton asked.

"Damned if he didn't finally phone Colonel Benedict, but only on the condition that Nebo Mota would not be a part of the delegation. So I agreed, figuring we'd find a way to appease Mota, God help us—and the colonel said yes. Why, I don't know, but he did. Maybe he just wants to get me off his back. Or maybe the colonel thinks he's above the law and doesn't care whether we see it or not."

Denton visited Toki's barracks to ask him to be a member of the delegation. While Toki's wife, Sumiko, sliced fish for sushi in the kitchen area, he and Toki went to the far end of the room. Toki sat in his rocker, his favorite chair. The Hondas' room was peaceful, with a tatami mat covering the floor, and a few simple blond wood furnishings. Two of Frank Murayama's abstract paintings hung on the walls, and an elegant obelisk of polished wood, sculpted by Sumiko, stood on a black, shellacked chest in the corner behind Toki's chair. Danny Honda was studying behind the wall of curtain that separated the living area from their sleeping room. He'd come out to greet Denton and then gone back to his books.

"We decided to eat dinner here," Toki nodded his head in Sumiko's direction. "That's why you find me at home. It was too uncomfortable in the mess hall for us last night. I didn't feel strong enough to return right away."

"What happened?" Denton leaned forward; Toki kept his voice so low it was hard to hear him.

Toki rocked without speaking for a moment. "Did I ever tell you how difficult it was for me when I first got here from the FBI camp?"

Sumiko looked over worriedly and then bowed her head over her work.

"My wife thinks I'm imagining the animosity, but I don't think so." Toki said in answer to her look.

"I know some of the Issei women accused you back then."

"That's correct. I only bring it up because last night in the mess hall I felt the same hostility that I suffered a year and a half ago. Whether or not it's true, I'd rather digest my food in peace in my own home tonight."

When Denton told Toki why he'd come by, Toki said, "I don't think so, Denton. You know I would do anything to help, but I'm not the man for the stockade inspection. No one would believe my perceptions anyway."

"Please, Toki. We need your calm and rational perspective."

"Is Nebo Mota going?"

"Someone from the *Daihyo Sha Kai* will go, but not Nebo."

"Oh?" Toki stopped rocking.

"That's the condition. Andross said we can only go in if Nebo isn't along."

"Does Mota agree to this? Or will he throw a monkey wrench into this, too?"

"We'll see. I haven't talked with him yet."

Toki brushed his hand down the back of his head, his thick upper arm straining at the fabric of his shirt. "In that case, why don't you ask me again after you've spoken with Nebo Mota."

The next morning Herm found Nebo at the predawn calisthenics of the *Hoshidan*. Herm told Denton that when he'd informed Nebo that they'd go to inspect the stockade whether or not Nebo sent a representative, Nebo changed his tune and said he'd send Chiura Tamagata so there would be a check on the administration's opinions.

About Toki's going, Nebo scoffed, "Honda is the same as the administration. Honda does your bidding."

Denton listened carefully to what Herm said. He put Nebo's statement together with the hostility Toki said he had felt in the mess hall. Something serious was brewing. He'd been thinking too much about Alice Hamilton and not enough about camp problems. He had to start concentrating on what was happening in the camp.

The stockade was in the army section, behind the director's office, but blocked from sight by the food and supply warehouses and the army's dining hall. Only the stockade's ten-foot-high chain-link fence, topped by barbed wire, was visible over the buildings as the four men made their way across the frozen ground. They've created another high-security prison within the high-security prison, Denton thought. They moved in silence, each man for his own reasons. Herm had said to Denton when he'd picked him up at the Co-op, "Don't think this is going to draw me back into this place. I'm leaving, I tell you. This is my last act of conscience." Just hours earlier, Toki had reluctantly agreed to come. Denton didn't have the damndest notion what the *Daihyo Sha Kai* representative, Chiura Tamagata, thought. All he knew about the wizened and weathered old man was that he was a fisherman and a transfer from Topaz Camp. But he liked Tamagata's intelligent eyes and the way his chin jutted forward as Toki spoke with him in Japanese. His rapid-fire response, even the shortness of his answers suggested to Denton that Tamagata was energetic, quick and smart. He didn't meander and grandstand as some of the older Issei men were prone to do in order to make themselves feel important. And it was helpful that Toki seemed to take a liking to this new member of the *Daihyo Sha Kai*.

The damp chill air penetrated Denton's heavy coat as they rounded the food warehouse. It was the coldest day in a week of wintry temperatures and he wished he'd worn an extra layer. Tamagata was a walking coat and hat. His small body was engulfed in a huge herringbone overcoat, a wide brimmed hat, and a gray muffler wrapped round and round his face, covering his mouth. Toki didn't wear a hat or a scarf and his complexion had gone quite gray as he leaned forward against the wind. Denton was worried about him.

"Holy cow," Herm whistled. "What the hell have we got here?"

Massed along the high metal fence were about a hundred

residents—men, women, and children, huddled in the cold, shifting for better position, calling out names, squeezing their hands through the fence to touch the prisoners who crowded close on the opposite side. As they neared the milling crowd, weeping could be heard, guttural and harsh. Young Caucasian soldiers on the inside stood back from the fence, their bayoneted guns held across their chests as though for physical protection.

"This doesn't look good," Denton said.

They were spotted first by an old Issei woman in wide pants and a man's coat and a teenage girl dressed in high heels and a coat with a velvet collar and cuffs worn shiny. Immediately they were surrounded by demanding, begging people, pressing in on them, shoving large packages in their faces. "Please, bring this in with you. It's food for my brother. It doesn't fit through the fence," a girl said. "Food for little boy, my little son," an Issei woman wept. "Please, my father, he's freezing. Take this jacket and these shoes," a large young woman with Hawaiian features cried as she dragged like a beggar on Herm's arm.

Herm yanked himself from the young woman's grasp. The girl grabbed him again. He moved aside as though she were contagious.

"Let's get inside," Denton said to Toki.

Toki began to push steadily through the throng with Denton, Herm and Chiura following behind.

They were jostled and shouted at as Herm shoved the Colonel's credentials through the gate to the frightened soldiers. Chiura had pulled his muffler down to argue with an Issei gentleman whose visage was as shrunken and wrinkled as his own. The soldier examined the memo. Herm stood stiffly, keeping his elbows raised at an angle to deflect the pressing bodies, his face a mask of detachment. He reminded Denton of shell-shocked Huey, on the verge of tears and rage at all times. Hold on, friend, Denton begged in silence.

When the soldiers started to open the gate, the crowd surged violently, and the young men rushed to shut it, clanking down the bolt lock.

"Sir, I can't unlock this gate if the Japs are going to rush through. You've got to do something."

Toki began speaking calmly in Japanese to the people who had gathered ten deep around them. They crushed in closer to hear. Chiura was wedged so tightly against Denton's side that the man's bony shoulder dug into his ribs through two layers of fabric.

"We have come to assess the situation in the hope of bringing relief to your sons and husbands inside," Toki said, switching to English. "Please stand back. Leave us unmolested to do our work on your behalf."

"Why we trust you, Honda-san, when you come with Head of Security and with Business Enterprise spy?" An older Issei bachelor spoke. He was John Seko, one of the original residents. Denton remembered that Toki had been instrumental in getting Seko to join the Co-op. "My nephew inside, because these two *keto*."

"Listen here, Seko-san, these are decent men. It was their idea to come here to ameliorate the situation for the lads inside. I'm ashamed of your insulting outspokenness." Toki was trembling. "I demand that you stand back and let us in. If you don't, we will have to leave and those inside the stockade will suffer, because they will have no one in the administration to act as their advocates."

Seko scowled, causing the multitude of wrinkles on his narrow face to deepen, as he grumbled to the old man standing at his side. Others began to speak out in Japanese.

"Toki, how are we doing?" Denton said.

"Not very well."

"What do you suggest we do?"

"Wait a moment if you're able."

"Foolishness." It was Chiura. His finger pointed upward, the wide sleeve of his overcoat falling back to expose his scrawny wrist. He pulled away from Denton's side. "You see sky. It will snow in few hours. You see those boys inside. No covers. Only tents. You want them freeze to death? Or you want us try? Foolish." He put his bony finger to his temple. "Who more foolish, you or me? I try. You yell. You more foolish, I think."

Mr. Seko shrank back from his bullying stance and was left glaring at Toki. The crowd began to call out to Chiura to go in, that they would trust him to tell them what he saw. "But not the white men," they yelled.

"So you want *hakujin* not go in with me? That what you want?" Chiura's voice rose to a squeak.

Denton worried. This was a mistake. The army would never allow Chiura to go in alone. What would happen when the crowd had to be told that?

"Yes, Tamagata-san. You enter and we will trust what you have to tell us." It was the young woman who had hung on Herm's arm.

"Wonderful move," Herm growled.

Denton was about to say something when Chiura laughed.

"Foolishness again. We need white men. But I tell them what to say, you can trust that. Okay?" He turned to Denton with the question. Chiura smiled, but the Issei's eyes held a demand that said, you'd better back me up if you know what is good for us.

"Correct," Denton said without hesitation. "The member of the *Daihyo Sha Kai* shall determine the questions to be asked." Denton didn't chance a glance at Herm, but only hoped that he didn't show even a twitch of disagreement. "So, may we proceed in peace?"

Chiura chuckled as the crowd parted. Denton thought, Chiura is one crafty guy.

Herm, Denton, Toki and Chiura, accompanied by a soldier, slogged through the slushy trodden snow and mud of the prison yard toward a line of army tents. The wet seeped through Denton's leather shoes. The prisoners remained at the fence, following their progress with angry shouts in Japanese.

Their delegation moved under the flaps of the tent entrance to find a dim, cold space, twenty feet long, lined with two rows of canvas cots. Men and boys lay on their thin beds wrapped in whatever scraps of fabric they had managed to scavenge. Two kerosene heaters had been set up in the aisle between the beds, but they gave off more stench than warmth. The prisoners outside had expressed angry outrage as they'd passed by; in here they found a sullen and listless silence. The boys on the cots—those who weren't trembling with chills—looked up with dulled eyes and mumbled through mauve lips.

Herm's hand covered the forehead of a young man who was tossing from side to side, his eyes glassy, his shirt soaked.

"He's burning up. Even out here."

The soldier accompanying them said, "We got a lot like this one."

"What are you doing about it?" Denton said, keeping his voice calm.

"We don't have no orders. I ain't a doctor neither. But I don't like it. Scares me. I don't care what they done, it ain't right."

"This very bad." Chiura Tamagata unwrapped his grey knit scarf and placed it lengthwise over the curled body of a boy who looked no older than fourteen.

"*Arigato*," the boy whispered as tears filled his eyes.

Denton recognized him as one of the boys who worked in the motor-pool. He'd heard that some of them were in here for the crime of speaking Japanese on the night of the disturbance.

"Anyhow, they shoulda thought ahead before doing all that riot stuff," the soldier said as they walked single file between the cots.

"Spare us the commentary," Herm snapped back.

"Sorry, sir, it was just my thoughts," the soldier said, and kept walking.

While a hundred men were detained outside in the five tents, a hundred more were crowded into five barracks dorms. The rooms were warmer from the heat of twenty bodies, but the air, malodorous from unwashed bodies, vomit and the stink of diarrhea, seemed devoid of sufficient oxygen for human existence.

No one approached them as they made their way through one dorm after another, but Denton recognized many of the prisoners. These were men taken in from Nebo Mota's earlier demonstration, the mass funeral Nebo had staged, when he'd used Seiko Kitamara's death for his own ends. Mota should come see what suffering his heroics had brought on these men. But to be fair, Denton thought, how could Mota have anticipated such cruelty from the administration? Denton made mental notes of all the names he knew. He could at least carry news out to their families. His chest ached even picturing his visits to their rooms. Denton had to fight against averting his eyes from the scene. He maintained his self-discipline by reminding himself that he was here to bear witness to this tragedy. But he felt ashamed to be seeing it. He was ashamed to be a part of a system that would do this to other human beings.

"What about the cage?" Herm asked the soldier when they left the last dorm. They stood outside, next to the reeking latrines. "We'd like to see it."

"Sorry. You can't see the cage." The soldier shook his head. His expression became more opaque than usual.

"And why is that, soldier?" Herm said. When he didn't answer, Herm said, "I'm Katz, head of Internal Security. Are you trying to tell me the cage is off limits to me?"

Denton watched Herm's face. Herm had hedged his bets on this one. Herm wasn't even sure if there was a "cage" employed here like the one used for solitary confinement in Manzanar. It looked like he'd won the bet.

"Sir, I think I have to call Colonel Benedict on that one, sir, if you please."

"Then why don't you do just that," Herm said, keeping his voice low and composed. "I'll go with you and we'll see if we can get him on the phone."

Herm left with the soldier, and the rest of them decided to check the latrines while they waited.

Denton was almost knocked over by the fetid stench when they entered. He had to hold his hand over his nose and breathe shallowly, but even so he gagged. There were no stalls around the toilet bowls. There were ten urinals and ten bowls, the latter caked with feces, set on floors that were pooled with liquid and more solid matter. It was as bad as the early days in camp when the latrines had erupted because the systems had been hastily dug and couldn't accommodate the sudden heavy use.

Denton squeezed his eyes closed as he backed out the prison latrine door. Clearly no lessons had been learned from the administration's early mistakes and omissions.

"I got permission. I don't know why that guy keeps giving it to me." Herm said, meeting them outside the latrines. "I hope you fellows are ready for this. They say they've got Koso Shinahara in there."

"Shinahara-san? He *Daihyo Sha Kai*," Chiura said, looking surprised. "He Hawaiian guy from Manzanar. Big guy. I know Shinahara."

"We can thank Mota directly for this one," Herm hissed at Denton as they entered a cement block building on the far side of the stockade area, set against the fence.

The door opened before Denton could respond, and a soldier moved aside to let them in. The square room had no windows and felt airless. It was cold but stuffy with the stink of urine, days-old perspiration and a hint of excrement. A bare, dim lightbulb hung from the low ceiling. Denton froze with shock. In the center of the room was a metal cage, a massive cube of shiny black steel, an enclosure more unforgiving than the herding pens for cattle on their way to slaughter. On the side of the cage nearest to them, the soles of a man's shoes, looking small and vulnerable, pressed against the grid of two-inch-wide strips of thick bolted steel. A body lay in checkerboard shadow on a metal cot that was held up by a chain fastened to the roof of the steel cube.

"Koso. Koso Shinahara. We've come to talk to you," Denton said when no one else spoke.

Metal screeched against metal as Koso slowly sat up. He shifted closer to their side until his dark eyes appeared in a two-inch opening in the steel grid. Through the other spaces they could see that he was wrapped in an army blanket. "Tamagata-san," Koso Shinahara whispered hoarsely.

"*Hai*, Shinahara-san," the old man barked.

"Speak English," the soldier said.

"We here visit, Shinahara-san," Chiura said, glancing at Denton as though to get permission. His voice trembled.

Denton nodded.

"What you want, Shinahara-san?" Chiura asked. "What you need?"

Denton felt Toki step back. Denton glanced over and saw that Toki was leaning against the cement wall, his face a sickly beige.

"Cigarettes. Tell the manager of the Co-op over there that I want cigarettes and I want to get the hell out of here. Hey, Honda, you hear me, I want cigarettes," Koso Shinahara challenged, his voice rasping from disuse but as aggressive as Denton remembered it. "I can't stand up in this damn thing." Koso Shinahara stood to demonstrate. His head hit the top even with his knees bent. Denton realized for the first time that the cage was only five feet high by five feet wide and the same in length. Koso was at least five inches taller than his cage.

"Don't forget me, Honda," Shinahara continued to reproach Toki.

Denton was torn between horror at what he saw and sympathy for Toki, who remained accused and silent against the wall. He couldn't understand why Toki should be attacked.

"How long have you been in here, Shinahara?" Herm asked.

"Since the demonstration. End of October. I don't know what day it is."

"It's November 17. You've been in here for over two weeks."

Shinahara sank down onto the steel cot, all his belligerence seeping out. "Fucking long time," he whispered.

They signed themselves out in the sentry house by the front gate. As the gate was opened, clanking and squealing, Denton saw a man his own age, dressed in dirty blue jeans and a traditional Japanese worker's jacket, and a woman, crouched on opposite sides of the fence. The prisoner and the woman cried unabashedly, their foreheads touching through the metal links.

The mass of men and women on the outside rushed forward begging, weeping, and screaming at Denton and the others.

"We're going to do all we can to help," Denton tried to yell over the din, but it was futile. They drowned his voice. Denton saw Toki being buffeted by the physical force of the desperate crowd. They had to get out of there before more harm was done or another disruption ensued.

After they'd gotten twenty yards from the stockade, the families seemed to give up hope of assistance, and began to drift back toward the stockade. Denton and Toki paused a moment to watch their sad retreat; a defeated people crossing the bleak expanse of black mud and slush. Herm and Chiura kept walking.

"Why do you think the colonel let us see the conditions? Let us see the cage?" Denton asked Toki.

"Perhaps he is issuing a warning," Toki said, his voice constricted.

"Of course. You're right. He wants word sent through the camp that this is what will happen if you rebel."

"I believe so." Toki stood very straight with his hands pushed into his coat pockets. His face, which had regained its ruddy color, showed no emotion except for a slight worry crease that had developed between his eyes. "We must be cautious. Must think each step through."

"Toki, I'm sorry about what happened in there."

"Shinahara mocked my efforts in the Co-op," Toki said. "His insulting behavior mocked all our efforts."

"He's been pretty beat up. Maybe we should make allowances," Denton said, surprised by Toki's response.

Toki turned stiffly and stared at Denton. "It is the Japanese way to maintain composure and dignity no matter what has been taken from us. I'm sorry, Denton, but I humbly disagree with you on this."

Toki began to walk and Denton kept pace with him. Denton felt frightened. He could hear Toki's hurt beneath his stern and stoic words; at the same time, he was dismayed by Toki's total lack of sympathy for Shinahara's situation. But maybe it was better to let Toki calm down, Denton thought. They were all shaken by this experience, all reacting irrationally. Denton wished he had someone to talk this over with. He thought of Esther. He longed to talk with her the way they used to.

Ahead of them Herm and Chiura disappeared around the corner. Denton and Toki found the two men leaning against the front of the warehouse, their heads back, breathing deeply, Chiura barely as tall as Herm's chest.

Herm opened his eyes when he sensed Denton's and Toki's presence. In spite of the cold wind, perspiration crept down the sides of Herm's flushed face. His curly red-brown hair was matted with moisture. He wiped his sleeve across his upper lip.

"This is my fault," Herm said.

"How can this be your fault alone? What about my part in this?" Denton said, carefully, sensing that Herm was close to the breaking point.

"Denton, pal, you're going to have to imagine a situation that doesn't involve you in a pivotal way, if that's possible."

Chiura and Toki began to walk away.

"Where are you two going?" Denton yelled, suddenly angered by their leaving. "You can't just leave like that. We're in this together, the four of us. We need a strategy before we face anyone in the camp, the administration or the residents."

Chiura opened his eyes wide in surprise, but he came closer. Toki remained where he was with a neutral expression on his face, as though he had nothing to contribute to the matter at hand. Denton knew how upset Toki was, but his impassiveness angered Denton further.

"This is my business," Herm shouted. "I'm the head of camp security. This happened because I wasn't firm enough with the *Hoshidan* and with my own security staff. I didn't keep control and this is the fucking result. I was a damn sob-sister and we're all paying for it."

"You're not helping matters," Denton said.

"Don't you worry that I'm going to turn in my resignation. I'm going to stay right here till the end. But you stay away, Jordan, with any highfaluting theories about this filthy mess. This is what you get when liberals like us forget the viciousness of those soldiers and Andross. We think we can make everything nice with decent acts. Instead we just leave an opening for the likes of Andross to do his dirty work."

"Sounds like you're the one with the fancy theories," Denton said.

Herm grimaced and looked up at the sky. He was silent for a moment as though listening to an interior argument. "You're right. I can't indulge myself this way," he said, pushing off the wall. "So fellows, how are we going to tell this story?"

Chapter Twenty-Two

Denton nursed his scotch as he waited for Herm in the mahogany-stained, wood-paneled barracks that served as the army's dining hall. He could be anywhere in America. There were red-and-white-checked tablecloths on square wooden tables. There were even old Chianti bottles with dripping candles in the center of each table. Ferdie Franza, who set up this franchise for the administration, brought his personal taste to the task. Denton disliked Ferdie, and suspected that Ferdie stole meat from the internees' supply warehouses, but he'd never done anything about it. The man was the least of the problems in the camp. Denton had set his sights higher, he used to say to Esther, and Ferdie was too low to bother about. Tonight he wished he'd gotten the bastard. He wished he'd gone after every single one of the creeps who thought they had a right to break the rules just because they were in power, and still saw themselves as morally better than the internees. In the stockade he'd felt the cumulative effect of all the little character flaws, snide remarks, racial slurs, half-truths and petty thefts that he'd turned his back on in camp, thinking the bigger picture was more important than the everyday dishonesties. He hadn't wanted to waste his energy on those petty incidents and his friendship with Herm gave them both a place where they could blow off steam. But all the little atoms put together could make for an explosion and that's exactly what had happened. This place had blown sky high, shattering into tiny pieces that were impossible to patch together again.

What they'd found in the stockade had sickened him like nothing else in his life. He knew that worse brutality was going on in the world, but this was his own land, his own people. The cruelty they'd witnessed wasn't supposed to happen in a democracy.

Herm had gone directly to Andross's office after their visit to the stockade. Andross had ridiculed Herm for his concern, stopping just short of calling him a traitor. Colonel Benedict had been worse, Herm said, "And that after the bigwig had given his permission." The colonel had said, "This is our charge, Mr. Katz. Your bailiwick has been clearly enough defined and it doesn't include the new holding area. I'm afraid you've overstepped."

At least Denton's visit to the hospital had been more productive. He'd met with Joe Miller about the doctor going to the stockade to check on the health of the prisoners. Alice Hamilton had sat in on their meeting, saying she might as well take notes, "for posterity, if nothing else." When they'd finished and Joe had agreed to go directly to Colonel Benedict, Alice walked out with Denton. Grabbing her coat as they passed the nurse's station, she said, "Could I ask for a favor?"

"Sure, what's that?"

"I'm off early and I wouldn't mind a lift," she said slipping one arm into her coat.

He reached over and caught the lapel to help her with the other sleeve, and felt her heat on his hand and wrist. Denton was about to say he didn't have the car, when he remembered he'd left it at the administration building. But he didn't want to meet Herm coming out of Andross's office. He didn't want Herm to see them.

"Sure thing," he said, struggling to calm his shameful giddiness. "I left the car at the administration building. I'll get it and come back for you."

"Hell, no. I'll go with you," she said. "I can use the fresh air."

She was silent during the drive. He kept thinking he should make conversation, but he couldn't come up with anything to say. He drove straight to her barracks.

"You found it all by yourself," she said when he pulled up and stopped.

"Your directions from the other day are seared into my memory," he said, laughing to cover up the truth of what he said.

"That's a good sign." She smiled at him, leaning closer. The right side of her face and her long hair were lit by the moon that sat over the roof of her building. Her skin looked smooth and silvery, and the deep side-dip of her hair was like liquid gold. "Maybe that means you're going to take me up on my offer of dinner after all."

"I don't think so, Miss Hamilton."

"Miss Hamilton?" She touched his arm.

"I'm sorry...Alice." He could barely speak.

"That's okay. I understand your conflict. All the same, I'd love it if you'd come by, and I sense you could use some company and a good listener about now." With that she opened the car door and stepped out.

He waited as she climbed the steps to her room. She went in, switched on a lamp and came back out to wave. Then she disappeared inside and he felt her absence in the cold air of the empty car. He touched the seat where she had been sitting and found it was still warm. Leaning over, he smelled the upholstery and discovered in it the faint scent of flowers.

Denton shook himself from his reverie when he saw Herm walking toward him across the half-filled dining room. The man's shoulders sagged.

"Hiya, buddy. I'm glad you suggested this. I can sure use it after today," Denton said.

"Same here."

Denton watched as Herm, with exaggerated care, unbuttoned his bulky tweed coat and slid out of it. Without the coat, Herm looked thinner than usual. He had dark circles beneath his eyes. His hair had started to grow back over his wound, creating a furry patch at his hairline. Denton remembered how Sylvia was fond of calling him her 'big bear'. Sylvia, a large woman herself, would grab hold of Herm, oblivious to company, and laughing, she would rub her hands through his hair and stroke his freckled face, saying, "I love my big brown bear." It was said with such affection that no one except Esther seemed embarrassed by it. Esther found this behavior more demonstrative than she liked to see in public.

Ferdie came over to greet Herm and take his drink order. He was a runt of a guy, short and skinny, which probably accounted for his swagger.

"Where the hell you been?" Ferdie asked Herm.

"I've been busy. There's a lot of work to be done out there, in case you hadn't noticed." Herm sat with one arm thrown over the back of his chair.

"Sure is. I always thought it would come to this. It's because of those liberal policies of the guy before, the other director, what was his name, Bennett? Yeah, that's it. You liked him though? You thought he was doing things right? Huh?"

Herm gave a slow smile back. He nodded his head. "Yup."

Ferdie laughed, seeing he wasn't going to get anywhere with that tack. "So how's the better half, Jordan, okay? I haven't seen her in a long time."

Denton reddened.

"She's in San Francisco visiting her parents for a week or two. Down there with my little girl."

"Hey, you should come here more often then." He laughed. "So what can I get you fellows? How about a round on me, seeing as how you're coming in here after a long vacation?"

"Why not," Herm said. "A bourbon for me."

"You, Jordan, how about it, another scotch?"

"Sure, Ferdie. Another scotch on the rocks for me."

When Ferdie disappeared around the corner of the bar, Denton turned to Herm.

"How are you doing?"

Herm shook his head. "I never thought I'd see such inhumanity in my own country."

"I was sitting here thinking the same thing," Denton said.

Ferdie reappeared with their drinks. "Bourbon for the big guy and scotch for the pacifist. Right?"

"Cut it out, Ferdie," Herm said.

"That's alright, it's what I am. Here's to you," Denton said, shoving his glass across the tabletop to tap Herm's. "Drink up, pal. See you later, Ferdie. We've got business to talk about."

"Don't want me eavesdropping, right?"

Denton sighed. "Right. Top secret government stuff."

Ferdie shrugged and left, sauntering across the room.

The murmur of noise from the other diners rose as Denton and Herm sat in mutual silence. Most of the customers were officers in uniform, and the only two civilian couples were Nancy and Tom McIntyre, and two Caucasian women who taught in the high school. Denton wondered what Esther was doing at this moment and whether she felt relieved to be away from here.

"I miss Sylvia really bad." Herm stirred his bourbon with his finger.

Denton returned his attention to his friend.

"I can see that." Denton took a sip of his drink, enjoying the sound of ice clinking against the glass, and the rush of alcohol through his veins. He allowed himself to imagine Alice Hamilton at the table, leaning toward him intimately.

"It seems like you never know how much you love your wife until she's away. Then you remember all over again why you fell in love. Do you know what I mean? Are you having the same feeling?"

"Maybe it's a little early to tell. Esther only left a few days ago. I'll tell you next week." Denton laughed. Had Herm guessed anything? He couldn't possibly have. He was the least suspicious person. Probably because he'd never had cause for guilt himself.

"You just wait. It's awful. I talked to Sylvia long distance after I got out of Andross's office. Needed her after what we saw today. I wanted to climb inside the telephone. I imagined her in there. I don't know how anybody as big as Sylvie could fit in the telephone, but I imagined that if I could make myself small I could climb in there and be in her arms in a second. It's hard going six months without real sex. Six damn months. Shit." He ran his hand over his face. Laughing, he blushed. "I don't usually talk about things like this."

"It's okay," Denton said, but felt himself drowning in his own erotic feelings. He'd been like that since dropping Alice Hamilton at her barracks. Barely fifteen minutes went by when there wasn't another illicit image floating into his consciousness, or another fantasy. He hadn't felt so constantly hard since he was an adolescent, and even then it hadn't been this bad. "I bet it's rough."

"You don't know the half of it. I think if I had those needs satisfied just once again, I wouldn't be feeling so terrible, so alone. Hell. I didn't even know this was what was bothering me. I thought I was all worked up about those bastards Andross and Colonel Benedict, and what we saw at the stockade, but maybe I just need a good... *fuck*." He whispered the last word, chuckling to himself as he drained his drink. "This is not my first drink tonight." Herm sat staring into the ice in the glass.

Feeling his own drink more with each sip, Denton thought how fine it would be to sit and share his real thoughts with this man. He'd never had that experience. When he talked intimately with anyone, it was always with women. The social worker he'd been infatuated with at the Farm Security Camp, or the Catholic woman at Berkeley who had counseled him on his choice to be a conscientious objector. Abby Holdman, that was her name. He had told her that he didn't believe in resolving disagreements with any kind of violence, even verbal, though he had to admit to verbal cruelty in the fire of political discussions. And marriage. Marriage, he confessed to Abby, had

191

brought him the closest to violence, even physical. "But have you actually ever raised your hand?" Abby wanted to know. "No, I haven't even come close," he admitted. "Maybe because I know Esther wouldn't stand for it, and I'd be on the street faster than my blow could land." That didn't count, Abby said. Would he consider violence if he stopped to think first, she'd asked? He hoped not, he said, but he couldn't be sure. That was as close as he'd ever allowed another human being—except Esther—into his real doubts and muddled thoughts. But even with Esther, had he ever really told her what he was feeling at the moment he felt it? Sitting across from Herm, he yearned to speak from his heart, to unburden himself to another man, and to share the peculiar, intriguing joy of lusting after a woman.

Herm looked up and said, "I sure would like another round. Why don't we let ourselves get a little pie-eyed?"

"I don't know." Denton began to make a mental list of all the things he had to do, the people he had to contact before the Co-op meeting with the *Daihyo Sha Kai*. And he had to cancel the dinner with Alice. "Hell, why not." He raised his hand for Ferdie, pointing to their glasses.

"Let me ask you a question," Herm's speech was slurred after a fourth round and a barely touched dinner of roast beef with mashed potatoes.

"What's that?" Denton had cleaned his plate, partly from hunger and partly because he was feeling out of control from the amount of alcohol he'd put away. On the third drink he'd lost all sense of his responsibilities, exulting in the possibility of success in work, love, you name it. Euphoria had swept through him, lifting his spirits up out of Tule Lake, to a wonderful future filled with passion and important contributions to the world, hikes in the snow-covered mountains, all a man could ask for. But after the fourth drink, he'd grown thick and groggy, and fearful that all his usual defenses were weakened to the point that he might betray himself. That's when he began to wolf down the dry meat and tasteless potatoes.

"Why do you love Esther?"

"Oh, God, what a question. I don't know. I love her because I love her. She's smart. She's beautiful."

"I don't love Sylvie for that. Nope. You know what I love about Sylvie?"

"Go ahead, tell me," Denton said, though he was worried about where this was taking them.

"I love how she smells." He wrinkled his flushed nose. "Everyplace. Her upper lip, behind her ears, her armpits. Her down there. Yes, especially her twat. I love it. Always did. From the first time I sniffed around it."

Denton glanced over his shoulder. A couple of officers had sat down nearby. But they were deep in conversation.

"I'm embarrassing you." Herm leaned closer and whispered. "I can tell. Don't you like how Esther smells?"

Denton laughed nervously. When he did his ribs hurt. He couldn't talk this way. It had been one thing to try to say he missed Esther, and over dinner he'd hinted at some of his and Esther's latest disagreements. Not easy at all, but he'd done his best, and for the most part Herm had been more interested in relating his own troubles. But now the guy was staring at him through foggy eyes, waiting for the truth that supposedly came with drink.

"Yes, of course, I do."

"How?"

"Jesus, I'm not going to say it. Stop this."

"Hmm." Herm sat back in his chair. He began to make fork trails in the mashed potatoes. "Sorry. Went too far with that one." He shoveled meat and potatoes onto the fork and brought it in an unsteady path to his mouth. "Another question," he said, chewing.

Denton didn't respond.

"Have you ever thought you could like how another woman smelled? Let us say, if you came up close to this other woman and you started to like how she smelled, would that be a betrayal?" He took another shaky bite of potato, and sat waiting for a reply.

"What are you trying to get at?" Denton asked, his voice sharp. "Are you trying to get at me with this? Is that it?"

"Hey." Herm's wide forehead creased as if he didn't understand.

So Herm had been playing with him all the time. Herm knew. Herm was angry about it. Herm was going to teach him a lesson. That's what this was about.

"Don't play games with me, damn it. Just ask directly."

Herm shook his head as though to clear it. "You've got me wrong. I was only being foolish. Drunken banter. A guy who doesn't want to talk about suffering. Wants a couple of hours forgetting what he's seen and not thinking about how crappy people can be to each other. If I've stumbled in where I shouldn't be, let me just back out quietly." He reached under his jacket and tucked his shirt down into his pants, shifting his heavy body from one buttock to the other. He looked up, suddenly sober.

Denton saw the moment of realization on Herm's face. Denton straightened his knife and fork on the plate, trying to calm his panic. What did Herm know? Had Herm seen him and Alice in the car tonight? How would Herm see it?—He'd see it as Denton with the goy nurse. Denton and the gorgeous nurse.

"It'll kill her," Herm said. He stared at Denton in dead silence. "No, I didn't have anything up my sleeve. That isn't my style. I just now figured it out. And I wouldn't be your friend if I didn't say I think it would kill Esther if she ever found out."

Denton hovered between suspicion and belief. He wanted to tell all, but he was too afraid.

"She seems tough, but she's fragile," Herm kept on. "And a shiksa, if you don't mind my saying, would be brutal on her."

Anger replaced Denton's desire to confide his feelings, but he battled against it. He chose restraint.

"Nothing has happened. Nothing. Promise. Scout's honor." He raised his right hand in the gesture of his childhood.

"But she taped you up, didn't she? She touched your body, your naked flesh." Herm swallowed.

"Yes, she taped me. She's a nurse."

Behind them the officers burst into loud laughter. The rest of the dining room had cleared out. Denton realized he hadn't even noticed the McIntyres leaving. Ferdie was standing in the archway that led out to the bar, counting numbers on a pad.

"Did you go to the hospital to be taped?"

"Is this the third degree?" He felt sweat running down his sides, soaking the bandages.

"Nope." Herm took his napkin from his lap and put it on the table. "All I knew was that you didn't report the attack. And I have to say that since our visit to the stockade this afternoon I've begun to sympathize with your motives. But now I've started to put two and two together. You could only have gotten away with keeping it quiet if someone else went along with you."

"You and Andross," Denton mumbled.

"I heard that. I'd prefer if you didn't equate me with that man." He breathed deeply. Leaning forward, and putting his large hand on Denton's arm, he said, "Listen. I love you. Don't get embarrassed. But I do. I admire you. But keep things untangled. Don't let one secret create another. People are going to get hurt if you do that. And I'm afraid it'll be all the people I love the most."

Denton sat frozen, Herm's hand like a stone on his arm.

"Well, the business about the attack is out in the open now. Andross confronted me with it."

"And the other business?"

"There's nothing, I tell you. I haven't had anything to do with her and I'm not going to."

Herm squeezed his arm. "Good. That's what I wanted to hear. I love you, you know."

"I know. You just told me."

"Hmm." Herm released his arm. "So I did."

*   *   *

Outside the dining hall Denton parted from Herm, who took off in his jeep. Herm didn't invite him over for another drink, and Denton didn't suggest it. It would have been too uncomfortable to pass even close to Alice Hamilton's room with his friend now that Herm had pried into his infatuation. Denton walked slowly through the night. The drink had numbed his pain, but he felt stiff and old, and very tired. He had no idea how late it was, but the absence of human activity made it seem like the middle of the night. Even so, when he walked by Sy Topol's barracks and saw the lights still on, he didn't hesitate to knock. Perhaps the whiskey had emboldened him, or maybe he had a new sense of himself since Alice had let him know she was attracted to him. Whatever it was, he felt he had a right to ask Sy if he had given information to Ted Andross.

"What the hell is this? Do we have another problem?" Sy asked when he opened the door and recognized Denton.

"No, I just wanted to ask you a question."

"I'm almost in bed. It can't wait?"

Denton felt himself sway and realized he was more affected by the drinks than he'd realized. He put his hand up to catch the doorjamb and Sy stepped back.

"Herm and I got a little tanked up," Denton laughed.

"I can see that. Wait a minute. I'm going to get my coat. I don't want to disturb Sarah." He closed the door.

Denton walked heavily down the stairs, wishing he hadn't done this. His judgment had gone all to hell.

He started to shiver, the damp air cutting into him through his coat. But he didn't really tremble from the cold, he trembled from the accumulated physical and emotional hurts, the confusion of the past few days, the conflicting desires that jangled through him as though trying to shake him into a different man. His teeth rattled. He clenched his jaw to make the chattering stop. Sy came out the door, backlit by a soft glow before he turned the light off. Denton felt timid and small as Sy came down the stairs.

"Do you want to walk a little?" Sy said in a low voice.

"I don't know," Denton answered. Why had he done this, come here? How was he going to extricate himself? He took a few steps in Sy's direction and realized that it was better to be moving.

"I'll walk you home and then I'll come back alone."

"That's not necessary," Denton said.

"I know it's not necessary, but it's good to be out. I feel cooped up in there after too many hours with the baby. It sure is a full-time job. I don't know how Sarah does it day in and day out, but she seems to love fussing over Annie." He chuckled. "She sure is cute. And you do get attached awfully quickly, don't you think?"

"Sure." Denton's body still betrayed him with its trembling. He could hear Sy trying to defuse the situation. Sy knew he was upset. He probably even knew why, and wanted to avoid a confrontation and thought he could by shifting attention to family talk. They were already at Tom and Nancy McIntyre's barracks. In a moment they would turn the corner and be at his place.

"Why did you go to Andross with that story?" Denton blurted out.

Sy stopped in the beam of the searchlight that was trained on the area. Sy looked so damn innocent, Denton thought. Incredulous that he might be accused of anything.

"What are you saying?"

"I'm saying that I was in Andross's office the other afternoon and he knew about my getting beaten up, something I'd deliberately kept quiet because I didn't want to exacerbate the situation any more, and then he seemed to know that Alice Hamilton treated me and didn't report the incident, and I thought to myself, How in hell, who in hell could have passed that information to the director and I thought, There's one man who has his fingers on the pulse, and there's one man who has access to our director and he is one and the same person." The words pounded out of him with a force and rhythm he wasn't familiar with, out through trembling lips, out of a body that shuddered with each phrase.

"You'd better calm down, Denton. Better get a hold of yourself. You're too involved. It's not going to help anyone if you can't stand back and be objective." His skinny face took on a stern, schoolteacher expression. He pointed at Denton with his left forefinger as he spoke.

"Stop jabbing at me, damn it. What does objective mean in this situation, Sy? Does it mean concurring with the decision to throw two hundred men into a prison within a prison without adequate clothing, housing, and food? Have you been there? Have you seen what those men and boys are enduring? If you have, how the hell can you stand there and tell me to be objective?"

"Yes, I've been to the stockade. And I've had my own informal discussions with Ted and the colonel about the adjustments I feel need to be made."

"Adjustments? What kind of adjustments?"

Sy put his hands to the sky and then clasped them on top of his head. "What is this? Did you get me out here to talk policy? It's hardly the time. We can make a date and do this tomorrow. I'd like nothing better than to have one of our good talks again. We haven't really spoken for far too long. I honor our friendship and our working relationship. I have the utmost respect for you. You don't seem to remember that these days."

"Did you tell Andross or not?"

Sy dropped his hands to his side. He squinted as though he couldn't properly see Denton. "I don't know what you mean."

"Did you or did you not tell Andross about my getting beat up? Shoot straight. No meandering, please. I'm cold, tired and too drunk to last much longer." His body had stopped shaking and felt like dead weight. It took all his strength to remain upright.

"I didn't have to tell him, he already knew."

"And about Alice Hamilton taping me up and not reporting it?"

"I think he knew that, too."

"You think."

"Yes, if I remember it correctly. I would have to check my notes."

"Oh, so you keep notes on the activities of your honored friends."

"You know I take notes on everything. It's my training." He no longer squinted. Instead he stared directly into Denton's eyes, a glint of malice destroying his attempt to look sanguine.

"Do you know who masterminded the attack on me?" Denton kept his voice noncommittal.

"Dent, c'mon. I don't know."

"Damn it, you must have picked up rumors out there during your daily rounds."

"I'm freezing. I want to go home. Let's stop this."

"Sure thing," Denton said disgustedly. "I'm pretty sick of this conversation, too." He turned without shaking Sy's hand.

As he walked away he could feel that Sy remained standing where he'd left him. He knew he'd upset Sy, maybe even hurt him, but right now Denton didn't give a damn.

*   *   *

He waited until he saw movement between the parted curtains of her lighted window. She walked by, combing her long hair. She stopped before the window in her robe, combing and combing that reddish-blond, streaked hair. How gracefully she bent her head as she swept the comb through. He wished he could will her out into this glorious night to look at the stars. She would find him here and invite him in. They would drink and make love and talk all night. He shook his head at his brazenness. Why the hell had he come here? He felt like a fourteen-year-old standing outside the house of a girl he had a crush on, hopelessly incomplete and unrequited.

He had no business being out here secretly watching this woman. He was drunk. Pathetic. Dangerous in his lack of control. He was on the rat's edge of existence these days, scurrying around this way and that, always on the verge of doing something shameful.

"Good night, Miss Hamilton," he whispered to the woman combing her beautiful hair. He turned and tried not to stagger as he found his way home.

Chapter Twenty-Three

"I have no knowledge where Mota-san is," Tony Kato said when Denton, having put off the inevitable long enough, had come to Nebo Mota's barracks for a talk. It was whispered that Nebo had gone underground for fear of being picked up by the MP's and taken to the stockade. Denton had heard Nebo was sleeping in a different barracks each night, but he thought perhaps the rumors were wrong and that he'd find Nebo here.

Kato stood belligerently in Mota's doorway, one elbow against the doorjamb, leaving Denton outside to endure the stinging sleet. Denton barely knew Tony Kato, had only met him a few months earlier when he'd arrived from Jerome Camp. Tony Kato had the air of a street thug, with an expression of derision cemented on his face.

"If you see him, I'd appreciate your telling him I'd like to talk," Denton said, shivering as the sharp wet moisture stung his face and ran into his collar. "Do you know that Andross has lifted the ban on the *Nihongakko*?"

Kato laughed. "I'm afraid Mota-san and the rest of us have bigger matters on our minds, like the fate of fifty farmworkers who are freezing in lean-tos and tents out at the farm while they protest the scabs Andross brought in. And the *Daihyo Sha Kai* is concerned with worse conditions at the stockade. Why don't you see what you can get the director to do about that, before you speak to us?"

"Don't you understand that I'm trying to do my best for you?" Denton thought he glimpsed a figure behind Kato in the lighted room. Nebo could be in there.

Kato laughed again, this time with scorn. He bowed extravagantly. "We thank you very much, Mr. Jordan-sama, for all you are doing for us. I will be certain to relay your message of support to my comrades."

When Denton reached the middle of the no-man's land between the administration and the residents, the sky opened. The sleet had turned to rain and drenched him through his wool coat, plastered his hair to his head, and filled his shoes so that each step felt like he was walking barefoot through a swamp. He continued to be a pitiful specimen. He had looked pathetic in front of Kato. Why hadn't he been able to figure out how to reach the guy? He began to run, slipping and sliding in the black mud until a sharp pain in his ribs brought him back to a slow sloshing trudge across the firebreak.

*   *   *

An hour later Denton opened his eyes to see Toki standing over him instead of Harry Huroto, the Co-op's barber, who had finished with the shave and was applying hot towels to Denton's face.

"What is it, Toki?"

"If I may speak with you privately?"

All talk in the room had stopped. In the mirrors Denton saw eyes averted down the line of barber chairs and knew that everyone was listening.

"Of course."

He paid Harry and got his shoes, which were still soaked. He lifted his soggy coat from the peg beside the door, bowed to the silent assemblage of men and boys, and went with Toki onto the outside steps.

Toki opened his umbrella. "No umbrella? No galoshes? My Sumiko would tell you that you'll catch your death of cold."

"My wife says the same. So what is it, Toki? What bad news now?" he asked as they began to walk.

"There's a rumor that the director ordered the last of the striking farmworkers back to camp and that he asked Colonel Benedict to send military police to the farm to bring them in."

Toki kept walking toward the sentry gate as he talked. His body was as erect as a soldier's, his head pulled back. Denton knew that the worse Toki felt, the more upright his bearing.

"I have heard the workers are expected in the motor pool shortly. I would like to witness it with my own eyes, if that's possible. I don't want a dispute at the sentry gate. That's why I'm asking you to accompany me." He hardly moved his mouth as he spoke and did not turn to look at Denton.

They sloshed through black puddles, lashed by wind and rain, until their trousers were wet to the thigh despite the umbrella. At the sentry shack, Denton shouted, "We're going for a meeting with the director." When they reached the motor pool garage, Denton looked up to where Castle Rock should have been, to find that it had disappeared into a shroud of torrential rain.

The mood in the garage was as gloomy as he'd ever seen it, the floor muddy, smelling of crankcase oil, and the cold cavernous room dimly lit with bare bulbs. The motor pool had been a hotbed of resistance during and since the loyalty questionnaires. Paul Smith, the manager, hadn't helped matters. He had no understanding of Japanese culture and would bark orders without leaving time for polite interaction. Today the young men who serviced the vehicles sat idly on piles of tires and oil cans along the back wall. They smoked. A few played cards. No one acknowledged Toki and Denton when they entered.

Denton spotted Paul Smith through the window of his office.

"I suggest we talk to him rather than try to break through the boys' wall of silence. Is that all right with you?" Denton quietly asked Toki.

"I agree," Toki said.

"How do you like my work force out there?" Paul Smith complained, brushing his hand across his blond crewcut. "It's the damned status quo strategy. No respecti, no worki. Excuse me, Mr. Honda, but I'm full up to here with them. They refuse to speak English. Most of them were born here, for heaven's sake. I think half of them are faking it, pretending to speak Japanese, but really talking gibberish, if you know what I mean."

"Perhaps," Toki said, his face impassive.

Denton guessed how angry Toki must be, but since Toki didn't speak up, Denton knew he couldn't either.

The floor began to rumble and the motor pool boys rose as one and moved toward the garage door.

"They must be coming in," Paul Smith said, taking his green mackintosh off the coat rack. "The great striking heroes, home from the battlefield."

Two army trucks drove into the garage and two more were left to stand in the thundering rain. Tarpaulins had been thrown over the tops of the vehicles, but the men underneath were soaked through. Denton and Toki stood back as dozens of farmworkers were helped down from the trucks by the younger men from the motor pool. The farmworkers were old Isseis, a hardscrabble lot—stoop laborers, fruit pickers, men who had once leased their own land. Men who could take a pounding from any kind of weather or any kind of person. Denton had seen them many times on the camp farm, never letting the ravages of wind, rain, or relentless sun stop them from plowing, seeding, harrowing, weeding, spraying, sorting potatoes, digging onions, harvesting broccoli, weighing and boxing the yield of beets, cabbage and beans. These men would do anything to bring in a crop, and they had succeeded beyond all expectation. The farmers in the immediate area and throughout the county were in awe of this Issei crew. Much as the local horseradish farmers wanted to disparage the Japanese, much as the community in the town of Tule Lake railed at having this "Jap prison in our back yards," they had to admire what these fellows could grow. Denton remembered all of this as he watched the men stagger off the trucks. They were emaciated, trembling from exposure, their skin the color of eggplants, their fingers like the talons of raptors, frozen wrinkled claws of bone and gristle.

"Jesus Christ," Denton said. "This is the way we've thanked them."

He could barely watch as the farmworkers huddled before fires the motor pool boys had built in empty oil barrels. He knew without being told by Tony Kato that when Andross brought the scabs in two and a half weeks ago these men had been kicked out of their bunkhouses. Since then they had been sleeping in tents and lean-tos in this inclement weather, and cooking for themselves. Denton knew from his days of doing arbitration for them how determined they could be. These men believed enough in their rights to push themselves to the brink of illness and even risk death.

Toki had been silent throughout. He only spoke as they were leaving the garage. "The question is, did Nebo Mota assist in their struggle, or contribute to the defeat of these brave men?"

Denton found himself without an answer to Toki's question.

*   *   *

Denton and Toki recruited Herm and Sy to help them get a meeting with Andross. The project director agreed to the meeting, but refused to have Toki present, asserting that he was not an official representative of any party in this matter. Denton argued with

Andross but, getting nowhere, he decided this was no time to stand on principle. Denton had to inform Toki of the director's decision in the outer office with Stella Andross rat-tat-tatting on her typewriter.

"Don't worry yourself, Denton," Toki said. "I have far too much work waiting for me anyway. I'm only glad I could bring the matter to your attention."

They had moved out to the porch of the administration building and were watching the cascade of rainwater pour off the eaves and flood the parade grounds. Herm stood out there with them, leaning with one leg bent up against the wall of the building.

"But here, Denton, take the umbrella. Without galoshes, you will catch your death," Toki said, thrusting his umbrella at Denton.

"Absolutely not," Denton said, backing off. "I will not take your umbrella just because I was too stupid to remember mine."

"I have a change of clothes in the Co-op," Toki went on.

"Herm, will you help me here?" Denton asked.

"My dear Mr. Honda," Herm said, bowing. "You've convinced me to take care of my foolish pal here and drive him back home when this damn meeting is over. Will that solve the problem?"

Toki grinned and bowed. "I accept the compromise. But you understand, I don't want to lose my advisor here to illness. You must stay with him until you're certain he has his galoshes, hat and umbrella. He may try to sneak out without them."

"I'll see to it that he's well covered. In every way. I won't allow any damn-fool sacrifices on his part," Herm said.

"Remember, he's tricky. Very Japanesey, in fact," Toki said.

Throughout this interchange, Denton recognized mutual sadness beneath the play and patter of humor. He knew that Toki was aware as well.

*   *   *

"In the first place I had no recourse, gentlemen. I had to bring in loyals from the other camps," Andross said. "It was a matter of national security. In the second place I had to remove those demonstrators. They could have frozen to death."

"Like they're doing in the stockade," Herm grumbled.

"What was that, Katz?" Andross shot back.

It was clear to Denton that Ted Andross was only putting up with this meeting and that it would come to an end the minute they stepped over some imaginary line of misconduct. He signaled to Herm to pull back.

"Nothing," Herm leaned forward, his elbows on his knees.

Herm had not wanted to come. "There's no hope with this guy," he told Denton. "I finally saw it when I came to him about the stockade. There's no budging him."

"I don't know what you fellows want of me," Ted Andross said. "I was caught like a fool between the *Hoshidan* and the army. The *Hoshidan* boys were using the farmworker holdouts as a rallying point. Anyway it's a *fait accompli.* All the strikers are safely back here. We'll get them medical attention so Mota and his fellows can't use their health as a rallying point. It'll simmer down in a few days, if you men will finally help me. We have to find that bastard Mota. He's gone underground. He's somewhere in camp hiding out, stirring things up. This proves he's nothing but a coward."

Andross swiveled to his left and got out of his chair. Coming around the desk, he pointed at Sy, who hadn't said a word and hadn't even taken his raincoat off, who sat there looking miserable.

"You agree with me, Topol, that things would be worse if I hadn't tightened the reins?"

Sy looked wearily from Denton and Herm to the director. Denton had never seen him so discouraged. Maybe if he took a stand once in a while, he wouldn't be so exhausted and hangdog, Denton thought.

"I don't know." Sy said. "I just don't know. All I can say is, I wish I didn't have to answer questions like that."

Chapter Twenty-Four

"**S**he's very tiny," Esther said to Parin as they hurried up Grandma Leah's street. Parin had met the old woman a year ago, but she didn't remember her. "She's almost as little as you are."

"How come?"

"Because she was always little, and now she's shrunk with age. I think she didn't eat very well when she was a child. She didn't grow properly. You'll love her. You'll love that she's not so much bigger than you are," Esther said, remembering how as a ten-year-old she had been enchanted to be as tall as an adult.

Esther would often go to stay with her on weekends, as she and Parin were going to do. Esther was hurrying because they'd left her mother's apartment later than she'd planned and the afternoon light was waning. She had to get to Grandma's before sunset, before the lighting of the Sabbath candles. She had always lit the candles with Grandma when she visited.

It had been clear all day, one of those perfect Bay Area afternoons when the sky is a piercing blue and the wind is constant but gentle. The gnarled oaks and cypresses that lined Grandma's street were silhouetted against a sky that was so luminous it seemed painted on glass. Leah had lived here for most of her married life, after a failed attempt at homesteading in North Dakota where three of her five children, including Judith, had been born in a sod house. But it was too difficult, Grandma had told her. "Like the Bible it was, with pestilence, with grasshoppers, and hail. No boils," she chuckled. "But the worst by us was the Jew-haters. They ripped our crops from the soil, on our faces they spat. By Saul, he would have stayed. By me, I could have stayed. But for the children, no."

Grandma stood on the front porch waiting for them, her hands clasped at her waist, her coat open, over a navy blue, perfectly pressed dress that reached to mid-calf of her bowed legs. On her feet were heavy black oxfords; the left shoe had the thicker sole to compensate for her shorter leg. Her gray frizzy hair was rolled away from her sweet, homely face. She looked like a frog, Esther had decided one day, a darling, benign but ugly frog.

"Grandma," Esther called. She knew by the way her grandmother turned her head toward the sound, but didn't look directly at her, that her eyes were failing.

Esther wrapped her arms around the tiny woman, smaller by inches than Esther remembered. Her back felt as strong and straight as ever. Maybe this was where Parin got her sturdy body.

"So, who's this?" Leah said, holding the hand that Parin had extended. She touched the top of Parin's head, her hair and her cheek.

"I'm Parin," Parin whispered.

"No!" Leah asked in mock surprise, her mouth curving into a smile. "Such a big girl, you've gotten?"

"I'm not so big." Parin said. "Am I, Mommy?"

"By me you are, my bubeleh, by me you are. And so beautiful, such a soft brown squirrel you are."

"I am?" Parin looked up to Esther.

Esther nodded yes.

"Like a squirrel, my bube." Leah turned and absently walked into the house. She closed the front door behind her, leaving them on the porch.

"What happened, Mommy? Can't we go in?"

"Of course, we can," Esther said. She's old, she thought. She's ninety years old. You should have expected this. "When people get old like Great-Grandma, they don't think as clearly as they once did. Just be nice to her. She's a very kind woman."

The living room was as it always had been, stuffed with heavy, fringed red velvet furniture and a dark red Oriental rug that Saul had bought from a Chinese man when he'd worked on the railroads in his early years in America. The elaborate brass menorah stood on the bookshelf under the windows that faced the street. Saul's desk was against the side wall, open, with his papers strewn about as though he were still alive, though he'd died five years earlier, just after Esther and Denton had married. Esther smiled to think of Grandpa Saul. He was so like Daddy.

Where Daddy was committed to his theories of evolution, for over forty years Saul had worked on his own life's endeavor, his book on

Jesus as a Jew and how Christianity was a bastardization of Judaism, and how the world would have been a better, safer place, if Jesus had remained true to his early upbringing. After his railroad job and his attempt at farming, Saul had ceased to earn a living. He spent his days "at his thinking and writing," Leah would say both reverently and with a mocking smile. Meanwhile Leah brought in the entire family income from the secondhand store in downtown Oakland. "Mother was a magician," Judith would say bitterly. "She could turn rags into gowns, and pennies into dollars, so that Father could continue with his absurd work. So that we could be fed and educated." But for all Mother's condemnation of her father and ridicule of her husband's private scholarship, Esther thought, Judith had picked her own father to marry.

Esther wondered if maybe she had also married a man like Grandpa and Daddy, one who was consumed by an overweening intellectual passion, a man with an iconoclastic way of life. Had she unknowingly recreated a Jewish tradition of supporting a man whose life's work existed outside a middle class norm, who would follow his conscience even when the rest of the world thought differently and condemned his choice?

"Mommy, I hear her," Parin whispered.

Esther did, too. She heard Grandma's deep alto voice intoning the prayer. "Shh," said Esther, putting her finger to Parin's lips. "Let's go to the kitchen, but you must promise not to talk."

They stood in the doorway of the kitchen. Grandma's back was to them. She had taken off her coat. The candle burned, but she still held the lit wooden match above its flame as she spoke the Sabbath prayer.

"*Boruch atah Adonai eloheynu Melech...*"

A peach-colored sky glowed through the window over the sink.

"*Haolam asher kidshanu...*"

The prayer entered Esther and filled her with sorrow for these terrible days and years of war. She listened as she had for many years as Grandma gave thanks, as Grandma paid homage to her beliefs, as Grandma lived the life of a Jew.

"*B'mitzvotav v'tsi-vanu...*"

The color outside grew more intense, as the emotions swelled within her. I am a Jew like Grandma, Esther found herself saying silently. I am a Jew. I am a Jew. I am a Jew. Shame engulfed her, inflaming her cheeks, as she remembered her conversation with Herm in the train station. He had tried to get her to acknowledge that Denton's decision to be a conscientious objector in this war was fraught with extra meaning because he was married to her, to a Jew. Herm had reprimanded her when she'd said it had nothing to do with religion. She heard him saying, "I know it's no longer about religion. In the Nazi's eyes we're a race." She had wanted him to shut up. She hadn't wanted anyone in that crowded waiting room to overhear them and discover she was Jewish. That was why Mother so enraged her. Mother kept pushing her to acknowledge that she was a Jew. But to admit that she was a Jew and to face the implications, was to be furious at Denton, was to want to scream at him, My people are being slaughtered over there and all you care about is your sacred, puny, self-serving pacifism. My people are dying and I am denying them and denying my mother and my father and denying my dearest grandmother.

"*L'hadlik ner shel yom tov.*"

She wept, though no tears fell from her eyes. What she mourned was too huge for mere tears. She mourned her people. She mourned the god that allowed their destruction. She lamented her own cowardice.

Esther gathered her daughter into the folds of her coat, held her close, rubbed her hands down Parin's cheeks, caressed her ears, and thought, I wish they were Jewish ears.

Grandma turned and stood in profile to the candlelight. Her little frog face, with its large nose and full lips, unseeing eyes and sturdy chin, was beautiful to behold. She smiled, obviously sensing that her granddaughter and great-granddaughter were there.

"*Boruch atah Adonai eloheynu melech,*" Esther began the Sabbath prayer again. Leah, smiling, joined with her, and speaking in unison they kindled a sacred light.

"*Haolam asher kidshanu b'mitzvotav v'tsi-vanu l'hadlik ner shel shabbos.*"

Chapter Twenty-Five

As the Director of Community Enterprises Denton usually attended the regular weekly meeting of the Co-op's Board of Directors. He was in a quandary today about how to handle the meeting, with members of the *Daihyo Sha Kai* in attendance. He hadn't informed Andross that they were coming to make a request. It was just the sort of information Andross expected him to report. Maybe afterward Andross would get wind of it and call him in, but he'd be damned if he'd let the man know ahead of time. What if Nebo came out of hiding and showed up? Denton would really be boxed into a corner. But even so, he couldn't bring himself to tell Andross.

Since their meeting, and after all he had witnessed in the stockade and the motor pool, Denton had grown increasingly ashamed of his unspoken complicity with the man. Why had he been so weak in the office that night? Why hadn't he spoken up, whatever the consequences? "No," he should have said, "I will not come back here carrying tales of what is happening in the community." He was certain Alice Hamilton would have done just that. Alice. He could hardly bear to think of her either. He'd let her draw him into her magnetic field. A magnetic field that attracted all kinds of wandering objects, like husbands on the prowl. Was that what he had become, a husband on the prowl? Just like his father. He hated it, but the truth was he couldn't keep his mind off the woman. He'd tried to think about his work, to develop a strategy for this afternoon's meeting, and the next thing he knew he was indulging in an adolescent fantasy about taking her to bed.

Esther had called late the night before. It had been a poor connection, with static on the line and noise from a party in the dining hall in the background. He was just as glad she couldn't hear him well enough to detect any insincerity in his voice as he shouted into the phone that he missed her, and asked when she and Parin were coming back up. She said she thought it would be another week, but that if she had her way she'd leave that moment. "I'd like to talk to you, Denton. I have things to talk about. I miss you. Do you miss me at all?" That's when he'd said he was as lonely as a stray puppy without her. He'd almost believed it as he'd spoken. "I'm all over the place without you to hold me down," he'd said and he'd believed that, too. But when he'd come out of the phone booth, seen the people talking in the smoke-filled room and heard the dance music playing on the jukebox, instead of imagining Esther in his arms, he'd thought of Alice, and how her hair would fall loosely around her shoulders and how her cheek would feel against his, and the way their bodies would fit together as they moved.

Denton walked through the now-completed gate separating the internees from the administration. He waved to the young soldier standing guard. The boy nodded back. Instead of thinking about how much he hated these guys, he wondered if Alice Hamilton could see him from the window of her barracks room. Would she recognize him from behind with his brimmed hat pulled down? Did she know his gait? Was she interested enough to have noticed such characteristics?

What a day for a hike, he thought, tipping his hat back to catch the sun. He imagined the light and shadow of the pine forest, the whirring sound of ponderosa high up. He wondered if Alice liked to camp out in the forest. On winter nights you had to retire at four o'clock, and the night could seem interminable. But not with Alice Hamilton, he thought.

"Jesus Christ, Jordan," he said aloud. "Get that woman out of your mind."

Entering the meeting room at Building 707-D, he was struck by how bright and warm it was and how quietly the men sat. "Good afternoon, gentlemen," he called cheerfully, stopping to hang his coat on one of the pegs that lined the back wall and to slip off his galoshes. Other pairs of boots standing in puddles of melted snow told him how late he was. The long woolen coats and felt hats of the board members were hung neatly above each pair of boots. They still wore their best clothes to these meetings. This reminder of better times made him uncommonly happy.

At the front of the room, the ward representatives and the officers of the Co-op board were convened around a long table. In the first row of chairs facing the table, Nebo Mota himself sat between Chiura Tamagata and Mike Kitamano.

Tony Kato, glowering, sat next to Mike, and Kanga Tomatzu, a transferee from Manzanar, was on Tony's left. Nebo appeared calm. He didn't look Denton's way, but stared straight ahead at the wall above the table.

"We've been waiting for you so we could start, Denton," Bill Nakamura said, from his position in the middle of the long table.

Toki sat on Bill's left and Ate Kashimoto, the manager of the tofu factory and a ward representative, was at Toki's left. Arthur Nagasaki, the Co-op treasurer, sat at the far end of the table. On Bill's right was Joe Hohri, the recording secretary.

Joe was meticulously layering carbons between sheets of onionskin paper, preparing for the formidable task of taking minutes. He set himself the almost impossible goal of transcribing in multiple copies every sentence spoken in these meetings, after which he typed them, also in multiple copies. Denton had suggested to Joe that he condense much of what was said, but the young man answered, "No. Who am I to make those decisions of what goes in and what doesn't?" Denton wanted to say, "That's why you have the job," but seeing Joe's earnestness, he'd decided to let it go, and accepted the twenty typed pages of notes after each weekly meeting. Denton took a place at the table between the representatives of Ward 5 and Ward 10, directly across from Bill. This left him with his back to Nebo and the others, but he couldn't ask one of the ten ward representatives to move to give him a better vantage point for watching Nebo and figuring out what the hell he was up to.

Bill rapped his knuckles on the tabletop. "Meeting of November 18, 1943, of the Tule Lake Co-op Board of Directors is hereby called to order. Let it be shown in the records that all member representatives of the various wards are present," and Bill proceeded to list the names of the ten ward leaders. When he had finished with their names he asked that Toki Honda, general manager of the Co-op, be counted present, as well as the other members of the Board of Directors. "Let it also be entered in the minutes that we have the honor of a visit from the representatives of the *Daihyo Sha Kai*, namely Mr. Nebo Mota, Mr. Chiura Tamagata, Mr. Mike Kitamano, Mr. Tony Kato, and Mr. Kanga Tomatzu."

As Denton watched Joe Hohri dutifully scribble the names with his indelible pen, he realized that unless he got up this instant and walked to the director's office, there was going to be the devil to pay when Andross saw these minutes.

"And our esteemed president, William Nakamura, is present," Toki rose to say. He tugged on his suit vest.

"Thank you, Mr. Honda," Bill nodded to Toki. "And let the records show that Denton Jordan, head of business enterprises for the WRA, is also present."

Every man around the table nodded in Denton's direction, acknowledging his official role. He was certain there was no such affirmation from the men seated behind him.

"Gentlemen," Bill said, "the preliminaries have been taken care of. I believe we can proceed. Why don't the *Daihyo Sha Kai* present their requests to the board? Mr. Mota, are you the spokesman?"

In the silence that followed, Denton heard children outside the building shouting to one another.

"Yes, I am," the familiar voice spoke behind him. A chair scraped.

Denton swiveled to look at the young man he'd been wanting to sit down with for the past two weeks. Denton stared hard at him. Nebo seemed thinner, but not unwell. There was a sadness around his mouth that hadn't been there before. He stood, legs spread wide, arms folded behind his back, shoulders squared. "Before I begin, I have a question for the Co-op representatives," Nebo said in his most formal English. "I wish to know if you are willing to listen to the *Daihyo Sha Kai* and our demands."

Denton turned back to see Bill sizing up the table. All the men indicated assent.

"Yes, Mr. Mota. Before you or Mr. Jordan arrived, we discussed our willingness to listen to you and our openness to your requests. You are all members of the Co-op, according to the records I checked when Mr. Chiura Tamagata came to me a few hours ago. Two of you have joined in the past week, I believe. As members you have every right to state your requests to the Board of Directors and the Board of Directors is duty-bound to listen to you with an open mind."

"Thank you, Mr. President, for making that clear. We will then proceed." Nebo shifted his feet, but kept his hands behind his back. "We wish to demand that the Co-op cease selling luxury items such as fruit, candies, ice cream, soda pop, tofu and fish to the residents of the camp." Someone at the table exhaled loudly. But Nebo continued without pause. "We demand this because we want to force the administration to do what we construe to be their duty; they should provide these goods to the populace without charge. Due to the incident on November 4, the invasion of the army and the subsequent establishment of martial law, the closing down of many resident-managed operations, and the importation of scab farmworkers, the majority of our people are without money, having been deprived of the means of earning it. We feel that there could be an even more serious incident within our community if you continue to sell these items to the few who can afford them while the others go without. We worry that our people will suffer from the divisiveness of such a policy."

Denton tensed as he waited in the ensuing silence for a response. Chiura sat like a statue, giving no hint of his position in the matter, whereas Tony Kato leaned back arrogantly, with one arm thrown behind the folding chair that he sprawled on. Kanga Tomatzu smiled and nodded. Only Mike looked uncomfortable. Maybe the young man likes his ice cream too much, Denton thought.

"Mr. President, may I answer Mr. Mota?" It was Toki, his voice pitched at its deepest, most modulated level. Denton knew this formal voice well from their earliest days together, when Toki was still uncomfortable with their "association," as Toki called it. This formal tone meant he was angry, nervous or trying to gain the upper hand.

"Go ahead, Mr. Honda," Bill said.

Toki cleared his throat and sat with his forearms on the table, rolling a pen between his palms. "Do I understand that you think we should cease supplying these items for the time being?"

"Yes, for the time being, until the camp is brought back to normal and is no longer under martial law, and until the stockade is investigated by an outside impartial group, namely the Spanish Consulate, which oversees such matters, and our people are given jobs at reasonable salaries."

"And I understand that you have other proposals that entail people refraining from doing certain Co-op jobs that are still open to them, thus refusing the administration's request. Is that correct, Mr Mota?" Toki gave a quick bow of his head.

"Yes, Mr. Honda, that is correct. Until the pay scale is adjusted, at the very least, we would like them to stop performing domestic service for the administration, as we've stated all along, and we've expanded that to include no longer taking care of the children of the staff."

Denton felt embarrassed as he thought of the Takaetsues.

"As you know, we have demanded that residents refrain from cleaning the latrines, either for pay or as volunteers, and we've called for and partially succeeded in a work slowdown in the mess halls."

"Yes, I'm all too aware of that," Toki said. "Getting back to the Co-op's distribution of products, which is the question on the table, what do you expect to happen, say, in the case of fruit, if the administration does *not* provide free fruit, especially to children? You know that our children and our older population suffer from constipation from the hard minerals in the water. Would you have them suffer further, without fresh fruit to move their bowels successfully?"

A flicker of discomfort crossed Nebo's features and was gone. "I failed to say, sir, that we voted and decided that oranges should still be sold. We were concerned about the constipation problem, and if the administration is slow in fulfilling their duties or fails to do so, we do not want the people to suffer any more than they already do."

"I see. Mr. Mota. Mr. Tamagata. Mr. Kitimano. Mr. Kato. Mr. Tomatzu. It is very considerate of you to think of the well-being of our residents. And may I ask, just which residents voted on these points?" Toki tapped the pen on the table as he looked sternly from one man to the next.

Denton saw Arthur Nagasaki, who had been hurriedly writing during this exchange, slip a note to Ate Kashimoto, indicating that he should pass it up to Toki. Ate tapped Toki and handed him the note without reading it himself. Toki opened the folded paper, read it, and gave Arthur a nod.

"Mr. Mota," Toki said, "before you answer, perhaps I could ask another question of you, a question that Mr. Nagasaki, our treasurer, has reminded me of." Without waiting for Nebo to answer, he continued with studied innocence. "We wonder why cigarettes are not included on your list of luxury items to be eliminated."

Nebo's eyes shifted almost imperceptibly. "We had at first decided to include cigarettes on the list, but when we talked to the people, they told us they didn't want to."

"Didn't want to give up the luxury of tobacco? I see." Toki paused. "Who are these people?"

Mike Kitamano looked down at the floor. Tony Kato leaned forward, his elbows on his knees. He stared hard at Toki.

"In particular, the kitchen workers," Nebo finally said. He was too smart not to know that Toki was trying to expose this inconsistency in their stand, this concession to a crucial constituency.

"Only the kitchen workers? They are the only ones who voted in your polling of the people?" Toki asked, his voice rising with false surprise.

"Mr. General Manager, we come here in good faith. We want the best for the people. This was a preliminary polling. We are at a disadvantage these days as you must know, our movement being restricted and our leadership depleted. The kitchen workers are among the few residents, besides your Co-op staff, who are still working since the incident, and we listened to them in this matter. They are important people in our community."

"Yes, they have a good deal of power these days," Toki said, tilting his head back arrogantly.

Denton wanted to tell him to stop, that he was unnecessarily antagonizing these men.

"As you do, too, Mr. General Manager. You are a man of great power in our community, particularly these days. I bow to you, sir," and Nebo bent deeply at the waist in a parody of respect.

"Excuse me, Mr. President." It was Tony Kato. He stood with his hand in the air. "May I interject?"

Nebo seemed taken aback by Tony's interruption.

"Is it all right with you, Mr. Mota?" Bill asked. "You do have the floor."

"Of course, I'm happy to have our member speak." But Nebo didn't look happy at all, he looked quite irritated with Tony, Denton noted.

"Thank you." Tony stepped forward. "I want it to go into the record that I detect sarcasm and disrespect in Mr. Honda's treatment of my comrade. Is that the American way? Because it is clearly not Japanese."

Denton watched the men carefully. Mike Kitamano sat straighter, more attentive. Chiura, trying to disguise an involuntary expression of disgust, massaged his jaw with gnarled stiff fingers. Kanga remained impassive. Nebo brought his arms from behind his back, folding them at his waist, and fixed his gaze on Tony Kato.

"I beg your pardon." Toki said, sitting back in his chair. "I meant no disrespect. Please forgive me if it slipped out unintended. But as *you* wish to see the people served, so do I!" His voice rose, betraying his anger. "I do not want to see them deprived needlessly, and choices made for them capriciously. And yes, freedom of expression is an American value. Which I've always thought included intonation as well as words."

"Most distinguished General Manager, I'm ignoring your last remark. As to the earlier question of the oranges, the people did vote on that. I believe our most esteemed Nebo Mota will explain." Tony backed his way to his chair and sat.

"Who are the people in this case, Mr. Mota?" Toki strained to keep control of his anger.

"We had more time because it was an earlier decision to exclude the oranges from the list, so we were able to canvass the wards in this matter, and they said that they agreed with us."

"Did you canvass the representatives of the population?" Toki glanced at the men who were the voices of the ten wards, but he wasn't seeking a response from them. "Or was it the people?"

"The people, of course." Nebo Mota answered.

"Were cigarettes on that original list of luxury items that you presented to the people? Did the people originally vote that the Co-op should not sell cigarettes?" Toki asked in a soft voice.

Nebo stood in seething silence.

"And there was no coercion?" Toki continued the questioning.

"Again I note contempt," Tony Kato jumped up.

"Can we do this without confrontation?" Bill Nakamura said. "Can we address the question of the feasibility of such a demand, Honda-san?"

Denton turned back to the table just in time to catch a look pass between Bill and Toki. He didn't quite know how to read it, whether to think there was some complicity between them, or that Bill was trying to let Toki know that he should lay off. Joe Hohri had his head close to the page, scribbling furiously. The other men were sitting at attention, not looking at one another, not exchanging asides. As Denton scanned the fifteen faces around the table, Arthur Nagasaki was the only person who met his eye, squinting as if to ask, What the hell is going on here? Denton gave a faint shrug in response.

"Certainly," Toki said. "What you must certainly understand, Mr.

Mota, from your tenure working with the Co-op, is that we run a business here and this country is at war and we are a segregation center and not much beloved by the wholesalers on the outside. They give us these preferential terms only because Denton Jordan has fought and finagled, and has petitioned the Office of Price Administration, as well as fighting like hell with them to get our sugar allotment increased. But you know all of that, because you were involved from the beginning. If we discontinue ordering from the distributors for even a week or two they will happily cut us off completely. And when the time comes when you want everything to return to normal, to what it was before your so-called status quo stand, we would not be able to make it happen. Furthermore, we have our membership to consider. We are democratically run, and we are, I repeat, a business. We have over eight thousand members counting on our success, both for their patronage refunds and for the future operation of all the stores. Rich—those with access to their money on the outside—and poor alike, are members. If we fail, if our wholesalers no longer want to sell to us, all must suffer, poor *and* rich."

"Am I to understand, Mr. Honda, that you are saying no to our request?"

The tension in the room was palpable. Denton knew how uncomfortable the older men were with this much hostility in a confrontation, no matter how polite Toki and Nebo had remained throughout.

"I have not said anything of the sort." Toki placed his fingertips on the table. Denton saw the strain in his thick fingers as Toki pressed his weight on them. "I am trying to remind you that the Co-op is not an amateur operation. It is a major enterprise. I am saying that we must poll our membership. We can do nothing as drastic as this without their approval. Our charter calls for one man, one vote. That is the situation, Mr. Mota. I will ask the board for permission to go to the membership with your request and we will let you know the results of the vote."

Nebo sneered and flicked his hand as though brushing away a fly. Denton hoped Toki would let it pass.

"Young man, under your proposal we would have to fire seventy-five to one hundred employees," Toki said, all pretense of politeness vanishing as he glared at Nebo.

"Yes, sir, I'm aware of the sacrifice entailed." Nebo crossed his arms higher on his chest. "I realize it will be a hardship, but out of such hardship success is born, and it's important that the evacuees raise a united front against this cruel administration. I presume your Co-op officials are evacuees and prisoners of this country as well, and that they still think of Japan, their native land. We believe we are at war with America. That is why we are asking you to cooperate."

Denton thought Nebo looked his way, but it happened so fast he couldn't be certain. Did Nebo expect Denton to carry this challenge of war against America back to Andross? Maybe Denton was supposed to be a messenger, tattling to Andross if the Co-op wouldn't agree to Nebo's demands. At least that way Nebo could stir things up, even if he failed to get the Co-op to collaborate. Had they beaten him up the other night to show how far they would go? Were scare tactics and bullying Nebo's means, and violent chaos and anarchy his ends? Denton hoped not. But he was jolted out of these thoughts by the anger in Toki's voice.

"I beg to differ with you. This Co-op is an American organization. We have built it from nothing, for the benefit of the evacuees, into an industry worth hundreds of thousands of dollars. You, yourself, young man, were a part of this proud venture. It has provided services and jobs for the residents. That is the form *our* loyalty to Japanese Americans takes. You are asking us to destroy it."

"May I propose, Mr. Honda, if you want to make money, that you ask for leave clearance and return to America and set up a business. You're certain to do very well."

Joe Hohri's pen scratched loudly across the paper as he took all of this down.

Just as Denton was silently begging Bill to intercede, to put a stop to this, Bill did just that.

"Gentlemen, I believe we have come to the end of this request. When our visitors have left, we can have a more open discussion among ourselves. If we have any questions for the *Daihyo Sha Kai*, I presume we can find a way to reach you."

A discernible relief settled over the board members. Joe Hohri stopped writing.

"I wish to have something added to the minutes first." Toki's voice trembled with emotion.

"Certainly," Bill said gently. "You still have the floor."

"I consider the reference by the esteemed Mr. Mota to my wishing to make a profit as an insult of the highest order, and I want it to be recorded that I pride myself on the work I have done in the name of the people sitting around this table, and in service to the membership. I do not wish to be vain, but it should be known that I have always attempted to promote the principles and the welfare of the Co-op. I have tried to remain selfless in the performance of my work. Thank you, gentlemen."

Denton saw that Nebo Mota's words had struck a public, physical blow and Toki was trying with every ounce of his will to conceal his agony until he could retreat to a very private place.

Nebo, Mike, Kanga and Tony stood and walked toward the back of the room. They moved stiffly, conscious of all eyes on them. In that moment Denton hated those four arrogant, self-righteous young men. They made him ashamed of his own support of Nebo. Chiura Tamagata had not risen with them, but instead seemed to be caught in his chair, unable to move. Under Denton's stare, he looked up. Placing both hands on his knees, the older man rose slowly, stooping, and followed the others to the back. He took his worn overcoat and hat in hand, bent to pick up his galoshes and slipped out the door, followed by Kanga Tomatzu. Nebo, Mike, and Tony pulled their jacket collars high and walked toward the same door. But instead of stealing out, they turned toward the men seated at the long table, lifted their fists high, and in unison shouted, "*Banzai, Banzai, Banzai*" and "Long live Japan." Then they were gone, the sound of the slammed door echoing through the room.

Denton walked to the window. No one joined him. He saw Chiura and Kanga trudging off toward Block 10. Tony and Mike trotted north toward the farther reaches. Denton looked to the east and the west. Nebo Mota was nowhere to be seen.

*   *   *

Bill began speaking. His words rushed together, revealing how upset he was, but he dealt with practical business. He asked Joe Hohri to state in the minutes that the ward representatives would hold meetings and poll their constituencies on the requests of the *Daihyo Sha Kai*. He asked Toki if he thought he could provide facts and figures that the representatives could use in their discussions. Toki simply said yes, without looking up from his papers. The man's pain was patently visible. Denton wished he could go over to Toki, slap him on the back and say, "Hey, Toki, it's okay. They just got carried away. They didn't really mean what they said." But he knew he could never do that. It would be a further humiliation for Toki.

Bill continued reading the lists of new products that had been received at the Co-op warehouse, "Toilet paper, five hundred rolls, mochi gome, fifty pounds, black beans, one hundred pounds."

Denton still couldn't understand why the anger of the young men had been directed at Toki. He was being used as a lightning rod, that much was clear. It could be because of the old rumors about Toki being picked up by the FBI in the early days and then released. Toki had mentioned it again the other night. Or it could be residual anger from the days before the roundups, when Toki had been a wealthy business man who had parlayed his retail business into a thriving wholesale operation. Denton knew Toki had lent money to people in the community, and he understood how complicated this could become among Japanese Americans who preferred giving to receiving. Denton felt protective of Toki, but Toki could have handled the situation with more diplomacy. Though how in hell was Toki supposed to react to such demands? What was *Daihyo Sha Kai's* ultimate goal? But then again, maybe such a militant stand would put pressure on Andross. Perhaps the board should consider some aspects of the proposal. They didn't really need to sell ice cream in winter. And soda pop wasn't healthy for children. But Denton knew he was grasping at anything to avoid facing up to his own responsibility for this. He had brought this humiliation on Toki. He had left Toki out in the open to take the fire alone. And Denton's spirits sank when he remembered how hard he had fought with the Office of Price Administration to get the sugar rationing raised so they could have soda pop in the camp. It had been part of the overall plan, supported heartily by Al Bennett, to render life in the camp tolerable. It seemed to him that ice cream and soda pop were symbols of how far they had traveled: he and Bill and Toki working from the top down to make the camp livable; Nebo working from the bottom up to deny people these small luxuries, in the name of fierce political commitment.

Before Bill adjourned the meeting, he reminded Joe that the minutes were not to be translated into Japanese, and he reminded the others that they were not to fall into Japanese in this room. Instead of staying around to chat as they usually did, the men exchanged muted goodbyes. Denton sensed that they were uncomfortable with the deep pool of silence that surrounded Toki. As Denton accompanied the men to the door, he glanced back into the room.

Bill, who had remained at the table with Toki, had taken off his jacket, rolled up his shirt sleeves, and was writing in his journal. It was his custom to stay after the meetings to set down his own recollections so he could check his perceptions against Joe Hohri's.

Toki was having trouble putting his folders in order. Sheets of figures kept slipping to the floor. Denton finished his goodbyes, giving promises to attend the various ward meetings, and walked over to where Toki fumbled with a packet, trying to straighten pages that stuck out in all directions.

"I'm sorry the meeting was so rough on you," Denton said.

Toki looked at him. His cheeks were slack and little pouches of flesh sagged at his jaw line. His eyes looked dull behind his glasses. "I am despised by my own people." He cradled the unruly folders to his chest, his shoulders hunched forward protectively. "They are going to circulate more virulent rumors about me. People will be contemptuous of me. And all I wanted was the best for everyone." He looked down, and absently patted the papers he carried.

Bill shook his head, meaning, Leave the guy alone.

"If there is anything I can do, Toki, please call on me. You know that I hold you in the highest esteem. You can't let those bastards get to you."

"That's kind of you to say." Tucking the folders under his arm, Toki turned, walked a few steps, then wheeled to face them. He bowed slightly. "Thank you, gentlemen. I'll be going now."

Denton watched as Toki slowly made his way to the rear of the room and out the door. From the back, Denton thought, Toki could be an old man.

Denton slumped in a chair waiting for Bill to finish, remembering his first meeting with Toki Honda in Toki's barracks soon after he'd been released from the FBI camp. Toki had sat motionless in his rocking chair, while Denton strained forward on the davenport, feeling like an excited colt, rattling on about his plans for the consumer-owned store. When he finally stopped talking, Toki took so long to speak that Denton almost began again, thinking he hadn't done enough to convince this sphinx of a man.

But a smile appeared on Toki's square face. "I'm very impressed with these ideas. They encourage me. This is the first good news I've heard in four very difficult months."

Sitting in the meeting room, Denton wished again that a man of Toki's stature and integrity might have been his father. Toki didn't change his position or personality to suit the situation or to charm some woman. He was a man to be trusted. A raw wound grew in the center of Denton's chest. Unfortunately, he was Stanton Jordan's son, and no amount of longing, or association with Toki Honda, would make him otherwise. Denton closed his eyes and listened to the sound of Bill's pen as his friend poured his thoughts onto the page.

*   *   *

The sun was setting behind them as Bill and Denton followed their own long shadows over the magenta-tinted snow. In a month it would be the shortest day of the year, Denton realized with surprise. Christmas would soon be here. Esther would expect a present. He usually disappointed her with his gifts. He had bought her an ironing board one year when they were in the Farm Security Camp. He had been thrilled when he'd made the purchase because he knew how much she needed and wanted it. But when he'd presented it to her in the suffocating heat of the tent, she had begun to cry. "It's utilitarian. Don't you understand? A useful gift is the last thing I want here." Remembering the incident he was filled with unexpected yearning for her and a desire to give her something particularly feminine. Perhaps he could get one of the women to make her a frilly blouse or a quilted bed jacket. That would surprise her.

"'Behold the wine-dark sea,'" Bill quoted, sweeping his hand over the expanse before them. He looked more handsome than usual in this light, his smooth skin absorbing the red of the sun. His glasses glinted with red as well. His knitted yellow scarf was tied round his collar, the tails blowing back over his shoulders as he walked. "The meeting was destructive, Denton, their demands were motivated by hatred. They are using us, using the Co-op, to further their own ideological ends. They don't have the residents' well-being in mind. I know my people. I know how rigid we can become when we get on a tack. Sometimes the single-mindedness serves us well, our communities, our families. But this is wrong-headed. It's taking on its own destructive momentum. They pushed much too far today."

Denton scuffed through the snow, kicking up the black dirt, muddying the sun-tinted crystals.

"I'm coming around to your way of thinking," Denton said in a low voice.

"What's that? What did I hear?" Bill grabbed Denton's arm to stop him.

Denton turned to face Bill who was looking intently at him. "I've lost my focus. I'm not a man who is comfortable without a focus. It makes me feel as though I don't care anymore." To Denton's shame, he began trembling again, as he had the other night. His teeth knocked together with such force that he couldn't get them to stop.

"I h-hate it that Nebo and his b-buddies beat me up. I hate how they treated T-Toki today. But I still h-hate it that Andross is s-such an arrogant bastard."

The cover of night was descending; in a minute the floodlights would come on. Denton wished he could hold that moment off. He needed the protection of darkness, the quiet of the moment after dusk, the patience of his friend.

"I figured as much," Bill said softly. He put his hand on Denton's arm again and held it there. "But we'd better get moving. It's late. There's a curfew on for some of us."

Chapter Twenty-Six

Denton surprised himself by showing up promptly at seven p.m. at Alice Hamilton's room. He usually got to meetings on time or before hand, but he was always late to social engagements. It was a habit of his that Esther particularly disliked, she'd told him enough times. Esther. Thinking of her gave him a sharp stab of guilt. He'd already promised himself that he wouldn't do anything to compromise his marriage vows, but even walking up these stairs, knocking on this door made him feel as though he'd committed adultery. Weren't thoughts as bad as actions? He'd certainly had the thoughts, much as he'd resisted them. They'd continued to crop up, in his sleep, in the moments before sleep, upon waking. He'd imagined taking Alice Hamilton in any number of ways. And she'd taken him against his will, as well. This was almost his favorite fantasy—it was certainly the one that exonerated him from blame. In his daydreams she came to him and said she had to have him and wouldn't he please touch her between the legs because it had been so long since she'd had a man. She would say he didn't even have to enter her, just touch, but when he did, she moaned and slipped her panties down and said to please, please fuck her.

Shit, Denton said to himself, trying to shake the thoughts. His groin was hot again and his penis beginning to harden. He stood on her doorstep willing it back into place, looking over his shoulder, hoping there was no one to see him standing in the light by her door. He was thankful that Herm's barracks was around the corner and out of sight, but at any moment Herm could come lumbering by and he'd be in big trouble trying to explain what he was doing outside Alice Hamilton's door on a Saturday night.

The door opened. Alice stuck her head out.

"Did you knock and I didn't hear you?" She looked puzzled.

He shook his head. "Nope, just standing here."

"Whatever for?" She opened the door wide. "Come in. It's cold out there. I'm having enough trouble as it is keeping this place warm."

"Feels warm to me," he said, entering the room.

"It must be the contrast," she said, rubbing her arms. She wore the same soft pale-blue wool sweater she'd worn the other night and a gray gored skirt. Over her clothes she'd tied a pink and gray plaid bib apron. Her cheeks were flushed, giving the lie to her complaint that she was cold.

She rubbed her cheeks as though she'd heard his thoughts. "I've been stirring a pot, so at least my face is warm." She laughed too loudly. So she was nervous, too.

"Well," she said, "let me take your jacket and then you can find a seat in my grand sitting room."

Her place was identical to Herm's in layout. One room with a minimal kitchen setup on the east wall and a cot on the other side of the room. But she had turned the cot into a sofa by covering it with a red hunter's blanket and piling it with worn needlepoint and dark velvet pillows. There was a braided rug in the center of the room beneath a chipped blue-painted wooden table and chairs, and a cheap rocking chair like the ones they were selling at the Co-op. A small, slightly soiled quilt was thrown over the back of the rocker. On the south wall, surrounding the entry, were family photographs. There were kids, adults, older people. Had she been married, he wondered? She seemed too young to be the mother of the ten and eleven-year-olds who stared into the camera.

"My nieces and nephews," she said from where she was working over a burner. "And the photo on the far right, that's me and my brother when we were growing up."

Denton moved closer to inspect a picture of a five-year-old girl in a dress and pinafore standing beside a much taller boy in riding breeches. The girl had a mischievous, impudent look about her, the boy was already imperious. They were posed on the porch of a large wooden house, with an elegant wicker chaise lounge and wicker chairs visible behind them. He'd guessed she'd come from money. This proved it.

"Here's all I have to offer in the way of drinks," she said, handing him a glass of scotch. "If you insist on ice, I'll chip it, but I'd prefer not to."

"It's too cold for ice," he said, taking the glass, careful not to let his hand touch hers.

"To health, healing and justice," she said, raising her glass. "How is your healing, by the way?" She sipped from her drink, her grey-blue eyes watching him over the rim.

"Sometimes I even forget about it. Last two days, the pain in my ribs is hardly noticeable. I've got a good nurse."

"You're a good patient."

The scotch warmed him and went immediately to his head.

"Whoa, this is good," he said.

"My folks gave me the bottle on my last trip home. They've stockpiled the cellar in anticipation of a calamity. There always is one." She laughed. "My dad wouldn't know what to do without his booze, especially his gin. He's your traditional flush-faced, broken-veined Anglo-Saxon. Mother has discovered Manhattans, even though she despises their namesake. New York is Gomorrah to her." She frowned.

"Where are you from?" Denton concentrated on getting his words out distinctly. The scotch was wreaking havoc with his senses. The scotch and her proximity. He thought of Esther's complaint that the women staff members and the wives of the staff members were practically teetotalers. "They're such goody two-shoes," she'd said on a number of occasions. He wondered if Esther would like Alice. But he couldn't get them together. It wasn't possible anymore.

"Boston," Alice laughed.

She went back to the kitchenette, or what could generously be called a kitchenette, Denton chuckled to himself. He liked how foggy his brain was becoming. Boston. The real thing. He'd never had the genuine article.

"Brahmins?" he asked.

"Brahmins," she answered. "Blue-blooded, straight-line Daughters of the American Revolution."

He'd known New England types, transplanted to California usually by way of Berkeley. But they came from Quaker families with a commitment to social change. He made his way unsteadily to a straight-backed kitchen chair. He knew enough not to sit on the bed-sofa arrangement. He took another big swallow, almost emptying the glass. She came toward him with the bottle to fill it again.

"Hey, wait a minute." He held up his hand. "I don't usually drink like this."

"It's medicinal." She smiled down at him.

Pretty smile, he thought. Damn pretty smile. He could smell her again. Lily of the valley. The scent of milk, mixed with scotch. He was going to have to watch himself. Or he was about to be in more trouble than ever before. He longed, though, to reach out and place his hand on her waist. Not a terribly slim waist, not like Esther's. "You're going to hurt Esther with this," he heard Herm whispering in his ear. But he could imagine the feel of Alice, solid, though fleshy, and her behind, really fleshy, and her breasts, full with pale nipples. He took a sip. She was still standing over him, her eyes on him, he knew, though he didn't look up.

"Are you a Quaker?"

"No. God, no." She turned and went back to the pot steaming on the burner. The room didn't much smell of food. He couldn't figure out what they were going to eat.

"You're pretty sure of that," he said, laughing.

"I'm pretty sure of a lot of things." She looked over her shoulder at him. "You'll find that out. No, I could never be a Quaker. I'm too violent, too angry. I know that about myself. If I were a man, I think I'd be hell on wheels." She hit the spoon against the side of the pot. "I hope you like rice. I hope you like fish from the Co-op. And canned corn, all bought especially for you."

He didn't give a damn what he ate. Everything and everyone in his life receded behind the scotch. He didn't care who he was supposed to be, how responsible he always prided himself on being, how he was married and how Esther would never forgive him. He imagined what it would be like to have Alice come over and sit on his lap.

"I'm a pacifist, you know," he said. He'd rediscovered the trail of conversation. He held out his empty glass.

She was there with the bottle. This time she held the glass, closing her hand over his. Her leg touched his as she poured.

"I'm not much for preliminaries," she said, still with her hand over his.

"I'm married," he said, but it didn't do a damn thing to deaden what he was feeling. He knew what was going to happen. It was only a matter of time. He didn't feel any guilt now.

"What does that mean?" She moved closer. Both her legs were against his.

"It means I'm loyal. Means I'm..."

"Celibate?"

He laughed. "No, I'm not celibate."

"Your wife hasn't been here for a while."

"Only a week," he said. The guilt crept back in. For betraying Esther. For becoming his father's son.

But she was taking the glass from his hand and she was lowering herself onto his lap and he felt the full weight of her warm thighs and buttocks. She took his hand and put it to her breast, and the guilt disappeared. She lowered her head and kissed him, her tongue found its way into his mouth, her mouth remaining on his as she raised herself and straddled him, her legs around the back of the chair. He was hard against her and this was better than he'd imagined. She moaned deeply, gutturally, and when she did that he wanted her badly. He fumbled with the buttons of his fly. He put his hand under her skirt and found she had no panties on. He moved his fingers up into her and she was wet, a thick wetness, and she moaned again and helped him with the buttons of his pants and then effortlessly he was slipping into her and he couldn't get enough of her.

Later they moved over to the bed. He had never been so virile. He would go soft, only to rise up again, either by her hand massaging him, or her teasing him with her lips and tongue. Or she would get on top of him and rub against him until he became huge and hard. Or he would initiate, in ways he never had before. He knelt and put his face into her, into the soft fur of her, and sucked and sucked like a baby at a breast, though she didn't taste of milk, despite her milky odor. Her come was sour and salty, coating his tongue as he dug into her and into her, until she lifted her hips, and cried out in a strangled call. The beam of a searchlight came through the crack between the opaque curtains, fell on her and showed that her face was flushed and her chest had broken out in a rash. When he moved up to lie beside her, she still had her fist in her mouth. He grinned at her, and she burst out laughing.

"I have to gag myself," she whispered, giggling again. "These thin walls. Everyone in the barracks will know our business."

He lay back. He was spent. The urgency of his sex had finally subsided. At the height of their second or third coupling, at a moment when it was impossible to stop, they'd smelled burning rice and he'd said, "Oh, God, we're going to burn the barracks down." She'd said, moaning, "Oh, fuck it, let it burn. Burn the whole damn place down."

They'd come, and then she'd scrambled up, staggering over to take the pot off the heat.

The acrid odor of the burned rice had subsided, but he suspected one could smell it on entering the room. And what about all the other smells, her sex, his? There would be no disguising them if someone happened by for a visit. His guilt returned and began to build in him. She got up and padded over to the window. He watched her shape against the searchlight's beam. She pulled the shade down cutting out all light. He heard her bump into the rocking chair.

"Damn it," she said.

"Careful," he whispered.

The table light came on, filling the room with a soft glow. He watched her as she walked across the room to the kitchenette, inspecting the body that he'd been touching for hours. She was stockier than his hands had told him. Her hips were narrow but fleshy and her shoulders were wide and strong. He thought she must be a good swimmer. Her breasts were large and heavy but shapely and they sat high on her rib cage. The nipples were darker and larger than he'd imagined. Her pubic hair was the same pale golden-red color as the shiny locks that were half pinned in a tangle high on the back of her head and half falling on her shoulders.

"I'm starving," she said, taking the pins from her hair. She drew her fingers through the knots, trying to make order. "How about you?"

He thought for a moment. He was exhausted, the pain in his ribs which had been dulled by passion had begun to throb. He had a slight headache from the scotch, and his mouth was dry and foul, but, yes, he was hungry.

*   *   *

While she cooked, he went into the tiny bathroom. It had a sink, toilet and iron tub; the same setup that Herm had. Denton turned on the bath water, and waiting, he urinated. After a while he stood before the sink looking at his reflection in the small round mirror she'd hung on the wall. His face still looked abraded. He was flushed red from lovemaking. And his eyes, what did they say to him? That he was beginning to feel very bad about what he'd done. He didn't love this woman. He didn't know her. Once before he'd slept with a woman he didn't even like, a secretary in the Economics Department at the

University of Washington. She'd typed stencils for him and afterward she'd asked him to walk her home to her apartment. He'd slept with her, but it was a rather perfunctory exercise. She had wanted him to spend the night and seemed so pathetic that instead of feeling sympathy for her, as he tended to for most needy and sad people, he couldn't tolerate being in the room with her, could barely contain his distaste for her. He'd left immediately. For the other three or four women he'd been with, he'd felt affection at the least, respect for their minds and their ways of seeing the world. With Esther, he'd been dazzled. She was the smartest woman he'd ever met, much more intelligent than he. She had the kind of braininess that he valued much more highly than his own brand of putting two and two together. He saw her smile, her intensity, the dark complexion and eyes, the unruly black hair. "A *shiksa* will kill her," Herm had said.

He put his hand to the wall and leaned his head against the mirror. Behind him the water roared into the metal tub. "Esther, forgive me," he whispered, certain it couldn't be heard in the next room. He had to say it aloud. The words would only have validity and provide salvation if said aloud. He thought of Parin, saw her sad little face, with her heavy glasses, her lazy eye, her tremendous, overpowering need for him. What the hell was he thinking of? But he hadn't been thinking. That was just it. What the hell had he been doing out there in the other room? Would his daughter sense his unfaithfulness as he had his own father's? Would she guess the betrayal? He didn't know if Bessie had known about their father. Huey was too crazy to notice, wandering in his own terror-filled world. Nothing was expected of the war-damaged grown man. Huey didn't have to bring their mother out of those hideous stuporous sleeps where she escaped from truth and responsibility and where she drowned her anger. Denton clenched his fists, his nails cutting into his palms, as if the pain would help him tolerate the memory. Whatever his father had done, he despised his mother more. Hated how she didn't fight back against his father, how she just lay there with her limp hand on his own arm, her skin waxy and transparent. Was this the way she lay beside his father, with phlegmatic hand and body? Was this why his father couldn't abide going up into her room?

But he had Esther and Parin whom he loved. He knew he loved them, even through these difficult last months, even though Esther's anger had been debilitating to him, had drained him of good feelings toward her, even though he worried about her treatment of his daughter, and worried that she wasn't the loving person he'd believed she was. He hit his fist soundlessly against the wall. What was the truth? What did he feel? How much of their discord had he himself brought on?

The water scalded as he sank into it. Alice had said not to soak the bandages, but he didn't care. He remained submerged while the heat seared his flesh. He wanted to burn in hell. He listened to what the pain had to tell him as it increased in intensity. He listened, and remembered as he endured the fire.

When they first married, they had continued to be passionate, but if he were honest, pretty early on their lovemaking became intermittent, possible only when Esther was not in a rage. Possible only when he was not afraid of her. She could, he found, be three people: an angry person, an erotic, loving person and yet another person altogether. That other one closed down, got as cold, as distant as another human could become.

Denton raised himself in the cooling water. He understood something he hadn't before. It was this disappearing, this withdrawing into herself, that had reminded him of his mother and her endless sleeps, those slumbers that had disgusted and frightened him when he'd been sent to wake her. When Esther's face became masklike, when she wouldn't answer him, she was like that sleeping mother, even though she was awake. When he became insistent, trying to get her to respond, Esther would abruptly turn vicious. Her voice would harden to obsidian, black and shiny. If she could have hurled her voice, it would have bruised him on impact, so hard and powerful was it in its cruelty. How did it affect a child, he wondered, taking a deep and sudden breath. What was it like for Parin when Esther turned on her? He began to cry, soundlessly and dry-eyed.

*   *   *

"Sorry there are no candles," Alice said as he stepped out of the bathroom dressed only in trousers and undershirt, his feet bare.

She'd set the table in the middle of the room and brought the lamp from her night table for a softer light. Her dark blue man's kimono was tied loosely at her waist and she wore getas over socks. She'd scrubbed her face so shiny clean that she looked about fifteen, and the braids she wore on either side of her head only added to the impression. How could this woman who had been so wanton in her lovemaking look so innocent? She even had freckles, pale and tiny, across the bridge of her nose and high on her cheeks. He saw that her full, swollen lips were freckled as well.

"Food smells good," he said, feeling his diffidence returning. He was a changed man, a stranger to the Denton who had walked into this barracks a few hours earlier, and no relation to the insatiable lover of half an hour ago. He was raw and open, newly shy, ashamed of what he'd done, of who he'd been. But he couldn't revert to the man who'd walked in here. He no longer knew who that man was.

"Sit," she said, pointing to one of the chairs.

He sat in the chair where his shirt hung.

"Eat," she laughed.

From the first bite of corn he was as hungry for the food as he had been for her body. He couldn't get enough inside him. She kept putting more on his plate until everything was gone.

"You've eaten me out of house and home," she laughed again, but seeing that he didn't laugh in response, she sobered.

Resting her chin on her open hand, she stared at him. She looked even younger, like a small kid at the dinner table, bored with the food. He thought of little Bessie, and how she used to scrutinize him silently when their mother had disappeared into her thoughts. Had he taken good care of Bessie? Had he protected her?

"You're feeling bad, aren't you?" she said.

He looked into his plate.

"Look at me," she said.

It was a fight to make himself hold her stare, her grave, gray-eyed stare.

"This is between the two of us," she said. "It won't go any further than this room, and it doesn't have to go past tonight. I'll remember it. You were wonderful. I never thought such a serious guy could be so good. I'll be disappointed if this is all, but I'll still be grateful." She smiled, like the mischievous child in the photograph.

He wanted her again, but he knew he shouldn't. Wouldn't. He was flattered that she thought him a good lover, but he was a fraud. Somebody else had been in that bed with her.

"I'm sorry," he said. "I feel like a heel about this. I led you on, promising something I'm not going to fulfill."

She erupted with laughter. She couldn't stop.

"Ohh," she gasped. "You sound just like an organizer. You talk like this fellow I knew down in Manzanar. 'I raised expectations too high, can't fulfill the felt needs.' Isn't that how you fellows talk?"

He tried to smile.

"Now I'm the one who is sorry," she said, lighting a cigarette. She held the pack of Camels toward him. "You want one?"

He waved it away even though he wouldn't have minded a smoke. He didn't feel like accepting anything more from this woman.

"Okay," she said. "Let's be serious. You're full of baloney that you're worried about me. You're worried about yourself. You've broken a cardinal rule and you're a highly moral man and you pride yourself on how perfectly loyal you are. Is that correct?" She picked tobacco off her tongue.

"Maybe we could be less glib about this," he said in a low voice.

Her expression changed. He had gotten the upper hand on that one.

"You can be a real bastard, can't you? What's that saying? 'Nice to the outside world, a shit at home.' Not that this is your home, of course." Tears welled and tipped over her lower lids. She brushed them away with the flat of her hand. Her face flushed bright red. "God damn it."

He didn't say anything.

"Don't worry," she said. "I'm not going to hold you with my tears. I just feel too much emotion. Too many violent feelings. Too damn much passion." She took a deep breath that turned into a sob. She threw her head back. "You're right, we shouldn't have done this. You've got a wife and a child and a hungry dedication to your work. That's what you are, Jordan, a very hungry man. I admire you. I admired what I'd been hearing about you, and then you walk into the hospital all beat up and you're willing to cover up what happened and I thought, here's an outlaw, a western cowboy, and I'm an Eastern girl with my own brand of lawbreaking." She shrugged. "That was it, just like in the movies. Technicolor and all." She drew deeply on her cigarette.

He stifled the urge to reach out to her, to guide her over onto his lap, or to get up and stand beside her so she could burrow her face into his waist and he could comfort her.

"What about one of those cigarettes, after all?" he asked.

She pushed the package across the table, followed by the matchbook.

He lit up, inhaled and immediately became lightheaded.

"Maybe I shouldn't have covered up for those fellows. I pulled you into it and there could still be trouble for you with Andross."

"Don't worry about that. I've been in plenty of that kind of trouble in the past. It's my middle name, that sort of mess. I do what I feel is right at the moment and I think afterward. Most of the time I'm right. Sometimes I'm not." She looked straight at him as though asking a question.

"I'm so damn confused," burst from him. He got up and walked around the room, to the bed, and then toward the door, and back to the bed. "I'm turned inside out. This isn't the way I am, I want you to know that. I've always known what I wanted. I've always gone in a pretty straight line; when I had problems with bosses and profs at the university, we usually couldn't see eye to eye because I knew all too clearly what I wanted. But here I am, shifting back and forth on an hourly basis and sometimes within the same hour about where I stand. We had a Co-op Board of Directors meeting yesterday. I even got confused about which side I was on. I'll tell you another thing, Alice, that I haven't told anyone. I'll prove to you how spineless I've become. I sat in Andross's office the other day. That's when he pulled the carpet out from under me about what he knew about me and the attack and how we hadn't reported it, and that guy almost had me going over to his side, almost had me willing to spy for him."

"That's like spying for the Nazis as far as I'm concerned."

"Don't make light of it. It's not the same thing, and you know it. It wouldn't be right to go back to Andross with information, but he's not a Nazi. He's nothing more than a weak authoritarian bastard who's way over his head in the job."

"Sounds like a good description of Adolf Hitler, to me," she said.

Esther couldn't even say the man's name. Judith Kahn would rise from her chair whenever Hitler's name was mentioned in discussion, as though she couldn't bear to be in a defenseless position with his presence in the air. Neither one of them would find the comparison amusing.

"Hitler's actions result in death and misery for people all over the world. He wantonly slaughters people. Andross doesn't go quite that far," he said. He didn't want to be in this room any longer talking to Alice Hamilton. He'd gone cold on her.

"He slaughters Jewish people, is what you mean." Her face twisted into a grimace as she stubbed her cigarette out in the ashtray. "Esther's Jewish, isn't she?"

"Yes, she is."

"I thought so," she said. "It must be hard for her. It must be especially hard that you're not over there." She tossed her head.

"You're the second person to mention that to me this week."

"Who was the other?"

"Andross."

"Hmm. Not the best bedfellow."

"I'll say." He didn't like her entering his life with Esther in this way. She had never suffered from discrimination, couldn't possibly understand Esther's vulnerabilities. Alice thought of herself as an outlaw, but he suspected that she'd always fit in, wherever she went, and she lacked depth and seriousness, the essential elements of his and Esther's love. "I'd better be going," he said.

"Have another cigarette," she said, touching his arm. "Come on, sit down. Talk to me. Don't leave angry. I said something to make you angry."

He felt himself being lured back into her orbit. He knew he should leave. But she was right. It didn't do to leave angry.

"Talk to me," she said again. "Maybe I wanted to make you mad at me. Take notice of me. I'm jealous of Esther. She has you all to herself. I know she's more interesting than I am, more exotic."

"What does that mean, exotic?" He shook off her arm, grabbing the pack of cigarettes off the table. He dug one out, lit it, drawing deeply. This time his head didn't swim. He could hear Esther, "She means I'm a dark-haired, swarthy Jew."

Her eyes got teary again. "Damn you." She took a cigarette. It was the last. She crushed the package and tossed it toward the wastebasket beside the sink. She missed. It rolled back toward them. "Please, sit down."

He didn't know why, but he did what she asked. They sat in silence, smoking, Alice blowing perfect rings into the air.

"Tell me about the Co-op meeting. Let's talk about that for a while. Then you can leave." She squinted. Her eyes were still filled with tears.

She seemed older. She could be in her thirties. No longer on top of this situation between them, she began to go slack, her jaw line, her breasts beneath the kimono. Even her hair wasn't as bright as it had been when he'd arrived.

"Sure," he said. "The *Daihyo Sha Kai* paid us a visit. Nebo Mota even surfaced for the meeting."

"Really?" She wiped the heel of her hand under her right eye, catching a tear that had escaped. Her voice sounded nasal.

"They're making more demands around the status quo strategy. They're demanding that the Co-op stop selling certain luxury items to the membership."

"What's the purpose of that?"

"To pressure the administration into providing the luxuries itself, things that people have gotten used to, knowing full well Andross will only dig his heels in deeper, and hoping that as a result the population will rise up against him."

"Andross is such a son of a bitch." She blew her nose on a lace-bordered white handkerchief.

"Toki Honda is pretty stubborn himself. He's our general manager."

"I know who Honda is."

Their relationship was shifting again. He felt comfortable talking with her. He liked her responses.

"Toki wouldn't budge when they made their demands, and then he got Nebo Mota all riled up."

"How bad was it?"

He didn't answer. When she spoke, he had heard music coming through the wall dividing Alice's room from the next room. He panicked. What if whoever lived there, and he couldn't think who it was, had heard their lovemaking and would now recognize his voice? "Could we turn on the radio, too?" he whispered.

She looked puzzled.

He nodded his head toward the music.

"Oh, I get it," she said, and wrapping her kimono tighter, walked barefoot over to the Motorola beside the bed and snapped it on. Dance music flowed into the room and Denton remembered it was Saturday night and this was ballroom music from San Francisco. He had a vision of dancing with Esther; she, anticipating his moves, and he, barely pressing her narrow, straight back to lead her. On the dance floor he was indeed master. A wave of love filled him and he wondered what the hell he was doing in this room.

Alice sat down, apparently unmoved by the surging strings of the big band. He guessed she had no interest in anything as romantic as dancing. He couldn't imagine her twirling with her eyes closed under a starry sky, as he'd seen Esther do on many a summer night.

"So?" she asked, waiting.

"It was pretty awful. Polite, but ugly."

"So you're confused. You don't know whether to let Andross in on this internal fight. Isn't that so?" She put her hand over his on the tabletop and he didn't pull away.

"Yes, that's part of it. It would mean showing our cards before we play them, if we ever get to play them. And I know what he'll say if he hears about Nebo." He rubbed his thumb over hers.

"What happens when Andross reads the minutes?"

"Of the meeting?"

"Yes, doesn't he get them as a matter of course?" She stubbed out her cigarette.

"How do you know all this?" He shook his head, crushing his cigarette in the same ashtray. He let his hand be held. He still caressed hers.

"I don't. But since all our reports eventually go into his files, I would guess yours do, too, especially now."

"Joe Hohri isn't the fastest recording secretary we've ever had."

"I see," she said. "A regular old slowdown."

"You got it, sister." He played with the dead cigarette butts in the ashtray. The memory of Toki's mortification returned. "But it isn't as easy as keeping the minutes from Andross. There's Toki to consider. He was humiliated by Nebo. Toki loves the Co-op. Mota and his boys don't care anymore what they destroy." He tried to ease his hand from hers but her grip tightened. "Alice, I'm not an outlaw. You got that wrong. I want a peaceful settlement as much as the next ordinary guy." He waited for her to tell him he was a coward, that he should shape up, come to some sort of conclusion. Why the hell didn't she speak? "Well, what do you think? Why do you just sit there? Don't you have a damn thing to say to me?" He pulled his hand from hers.

"Hey, hold it, honey."

"You must have an opinion. You're not some sort of dizzy dame, are you, or a dumb bitch with nothing in your pretty head? Or a ball breaker who wants to torture me with silence?" He horrified himself with the anger fueling his speech. He had never spoken to anyone and certainly not a woman in this way. His groin was tight. He was as hard as he'd been at the height of sex. "I'm sorry."

"Forget how sorry you are all the time, brother. I can't solve this dilemma you're in. If you want to know, I admire Mota. I think he means well. Somebody has to say something. Even when people get hurt along the way."

"You don't know Toki. How principled he is. How loyal. Talented. Without Toki we wouldn't have the Co-op the way it is."

"But he holds to the middle ground. Practically the administration line, from what I've heard."

She still excited him. The more she contradicted him in this way, the more he wanted her. Her face had grown beautiful as she spoke, her eyes an even paler gray-blue, her eyebrows darker by comparison to her hair and pale skin. Her lips were bruised a reddish-brown and he could see the tips of her white teeth. The kimono had slipped loose and he saw the rise of her breast and the slight rash left from their lovemaking.

"It's more complicated than that," he said.

"I just prefer people who shake things up. It's what I liked about you, what made you so attractive to me."

"I love the guy," his voice came out in a husky whisper.

"I can see that," she said. "That counts for a lot between two people, no matter what the differences." Her leg touched his lightly beneath the table.

"I felt so much pain to see him hurt."

"That's a nice sentiment," she said.

"Are you ridiculing me for being sentimental?" His anger rose again with unusual force. What right did she have? He clenched his fist to keep from slamming it on the table with all his might. He jerked his leg away from her.

"Absolutely not. I'm saying you're a man who's pretty torn up and not used to it at all."

He watched, not understanding, as she rose and came toward him and for a moment he thought she was going to ask him to dance, which he decided he should decline out of some convoluted sense of loyalty to Esther, and because he didn't recognize the song the band was playing on the radio, and because he still felt irrationally angry at

Alice. Her robe slipped open. She hadn't pulled it tighter this time. Her nipples were full and soft and then began to harden. She wore no underpants, and he saw the mound of hair on her pubis which he knew by touch and odor. He was overwhelmed by desire for her, even stronger than it had been when he'd first entered this room, because he knew now, through his entire body, exactly what waited for him in her bed.

She reached down and took his hand and put it between her legs like a cup, pressing his fingers into the wetness of her, and he knew it was more than he could manage to say no.

Chapter Twenty-Seven

E sther sat by the open window in her old bedroom in Grandma's house. The sabbath had been over for hours, and she could have turned on the lights but she didn't. It was pitch black outside; the street lights had been extinguished; the moon and stars were obscured by the fog that had rolled in this afternoon. She was in a little cocoon of mist and darkness and it suited her mood. Her chest was still filled with emotion from the realizations of the night before. The grief had lived with her throughout the night and during the morning as she'd stayed with Grandma in the parlor and later when she'd taken Leah for a walk around the neighborhood. The tiny woman with her aching malformed feet could still go at a steady pace for a few miles. Leah had held Parin's hand and from time to time would bend down and kiss Parin on the top of her head, chuckling and saying, "My little squirrel."

At one point Leah gazed up at Esther, her blind eyes a milky gray in the bright light, and asked, "so who does my little squirrel look like, Esther?"

Esther brushed the frizzed gray hair from grandma's forehead, feeling the softness of her skin. Jewish women keep their skin, her mother had always said. "She favors you, Grandma, in a certain way."

Esther put her finger to her mouth and shook her head when Parin seemed about to protest.

Grandma stared into the distance. "What I look like I don't know anymore. What I used to look like wasn't so beautiful. I hope this one is more beautiful."

Esther laughed. "We're not talking about features exactly, Grandma, but spirit. She has your demand for life. And she is quite beautiful, at least *I* think so." Esther smiled down at her daughter who was quietly taking in this last sentence with a private smile curling her lips.

Shivering, Esther got up to close the window against the cool damp night. She remained there with her head against the cold pane. How little it took to make her daughter happy. Why hadn't she been more understanding and sweeter to her over this past year? Where had all the anger at her daughter come from? She thought again of how she'd worried about Parin's ears, that they were Jewish ears. So what if they had been, and for that matter what the hell were Jewish ears really? She'd seen plenty of Christian people with ears that stuck out, especially among the dust bowl farmers and their skinny wives and children.

Esther remembered how after Parin had been born she'd been afraid to look into her baby's eyes. She'd heard that mothers fell in love the minute they met their babies' eyes. When the nurses brought Parin for her bottle, Esther didn't look down, instead she found the tiny mouth with her fingers and guided the nipple in, working against the temptation to soften to the living creature mewing and struggling in her arms. Not until the fifth day did a voice inside Esther say it was safe to look into the baby's eyes. When she met the infant's gaze a love rose up in her, fearsome and thundering like the passion she would feel for Denton when they made love. She had thought at the time that people weren't allowed such hunger, such love for a child; it couldn't be normal.

Esther blew on the window glass, creating a wide circle of fog. Her eyes had adjusted to the darkness and as she traced the names with her finger she could just make them out. Esther Kahn. Denton Jordan. Parin Kahn. "Parin Kahn," she said aloud, trying it out. How beautiful it sounded.

She went to the bed, turned down the fresh covers and sheets and slipped under, releasing the aroma of laundry soap, and pulled the bedding to her chin as she had as a child, as a teenager, as a college coed when she'd come here to get succor, to do her homework in peace, to find herself. It was only at Grandma's that she could escape her mother's cruelty and iron hand.

Now that she'd opened the door to possibilities, the memories kept pouring in, things she'd long ago put aside, not to be reconsidered. When she and Denton had married, they had decided to relinquish all religion; he would no longer be Christian, which was no loss, he'd joked, "Because I don't believe in God"; and she had said she would no longer follow Judaism, they would have no seders, she wouldn't observe the high holidays, her daughter wouldn't be considered Jewish. "It's for the best," she said, "we don't want religion to get in the way, to divide us." They had gone by themselves to a Justice of the Peace and the nutty little ceremony was one they recounted ad infinitum to their friends, how the Justice was drunk and got his lines all wrong and ended up asking Esther if she would love and honor her wife and if Denton would love and obey his husband.

Esther hugged her knees to her chest and allowed herself the thought that she might have liked to stand under a chuppa with Daddy at her side and she might have liked it if Denton had smashed the glass and everyone had yelled, Mazel Tov! How could that have harmed their love? How strong could a love be, if such a simple act could have divided them?

*   *   *

Esther woke to the clatter of dishes. When she opened her door she saw light from Grandma's bedroom and went to look, but no one was in there. From downstairs, she heard the sound of dish shards being swept up.

Every light was on: the fixture above the sink, the ceiling lamp, and the deep green glass-shaded lamp over the table.

Her grandmother was bent over at the waist, brooming crockery bits into the pickup. She wore an old blue wool bathrobe that had belonged to Grandpa Saul. Her feet were bare and so twisted and calloused that they could hardly be called much more than stumps.

"Grandma, let me," Esther said.

"*Wer iss dos?*" The old woman jerked up in alarm. "*Wer iss gekummen?*"

"It's me, Grandma, Esther."

"*Wer?*" Grandma stepped back from her, holding up the brush for protection.

"Esther, your granddaughter, Judith's daughter. I'm sleeping here tonight," Esther spoke quietly as she approached her grandmother.

Leah's mouth continued moving, though not uttering a word, and her eyes fluttered in confusion. Then she smiled, feigning knowledge. "Ah, of course. Ruthie, bube, Mama forgets. Come, come bube, let's Ruthie and me have some warm milk."

Esther caught the hand Grandma reached out and guided her to the icebox. She knew Grandma would want to get the milk herself, heat and serve it to this person who had invaded her home.

They sat side by side at the table drinking the rich warm liquid. Every once in a while Esther caressed Grandma's hand and the old woman let her.

"Grandma, you haven't asked about Denton," Esther said after a long silence.

"Denton?"

"My husband."

"When did you marry, Ruthie? Ruthie never married. Ruthie married her work."

Esther laughed to herself, yes, in a way that could be said for me, or for that matter for anyone in the family, not just Aunt Ruth who was wed to her job as a librarian.

"I married Denton, the man who likes to eat your food and who laughs so nicely."

Leah thought, but then shook her head. Tears came to her old folded eyes, seeping out and down her cheeks.

Esther wiped them away with her fingers. "It doesn't matter Grandma. You love him. When you remember again, you'll know how much you love him. And he loves you."

Leah sat in profile to her, her stubborn head held at a tilt. Mucus hung on the nub of her nose, but she seemed oblivious to its presence. Her hair was matted in clumps from where she'd lain on it. Esther decided that Grandma must have slept because her cheek was creased with the pattern of wrinkled fabric. Leah had gone up to bed at six o'clock right after dinner and it was now close to eight. She was still probably halfway into sleep in a safe place of deep forgetfulness.

"Denton is a good man, Grandma. But I have something I want to tell you about him. I haven't told Mother or Daddy." Esther stroked the bathrobe's wool sleeve, feeling the bony arm inside it. She slipped her hand down to Grandma's wrist, and was surprised to find it quite fragile. Grandma's bones had always been so dense and strong. She took the warm hand in hers and held it. "Denton has decided that he cannot fight in this war. Or any war. He doesn't believe in killing. I've said to him that it's fine, that I believe in what he's doing, that I admire his courage. I try to not listen to what mother says about the massacre of Jews. I try to remain angry at mother so I don't have to hear her. But I'm really angry at Denton and at myself." She had to stop. If she didn't she would begin to weep inconsolably.

Grandma didn't move. She didn't even blink. Esther calmed herself. There was one more thing she had to say. Esther waited until she was able to speak again.

"Grandma, I am not kind to my daughter because of this anger. I take my fury out on her."

The old woman turned to Esther with a face that was suddenly alert. Her eyes seemed almost to be seeing.

"My Esther is two sides of a coin, *nu*? And so much more. So many sides, she is. Like a gambling dice. So which side will come up today?" She continued to stare intently, boring into Esther, and then her clouded eyes widened and she grabbed Esther's shoulders and with great strength pulled her to her breast and wrapping her arms around Esther she held her so tightly against her body that Esther couldn't move; Grandma kept squeezing harder and harder, crushing Esther to her.

Grandma released her hold slightly and kissed Esther passionately on the cheek with wet lips, and whispered, "Don't you tell to Judith and Harry. You told to Grandma. It's enough to Grandma you should tell. Not to them. By me it goes to my grave."

Chapter Twenty-Eight

When Denton opened the door of his apartment he heard a piece of paper fall to the floor. He groped around on the top step until he found it, and went inside. The room was warm and stuffy. He'd left the gas heater on. He immediately wanted to race back out into the frigid night, to free himself of a suffocating, heat-induced attack of self-loathing. Instead he turned the heater down and opened the living room window an inch, letting in a rush of cold air. He had to find a way to live with what he had done; he didn't have time to let it consume him.

Remembering the paper in his hand, he went over to the standing lamp, turned it on and read. "Your wife called. 21:00 hours. Says she's returning a week from Sunday on the afternoon train. Can you or someone meet her? Says no need to call back unless you can't come. Ferdie Franza." Jesus, what time had Ferdie brought this by? He wouldn't have closed up the canteen until well after midnight on a Saturday night. It was three now. Had Ferdie looked for him at Herm's? Who had been asked about his whereabouts? No, Ferdie wouldn't have gone looking for him if it had been that late. He'd know better than to disturb anyone. But had he asked at the McIntyres'? Denton's face grew hot, his back prickled with burning fear. He must find out where Ferdie had looked for him, before Denton saw anyone else. But how could he question Ferdie without drawing the man's suspicions? No, he'd let it go. He would not volunteer anything until he saw Herm or Bill. No, not Bill. Ferdie would never have gone into resident territory. Ferdie was a bigoted coward, he could count on that. No, only the homes of Herm, Sy, or Tom McIntyre would be possible places where Ferdie would seek him out. So his story had to be that he'd been at none of those, but rather with Bill or maybe Toki. Yes, that was it, he'd gone to Toki's to talk with him after the confrontation at the meeting. But no one should find out about that

245

confrontation, not if he didn't want Andross to know that he'd kept silent for an entire twenty-four hours. He'd trapped himself with too many lies.

Denton stalked the room, his heart pounding like a captured animal's or a boy who's been caught stealing. This was such a familiar sensation. When had he had it before? When? His breathing came in short, shallow tugs. His chest felt hollow. He remembered coming up the front walk. It was a dark winter evening, not quite six o'clock. He'd put off going home as long as he could. But short of running away, he had to return. He saw a shadow on the front steps. The porch light had not yet been turned on. The shape didn't move as he came closer. He was frightened, but not because he didn't know who the shadow was.

"Denton," his father's voice came through the darkness.

"Yes," he answered, waiting for the first blow.

"I got a call at the office today from Mr. Teller."

"Yes." He would lie. He would say that Mr. Teller had made it up. Or that another kid had been cheating and he had covered for him.

"You know what he told me."

"Yes." With the acknowledgment he felt both relief and nausea.

"Why?"

Was this all? Did he merely have to explain why? "Because I wasn't prepared." Because I didn't want to fail, he cried inside. Because I was afraid to miss the answers on the history test. He'd been lazy and hadn't studied for months. He'd tried at the last minute to cram all the information in, but it had been too late. He'd brought the facts on a crib sheet, the dates and places that he couldn't possibly remember.

"You've hurt me, Denton. I'm ashamed of you. A man's honor is all he has, especially when he's lost everything else. How do you expect to go to the university after this?" His father stood up, looming over Denton from the top step. Without another word he turned and went into the house.

"What happened after that?" Denton asked aloud in the privacy of his barracks. "What the hell happened after that?" He knew what struck the household two weeks later. What he couldn't recall were those intervening two weeks. What the hell had gone on between his father and himself before that night his mother woke him, screaming, "Your father! I can't make him breathe!"?

Denton lay like a traitor on his bed, staring at the blurred pattern on the ceiling, made by the flood lights penetrating the sheer curtains. He had never told Esther about the confluence of those two events, his cheating and his father's death. He'd never even told her he'd cheated and been caught. He hadn't breathed it to anyone his entire life. He wasn't certain if his mother knew, though he thought not. His father probably kept to himself his shame about Denton's crime. Kept it inside until it killed him. Had he killed his father with his deceitful act? How could that be? His father who had cheated over and over with other women, how could he hold his son's one act of dishonesty so close to his heart that it could kill? If only he could remember what had happened during those weeks. He had no recollection of returning to school until after his father's death, when everyone had sympathy for him, and whatever punishment might have been meted out never materialized. He graduated with respectable grades and he went on to the university. His father's death had saved him. But he could remember neither any additional reprimand from his father, nor a reconciliation. No, he didn't think there had been an offering of peace or understanding. It had been fourteen days in a wasteland, devoid of love, or even hatred. Nowhere to turn.

*   *   *

Denton woke before dawn. When he got out of bed his body was even stiffer than it had been in the days following his beating. These new aches recalled the night before, but he shook off the memory. He had too much to do today. He wanted to catch Bill before he left the house. They could go to the Co-op together and try to have a talk with Toki, after which he'd track Herm down and cover himself about last night. When he had time he would explain to Alice that what he'd done was wrong. He would never tell Esther. Herm was right, it would kill her.

Denton filled the sink with water and lathered his face. He made tracks through the white foam, down each cheek and under his chin. To his surprise, the face that emerged was not that of a villain. It was open and smooth. From today on, he thought, staring into his own eyes, you're going to walk the straight and narrow. When Esther came back, he'd give more attention to her and Parin. He would prove he deserved his wife and daughter.

Chapter Twenty-Nine

Denton arrived at the Nakamuras' room at seven-thirty to find that Bill had already left. Mitsue came to the door in a grey suit with a white blouse beneath her jacket. She had a comb in her hand, and her hair was half wrapped into a pompadour and half falling down over her right eye. She looked tired.

"Denton, I'm sorry I'm such a mess. Dori and I are getting ready to go to the Buddhist Center. Bill just left for a block meeting and then he's going to the Co-op office. He should be there by nine."

She insisted that he stay for a cup of tea.

Denton removed his shoes at the door and went to the table where Dori sat on two pillows piled on a chair, eating cereal from a turquoise bowl. As usual she stared dourly at Denton.

"Hi, chicken," Denton said, touching her round cheek. He had a bitter pang of missing his daughter, feeling her body against his chest, and the softness of her fingers stroking his neck.

Mitsue brought the Chinese teapot and cups on a lacquered tray. "When are Esther and Parin returning?" she asked.

"She called yesterday to say she's coming next Sunday," he said, relieved to have the answer ready.

"How wonderful. Is she feeling better?" Mitsue absently smoothed Dori's pigtails.

"I didn't get to talk to her." The memory of his night with Alice threatened to roll over him. He pushed it away. "I was out all afternoon and evening and I only found the note when I got home."

"I bet you'll be glad when you're no longer alone *and* overworked," Mitsue said, pouring the tea.

The danger had passed.

"Bill is beside himself with what happened on Friday. I don't know what those No-No-boys think they're doing." She handed him his cup. "Be careful, it's hot. They don't seem to understand that more than ever we have to pull together." As she poured her own tea her mouth formed an angry line. "Bill says you're coming to your senses, finally."

"Mitsue, ever the plain-spoken one in the family." Denton laughed.

"Yet another way I deviate from my cultural heritage. Mama still calls me to task for it, saying she can't imagine how I found a man. But Bill seems to appreciate it." She sipped her tea demurely, her eyes glinting with ironic humor.

"I think Bill appreciates everything about you."

"Don't idealize me, dear Denton." She lifted her cup in a toast. "To Esther and Parin's homecoming."

"Yes," he said, solemnly. "To their homecoming."

They drank in silence, until Dori began to tell him what her Daddy had done the night before.

"He tooked me and swunged me in the air, and Daddy said when we go away again, when we go where Grandpa lives, we can have a doggy. Daddy said that, didn't he, Mommy?"

Denton looked questioningly at Mitsue. Had Bill decided to take him up on his offer to find placement in New York?

Mitsue shook her head, and turned to her daughter. "Are you done, Dori, sweet pea? Ready for Sunday School? Go get your coat and leggings from the bedroom, please."

When Dori had disappeared behind the curtain she spoke sharply. "He should never have said that to her. I'm very angry. He has no intention of leaving."

"You never know."

"Of course I know, Denton. Don't be silly. He's as dedicated and hellbent on straightening this place out as you are."

But I'm losing *my* dedication, he thought.

Mitsue dressed Dori in her blue leggings and gray flared coat. She tied a white knit hat around the child's head, leaving only straight black bangs to frame her ivory face.

"What a doll," Denton said. "A perfect American Beauty rose."

The child, who he'd been trying to charm for at least a year and a half, smiled back, revealing little pearl teeth, and her black eyes gleamed with pleasure.

Denton laughed full out. "I'm yours, princess, totally yours."

Dori let Denton hold her hand as he walked them to the Buddhist Center. It had turned into an extravagantly beautiful day. Last night it had snowed again and the dirty gray grounds had been dusted a perfect white. The clouds had moved off and were sitting like observers in the west, above the mountains, leaving behind cold but dry air with almost no wind. Walking with Mitsue and Dori, the warmth of her tiny mittened hand in his, he felt curiously cleansed, pure, absolved of his transgressions, hopeful that the political situation wasn't as dire as it had seemed yesterday. If only this renewed sense of the world and his place in it could continue, at least until Esther arrived.

*   *   *

He found Bill in the Co-op's business office where Mitsue had said he'd be. No one else was around.

"Morning," Denton said, standing in the doorway to the inner office that Bill often used to do his paper work. Denton's cubicle was down the hall.

"Hi, there," Bill said, looking up from his work.

"Pretty empty."

"You're right. I'm afraid these guys have really done their job. They've been intimidating everyone."

"When? Everyone but Toki seemed okay after the meeting."

"Yesterday afternoon. The *Hoshidan* gang went to the youth meeting in our block and threatened the kids, especially the jitterbuggers, telling them not to dance western style. The Sacramento kids defied them. Nobody is going to insult their way of life! But in the end only a few of the kids held fast. The majority left, and when they got home their parents were so upset they wouldn't let them out again. There was cabin fever in the barracks by dinnertime last night. And to top it off, Nebo came out of hiding long enough to go with his henchmen, Tony and Mike, from door to door, barracks to barracks, trying to lobby votes by saying that a vote against their position was a vote against Japan and when the war is won the Emperor will know who voted with him and who against. How do you like them beans?"

Denton felt faint. He hoped against hope that Bill wouldn't ask him how he'd spent his Saturday.

"And I happened upon some of the rowdies on my way to the temple yesterday. I was with Mitsue and Dori and there was a pushing match. I don't know why I was such a fool, but I answered when they

250

taunted, and one dark-skinned fellow came up to me and..." He stopped, removed his glasses. Without the cover of reflecting lenses his eyes looked tired. He put the glasses back on. "It was terrible. Mitsue was frightened. Dori was terrified. To think they would harass a father with his baby near. Denton, I don't know what these guys won't resort to."

"I just came from your barracks. Mitsue seemed a bit tired, but she never let on."

"Mitsue wouldn't, not with Dori there. How was my daughter?" His face was pale and strained.

"She seems to have bounced back. In fact, she chattered on about her wonderful daddy and how he picked her up in the air."

Bill's expression relaxed for a moment.

Denton moved into the office without being invited. "Can I join you?"

"Of course, I should have asked. I'm so preoccupied." He moved a pile of papers off the chair beside his desk, piling them on the table under the one window in the room.

Denton watched him, thinking how much he liked this guy.

"Toki?" Denton asked when Bill had sat down again behind his desk.

"He needs the day off. He came in here looking ill. I sent him home."

"And he went?" Denton couldn't believe it.

"Yes," Bill sighed. "With very little resistance."

"We'd better start thinking fast. We can't lose the Co-op to those thugs," Denton said quietly. He leaned forward, examining his hands, rubbing the knuckle of his thumb. "We've lost time. Let's try to make it up."

The two of them spent the next few hours working out strategy for the ward meetings. They went over the modifications from the Office of Price Administration. They decided that they wanted the membership to know just how complicated it had been to get a special government allocation of sugar to the soda production companies and to the candy manufacturers, so that they in turn could supply the unusually concentrated demand from the eight-thousand-member Tule Lake Co-operative. Denton and Bill agreed that not only would this illustrate to people why it would be difficult to cancel orders with no prior notice, but also why they couldn't expect the companies to jump back into action and restart the deliveries at a moment's notice, if the membership decided to go ahead again. Denton and Bill designed a large inventory balance sheet that they could take to the ward meetings and that Bill would get stenciled to add to the newsletter going to press. "Maybe I can get it into the Tulean Dispatch," he said. "Yes, that is exactly what I'll do. If everyone sees exactly how much money is entailed, and how extensive our inventory is, they'll know we can't just stop and start this elephant on the whim of some splinter group."

When they turned to figures for the fish market and tofu factory, the two of them became elated.

"Holy cow," Denton said. "Do you realize what a beautiful monster we've created?"

"It's true, isn't it?" Bill became pensive. He straightened and stretched. "This is good for us, too, isn't it, to take inventory, not only of goods and services, but of our own labors?"

They sat on opposite sides of the desk, the pages piled between them, and there were stray sheets scattered across the office floor. They'd taken off their jackets and rolled their shirt sleeves above their elbows.

"Maybe that was our ulterior motive in doing this appraisal," Denton said, laughing.

"Rebuilding our own morale?" Bill finished his thought. He took his watch from his pants pocket. "Almost twelve. You ready for lunch?"

"Shall we go to the mess?"

"Is there a choice?"

"But let's get right back to this afterward. No dillydallying."

"Yes, sir." Bill gave a mock salute, and together they took their jackets and coats from the backs of their chairs.

*　　*　　*

By the time they reached the mess hall in Block 10, a long line of people had formed outside. Though the sun still shone, glaring off the snow, a wind had picked up and it was much colder than before. Denton turned up his coat collar, wishing he'd worn a hat or at least a scarf. But as cold as the wind was, it wasn't as chilly as the looks they got as they walked to the back of the line. As it grew longer, Bill turned to greet the family behind them, but they averted their eyes. Denton and Bill glanced at each other and shuffled along in silence, as did everyone in their vicinity.

Inside they found the cavernous room not much warmer than it was outdoors. They could see their breath as they went through the cafeteria line. The cooks and servers had wool scarves wound around their necks and tied on top of their heads. Gloves, with the fingers cut off, covered their hands.

"Why haven't they winterized this mess hall yet?" Denton said under his breath to Bill.

"Ask the administration."

Denton took a plate of macaroni and cheese. It looked the least unappetizing. The other choice was congealed chipped beef. Bill took the macaroni and cheese, too.

They found places at an empty table halfway down the long room. Denton felt that if people had been seated there, they would have moved away when he and Bill arrived. The discomfort with his presence, and perhaps with Bill's, too, was obvious. People Denton knew well barely nodded.

"What the hell is going on?" Denton spoke quietly, with his head bent over his plate. He poked at the pale gooey mass before him.

He needn't have bothered to keep his voice down. The crash of metal trays and crockery plates being slammed around behind the serving counter and throughout the uninsulated room was deafening. He'd forgotten how, in the early days, the older evacuees had hated the din. "Eating is quiet time," an old Issei man told Denton in confidence, ashamed to be complaining to a white man, but beside himself with distress. "It quiet but social time. Time to hear soft voices. Can't hear nothing in this noise. Can't hear what I think, even."

"Like I told you," Bill said, being careful not to look around the room. "They used strong-arm tactics, barging into rooms last night. Real terror tactics. The oppressed learn from the oppressor, no? Isn't that what you taught me?"

"Damn it, stop that. You didn't need me to teach you that."

Bill winced, visibly pulling away from Denton.

"What is it?"

"I think we should maintain our respect for each other, and courtesy through this," Bill said. His voice had taken on an old formality, one that hadn't come between them in a long time.

"I'm sorry, Bill. This place is putting me on edge. Let's get out of here before we lose our tempers." He tried to smile.

"You're right. Let's go." Bill bowed his head and shoveled the last of his food into his mouth.

Silence moved like a wave as they passed up the aisle carrying their trays. Conversations stopped, picking up after Denton and Bill had passed. Just as they got to the end of their seemingly interminable walk, he heard the inevitable.

"*Inu,* informing dog," a male voice called. A chorus of barking followed.

He felt Bill stiffen beside him.

"Let's just keep going," Denton said. "Don't respond."

They reached the kitchen. They pushed their trays through the hatch for the dirty dishes. No more verbal taunts sounded behind them, but anger and hostility was in the air. It was circulating around them. It was in the icy looks that met theirs. Bill was a dog, a traitor, an informer, for being in Denton's company. Many of these people were too new to the camp to know Denton. For the first time Denton fully understood that the *Hoshidan* were plowing in fertile soil. Why hadn't his vision been clearer a few weeks ago? He could have anticipated this and acted on it. But what could he have done, realistically, with Andross hellbent on forcing the *Hoshidan*'s hands? He couldn't take the blame on himself. It went back to Andross. The director had primed the camp until it was a sinkhole of doubt, fear, and hatred, imploding with suspicion, rumor and dissent.

Out in the cold, Bill walked ahead at a madman's pace.

"Hey, pal, wait for me." He trotted to catch up.

"These are my people," Bill shouted into the stiff wind.

Denton shielded his eyes from the blowing sand. Clouds had filled the sky and it looked like a heavy snow was on the way.

"I feel just like Toki. All the hard work we've done for them is manure in their hands. Like the manure we were forced to sleep in when they took us from our homes. When they put us in horse stalls. They had to work so fast to protect the nation from us that they didn't even have time to clean the stalls. Poor overtaxed workers. Do you know what it was like to be treated like a horse?" He stopped abruptly and spun around to confront Denton with his fists raised.

"I can't begin to imagine," Denton whispered. His friend had never lost his composure before, never shown how humiliated and shamed he had felt by the way he'd been treated.

"Thank you for not pretending to be able to," he shouted. "No, you cannot imagine. How could you? Have you ever been housed like an animal? Have you ever been made to feel less than a man before your wife? And now my own people are doing the same. Humiliating me publicly, pushing me around in front of my child." He stopped. The expression on his face said he realized he'd lost control. The wind whipped his hair, and his nose was red with the cold and with fighting back tears. His eyes squinted with suspicion behind his glasses. "Don't you ever feel discouraged, Denton?"

"Of course. You remember the other night. I shook so badly I couldn't stop. Perhaps that was my moment of realization, and now you've had yours. Let's go find shelter. I'm freezing."

*   *   *

In the office they sat for a long time without speaking. They had to turn the lights on eventually because the sky over the camp had blackened with storm clouds.

"The saddest result is that I've lost my enthusiasm for all this," Bill said, moving his hand in a wide arc that seemed to encompass the Co-op and the camp beyond. "Why should I care when everything I do is interpreted by them as being traitorous? How ironic, really. I'm in here because my government thinks I'm going to commit some treasonous act against the United States. And my own people think I'm in the process of betraying them. I guess it's the fate of the Nisei, no? Neither this nor that. Neither white nor yellow. Neither Yankee nor Jap."

"Please don't talk like that," Denton said. "I hate hearing this coming from Bill Nakamura."

"I've been thinking about getting out of here after all."

"That's news to me." So Mitsue had been covering about that as well.

"We've had these discussions ad infinitum in the past, and you used to try to push me to get out when the going was good. Now the going is bad, and I feel the toll it's taking on me and my family is too great. I'm also going to have a talk with Toki. For his own safety he and his family should leave."

"Safety?"

"They mean business. If they dared to beat you up, I don't know what they'd do to Toki. He's expendable to the higher-ups in the administration. Namely Andross. I think the populace is so intimidated by these thugs that if anything happened to Toki, nobody would talk. And I don't think Andross would press them for more than a minute, either." He frowned. "You should get out of here, too."

"I know, you've made that clear. Why should I possibly want to stay in this place?"

"I apologize for that, Denton. I know why you've remained with us. You care about us, that's evident. You were misguided about Nebo, but only because you cared too much. I admire that. I do. But you must see how easy it is to be turned from hero to enemy. They could hurt you seriously the next time."

"What will you do?" Denton asked, wanting to shift the attention from himself. He wasn't ready to leave. He had to stay, now more than ever.

"I thought you might find me a co-op to work in for starters, near a university so I could finish my doctorate."

"What about going back to the University of Washington? I've heard that any day now, Roosevelt is rescinding the exclusion order that kept you off the West Coast. Maybe you were right to wait."

"Nope. I'm not going back to the West Coast. I have too much resentment. I'd rather try the Midwest or New York City. Preferably New York where my family is. I hear a person can disappear there, what with so many different kinds of people living together. Oh, boy, how I'd love that."

"I could talk to the co-op wholesaler in New Jersey again for you."

"I hoped you'd say that."

"When were you planning on leaving?" It was taking everything in him to keep from breaking down. His sorrow grew, frightening him with its intensity. What would his days be like without Bill, Mitsue, Herm, and maybe Toki? Everyone was leaving him. He shouldn't just think of himself, but it hurt.

"I can't take much more than a month of this."

"I'll get right on it."

"And Toki? What could you find for him?"

"I'll do whatever he wants. But he'll have to talk to me directly.

He'd hate to think you interceded. He's so darned proud. I only hope we don't run into any roadblocks with Andross. I've never approached him on leave clearance. And I haven't exactly endeared myself to him lately."

"We'll take it one step at a time and we'll take whatever we can get," Bill said. "I don't think you're God, you know, even if *you* sometimes do." He grinned. "Let's get back to work. I'd like to defeat Nebo's proposal before I get out of here."

*   *   *

It was after six by the time Denton and Bill finished their work. They had been concentrating so hard that it was a surprise to look up and find heavy flakes blowing gently against the blackened window. The sight reminded Denton of snow falling in a Japanese landscape print. Denton leaned back in his chair, exhausted. He wondered if the older Issei, who remembered Japan, got particularly homesick at this particular scene tonight. With the thick snowfall, the fences and watch towers were obliterated. Only the white flakes existed, a veil of purity obscuring the flat ugly expanses of rutted land with its starkly repeated rows of tarpapered barracks. Denton wondered if the images of this place would always be with him. How would the camp translate in memory? Would it take on a nostalgic tint, the way the Farm Security Camp in the San Joaquin already had for him? But that camp was a place of hope, a step out of despair. Here it simply got worse and worse.

Bill flipped off the desk lamp.

"You want to come home with me?" He stretched his arms and dropped his head to one side and then to the other. "Oh, my shoulders are so tight. What do you say? A little tofu for the *hakujin*?" Bill joked.

"I thought I might go by to see Toki. Give him some moral support."

"I don't think that's such a good idea."

"Why not?"

"You don't know how much he's said to Sumiko. Maybe he doesn't want you to bring the humiliation into his home. Better to see him in the store tomorrow."

"You think he'll show up?"

"He won't stay away. He won't want to look like a lazy man in his wife's eyes. He certainly won't play *Goh* with the old bachelors. How about it, come by and spend the evening with Mitsue and me."

How was he going to fill this evening? He got up and put on his jacket. He felt the pull of Alice. He'd almost forgotten about her during the hours of work. She was on the evening shift. He could stop by.

"I don't want to impose on you," he said. "I already had tea with Mitsue this morning. You two can use a quiet night together, before we begin making our rounds to the wards tomorrow. We'll be out every night for the next week. Let's try to get some rest." How easy it was to build this alibi. When had he become such a talented liar?

"I'm sorry your wife isn't here," Bill said.

"I am, too," Denton said, surprising himself with a wish to see her. He was lonely. That's what it was. He imagined crawling in beside Esther, fitting his body to hers and his mouth into the softest parts of her neck. After yesterday's hungry, angry eroticism, the thought of Esther brought a different sort of passion to mind, one that was both reassuring and more intimately sensual than anything that had happened with Alice.

Outside, he and Bill stopped a few feet beyond the office barracks in the silence of the falling snow. Denton tilted his head back and stuck his tongue out the way he had as a kid, catching the cold flakes, feeling them melt, catching the snow's whiteness.

From far away he thought he heard a wailing. It had to be the wind. But it got louder and more insistent than any gusts that blew through camp, and besides, tonight the air was still. The wailing stopped.

"Did you hear that?" Denton asked.

"It sounded like a siren. Like the ambulance."

"Where do you think it went?" Denton licked his lips. His mouth had gone dry.

"I'd say about Block 15."

"Why do you think it's out?" Denton kept talking, trying to hold down his fear.

"It could be anything." Bill said.

The porch light was bright enough for Denton to see the concern on Bill's face.

"Like a birth?" Denton said.

"Sure, anything like that."

The siren rose again in a high-pitched moan. It must have been what they were waiting for, because they took off running.

"I have to see," Denton shouted. "I won't be able to sleep."

They ran through the endless curtains of snow. Denton raced as he had in cross-country in college. There was a freedom in this running. As it had in his youth, it kept him tonight from real thought. He had to concentrate on his footing, not to stumble in a hole, not to slip on the new covering of snow. The siren came nearer, off to their right, which he supposed was the direction of the hospital. He was disoriented by the dense snow. They turned toward the sound. Denton ran faster. Bill kept pace at his side. Bill was stronger than Denton had imagined. Denton felt his breath burning in his lungs. His legs began to grow heavy and ache from lack of oxygen. He remembered himself in those races, scrambling up the hills, leading, unwilling to let go. He was not going to give in to the pain until he had won. He was breaking the tape, gasping, clawing for breath.

When they reached the hospital, the main doors were wide open and the ambulance drivers were carrying a stretcher up the stairs. The drivers were two young Nisei men whom Denton recognized.

"Tommy, who is it?" he called.

The boy turned and stared, but shook his head. His face was shrouded in shock and pain. Suicide, Denton thought. He recalled Gozo Horokawa's attempted suicide, how he'd slashed his own face, arms, and legs, and later tried to hang himself. He remembered the bloody violence of the ripped-up barracks room.

He gripped the railing as he and Bill followed the stretcher. Bill's face looked pallid in the cold hospital light. Denton felt like weeping; for a moment he felt that they were one and the same man.

He spotted Alice immediately when they entered the bright reception area, her fair head bent among the dark ones. The stretcher was on the floor and a group of hospital attendants and the ambulance drivers knelt in a circle around it. Alice looked up as though she'd sensed his presence. Her eyes held warning when they met his.

She stood and came over to Bill and Denton.

"Is it suicide?" Denton asked.

She shook her head. Her eyes were the palest gray, as though all the color had been drained from them.

"Is he dead?"

"Yes," she whispered in the increasingly noisy room. People were shouting orders. Other nurses rushed in, young Nisei girls in crisp white uniforms and starched caps.

"Who?" he asked her.

"Toki Honda." Her voice came out flat and harsh.

Bill clutched his arm.

"Oh, God," Denton said. "Oh, my good friend, dear God."

Bill pushed his way into the crowd surrounding the stretcher. The blood-soaked sheet had been pulled away. Denton stood motionless, staring at the dead man lying at this feet. Toki's red-stained white shirt was ripped open to reveal his barrel chest, a bloody mass of viciously torn flesh. His eyes had been closed by someone, or maybe they'd closed naturally. Oh, please let that be the case, Denton thought. Toki's mouth was set, the corners turned down slightly. A clot of blood clung to his lower lip. Otherwise, it was Toki's same square, kind face. Denton remembered his last sight of Toki at the meeting, and how sad and angry his face had been.

There was a commotion at the front door. Herm rushed in with Everett Pfeiffer, the army's head of security. Herm's cheeks were flushed and a layer of snow covered his unruly hair. Everett Pfeiffer wore his regulation cap and it, too, was covered with snow.

"Where is he?" Herm yelled.

"Over here," Denton said.

"What the hell are you doing here?" Herm asked. "How did you hear?"

"Bill and I were leaving the office when we heard the siren."

"Is this the murder victim?" Pfeiffer stood beside the stretcher. He glanced down at Toki. "Name?"

"Tokuro Honda," an ambulance boy said, his voice trembling.

The teenager had carried out his duty, but the significance of the violence was only beginning to sink in. He drew his hand through his hair and across his face. Denton saw with horror that blood from the boy's hand had smeared across his face. Denton moved over to him. He said, "Jimmy, perhaps you'd like this." He handed him a handkerchief. The boy looked at him in confusion. "Your face, there's blood on it and your hand."

The boy stared mutely at Denton as he lifted his palm. He

shuddered and grabbed the handkerchief, wiping frantically at the blood.

"Do you know what happened?" Denton asked.

"They stabbed him to death," Jimmy said.

Denton listened in shock as the other ambulance worker was explaining to Everett Pfeiffer. "Looks like they stabbed him about ten times, sir. He didn't have any chance. We found him at the bottom of his steps, nobody in sight except his wife, Mrs. Honda-san, standing at the top, screaming for help. She's still back at the barracks. Somebody called from the block office, but we don't know who. Nobody's talking. Not one person came out of his room. Just talked from behind their doors, sir. Even with the wife crying her heart out." He, too, seemed about to weep. "He was dead, sir, as a doornail, sir, by the time we got there. Blood coming out of his mouth, they must have punctured his lungs, he must have gone pretty fast."

"Bastards," Herm said, slapping melted snow drops from his jacket.

The nurses, mere girls, held each other, the stiff wings of their caps touching. Two of them were sisters whose parents were members of the Co-op, who knew the Honda family, Denton recalled.

Bill stood quietly with his head down.

Dr. Oshimoto, in surgical scrubs with his hands held high, came rushing through the interior doors. He was the doctor who had delivered Annie Topol. He was the best surgeon in camp.

"Where's the patient?" he said. He was furious. "Why didn't anyone bring him in to me?"

"I'm afraid you won't be needed, Doc," Pfeiffer said. "He's been dead for a good half hour according to your drivers here."

"What in hell's name?" The short, round-faced doctor ripped off his cap and threw it on the floor. He stared at the group in the waiting room as though not seeing any of them. Without another word, he moved brusquely through the crowd, rudely pushing a nurse aside to get to Toki.

There was no denying it, Toki Honda was dead.

"I'm going home," Bill said. "I have to tell Mitsue before the news reaches her. This is probably moving like wildfire through the barracks." His eyes were bloodshot, his voice sad, but he had control of himself. "Mitsue loved him." His voice broke. He patted Denton on the shoulder. "I'll call a meeting for tomorrow at two if that's good for you."

"A meeting of what?" Denton watched as they rolled the bloodied body of Toki Honda through the doors. He hadn't said goodbye. He hadn't gone to see Toki tonight. He realized he could have arrived just as Toki was being attacked. Toki could have died in his arms. Denton dreaded what was to come: confronting the sorrow of Sumiko Honda and her children when he went to pay his condolences, the effect on the Co-op board, Andross' reaction, and finally the funeral.

"Of the Co-op board," Bill said. "We must talk out what we are going to do for the family. We must all go together to the widow. That's the way it must be done."

Through one of Pfeiffer's men, Denton got Bill an escort, because the curfew had started while they'd been at the hospital. Then Denton didn't know what to do. Where should he go? Alice was behind the reception desk. She was watching him as if asking, Do you want me to be with you? He gave a tiny shake of his head. No, he couldn't, even though he longed to go to her, to be held and caressed. In a different world, at a different time in his life he might have done that. Not now. Never.

Herm sat writing in an armchair desk that he'd pulled over to the west wall of the waiting room. Denton went over to him.

Herm kept writing. Denton watched his large freckled hand move across the pages, back and forth. How could he have so much to say? What more to say than that Toki Honda was dead, stabbed to death on a snowy night in November, 1943. Denton imagined the blood spread on the snow. By now it would be powdered over, dusted to pink.

"You satisfied?" Herm said, not looking up.

"What?"

"You satisfied with what your hero Nebo Mota did with his rabble-rousers?" Herm said, continuing to write.

Denton turned and walked numbly to the door. He heard Herm get up, and knocking into chairs, come after him. But Denton went out the door and trotted down the stairs, buttoning up his coat, pulling up his collar. Yep, he thought, it was still snowing. He trotted for a short spell. Then he slowed down, relishing the silence, the vacuum that closed around him like a cocoon, grateful that it muffled the calls of Herm's voice as he shouted from the hospital porch.

*   *   *

With two large glasses of scotch in his belly, Denton slept through the night without moving, waking at dawn from a dream in which he was sucking on Alice's breast. He had an orgasm and after the pleasure had passed, he was filled with shame. He sat up, reached over to the chair and into his trouser pocket for his handkerchief to wipe himself. He saw the blood. Shocked, he dropped the stained cloth.

After a few minutes Denton got up and went to the iced-over window. He scratched at the filigree pattern until he'd cleared enough space to see out. The sky was red on the horizon, and the wispy striations of clouds rising from it were red as well. The snow was red, except where, in the shadow of the building, it was purple. The colors of blood and mourning. "Blood and mourning," he said aloud. But these were words devoid of meaning for him. He was as frozen inside as the ice that had formed on the window, untouched by the heat of sorrow. Toki Honda was dead and he couldn't feel a thing.

Chapter Thirty

A s Bill had promised, the meeting convened at two o'clock the next afternoon. Everyone was present, fourteen men around the large table in the meeting room in Building 707-D: the delegates from the wards, the officers, and Denton. The room dazzled with white winter light. It seemed incongruous to Denton that there was such brilliance on so solemn an occasion. It was out of keeping with Toki's personality; a mellow glow or the mauve of evening would have been more fitting for Toki Honda.

"Without further ado, I call this special meeting of the Board of Directors of the Tule Lake Co-operative to order," Bill announced somberly.

Joe Hohri raised his hand. "Am I to take notes as usual?"

"Certainly," Bill said. "This is a business meeting."

Harry Huroto, the camp's main barber, stood. He was a portly man in his middle fifties, the same age as Toki Honda. "As vice president, I wish be recognized."

"I recognize you, Harry."

"I wish turn in my resignation. All other members do, too."

Denton wasn't surprised. Bill had prepared him. The board members felt shamed by what had happened to Toki and felt it reflected on their own leadership. "They're convinced they don't deserve to remain on the Board, and they're frightened," Bill had told him. "There is talk of requesting protection from the administration for themselves and their families."

"May I be recognized, Mr. President?" Denton raised his hand.

"Of course, Mr. Jordan," Bill said.

"You know I don't usually interfere in matters of the Board. I've always honored the positions you've taken. I've followed your initiative and acted only as an advisor in matters of economics, though my advice was redundant most of the time because our

264

esteemed general manager, with his enormous know-how, was in complete charge." Denton's emotions began to rise. Why did sorrow choose this moment to overwhelm him? "But I wish to suggest that this is a terrible time for you to resign. It's more important than ever to remain united. If only for Toki Honda's sake, for the honor of his memory. He wouldn't want all he has worked for to erode to nothing."

Harry's hand shot up.

"Yes, Harry," Bill said.

"I beg differ with our advisor. To us it is act of honor to resign, to make statement that others must now take care for Co-op, because we have fail to do so properly. I for one cannot continue assume false authority."

The other men nodded. Foshiko Kaminyo of the eighth ward. Kamu Kaminaki of the seventh ward. Jim Hanani, Ward 10's representative. George Yamaguchi from the fifth. And all the others.

Fred Tokami of Ward 3 raised his hand when Harry was seated.

"I agree with Harry. I cannot face the community after this, and I have my family to think of. My wife will not leave her room, for shame and out of fear. She has not even paid her respects to the widow, which leads me to the next part of my three-part statement. We must get this vote out of the way before deciding what the Co-op should do for Mrs. Honda-san and the children. And another matter for you, Denton. If you could speak with the Director about our receiving protection." He sat down.

"If I may," Denton said. He remained seated. "Yes, Fred, I will speak to Director Andross. I think it's not a bad idea. I don't know if you want guards, which I personally feel might be upsetting for the rest of the community." Several of the men nodded. "Perhaps a better solution would be to find you other quarters, away from the general population." Harry and Fred looked alarmed. "Certainly not in the stockade. Please don't think that. Perhaps the new addition on the hospital can be adapted to your families' needs." Denton wanted to assure them he was including their families. "But regarding your resignations, perhaps that can be held off until after the discussion of the widow Sumiko Honda and her family. Because if you no longer constitute a Board of Directors, then the gesture wouldn't be coming from the Co-op and would not carry the same honor. Remember how important the Co-op was to Toki, and how important a formal courtesy call from the full Co-op board would be to Mrs. Honda." As he spoke he leaned forward casually, with his elbows on the table and his hands folded under his chin, so that his recommendation wouldn't be mistaken for an ultimatum. "That's my humble opinion," he finished.

Denton didn't look toward Bill so as not to raise suspicion among the others that he and Bill had planned his statement. If he could get them to hold off on their decisions until after seeing Sumiko Honda, he was certain they wouldn't quit. Across the table a hushed conversation was going on between Harry, Fred and Ate Kashimoto. In the lull Joe was sharpening his pencil with a pen knife. A neat pile of shavings grew on the table before him.

Harry stood and asked to be recognized again. "I agree with Denton. We putting horse before cart. Principal concern as group is to honor memory of departed general manager and pay homage to family as complete group. I move we discuss how we pay respects to widow Sumiko Honda-san and children."

So it was decided that the meeting would be adjourned while two of the members, Fred Tokami and Harry Huroto paid a visit to the widow to ascertain what she most needed. Bill had declined, saying he needed the time to stop by the store and see how things were going. He had left it in the hands of the store manager, Yoshi Nakamata, and Mary Makado, and he feared they were so saddened that they would need moral support. Denton had declined, saying he didn't think it was appropriate for him to visit the widow until it was decided what the group would do. He knew they didn't want him to go, but were only inviting him out of politeness. He, too, wanted to stop by the main store.

There followed discussion of just what they would ask Mrs. Honda.

"You ask widow Honda if she wish traditional burial," Ate Kashimoto suggested. "She be the one to say so."

A loaded silence followed. This was how the trouble had started, with Andross's refusal of a traditional burial for Seiko Kitamara.

"Hondas are Protestants." Tano Osaka spoke. He was the ward representative from Ward 1, an old Issei farmer not given much to speaking in public, but highly respected.

"That's correct," Bill said with relief. "Thank you, Osaka-san. The Reverend Takano has been their pastor since before they came to camp, back in Tacoma. It's a blessing that he's here. I understand that he returned just two days ago from his visits to the other camps. That will be a comfort to the family."

Osaka nodded gravely.

Yes, a blessing, Denton thought, and he nodded in confirmation with the other thirteen solemn men around the table.

A few minutes later they adjourned until four o'clock.

*   *   *

Denton and Bill drove across the camp in the Co-op's pickup truck. Denton had signed it out of the car pool in the morning. The army had taken over the garage, replacing the young men who Andross claimed were responsible for the agitation among the farmworkers. Denton disliked going into the garage. It recalled the day he and Toki had witnessed the return of the farmworkers, those exhausted, frozen men. He remembered the meeting afterward when Andross had refused to let Toki participate, and he had watched the man walk across the rain-whipped parade grounds, bent into the wind, his trousers getting soaked. Denton was further upset to learn from Paul Schmidt that two of the farmworkers were in the hospital with pneumonia and that Andross had sent the leader of the renegade group to the stockade.

Denton turned into the main firebreak, working the rattling vehicle over the ruts. He glanced over at his silent friend who stared straight out the windshield. Bill's yellow scarf was wrapped up to his nose. Flashes of sky and camp were reflected in his spectacles. His arms were folded tightly around his waist.

Denton wondered what his companion was thinking. Denton knew where his own thoughts kept leading him, and he was frightened by the path they took. As hard as he tried, as many times as Denton went over Toki's murder, he couldn't picture himself responding nonviolently if he'd come upon the killers. Even if he'd pulled them off Toki, Denton knew his rage would have been so great that he would have grabbed the knife and plunged it into the attackers.

The truck clanked noisily as they shimmied and bucked over the ruts and the blinding drifts of snow.

"They can't get anyone to come forward, just like I predicted," Bill suddenly shouted over the racket of the truck. "I know people saw what happened, who killed him. But no one will speak up. They're scared, but hell, someone could show a little courage. Katz's Internal Security Force has just disappeared. Herm said most of them aren't showing up for work. What a courageous lot of J-A.'s." He slammed his fist down on the dashboard. "I want to kill whoever did this. I want to make them pay for what they did." He hunched forward, squinting into the light, his lips pressed tightly together.

Denton wanted to weep for Bill, for the rage he felt. He wanted to run amok, go crazy, create chaos, terrify the world with wild confusion. He wanted to drive this damn truck and find Nebo and Andross and the killers and run them down, crushing their bodies beneath his wheels. He wanted to kill and maim even if it meant taking a chance with his own and Bill's life in order to accomplish his ends. Goddamn it, he could live as cruelly and dangerously as the next person. He could wreak havoc on this evil world.

A stabbing pain shot through his left temple, down his cheek and neck. No, he screamed inside, I will not get a headache!

"Goddamn fucking everything!" Denton yelled, gripping the steering wheel and gunning the motor. The tires whirred on the ice beneath the snow as the truck swerved and righted itself and took off down the firebreak. He drove at breakneck speed down the center, passing block after block of black structures sitting on dirty snow. The sides of the buildings were spattered with mud. Through the openings Denton had glimpses of people, filthy coal bins, clothes hanging to dry on lines. He sped up until the camp became a blur of white and black. Bill braced himself with both hands against the dashboard, but didn't tell him to stop when Denton pressed down harder on the gas. They passed Block 20. They kept going. He raced toward the fire station on the hill and the water tower and the fences at the end of camp. They should have cut into Block 23, but Denton didn't turn. He wanted to ram the damn truck right through the chain link fence and barrel out to freedom.

Nebo's face appeared before him, a haughty face against the blur of white. An image of Toki's calm, sympathetic face came to him as well. He envisioned Toki in the moment before the assault, looking out his door into the thickly falling snow, wondering at a noise in the square, walking down the stairs to get a better view, when from the shadows men came running and plunged long kitchen knives into Toki's barrel chest, into his gut, plunging up under his shoulder blade, sending blood spurting as he crumpled to the ground. Toki, never having the opportunity to defend himself, while Sumiko cried for help, and no one came to their aid. Denton slammed on the brakes, sending the car into a swerve and a spin. He worked the steering wheel into the skid, letting the truck go where the wheels would take them. Bill reached out and grabbed the wheel, helping him to turn, until the car came to a stop.

They sat breathing heavily. Bill let go of the wheel and slid back over to his side of the car. The truck faced in the direction they had come from—back toward the front gate towers, the blocks of resident barracks, to the no-man's land between residents and administration, to Alice Hamilton's room, the barracks he shared with Esther and Parin, Building 707-D, the stockade, the sharp outline of Castle Rock, and beyond that, to Mount Shasta and San Francisco. But everything was different than it had been two days ago.

It didn't matter who had done the killing, nor who was to blame. It didn't matter that Andross had created an atmosphere that made murder possible. It didn't matter if Nebo was reacting to racism. It didn't even matter if Nebo had no direct hand in this killing, but had only encouraged it with his actions. It didn't matter anymore if he himself had played a part by keeping information from Andross, by closing his eyes to the escalating violence. What mattered now was that he knew he would have picked up arms against the bastards who'd come for Toki Honda. He would have protected Toki by any means, even if it meant killing.

*   *   *

At the main store there was a sign in Japanese posted on the door. Bill read it to Denton:

"Due to the death of our general manager we are closed today."

"Did you know about this?"

"No. They were open when I left." Bill knocked.

Mary Makado came to the door. When she saw Denton and Bill she smiled sadly, opening up for them. Denton felt calmed by her beautiful smile.

"We decided to close," she said after she had greeted them. "The store was empty until Mrs. Hoji and Mrs. Ito came by, and you know how those women can be. They made us feel so bad. They said it was not right to be doing business on the day after Mr. Honda's death,

269

that it would hurt and insult the family if they learned. They said the fish store was closed and the tofu factory. She made us so ashamed that Mr. Nakamata and I decided to close. But we're working up the inventory that Mr. Honda would want completed by Tuesday. We took it out of his office. We couldn't sit in his chair." She began to cry. "Oh, no." She wiped her eyes on her sweater sleeve and covered her face with her hands.

"You did the right thing, Mary. Didn't she, Bill?"

"Yes." Bill put his arm around the girl, and walked with her into the deepest reaches of the store to find Yoshi Nakamata.

Toki's office was open and Denton went in. The desk looked just as it had on Friday, Toki's last day at work. Yes, it would have been Friday, Denton thought, walking around the desk. He'd probably come by for an hour or two before the Co-op board meeting. Denton sat down in the wooden chair with the wool pillow Toki used to cushion the hard seat. He'd proudly bought it from the initial shipment of household goods to the Co-op. "For my fanny," he'd laughed. Denton looked through the papers on the desk. There was Toki's handwriting, lists of extra items for the inventory. A list of orders. There were scratch papers in Japanese, and notes between Toki and some other person, judging by the ink and the differences in the formation of characters. All in Japanese. Fluent as Toki was in English, he'd told Denton, for some reason adding and subtracting and making decisions about inventory remained easier in his native language. "Perhaps because I learned those skills as a young lad," he said. "From my father." When he remembered this, it was as though someone had grabbed Denton's shoulders from behind with no warning and begun to shake him so hard he couldn't breathe. Sobs heaved up from deep in his belly. He pressed his palm tightly over his mouth to stop the sound, but the tears rolled down his face until his chin dripped and his neck was soaked, and he swayed with the waves of grief.

When the animal pain had passed and Denton opened his eyes, he was struck by how much smaller and shabbier the room looked. The paint was dingy with lava dust, the woodwork was scuffed. And it was messier. Yellowing papers were piled everywhere, their edges curling, and the labels on the filing cabinets were askew. The room had shriveled. Like a skin that has lost the person inside. Like a skin in need of a great man.

*　　*　　*

Fred and Harry returned to the Co-op board meeting to report that Mrs. Honda had already made arrangements with Reverend Takano to have a Protestant service. Reverend Takano had reviewed the plans with Director Andross, at which time it was decided that they could have the viewing of the body in the Hondas' room. This was highly unusual but what the family desired. In fact the body was already there. Sumiko and her son, Danny, Sally and Sally's husband Frank would sleep at neighbors' in the adjacent barracks, but a family member would be with the body at all times.

At least Andross had some decency left in him, Denton thought, though he suspected a political ploy as well. It was a way to ingratiate himself with the family and by extension with the residents of their block, and the members of the Co-op. Maybe it was just political but it was better than nothing. Perhaps the man was learning after all.

In the short meeting, the board decided to get *kan sha jo*, traditional mourning wreaths, from Charlie Hokinama, manager of the produce department. Hokinama had been a florist before internment. They relied on his skills on such occasions.

"Hokinama make good mourning wreaths," Harry Huroto said. "Fine wreaths. They honor the dead."

They would all go together to pay their respects to the family.

Before they adjourned, a motion was passed that the next meeting would take place two days hence, at which time they would hand in their resignations as a group. Denton was glad to have the extra time, but he was afraid the conclusion had become inevitable. The men asked him to pursue the possibility of safer housing with Director Andross. "After what he has done for Honda family, he sure to give us safe place. So good, too, to allow body to lie in state in house. So good of Director," Harry Huroto said.

As they walked in a cortege through the cold early evening air, with the wind blowing at the hems of their dark coats, Denton reflected on the meaning of what he was taking part in. Here he was, the fourteenth man of a mourning party, marching solemnly across the white land of the camp. In a curious way, this was the closest he had ever been to these men or any of the other evacuees. He was not a representative of the administration on this night. He wasn't trying to find a way into their world nor was he searching for a role for himself, so that he could better understand them, could be trusted by them, could get them to join with him and each other. No, ironically, the actions of Nebo Mota—or at least his men—against Toki Honda had served to make him an unquestioned equal among these men. He suffered as they did. They mourned the same man. They had esteem for the same man. They walked across the same cold expanse to pay their respects to his widow and his children. And in doing so, they acted for the first time as one.

Two army guards stood on the lowest of the three steps leading to the Honda door, their legs spread at ease, their rifles held muzzle up between their legs. They looked frozen through, Denton observed with a certain satisfaction. At least their memory of this night would be of discomfort.

The room was filled. The mourners were seated in rows of borrowed wooden folding chairs on either side of the coffin. All the furniture had been removed to make room for Toki and for those who came to grieve. When the Co-op entourage arrived, many of the men inside got their coats and retired to the cold night, bowing and murmuring good evening to the new arrivals. Denton was greeted as warmly as anyone else, with great sadness and looks of commiseration. When he approached the widow, she bowed her head and then raised her face to him. She smiled kindly and said, "Thank you for visit husband. He think high of you."

"Not as highly as I thought of him, Mrs. Honda-san. Not possibly."

Then there was Toki himself. Or not himself. Denton almost had to laugh when he saw the job the undertaker had done on him. Who the hell had they gotten to do this? He was certain they'd sent out of the camp. There were men in camp who had been undertakers by profession, but they had no equipment here. Well, this undertaker was a doozy—without question a Caucasian who had never touched an Asian. Denton was almost grateful that such a terrible job had been done. The body looked nothing like Toki. He wore lipstick and rouge over white powder. Dark purple shadow made his eyes exaggeratedly oriental, as if he were a white man done up for the part. Denton looked up at the enlarged photo of Toki that hung over the coffin, draped in black and purple mourning satin. There was his friend smiling out, dressed in dark suit and vest and tie. It was a photo Toki had sat for not six months before. He had rather liked it, Denton recalled. "I don't look like such an old man," Toki had said. "My wife says it reminds her of how I used to look, out in the world, when I was a big shot." Gazing at it, Denton thought this was exactly how *he* remembered Toki, open, forthright, with an ironic twist to his grin.

Denton was leaving, bidding goodbye to Bill and the other men who were collecting their hats and shoes near the door, when Herm arrived. Wind rushed in with him, bringing dampness and cold, and the conversation stopped. Everyone looked up to stare at him, towering over them. Herm half-bowed to those present, and was acknowledged with cool courtesy. Denton noticed that some of the newer internees glared at him with suspicion. But it didn't affect Herm. He took off his cap and bent to untie his shoes. When he had toed them off, and before going over to Mrs. Honda, he turned to Denton. "How about waiting for me? I owe you an apology."

"Sure," Denton said, relief and pleasure flooding him. He hadn't realized how badly he'd been wounded when Herm had all but blamed him for Toki's death. Denton had had too many other emotions to grapple with to give it much thought, but the intensity of his present joy told him how injured he'd felt. "I'll be outside. It's too crowded in here for everyone's comfort." He bent and finished tying his own shoes.

In the square, surrounded by the barracks of Block 14, there were forty or fifty more people grouped in the pools of light from the stationary search beams.

Denton waited with Bill. They were joined by Mitsue, who had just arrived. She wore the dark gray gabardine coat that Denton knew so well. She'd had it on that first day, against the cold May wind.

"I must go in," she said. "How is she?"

"Sumiko is a strong woman," Bill said with a sad smile. "She was always strong support for Toki. He'd be proud of how brave she's being."

"Outer strength can conceal a soft inside," Mitsue said.

Denton thought of Esther, of how she used to say, "Don't believe how tough I seem. I need you to hold me. I need you to keep me in one piece." But it had been so long since she'd revealed that part of herself. He thought with chagrin of Alice and how she had professed not to care if anything came of their tryst—and then had begun to cry.

"I believe that, Mitsue," Denton said.

Bill looked at his wife with admiration and love.

"When I'm through in there I'm going to the Buddhist Center," Mitsue said. "Unless you need a place to rest, Denton, and eat. I could make you a small supper."

"Thanks," Denton said, leaning forward against the cold, his hands dug into his pockets, feeling lonelier than he had in weeks. "But Herm said he wanted to have a talk. Maybe we bachelors can find a little consolation in talk."

"But you'll come by soon?" She put her hand on his arm.

"I'll do that. I think we have a few matters to talk about."

Bill nodded. "I'll see you anyway at Toki's office tomorrow, no?"

"Yes. We've got a heck of a lot of work to do if we're going to save the Co-op." Denton said. "Let's get started early. Say eight?"

Chapter Thirty-One

Bill followed Mitsue back into the Hondas' room, holding open the door for Herm as he came out. Denton watched Herm maneuver awkwardly down the steps, moving sideways to favor his left leg. He must have injured it when the jeep went over, Denton thought. He'd have to ask.

Out of habit, they went to Herm's room. Denton couldn't imagine inviting him to his own apartment. It was the place he went to sleep and that was it. Much as he'd felt lately that it wasn't a warm home even when Esther and Parin were there, today it seemed less than a dormitory. It had become a stark, inhospitable place that encouraged unhappy thoughts.

He hadn't been at Herm's since the night of the military takeover of camp, light-years ago. While Herm restarted the fire—he'd left it with just a glow hours before, he said—Denton stretched out in the recliner and watched him work, and let the bachelor-quarter comfort of the room embrace him.

"These are bad times." Herm handed him a bourbon, the ice clinking.

"I admit this hasn't been an easy couple of weeks for me, or for any of us."

"I owe you an apology for the other night," Herm said, sitting on the davenport. "I don't know what got into me."

"Anger, probably."

"I guess you'd know about anger." With his head down, Herm's bushy eyebrows concealed his eyes, but Denton could see his grin.

"Yep. It feels like I've been living inside a tornado. As though I've been beating myself up mentally as well as physically."

"I'd call it being disillusioned."

"Oh, would you?" Denton said. "And what would you know about that?"

"I'm only too familiar with it," Herm said.

Denton took his handkerchief out and mopped his face and the back of his neck. He was suddenly pouring sweat.

"How's your left leg, by the way?" Denton said, not wanting to talk about what was on his mind. "I noticed that you favored it when you came down the steps at the Hondas."

"You're right." Herm extended his leg, massaging the thigh. "Ever since the other night when I had to crawl out from under the damn jeep, it's been bothering me. It's getting better though."

"Perhaps I am disillusioned," Denton said.

Herm listened.

"I'm so enraged about what happened to Toki I feel as if I could take the world apart with my bare hands." Denton felt tears rise in his throat. "If I could find out who did it, I'd kill the sons-of-bitches. I mean it, too." Denton stood. He went over to the kitchen counter and filled his own glass with bourbon. He let water run in the sink, and leaning on his elbows he splashed his face. He kept his back to Herm as he slowly wiped his cheeks and forehead dry.

"I haven't told you about my thoughts," Denton said, turning to Herm. He sipped his new drink. "I haven't told anyone, not even Esther."

"Tell me." Herm rotated his glass between his palms as he watched Denton, his face as compassionate as ever.

"I'm thinking about enlisting, going down to San Francisco first opportunity and asking my Selective Service Board to pull my conscientious objector papers." Denton sat down.

"You're thinking about this or you've decided?" Herm asked matter-of-factly, almost as though he'd been expecting it.

"I don't know yet. I've been mulling this for some time, but yesterday, I realized I can't go on letting other people do the dirty work for me. It's not that I want to kill, but I know I would in certain circumstances. I can't deny that. I really would kill Toki's attackers if it came to that." He began to tremble.

"You know that war is not just defending yourself and your buddies? They tell you when to kill and when not to."

"What are you trying to say?"

"I'm just letting you know what I know. Not that I've ever been through it, mercifully, but I remember my dad telling me that the hardest thing for him was having some guy he didn't respect order him to shoot some poor devil across the lines. A father or brother sitting in the same kind of rotting trench that he was sitting in. I don't think my father ever got over that part of it—knowing he'd followed along, hadn't killed to save himself or his buddies, or even his country. He'd say, 'Son, we weren't even protecting our own country over there, just fighting somebody else's war, marching to somebody else's orders.' Don't misunderstand me, it's not that I don't have days when I wish I could be over there. When I wish more than anything I could do my part."

"I'm sorry for you, that you don't have a choice. It's funny, not so many days ago I envied you in that regard."

"I bet you did," Herm said.

"Hell, they may not even take me with my migraines. What an irony that would be. Or maybe they'll give me a desk job. At least do my part that way."

"Or you'll decide to maintain your status," Herm said, his voice soft.

Denton leaned back in the recliner. "I remember when I was counseled by the Friends. This woman down in Berkeley. She said, 'Killing makes us a savage society. A civilized society sees that we control our basest instincts. When that covenant is broken, we have war. But there must be some people of conscience who say, No, I will not kill. I will contain my impulses.'" Denton's voice cracked. He cleared his throat. "I understood what she meant at the time. I used to think nothing would be gained by my killing another. But today I ask who the hell is going to save the others from destruction if I'm not willing to? Would I have turned my pacifist back on Toki? Who does the job of saving Jews if I won't?" He put his hand over his eyes to cover the tears that seeped out. All the pent-up sorrow pressed against the walls of his chest.

"I don't know the answer for you, Dent. I damn well don't know. In my crazy hours alone I fantasize about how it would be if Roosevelt had immediately opened our country to every Jew in Europe, or if Stalin hadn't signed the Pact and had taken a moral stand against Hitler. Simple, honorable and logical. But they didn't. And they're still not doing it. So young men are left with a terrible choice. We either refuse to participate and feel like hell, or we do what my father did and kill." Herm got up. "Refill?"

"Sure." Denton's eyes had dried. He sat forward. " Or I could insist that they call me up so they at least have to put me in prison when I refuse to fight. I'd be an honest man then."

"Yeah. Honest and in prison. How many people would be helped by your being in prison? Would it do Esther any good? I don't think so. Talk to Esther. See what she says."

Denton looked around the familiar room as Herm chipped ice from the block in the icebox. He watched the pick attack the block, sending up transparent slivers. He tried to picture himself in prison. He saw the cage in the stockade. His heart raced with the claustrophobic cruelty of it. Denton knew he wouldn't last a week alone in a place like that. He tried to imagine himself out in a field of snow and ice, with a gun in his arms, waiting to fire, waiting to kill another man. He knew it wasn't the same as defending a friend. He imagined an officer, his age or younger, a man whose politics he probably wouldn't agree with. The officer he was supposed to follow into battle, telling him who to kill. He knew he'd be terrified every single minute while he was doing his service. He would question strategy, tactics, the reason for being in that particular position on that particular day. He would question his right to be on another continent, in another man's land, destroying the people and the homes and the countryside. But hundreds of thousands of men were over there fighting at this moment and at least some of them must be plagued with doubts and still able to carry out their duties, and some of them even had to be philosophical pacifists like he was. He had to remember his killing rage over Toki's death, and he knew his fury in that instance was not a new sensation. He'd felt this urge to destroy— to kill—innumerable times in his life. Even though he kept his rage under control, didn't go into the streets and commit mayhem, hadn't yet broken the social covenant, he felt it was a lie to continue pretending he was too pacific a man to participate in war in some way.

"So what are your plans, your timetable?" Herm asked, handing him the fresh drink.

"I'll call Esther. See if she wants to wait for me down there for another week or two, or if she'd rather come up here, as she's planning to, on Sunday."

"She's coming Sunday?"

"That's what I hear. I haven't talked to her but I got the message." As he said it, he had a desire to tell everything to Herm, to confess.

"First I want to get certain problems taken care of. Talk to Andross about giving the Nakamuras leave clearance."

"Bill wants to go? Finally get out of here?" Herm raised his eyebrows. "Looks like this whole shebang is really coming to an end for the likes of us. I won't be the only one deserting the ship after all."

"It does seem that way." Denton sipped his drink. It felt good to be talking like this again, quietly, intimately. He wouldn't mind sitting here through the night, discussing one topic after another with Herm, maybe even circling back to the subject of the war. They wouldn't have many more times like this. Once they dispersed, that would be it, especially if he got shipped overseas or sent to prison. "I feel responsible to him and Mitsue, and I also can't leave until we find out who killed Toki and some sort of justice is done. What have you heard?"

"The same as you have. The obvious suspect is Nebo, or someone ordered by him, but not a soul is talking. The MP's found him out in the far reaches of camp, hiding out in Block 40's bachelor quarters. He's been taken in for questioning."

"No informants?"

"Not a goddamn one. It's unbelievable. Either they're scared or people wanted it."

"Nobody wanted Toki Honda dead."

"I know what you think of the guy, Dent, but to be honest, he was a tough nut at times."

"He was respected," Denton said angrily.

"The man had power. Power is resented in a place like this and you know it. You remember how they suspected him in the beginning?"

"But he'd proved himself again and again to people."

"That's true. That doesn't mean others didn't harbor their resentments though, and those old feelings are easily torched by rumors. I haven't gotten to the bottom of it, and Sy is working on it as well, but apparently there was a lot of rumor-mongering in the last week, and Toki was the focus of most of it."

"I thought I was," Denton sat forward, putting his drink down by his foot.

"You were, earlier on, but they couldn't get a rise out of anyone off you. Even beating you up didn't do the trick. It frightened folks more than anything else. It felt like all the rules were being broken. It was too crazy. So they switched all their attention to Toki, or so Sy seems to think. And that worked better. But who started the rumors or passed them on, and who was mad enough or fanatical enough to kill him, we just don't know. That's the way it is in these matters. That's the way it's been in the other camps, too."

"Are you trying to tell me you saw this coming?"

"Goddamn it, of course not. Or at least no more than you saw it." Herm rose from the davenport and walked around it.

He looks guilty, Denton thought. "You guessed what might happen and you didn't come to me. You and Sy knew what I didn't know and you didn't tell me." His voice got louder with each word.

"Stop it, Dent. There's nothing that any of us could have done. Of course we didn't know. We've had plenty of these rumors all over this camp since we started."

"But the situation in camp was never this critical before."

"And none of the residents has ever been killed before by another resident." His face was bright red. His freckles were dark brown. "Don't go and rewrite history and start blaming me and Sy."

"It's hardly history. It's a fresh wound." Denton clenched and unclenched his hands. "It's Sy's job to figure these things out."

"So now Sy is more godlike than either you or I?"

"What do you mean by that?"

"Sy came in with as many ideals as we did, thinking he could work miracles. No, I amend that. Of the three of us, Sy was the most realistic. He always knew what couldn't be done. Sy knows how complicated the human race is. He didn't expect anyone to be all good or all bad."

"Like I did."

"Yes, like we both did."

Herm walked over to his kitchen again and poured himself another drink. He turned toward Denton and silently held the bottle out. Denton drained his glass.

"Sure, why not?" he said.

Herm filled his glass, the rich brown bourbon rising almost to the brim. It felt good to drink. He needed this. He might feel like hell in the morning, but tonight he'd be at peace. He drank, remembering the scotch at Alice's place and the passion it had spurred. He knew he'd have to go back there and talk to her, and say goodbye definitively.

"We through it now?" Herm asked. "We having a truce?"

"I can't fight with you, not for any length of time."

"Pals to the end." Herm was sprawled on the sofa, his head on the arm. His curly hair stuck out in all directions. His shirt had come open over his belly and his socks had slid down around his ankles. "But there is one more item I've got to talk to you about, to ask you."

"Shoot." He was feeling more relaxed by the moment. He needed this restful time, to get the burden off for a few hours. The Irish knew how to do it with their drinking wakes.

"Tell me about Alice Hamilton." Herm didn't look his way, but stared at the ceiling instead.

"What do you mean, what about her?" Denton's head began to buzz with fear.

"You tell me."

Denton didn't answer. If Herm knew, let Herm tell him.

"It's only because I'm looking out for you that I'm talking to you about this. What's going on between the two of you isn't a big secret, my boy."

"How did it get out?" Someone had heard them. Who the hell lived next door to her?

"Don't try to figure it out. This place is a rumor mecca, you know that. She's got some style, that gal. I hear she stood up for what she believed down in Manzanar. She's the kind we Jewish boys always fall for. How come *you*, pal?" He sat up and reached across the space between them and swatted Denton's knee.

"How far has this gotten around, do you think?"

Herm grew serious. "Mum's the word with me, that's for certain. Sy knows. We had a talk about it. I made him swear on the old testament not to tell Sarah. I shamed the Jew. I said, 'Don't let one of them hurt one of ours this way.' I even confessed some of my own sins, that's how honorable I was on your behalf. Yep, that's right, I lied to you the other night." He laughed. "And Andross. Who cares if he knows? You're getting out of here."

"I still need some favors from him. For Bill. For the Co-op Board of Directors and the ward representatives. I don't want him telling Esther."

"He's not going to tell Esther. He's not the least bit interested in that kind of thing. I don't think he even has a pecker."

Denton half-smiled. Was it from relief at having his secret laid bare? "I only care about Esther in this. I'll tell her myself in my own time, but I don't want..."

"Don't you be a goddamn fool," Herm roared. "Don't you tell her about it. Just don't do it. What went on with you and that woman doesn't mean a thing. You were down, about as far down as you've ever been. She took unfair advantage."

"I'm a grown man. I can take responsibility for my actions." But hard as he tried to imagine telling Esther, he couldn't. It was too terrifying to think of getting the words out.

"Not for that thing," Herm said, pointing to Denton's lap. "Not when you've got a bush coming after you, all nice and wet and smelling good. Forget it, brother. There are times when all the years in the world can't keep you from acting like a panting adolescent. And if I haven't convinced you yet, let me say it again as a Jew to a Gentile, don't tell my Esther that you did it with a shiksa. Just don't. Especially not these days."

Chapter Thirty-Two

B efore going to the Co-op in the morning to meet Bill, Denton stopped off at the army's dining hall and made a long-distance call to Esther. He asked the operator to place it person-to-person. He didn't want to waste money if he happened to get Judith or Harry, and he didn't feel up to talking with them anyway. He had a splitting headache. His own fault, he knew, but nonetheless, he was suffering. He'd taken an aspirin, but it only gave him a raw, bilious stomach. He ordered sunnyside eggs with Spam and biscuits from the kitchen before he placed the call. Though the thought of the eggs nauseated him, he knew from experience that food was the best cure.

He sat in the hot, airless phone booth with the receiver pressed to his ear, hearing the distant sound of the ring. He realized that he hadn't prepared for this conversation. He didn't have any idea what he was going to say to his wife. Except that he loved her. That would always do, and this morning he felt it with an ache almost as strong as the throbbing in his head.

"Hello," a woman's voice answered.

"Esther?"

"Person-to-person for Esther Jordan," the operator interrupted. "Is this Esther Jordan?"

"Esther, it's me." He felt like a kid. He wanted her to hear him, not hang up on him.

"Of course I'll accept it." Her voice was clear, crisp and precise with that deep alto pitch he knew so well.

"Esther, my love."

"Denton, please," she said. "The operator will hear. And this is extravagant. Didn't you get my message? I'm coming on Sunday. Does this mean you can't meet us?"

"No, I'll be there. I miss you so much," he said. He believed it. He knew he missed her desperately. "And Parin?"

"She's fine. She's down with her grandfather in his lab. She adores him."

He felt a stab of jealousy.

"But you're still her idol, Denton. Don't worry."

"You read my mind."

"She talks about you every other sentence, my daddy this, my daddy that."

"You jealous?"

"Denton, why are you calling? We shouldn't waste this money."

He saw it had been a dumb idea to phone. How was he going to explain to her that he was considering giving up his C.O. status? He couldn't even say that he wanted to come down to San Francisco to have her help him decide, that he felt like a baby about this and he needed her to coddle and guide him. Nor could he confess that he had to get out of here before he heaped further betrayal on their marriage.

"I wanted to hear your voice." His throat constricted. "We've had some difficulties up here."

She was silent. He knew she was thinking, Here we go again.

"It's been particularly difficult," he said, lowering his voice.

"I can't hear you," she shouted.

"It's been hard here," he said. "Toki Honda was killed."

"Oh, no," she said in a tiny faraway voice.

"I've been doing a lot of thinking. I have a lot to discuss with you. I thought I might come down to San Francisco to deal with some things."

"But when? This weekend? Oh, Denton, I'm so sorry about Toki. When did it happen?"

"On Sunday night." He coughed. "I don't know quite when I'll be ready to come down, but as soon as possible."

"Honestly, if it's not this weekend, I'd rather come up. It's time to leave, and I have matters I'd like to talk to you about, too," she said, with special meaning in her voice.

"You want to tell me what?"

"Not on the phone, Denton."

"You don't want to say what it is?" His head hurt. She couldn't possibly know about Alice. No one would have called to tell her.

"No, Denton, I said I don't."

"Okay, let's keep the plan as it is and we'll talk up here."

"You're certain you want us to come?" Anxiety inflected her voice.

"I can't wait to see you." For a split second he thought, If I were still carrying on with Alice, would I say that? "I really can't wait," he repeated, putting more conviction into the sentence.

They made arrangements for him to pick her up at the Klamath Falls station. "If you can manage to find the time for us," Esther said.

"Honey, please don't. I promise you I'll be there," he said. Though as soon as he'd offered, he'd begun to wonder how the hell he could fit it in. But he had to go. This time he could not possibly send someone in his place. "I love you."

"Oh, Denton," she sighed. "I love you, too."

When he hung up and went out to the dining room, Ferdie was carrying in his eggs. The smell turned his stomach, but he sat down at a table in the center of the empty dining room and dug in.

"That your wife you were talking to?" Ferdie went around the bar and began washing glasses.

"Yep."

"When she called the other night, I'm glad she didn't insist I find you. I wouldn't have known where the hell to look for you. I told myself, he's out there deep in the colony and I'll get myself killed going after him."

"Yep, I was out working," Denton said. He forked Spam with egg yolk on it into his mouth. It started to taste good. His stomach was settling.

"Always working. You should try to have some fun. Do you good."

Denton shrugged and continued eating.

"Okay, I get the hint. I'll leave you in peace."

"Thanks," Denton said.

He was wiping the last bit of yolk off his plate when he looked up to see Ted Andross in his overcoat, looking freshly scrubbed and shaved.

"Mind if I join you?" Andross asked, coming over to the table. He grinned at Denton as though they were old allies. Well, this would save Denton a trip to the office.

Denton wondered if this straight arrow ever got himself into any nasty trouble, or did he always toe the line? Andross no doubt believed he was irreproachable, thought his rules were the only rules worth living by. He probably never swerved from the standards he'd set. It was the way Denton used to see himself, and that's what really rankled. He used to believe he had his own brand of morality, his own code that would eventually lead to an equitable world. He had guiding principles for dealing with people of other races, with the downtrodden, with his colleagues, and his wife and child. But lately the world of his ideas, actions and morals was spinning like a pinwheel, confounding him and tripping him up at every turn.

He must not have answered Andross, because the man said, "Well?" with a look that screamed, "Hey, I'm your boss and you're not responding to me."

"Of course, sit down." Denton stood and pulled a chair out for Andross.

Andross removed his overcoat and draped it over a chair at the next table. He wore an immaculate brown suit, vest, and white shirt.

"What're you having?" he said, sitting down.

"I'm finished. I had eggs and Spam. It was good." He felt self-conscious about the way he was dressed. He'd thrown on a day-old, open-collar shirt, with pants that hadn't been pressed in a week. Over the shirt he wore an old tweed jacket that had elbow patches and a lining that Esther mended regularly "to try to put another year of life in this old thing." He couldn't even be sure he'd shaved properly, since he'd been red-eyed and bleary as he'd stood before the bathroom mirror. But his appearance hardly mattered anymore. Neat clothes couldn't salvage his reputation in front of Andross. So be it, he thought, if the bastard doesn't approve of me.

Ted Andross ordered the same meal Denton had just finished, and toast to go with it. "And some real java if you have it, none of that chicory," he said to Ferdie.

Ferdie said he would see what he could do, with a wink and a nod to Denton to ask him if he'd like the same. Denton's reflexive response was to refuse. He never liked to have special treatment. But hell, why not?

"Thanks, I don't mind if I do," he said. As soon as he said it he found, to his surprise, that he felt on better footing with Andross.

Ferdie brought a steaming red enamel coffee pot to their table.

"Here you go." He poured the fragrant coffee into Andross's cup and then into Denton's.

Denton sipped the rich dark brown, barely bitter liquid, breathing the delicious aroma. This was worth the burden of sitting with Andross for the next fifteen minutes. Maybe sin paid after all.

Ferdie brought Andross his eggs. No one else had entered the dining room. Denton had imagined that the top army men came here each morning to have their meal together the way small-town elders ate breakfast at the local diner to thrash out the business of the day. Seemed not to be so.

"Sure you don't want anything more to eat?" Andross asked.

Denton shook his head.

"Glad I found you here, Jordan." He chewed with his mouth meticulously closed. He'd tucked the napkin into his shirt collar. He picked up one edge and wiped the corners of his mouth. "This Tokuro Honda business."

Denton drank his coffee.

"He was a good friend of yours."

"Yes, we worked closely together for over a year and a half. We grew to be partners over time."

"Well, I'm sorry."

"Thank you. But I think the sympathy really belongs to his family. It was good of you to allow the body to lie in state in the home. It means a lot to them."

"No need to thank me. She didn't ask for a traditional burial and ceremony. You remember where that led us, or shouldn't I remind you?"

Denton poured more coffee from the red pot, remembering how his mother had had a similar red tin coffee pot, and how he'd especially liked it as a boy. He thought of his mother's kitchen in Ballard, and how he'd grown attached to it. It was a place of solace when his mother lay upstairs in bed. He often sat there, looking out the windows, watching the light change as the sun shifted position through an entire morning or afternoon. What had occupied his thoughts those long hours alone in the kitchen? They must have been peaceful because he felt a certain state of grace in recalling them. It gave him the strength to talk to this man about Toki, which he didn't want to do but knew he must.

"The Co-op board is concerned about their safety. They're asking for protection."

Andross cut his toast into neat squares and used his fork to steer them around the plate. Watching another man mop up his eggs when you had a hangover wasn't pleasant. Denton tried to keep his eyes off the plate, out toward the kitchen where he could see Ferdie appearing and disappearing as he moved in and out of the door carrying platters and containers.

"I've heard that," Andross said.

I wonder from whom, Denton thought.

"We're going to put guards in their various blocks, but we can't keep that up forever. The army is champing at the bit and, between you and me, I don't know how much longer they'll uphold martial law."

"They're thinking of pulling out?" Make a mess and leave us to clean it up, he said to himself.

"That's what I got wind of. Don't know how much truth there is to it."

"Bill Nakamura and I were talking and we came to the conclusion that it's not the best idea to have guards directly in the blocks. It calls too much attention to the ward reps and the board members."

Andross didn't look at him, but went on eating. Ferdie came out of the kitchen and went behind the bar. A new teacher at the high school, a Caucasian woman from the town of Tule Lake, came in and chatted quietly with him.

"And?" Andross asked.

"We were wondering if the new extension on the hospital could be used by the men and their families. It isn't occupied yet. I hope this will be a temporary situation."

Andross tapped his forefinger on his temple. He nodded. "Good thinking. That is, if you really think it's necessary. Do you, Jordan? Do you think they're in that much danger?" He put his fork down and gulped some coffee.

"One man's been killed, sir, a leader in the community. Highly respected. Yes, I think there is danger for all those concerned."

"Yourself included?"

"I'll get to that, sir, but I'd like to talk about Bill Nakamura before I deal with my situation." He might as well get everything taken care of while Andross was receptive to his suggestions.

"The Nakamuras will go with the others, don't you think? He's the president of the board."

"Bill wants to leave camp."

"You don't say." He shifted sideways in his chair and stretched out as he pulled his napkin from his collar. "I thought Nakamura and his wife were staying here on principle."

288

"That's right. We've had our arguments about it. I thought he should leave. He's a bright man, the brightest. He has very few course hours left to complete to get his Ph.D. and he's been working on ideas for his thesis here in camp. He could have left long ago. I could have set him up with work, but he felt a responsibility to his community."

"I see what your fellowship must be based on." His smile changed to a grimace filled with distaste.

"Yes, sir. But now he'd like to get out. He wants to protect his family. I'd appreciate your assistance in getting his leave clearance okayed."

Denton watched Andross. He'd been put off the scent before by Andross's benign manner. He observed a hint of malice in the way his smile disappeared too fast and never really lived in his eyes. They were a good match, Denton thought with sadness. They both had hidden agendas that motivated all their actions, all their choices. Keep your eye on him, buddy, Denton said to himself. He's as sneaky as you are. Watch out that he doesn't attack and if he does, be sure you're ready for him.

"I'd like to find him some place where he could finish his degree and also get work to support his family. I have contacts in New York City, and I thought I might ask them for one more favor."

Andross looked tired.

"You've placed people in New York City before."

"Yes, and thereabouts. In the beginning, when we were trying to move people out of here quickly, I contacted the Co-op League out there."

"You've got plenty of friends, don't you, Jordan? Plenty of folks who are happy to do for you."

"I've helped people in the past. And they've been disposed to return the favors."

"Lots of friends all over the place."

"I don't know what you're getting at."

"Nothing. Have these friends ever *not* done for you in return?"

"I've had my share of disappointments."

Ferdie was moving from table to table filling the salt and pepper shakers. Denton wondered if he was doing this so he could eavesdrop.

"I thought *we* were friends, Jordan."

"Sir?"

"I wish you wouldn't 'sir' me. We're not in the army. I'm not much older than you are." His voice was low. He still sat in a relaxed posture, but it belied the anger that played across his face. Denton saw what he'd always suspected: when you got past this man's rigid manner, there was bitterness, a feeling that he wasn't getting his due, and a desire to take it at any cost.

"I didn't know that we were friends, per se. Colleagues, yes. A working relationship, hard won, but beginning to develop." He felt he was in dangerous territory here.

"Yes, I thought we'd come to an understanding at our last private meeting." Andross reached across the table and picked up the salt and pepper shakers. He poured a mound of salt on the tabletop and shook pepper into it. With his finger he began to mix them together. "I'd tell you. You'd tell me. Thought we'd found a modus operandi for our dealings."

"And I didn't live up to that?" Denton decided to remain innocent as long as he could. He saw the agenda, at least part of it, peeking through.

"You know what I'm getting at, Jordan. You know what you didn't tell me about Nebo Mota and the *Daihyo Sha Kai* coming to the meeting. Maybe it's fellows like you who are responsible for the Honda death. Have you thought of that?"

In another situation Denton would have thrown his coffee in Andross's face, or grabbed him by his fancy tie and pulled him to his feet and shouted that Toki Honda was like a father to him, and that he'd like to kill any man who used Toki's death for his own power plays. Instead Denton pushed his rage down deep into the pit of his stomach, put it as far out of reach as possible, told himself not to get into more trouble, that he needed Andross to get Bill out of here, that he'd be needing him a lot more in the next few weeks.

"Perhaps I made a mistake," he said. "But I don't think I can be blamed for my good friend's death. From what I've heard, you got the information as fast or faster than I could have reported it."

Andross continued playing with the pile of salt and pepper. A tiny smile appeared on his lips.

"Now what was this about Bill Nakamura?" Andross asked, pushing back from the table. He rubbed his hands together to brush the salt off. "If you want me to process his leave application, it would be best for him to come in himself and sit down with my Stella. They can write it up and I can look it over. You'll do the preparatory work for me? I'll need copies of your letters to the sponsoring people and organizations."

"I have another matter before you go, if I may?" Denton wanted to get it all done. He didn't want to have another of these meetings if he could help it.

"Go for broke."

"I'm thinking about enlisting."

Andross, who had started to rise, sat down again. "This is news. What brought you to this?"

"I don't think you'd find it particularly interesting."

"Oh, but I would. Very interesting to know why a man considers changing his highly principled position. You're more and more of a mystery to me, Jordan."

"Let's say I decided not to stay above the fray." He was about to say "sir," but he stopped himself. "Let's say I learned a thing or two here that shook up my way of seeing things."

"Can you be more specific?"

"It's pretty personal and not entirely thought through. I'm not completely decided on this, and I haven't yet talked it over with my wife. I'd rather not discuss it with anyone else before I explain it to her and hear what she has to say. But no matter what, I've decided I'll be leaving Tule Lake."

Andross considered Denton for a few seconds. Denton saw him thinking, Should I go after this guy for all he's worth? But Andross knew when his opponent wasn't going to give. Checkmate, Denton thought.

"Looks like we'll be losing all you liberal fellows. I hear Herm Katz is leaving, too. Going to be quite a different place without all of you. Quite a different camp." He shook his head as he stood.

"You'll need a different strategy without us to interfere," Denton said, resisting the anger that was emerging from hiding. He thought, There will be two autocrats battling each other. A perfect pairing, the *Daihyo Sha Kai* against a recalcitrant director, with no intermediaries.

Andross nodded and, without as much as a "see you," he grabbed his overcoat, turned and walked across the room and out the door. Denton's body went slack. He heard the outside door slam. Andross would be going over to his sedan, getting in, putting it into gear. He must be mad as hell, Denton thought, even if he doesn't know why. Poor bastard, he was losing all the trouble-making foot soldiers who gave definition to his authority.

Denton looked around the room at the few people sitting there. They were all white. This is what he would be going back into, a world populated primarily by Caucasians, people who didn't have to prove that they were loyal citizens, or that they were human beings worthy of existence. But he knew that he would never again live innocently in America. He would be a loyal citizen, maybe even an honorable soldier, but his loyalty to this nation would be permanently shaded by what he had learned here.

Chapter Thirty-Three

"They've all resigned," Bill said when Denton caught up with him at the fish store.

Bill had pulled him into the tiny office off the tank area to talk to him. Beyond their closed door business went on as usual, unlike the other stores, which had been almost empty when Denton had stopped in to look for Bill. Here there were ten customers.

As Bill carefully checked through a stack of papers on the desk, Denton stood at the plate-glass window separating him from the tanks and counters. Denton observed old Mrs. Nitari dressed in wool coat, slacks, and getas, as she watched the countermen work. She was a regular fixture here, lingering for hours watching others buy fish, never getting in line to make a purchase of her own. They'd offered her a job once because she spent so much time there. She'd declined, saying her husband wouldn't want her to work. But she remained, day after day. They didn't know what she wanted. Did she love the fish or the transactions? Or did she like the company, since she had only her husband Hisao for a companion? Hisao Nitari sat all day in their room in a depressed state, and when he wasn't completely silent for hours on end, it was said that he assaulted her with words, and had on a number of occasions struck her.

Denton sighed, turning from the window. Since his breakfast with Andross, the sadness and futility of the lives here was overwhelming him.

"They've all resigned, and as far as I can tell they won't be talked into returning."

Denton moved a stack of flattened cartons off the chair that was wedged in beside the desk. He pulled out the chair and sat down.

"Let's see," he said.

Bill shoved over the pile of letters he'd been going through. "I'm

293

giving up. I tried to talk them out of it, but they're not willing to listen. All they cared about was whether they were getting protection."

"You can tell them yes." Denton flipped through. Kamu Kaminaki. Foshiko Kaminyo. Henry Kido. Jim Hanani. Arthur Nagasaki. Harry Huroto. Every damn ward representative and every board member except for Bill. "Andross didn't even blink an eye. He must have already known that's what they wanted. He said yes to the hospital annex, thought it was a brilliant idea."

"When can it happen?"

"You know, I didn't even ask." Denton threw the letters onto the desk. "That's it, isn't it? It's over. Everything we've tried to do has gone down the drain."

"We'll call for new elections," Bill said.

"Who do you want to bet will win?"

"*Daihyo Sha Kai* and *Hoshidan* members."

"Damn right. What kind of a fool was I?"

"Look, they may be what people need. Maybe they'll be good for the Co-op. Maybe re-energize it," Bill said, picking up the letters.

"Do you believe that?"

Bill shrugged. "I'm seeing that all the things I believed in aren't necessarily the case. Nothing has turned out the way I thought it would. Maybe they have better ideas. Maybe...oh, forget it." He fanned himself with the papers. "I talked to Mitsue. She agrees we should leave."

"I talked to Andross and he agreed that he'd let you."

Bill put his hand to his brow as though checking for fever. "That means it's really about to happen, doesn't it?"

"Yes, my friend, it does. I'll do the correspondence to get you a job. And then I'm afraid it's *sayonara*."

*   *   *

The two of them worked for a while on strategy, trying to figure out how to salvage the Co-op they had built and believed in, by campaigning to get some of their people onto the board. They thought they could put off the elections for a week or two without too much resistance. It would give them time to lobby the members. Maybe they could even convince some of the original board to stand for re-election, once they were housed in safer surroundings and their terror had subsided. Denton didn't know if either he or Bill believed what they were telling each other, but working together today was almost like the early days. Who were good new people? Who had leadership qualities? Who did not? There was that fellow in Block 18, the Issei from Manzanar, Don Naburo, who seemed to have the respect of the old-timers. "Where was he on the more militant policies of the *Daihyo Sha Kai*?" Denton asked Bill. "I thought he held back from endorsing them. I've never heard anything he's said pro *Daihyo Sha Kai*, anyway," Bill answered.

"Excuse me. You go to Toki Honda funeral?" A voice interrupted them.

Their excitement evaporated.

"Is it time already, Mr. Seko?"

"Yes, Mr. Jordan-san. They say seven o'clock. Widow tell me seven in Protestant church."

*   *   *

The tarpapered barracks church was filled when they arrived. Toki's body was at the front in a closed coffin. The photo that had been in his home rested on an artist's easel next to the coffin. There were five funeral wreaths to the left of the altar, all made by Charlie Hokinama. Denton wondered which wreath was the gift of the Co-op board. He scanned the room for members of the board and spotted Harry, Arthur and several others. Harry turned to look around the room and when he saw Denton, he nodded. Denton nodded back. Herm sat in the back of the room on the aisle. He always did on such occasions because he was so tall. Bill beckoned Denton to the middle of the room where he'd found Mitsue. She'd saved seats. Herm grabbed Denton's hand as he passed and squeezed.

As he sat down he saw that Alice Hamilton was two rows ahead to his right. She must have felt his presence or been waiting for him, because she looked back and their eyes met. She started to smile, but caught herself. She turned to the front. His emotions raced at seeing her. He didn't care what Herm thought, he had to talk to her. For himself, to resolve it. For her, to be fair.

The Reverend Takano led the widow and her children down the center aisle. The family was dressed in white. Sumiko walked on the arm of her son-in-law Frank. She was a tiny, fragile figure of abject sorrow, her back curved. Frank was supporting her as if she might collapse. Sally, Toki's daughter, walked behind with Danny; Denton was comforted to see Toki's familiar features on her face. Little Danny was one of Esther's favorite students, "So solemn," she always said. "Always trying to be the little adult." Well, today he was a bereft child. His pudgy face was tear-streaked. His barrel chest, a smaller version of his father's, was heaving as his sister put her arm around his shoulders and held him close. His muffled cries could be heard throughout the still church.

Mary Makado entered from a side door and sat at the piano. She wore a black skirt and a demure white blouse. Her hair was neatly rolled around her head, with the front held off her forehead with dark, shiny combs. Mary sat for a moment with her hands in her lap. Denton knew how nervous she was. She had told Denton that she feared she would cry in the middle and spoil the music. Nonetheless, when Denton had suggested she might want to pass the duty to another pianist, someone less connected to Mr. Honda, she refused. "I must do this for him. He loved my playing." Slowly she raised her hands to the keys and from them emerged a simple, clear version of a Bach Passion. The music entered Denton, and it was like weeping itself.

Mitsue sat between Denton and Bill with her hands clasped in her lap. Denton glanced sideways and saw that even with the sweet smile on her lips, tears glistened on her lashes.

The Reverend Takano rose from the bench at the back of the altar and took his place behind the simple pine podium. He silently surveyed the gathering before he began.

"Family, friends, members of the congregation, we are together this evening to honor the life of Tokuro Honda, one of our finest members. We ask God's forgiveness for any angry thoughts we may harbor at his untimely death. He was a man who lived an exemplary life in his community in Tacoma, and here, as well, under unfortunate and difficult circumstances. He never failed to be a responsible husband and son-in-law and father, and to fulfill his civic duties. He personified our American values of perseverance, honesty, patriotism and hard work. In fact, he was more American than many of those who purport to be the preservers of American values, those who wish to protect their land from the complications of other cultures, or other races. But it is people like Tokuro Honda who make America great, with their diligence and commitment to family and community and religious beliefs. Tokuro Honda's life in Tacoma, Washington, and here behind barbed wire, was a constant heroic struggle to try to reconcile the conflicts of living as a perpetual alien in his chosen land, to try to remain a man true to himself and his ancestral values and those of the new world. Even when a vast and grievous injustice was done to him and even though he was misunderstood by all sides, Tokuro Honda remained a leader, always trying to find the right, true path.

"Perhaps it is presumptuous of me, as an alien myself, to speak in this way. As most of you know I came of age and was educated in England, but please understand that I speak humbly out of my respect, my honor, my esteem for this country. And please know that I, as all of you did, loved and had the highest regard for this friend and teacher, Tokuro Honda. My personal, selfish sorrow is that he will not be with me in the years of our eventual freedom."

Denton saw Mitsue grab Bill's hand and hold on tightly. He wished he had Esther here, to feel her hand in his.

The Reverend Takano went on to address the widow and the children and members of the congregation in which the family had played an active role. Then, he apologized to the English-speaking mourners, explaining that he wished to switch to Japanese, "into this first language of Toki's homeland." He mentioned the restrictions on using the Japanese language in camp, but assured the mourners that nothing rebellious or traitorous would be said.

While he listened to a language that he still didn't understand, Denton thought, Toki Honda is dead. Killed by intolerance. Toki Honda is dead, killed in a prison camp by his own people, those he dedicated his last years to protect. Killed by the American government which put him here.

"First I will read from Romans, Chapter 8, passages 26 and 28. You are welcome to follow in your Bibles," the Reverend Takano said, addressing them again in English.

There was a shuffling while prayer books were opened and the page was found.

"'Likewise the Spirit also helpeth our infirmities. For we know not what we should pray for as we ought: but the Spirit itself maketh intercession for us with groanings which cannot be uttered. And we know that all things work together for good to them that love God, to them who are the called according to His purpose.'

"And now please join me in the reading of Corinthians 13."

"'Though I speak with the tongues of men and of angels, and have not charity, I am become as sounding brass, or a tinkling cymbal,'" the congregation began, the various accents coming together into a unified sound. "'And though I have the gift of prophecy...'"

Denton joined in, thinking, I don't believe in your god, Toki, but I salute you with my prayer, for you, my dear proud friend. Here's to what I've learned from you. Here's to our work together. Here's to your goodness. And to your charity.

"'And now abideth faith, hope, and charity, these three; but the greatest of these *is* charity.'"

*   *   *

The sun was setting when he knocked on her door.

"Who's there?" she called.

"It's me," he said.

She still wore the white blouse and navy blue suit skirt from the funeral. He slipped inside her apartment, and standing by the door, needing the wall for support because he was faint with wanting her, he began to unbutton her blouse. She helped him. Roughly he sank both hands into the cups of her brassiere, forcing the straps off her shoulders, pulling it down until he held the full weight of her heavy breasts. Her large nipples were erect. He slid his hands up under her armpits and he turned her and pinned her to the wall as he began to suck and bite at her fleshy breasts until she moaned and spread her legs wide and pushed her pelvis into him.

"I want to suck you dry," he said hoarsely, and grabbed her skirt high and ripped down her garter-belt and her underpants.

"I'll never be dry with you around," she whispered, digging her nails into his back. "Put something inside me. Please. Your hand. Anything."

"We have plenty of time," he whispered, sinking to his knees. He bit and licked her thighs as she begged him to enter her. She seized his hair in her fists and pulled him higher and he pressed his mouth into her mound and following the distended, bloated lips of her sex, he pushed his tongue up into her pulsing wetness.

Later, when she pretended to refuse him, he forced her legs apart and hammered into her until he came in a frenzy of excitement. And when she sucked his penis, she suddenly squeezed his testicles painfully hard and it stirred him even more and she kept doing it until he moaned in ecstasy.

Finally sated, they lay naked and sticky in her narrow bed, Alice with her head on his chest and her heavy leg over his. He drank scotch from a jelly glass, and when he offered it to her, she lifted up on her elbow and let him hold the glass to her lips as she finished off the last.

"I'm going to enlist," he said.

"You're sure about this?" she asked, frowning, before returning her head to its resting place, her hair pleasantly tickling his skin.

"No," he answered honestly, "And I don't even know if they'll have me." He picked up a strand of hair and let the end curl around his finger.

"What I don't understand," she said, speaking slowly with an undercurrent of anger, "is how a serious person can change his mind on such a serious matter from one day to the next. 'Today I won't kill another human.'" She snapped her fingers. "'Tomorrow I will.' Or even for you to be unsure about it. I thought this was a deep philosophical decision." She didn't move or look up at him.

His first impulse was to lash back at her that she didn't know what she was talking about; she was a woman and didn't have to grapple with this choice; she wasn't Jewish and wasn't married to a Jew.

"But I'm a violent man."

"Sweetheart, I know violent men and you're not one of them. Wanting retribution for a friend's death and being sexy-violent doesn't negate your being a pacifist. Violent thoughts and wild play have nothing to do with a philosophical stand, from what I've heard. If they did, nobody would be a pacifist. Nobody could be that pure. But if a few good men don't take a stand then there's no hope for the rest of us. There's no chance of another way than endless slaughter and cruelty. In case you're thinking otherwise, *I* think choosing to be a pacifist is a pretty damn courageous position to take, considering the nature of man. I really counted on you to hold on for all us who aren't that brave. And in case you have any doubts, I think it's a very manly choice to make."

He was so overcome by a sense of relief that he couldn't speak; his spirits soared with the possibility of being that courageous man and a voice inside whispered, You can be a manly man and a pacifist. It felt as though his deepest fear had been revealed and, yet, the walls of the room still stood, the lamp glowed, and he breathed on evenly.

"I haven't told you what happened down in Manzanar," she said. "I won't go into detail because it's too painful for me, but during the riot the military guards shot people, and I had to tend to the ones they shot, and even though I'd seen a lot of blood in my life, before that night I never had to treat anyone on the battlefield, never had to take care of anyone shot in a prison in this country." Her fingers pressed into his side. "Two men, internees of course, died. That's all I want to say about it, except that I know about feelings of retribution. And I know about not acting on them."

"Alice." He smoothed her hair off her damp forehead. "I'm sorry."

"There's nothing to be sorry about. I'm just telling you what was." She shrank away and sat up with her back to him.

He put his hand on the naked curve of her spine. "I should have been kinder to you tonight."

"Oh, no, mister, you've got that dead wrong. It's exactly what I needed." She turned to him, her cheeks flushed and her lips still swollen from their lovemaking. "And so did you. If you remember nothing else about us, you'd better remember that."

Smiling, she curled back in beside him and then slid on top of him, her lips opening over his and her femaleness as wet and full as ever.

Chapter Thirty-Four

On Saturday morning, Esther left Parin with Harry in his garage lab and walked up to the campus. Despite Grandma's admonition, she had decided to talk with Mother, to tell her what Denton's real situation was. She could return to Tule Lake having finally done what he'd asked of her from the start. She would be honest with her mother, explaining her own resistance to his choice, but making it clear that she supported Denton. She could tolerate it if mother were furious; she and Parin would be leaving on the night train.

It was cold and damp as she entered campus through the high iron gate; the western wind brought fog and chilly air off the ocean. How strange and disorienting to go up the central walkway. She could sense Denton here, see how they'd moved around campus, recall how she'd felt so important, so safe with him at her side. She could almost feel his arm around her waist and hear his laughter.

The buildings looked large and imposing as she turned right toward the biology department. Her mother oversaw a morning lab. Esther knew it to be her mother's favorite class. Judith said these were her best students. Many of them worked during the week and could only come in on the weekend for a four-hour lab. Judith accommodated herself to their schedules.

Esther hadn't told her mother that she'd be coming. She had wanted to take her by surprise, for once to catch Judith off guard. Esther entered the biology building by the basement door. She walked down the silent dark hall, her steps echoing as she passed several closed-up labs. At the end of the hall was her mother's lab. Judith had the worst room in the department because, as she said, she was a woman. Despite the snub, Judith, with her national reputation, had high-school teachers from as far away as the East Coast steering their finest pupils to her.

Esther stood at the open back door, breathing the familiar piercing odor of formaldehyde. Ten women and three men sat on high stools up and down the long metal lab tables, their backs to Esther as they bent over their dissections. Lamps hung from the ceilings, casting pools of light over the students' positions, infusing the room with a warm glow that contrasted with the grayness just beyond the line of windows on the far wall.

She could remember innumerable occasions when she'd stood in this very spot as Judith diagrammed a dissection on the blackboard. Ever since she was a small child, she had come here after school to remain until her mother finished for the day. She would open the door and quietly slip in, trying not to disturb the students. But they always spotted her, as though they were waiting for her entrance. They would turn and smile at Esther as she walked to the end of the last table, climbed up on a stool, and began to do her homework or, if she had none, to read a book. They seemed to love that the imperious Dr. Kahn was human, had a child, a little girl. Esther in turn had been filled with pride to have a mother who was so important, who was looked up to and listened to by these grownup people.

Tears choked Esther as she observed her mother come out of her office carrying a handful of metal tools. Judith didn't see her, so intent was she on making her way over to a slender blonde coed who waited expectantly for the professor. Judith set to work, her gray head low over the laboratory animal, speaking softly to the girl as she began the instruction. Esther couldn't make out the words, but she knew her mother was patiently explaining how to pick up the muscles and how to avoid dislodging the dye-filled veins.

Esther backed out into the hall, momentarily overwhelmed with compassion for this other mother, this woman who more naturally belonged in the arena of a biology laboratory, finding excitement and stimulation in following her own research and in teaching, molding and challenging potential scientists. Though Judith was known as a taskmaster, Esther remembered that her mother could be kind to a slower student and was willing to "take as much time as necessary, as long as I see that the person is trying."

She just should never have married, Esther thought, and never have had a child.

Esther walked down the hall, away from her mother's lab. She no longer felt a need to talk with her mother, harbored no need to hurt her, nor to make Judith's life any more difficult or sorrowful than it already was. Her secret would stay with Grandma.

Chapter Thirty-Five

Nebo Mota was released from the stockade the day after the funeral. He and numerous other residents had been brutally interrogated about Toki Honda's murder, but no one had broken ranks. Not one person in the entire population had come forward. The War Relocation Authority in Washington, D.C. telegraphed Ted Andross with instructions to drop the matter if he was making no progress. Without Washington pushing him, Andross was not going to concern himself with the death of one Issei. He was happy to abandon the inquiry.

*　　*　　*

Denton left Alice's on Sunday at dawn, after a final night of lovemaking. Even as he walked away, the sensual pleasures were transmuting to vivid memory: the feel of her hair through his fingers, her full breasts weighing in his hand, the sour, salty taste of her. They would surely encounter each other around camp, but they had agreed and vowed they would never be intimate again. Out in this fresh new day, with the sun coloring the clouds a vivid fuchsia over the eastern hills, remorse and sadness battled with desire, and tore at him for what he had done to his wife and daughter. He thanked himself for at least not telling Alice that he was already missing her. In a few hours he would be meeting Esther and Parin; he would put his arms around Esther's delicate waist and look into her dark, serious eyes, and feel Parin's soft breath against his neck. The most he could hope was that one day he would redeem himself. But it would have to be a secret and lonely redemption, judged and recognized only by him.

He'd taken a bath at Alice's place and was on his way back to his own barracks to pick up the car to drive to Klamath Falls train station.

He went the long way around to avoid suspicion, which meant he had to cross the parade grounds. As he turned the corner of the end barracks he spotted Nebo leading a phalanx of *Hoshidan* across the parade grounds toward the firebreak. They were returning from morning exercises and greeting the sun. Denton was astounded that Andross was allowing such militaristic grandstanding. But it was not Denton's business anymore. Nebo's troops were marching parallel to the line of buildings where Denton stood. Denton stepped back against the wall. From there he observed Nebo pass by. Nebo marched unquestioned through the military police gate. Denton watched until Nebo and his men turned into Ward 4 and disappeared into the block of barracks. When Denton resumed his walk across the firebreak, two soldiers were arriving to raise the flag.

An hour later, Denton drove through the camp gates, feeling some trepidation, but mostly a bittersweet longing. As he passed the tower gate and the guard on duty, he thought, This is the beginning of my leave-taking. He had a month or two of work, but after that he was finished with this part of his life.

He understood better what the internees felt when they imagined leaving. For all its tragedy, the camp was a protected environment. Everything was provided: home, food, even some sort of job; schooling, entertainment. There was safety, too, in knowing that if you didn't leave, you wouldn't have to make large choices. He knew they were afraid of what they might find out there in the white communities where they would have to settle, where they would start new lives with a profound sense of their own differentness, with knowledge of the whites' suspicion and downright hatred of "Japs."

Though he had none of that to contend with, he did have his own struggle ahead of him.

He turned onto the road that led up through the flat lake valley of northern California, over the border into Oregon. The clouds were high today, with patches thin enough to let the pale blue winter sky through. He drove directly north on Route 139. A freight train rumbled by on the track from Klamath Falls, steaming down past Tule Lake Camp. The train was endless, clacking and chugging down the line.

Moving through the countryside he felt a vibrant yet troubling sense of freedom because over the last two days he'd come to a final decision: he would remain a conscientious objector, no longer toying with the idea of enlistment. He could not and would not fight in this or any war. What he'd told Esther two years ago still held. He couldn't kill another man, even a man he hated, a man he felt sinned against humanity, against Esther's people. He didn't see this stand as courageous, as Alice had described it. That was too romantic and naive a way of looking at an ugly, messy, tormenting choice. But Alice was correct when she said that being a pacifist wasn't about a simplistic notion of violence. And it wasn't about not being masculine or brave enough to kill another man or to face his own death. He understood for the first time that it was about believing to the bottom of his soul that there was a way, other than committing extreme and cruel acts, to make change in the world, and believing that this way could eventually bring peace for all and wouldn't leave an aftermath of wounds that could never, ever heal, even over centuries.

When he had declared himself a conscientious objector, he hadn't understood the full gravity of what it meant to be a pacifist. He'd never been truly tested; nothing he'd met in the university, at the gates of the corporate farms in the San Joaquin Valley, in the faces of the dust bowl farmers, in his own brother's postwar disturbance had equaled what he'd learned here. It took being beaten up himself, witnessing the brutality of the stockade and having his friend murdered to show him just how hard it was not to retaliate, not to meet violence with more violence.

He wondered, too, if the affair with Alice had somehow freed him to be more confident in his beliefs. He'd broken his own moral code by betraying Esther. He knew the worst about his private self. In a curious, roundabout way, this knowledge made him less frightened of what was to come.

What he had to do next was have a long talk with Esther. He would try to explain his reasoning to her, and he'd beg her to be forthright with him about her feelings, beg her to hold nothing back. He was willing to assume much of the blame for their failure to openly talk about his pacifism, but he needed to remind her that theirs was a love based on candid discussions of their deepest convictions, and to get her to recall the delight and almost sensual pleasure in doing so. He also needed to divulge the truth of his draft status to Judith and Harry. He had to make Esther understand why he could no longer hide his decision from her parents. After he talked to Esther, and after he'd finished the business in Tule Lake, he would go down to the draft board and insist that he be called up and that a ruling be made on his future.

To the east, the rolling hills of sheep and cattle land were softened by a fresh fall of snow. Beyond the hills the mountains rose above the cloud cover. He imagined their white slopes, the pines with snow weighing their branches, the peace beneath them. He checked the time on his pocket watch and saw that he was well ahead of schedule. He had a great desire to stop the car, get out and listen to the silence and smell the air. A few miles up the road he found what he was looking for. Past the turnoff for the town of Tule Lake was a small road that sliced up to the northeast. His heart beat with anticipation. He had not been here since the spring of 1942. The dirt road was narrow, bumpy, and unplowed, but lightly packed down by other travelers. He saw water glistening in the distance. He stepped on the gas and the car rocked and lurched as he plunged ahead. He stopped and parked in the center of the road, hoping no other vehicle would come down here. Leaving the road on foot, he sank knee-deep into an untrampled snowfield and walked slowly, lifting his legs high, toward the lake. The wind blew hard against him. When he reached the shoreline, a squadron of snow geese whirred up in a mass, frightened by his approach. He thrilled to watch as they careened and veered, making wave-like patterns against the gray sky. They flew a good half mile away and then dropped singly or in groups into the choppy gray and white lake. He hunkered down beside a stand of tules, sere and pale gold. Denton stayed like that for a long time, breathing the air that was part moisture, part freshness, part dried vegetation, and he found deep comfort in the silence, a quiet punctuated only by the slight lapping of the water and the gentle honking of birds in the distance.

Acknowledgments

My shelves are overflowing with books and documents about the Japanese American experience during World War II as well as the social history of this nation, so I must regretfully name only those who most influenced me during my journey into my own past: Michi Weglen's early and still seminal **Years of Infamy: The Untold Story of America's Concentration Camps**; Bill Hosokawa's comprehensive **Nisei: The Quiet Americans**; Thomas James's **Exile Within: The Schooling of Japanese Americans 1942-1945**; Charles Kikuchi's **The Kikuchi Diary**; Daisuke Kitagawa's **Issei and Nisei: The Internment Years**; Jerry Voorhis's **American Cooperatives**; Arthur Morse's **While Six Million Died: A Chronicle of American Apathy**; Stan Turner's **The Years of Harvest: A History of the Tule Lake Basin**; The Tule Lake Committee's **Kinenhi: Reflections on Tule Lake**; and Takasumi Kojima's pamphlet, **Tule Lake Pilgrimage: August 26-28, 1994**. Just as my book was going to press, I came upon Harold Jacoby's judicious **Tule Lake: From Relocation to Segregation**, too late for use as research, but I thank Dr. Jacoby for sending me a wonderful photo of my father at thirty years old, hunkered down on the slope of Castle Rock just across Highway 139 from Tule Lake Camp.

In the National Archives in Washington, DC, with the kind and astute assistance of Aloha South, I found my father's memos and letters from his tenure in Tule Lake, and at the University of California at Berkeley in the Bancroft Library, I discovered voluminous diaries of Nisei intellectuals, in which my father figured prominently. I would like to make special note of Elizabeth Stephens, Curator of the Japanese American Relocation Camp Collection at the Bancroft Library, for being enormously helpful.

I thank the Virginia Center for the Arts, Duxbury Colony and Janet Gordon of Bromica for providing me with safe retreats from telephones and the business of life. I am indebted to Faith Sale who long ago encouraged me to write this story; to Carol Ascher for many insightful, supportive conversations and close examination of the text, to Sandy Solomon, Deirdre Bonifaz, Alice Blanchard, Fred Pfeil, Barbara Rosen, Jane Blanshard, and Haruno Tsuruoka for careful and conscientious reading of the manuscript; to Mary Mon Toy for her assistance with the Japanese language; to Bonnie Bellow for helping me with the Hebrew; to Berti Held for going over the Yiddish; to my aunt and uncle, Harriet and Ed Nathan, for their frequent gifts of books and articles about the camps, and for just plain being there; and, of course to my agent Rhoda Weyr who continues to work ardently on my behalf.

But there never would have been a completed manuscript if not for Lorraine Bodger, my friend and colleague, who coaxed, coddled, queried and edited this novel into fighting shape.

And, finally, my loving gratitude to Fritz Mueller whose optimism has a set a standard for me over the years and whose very existence sustains me.

MARNIE MUELLER was the first Caucasian born in Tule Lake Japanese American Segregation Camp in northern California where her father, a pacifist, and her mother, a teacher, worked. Both her parents maintained a lifelong commitment to fighting for social justice. Because of her father's activities as a political organizer, Mueller lived in many different localities of the United States throughout her childhood. In 1963 she joined the Peace Corps and spent two years in Guayaquil, Ecuador. Subsequently she served as a community organizer in East Harlem, as the Director of Summer Programming for New York City, and as the Program Director of Pacifica Radio in New York (WBAI).

Drawing on her Peace Corps experience, Mueller wrote her widely acclaimed first novel, *Green Fires: A Novel of the Ecuadorian Rainforest* (Curbstone Press, 1994). *Green Fires* won numerous awards, among them the prestigious American Book Award from the Before Columbus Foundation and a Maria Thomas Award for Outstanding Fiction. *Green Fires* was also selected by the New York Public Library as a Best Books for the Teen Age. A German translation, *Grüne Feuer*, was published in 1996 by Goldmann/ Bertelsmann. As a result of the publication of *Green Fires*, Mueller was chosen to write a first person narrative about her experiences in the Peace Corps as "one of the voices of the Twentieth Century" in Peter Jennings and Todd Brewster's *The Century*.

With *The Climate of the Country* she once again transforms her remarkable personal experience into rich and exciting fiction.

Marnie Mueller currently lives in New York City where she continues to be active in community action projects.

CURBSTONE PRESS, INC.

is a non-profit publishing house dedicated to literature that reflects a commitment to social change, with an emphasis on contemporary writing from Latino, Latin American and Vietnamese cultures. Curbstone presents writers who give voice to the unheard in a language that goes beyond denunciation to celebrate, honor and teach. Curbstone builds bridges between its writers and the public – from inner-city to rural areas, colleges to community centers, children to adults. Curbstone seeks out the highest aesthetic expression of the dedication to human rights and intercultural understanding: poetry, testimonies, novels, stories, and children's books.

This mission requires more than just producing books. It requires ensuring that as many people as possible know about these books and read them. To achieve this, a large portion of Curbstone's schedule is dedicated to arranging tours and programs for its authors, working with public school and university teachers to enrich curricula, reaching out to underserved audiences by donating books and conducting readings and community programs, and promoting discussion in the media. It is only through these combined efforts that literature can truly make a difference.

Curbstone Press, like all non-profit presses, depends on the support of individuals, foundations, and government agencies to bring you, the reader, works of literary merit and social significance which might not find a place in profit-driven publishing channels, and to bring the authors and their books into communities across the country. Our sincere thanks to the many individuals who support this endeavor and to the following organizations, foundations and government agencies: Adaptec, Josef and Anni Albers Foundation, Connecticut Commission on the Arts, Connecticut Arts Endowment Fund, Connecticut Humanities Council, Lannan Foundation, Lawson Valentine Foundation, Lila Wallace-Reader's Digest Fund, Andrew W. Mellon Foundation, National Endowment for the Arts, the Open Society Institute, Puffin Foundation, and the Samuel Rubin Foundation.

Please support Curbstone's efforts to present the diverse voices and views that make our culture richer. Tax-deductible donations can be made by check or credit card to:
Curbstone Press, 321 Jackson Street, Willimantic, CT 06226
phone: (860) 423-5110   fax: (860) 423-9242
www.curbstone.org